WALLFLOWER

WALLFLOWER

William Bayer

A Janek Novel

VILLARD BOOKS

1 9 9 1

LIBRARY OF CONGRESS CATALOGING-IN-PUBLICATION DATA
Bayer, William.
Wallflower / by William Bayer.
p.   cm.
ISBN 0-679-40047-8
I. Title.
PS3552.A8588W35 1990
813'.54—dc20   90-25452

9 8 7 6 5 4 3 2
First Edition

For Paula

Flower in the crannied wall,
. . . if I could understand
What you are, root and all, and all in all,
I should know what God and man is.

—Tennyson

WALLFLOWER

1

She Remembered

Even years before, when it first came to her, she had relished the idea for the sheer cunning of it, treasured and cherished it for its craft and guile.

She remembered: It had been a sour, rainy day, much like this one, in Cleveland, smelly old Cleveland where the air always stank of iron and dust. She'd been sitting in the window seat, the one on the landing that broke the stairs in the gloomy old Tudor-style house—sitting there, knees drawn to her breasts (such as they were), arms wrapped about her legs, looking out at the rain spattering the sidewalk below. Thunder was rumbling in the distance, and an old kindergarten chant was running through her brain: "Rain, rain, go away/Come again another day. . . ."

Then, suddenly, lightning struck, a real bolt that zigzagged, crack!crack!crack! across the sky.

She sat up straight, and the singsong chant was forgotten, for she saw something then, something dark and scary she would remember all her life. There was a moment, just a split second really, when the tight gray fabric of the sky was torn. And then she caught a glimpse of the inky black—the other side. She would never forget that shade of black.

A second later the thunder clapped, and the rain poured down furiously as if a huge bladder had broken open and was emptying itself upon the earth. It was before that, just an instant before, between the bolt and the clap, that the idea was born. It was a very simple idea yet most profound. Only later would she come to understand how there was a cosmic view implicit in it.

She remembered: She had been fifteen years old when the concept came to her. Every day after that she harbored and nurtured it. And now, many years later, it was about to bear fruition.

She smiled as she remembered, smiled at the sheer cunning of it.

The cunning.

2

Janek in Love

There was in Frank Janek a certain imperturbability as the speedboat raced out of the dawn mist, then cut hard across the lagoon. A slapping sound, water against wood, as the boat sliced the tiny waves. A faintly rancid smell, too, seaweed and shellfish, hung on the vapor that rose from the salt marshes just touched by the morning sun.

The shadowy form of an oil tanker loomed on the horizon while ahead an islet fortress, deserted, trash washed against its seawalls, resolved out of the mist. He'd read about the place. He remembered now. It had been a lunatic asylum not too many years before.

The boat turned again, then charged forward faster, its sharp prow high and haughty, its wake a churning river in the smooth expanse of water behind. Then, in an instant, the fog broke, and his destination, pink and gold, was finally revealed. Towers, domes, arches, bridges, sculptures, pilings angled against a sinuous façade. The soft cries of men stroking long boats through the water merged with the muted tolling of church bells in the shimmering baroque city ahead.

She was there, all of her, all at once, suddenly, and as her remarkable presence hit him full force, Janek stood up in the boat and shuddered with rapture. He couldn't help himself. He had arrived, finally, in Venice.

It had been a dream to come here, a dream of seduction so long harbored he'd sometimes thought it would be better left unrealized. What if the legendary city, La Serenissima, failed to charm him with her wiles? She had fallen on hard times, he'd heard, was rotting, sinking, choked with tourists in her season, flooded and fetid the remainder of the year. There was a good chance, he knew, that he'd be disappointed. But rather than deter him, that possibility made him eager. If Venice had gone to seed, well then, hadn't he gone a little to seed himself? And if he was going to be disappointed, then perhaps disappointment was something he could savor. A depressed middle-aged detective with his greatest case behind him—might not a city well past her glory be the perfect place for him just now?

It had been ten years since he'd taken a vacation. And that was deliberate. "I just can't imagine myself doing nothing," he'd told people, "lying in the sun, broiling myself on some damn beach."

But there was a lot more to it. Perhaps, as he now suspected, he had been afraid of the feelings of emptiness a real vacation could expose. He had always considered himself fortunate: He had found his vocation early, had discovered the joys of investigating crimes, probing deeply into the motives of others. But the one kind of probing that was not pleasant for him at all was the examination of his own quite troubled soul.

Lately his despair seemed to have deepened, something he attributed to the Switch Case, which should have been his crowning achievement but which, instead, had left him feeling depressed, at times almost numb. Every case had its cost—he knew that, had been aware of that for years—but with Switch the price had been very high. No matter the glory, the fame, the adulation of young colleagues, and the respect of contemporaries, in Switch he had come face-to-face with a degree of blackness which haunted him even now, two years after the final trial.

After the book came out and the miniseries was broadcast, they'd tried to take him off cases. "We've got a thousand detectives to work cases, Frank," his chief had told him. "But you, you're something else, you've become a real asset. What do you say we put you on the fast track, get you ready for a field command?"

When he replied that he didn't want to go on the career fast track and that a command position wasn't for him, he saw the same skeptical expression he'd seen on superiors' faces since the day he'd come on the force, the look that told him he was being regarded as a maverick. He didn't care. Without cases to perplex him, taunt him in the night, he would begin to think about himself. And then he would have to deal with his greatest failing, his apparent inability to sustain a relationship with a woman.

For years he and his best friend and partner, Aaron Greenberg, had laughed over his "poor choices," his "bad luck," his weakness for "problem females." But lately the joke had stopped being funny. He had begun to fear the loneliness of middle age. Twice in the last six months he'd driven alone down to Atlantic City, walked into a casino, tanked up at the bar, bet and lost a week's pay at the blackjack tables. Then he'd driven back home in the dark, almost reveling in his loss of self-esteem.

Those episodes had frightened him. He didn't want to end up like so many detectives he had known, men who'd put in their time on the streets, done the job, retired after honorable careers to lead quiet, lonely, orderly lives. Until, usually on the eve of a winter holiday, the family next door would be awakened by a single shot in the middle of the night.

What he needed now was a chance to focus on who he was and where he was going with his life. And to consider, too, what form his redemption should take, redemption from his melancholy and despair. But it would never have occurred to him to combine that quest with his long-held dream of seeing Venice if Kit Kopta hadn't decided to send him to Lugano.

"You need a change, Frank. I've got just the thing for you," she said when he presented himself, obedient to her summons, at her office.

The room, large and square, seemed to dwarf her, for she was a small, lean forty-five-year-old woman with fine, sharp features, a mane of thick black hair, and dusty Mediterranean skin. Her eyes were her most prominent feature: big brown eyes that burned beneath dark Grecian brows. She'd been appointed Chief of Detectives three months earlier, the first woman ever to hold the position, the highest-ranking female cop in NYPD history. Now she was looking after her own.

"There's a detectives' conference coming up in Switzerland. A couple hundred of the top people from all over the world. We've been asked to send our best man. That's you, Frank. You're the one they want."

He squirmed in his chair. "Uh-uh, Kit. Please . . ."

She grinned, then shook her head. "You're not getting out of this one. They asked for you. They'll pay for everything. All you've got to do is give a little talk."

"About the Switch?"

She nodded. "I know you're sick of it. But a whole bunch of European detectives want to hear how you solved it."

"I got nothing new to tell them. It's all in the goddamn book."

"Doesn't matter. They want to hear it out of your mouth. Face it, Frank—you're a star. So you might as well enjoy it instead of acting like it's a heavy burden you have to carry around." She squinted at him. "Anyway, it's not an option."

Janek laughed. "You're *ordering* me to go?"

"We take a bad rap here. Murder City. Five to ten fresh homicides a day."

She linked her fingers, then set her hands straight in front of her. *Just like a chief,* he thought.

". . . so if some big shot foreign cops want to hear what it's like playing detective in New York, we're going to accommodate them." She paused. "I checked your caseload. You've got nothing much going. When you get back, that's going to change. I want you to attend the conference, then take a vacation, two, three weeks,

8

anywhere you like. The point is get some rest, come back here feeling good. A month from now I don't want to see you dragging your ass around. Okay?"

"Look, I appreciate—"

"This isn't charity, Frank. I need you in good condition."

"For what?"

"We'll discuss it when you get back."

Janek looked at her. He knew her well. They'd been lovers for two months twenty years before and then had parted bitterly. Five years after they split, they ran into each other at a police banquet, hit a bar together afterward for a drink, discovered they liked each other, and started dining out once a month. What had begun with sex, then soured to dislike had developed into a deep and mellow friendship. Janek thought of Kit Kopta as one of his half dozen closest friends in the department.

"Thinking of making me your special assistant?"

"Maybe something like that."

"People will talk, Kit."

"Let 'em talk. We won't give a shit, will we, Frank?"

Janek smiled. "Still the ballsy broad."

"I don't define myself that way. I like to think I'm . . . feline."

"Feline!"

Her eyes burned defiantly. "What's the matter?"

"Nothing. Just that in a Chief of Detectives 'feline' isn't what people expect."

She nodded. "People, as you call them, are going to have a lot of novel experiences now that I'm chief." She stood to signal the interview was over. "So it's settled. You're going to Lugano, then taking leave. Who knows, Frank? You might even enjoy yourself." She smiled. "Wouldn't that be different?"

"It would be," he said. "It sure as hell would."

Kit stepped out from behind her desk. "Give me a hug," she ordered. Janek hugged her.

" 'Ballsy broad'!" She laughed. "You gotta be kidding, Frank."

He didn't much enjoy the conference, even though he was lionized. British, French, German, Dutch—every detective in Europe seemed to know about Switched Heads. "I'd give my left ball for a case like that," one Australian inspector confided.

His talk was well attended. After he finished, he politely fielded questions for an hour and could have gone on indefinitely except that the hall was needed for a symposium on computer crime.

Afterward a mustachioed Spanish police captain, famous for single-handedly tracking down a cell of Basque terrorists, asked Janek to join him for a drink. The Spaniard, proud of his own achievement, said he would have preferred to have solved a great psychological case like the Switch.

"The young ones here, all they talk about is DNA fingerprinting," he said, gesturing at a group of husky young detectives hovering around the busy hotel bar. "They don't understand that the great cases, the only ones that can justify living the best part of your life in the gutter, are crimes of the wounded spirit. And the detectives who solve crimes like that are men like us, men who have wounds of our own. . . ."

After dinner Janek walked by himself through the deserted arcade of shops facing Lake Lugano, then crossed the avenue and paused to gaze across the water, seeking out the farther shore. It was lost in mist. The lake's surface was smooth, like an expanse of black glass, and the lamps along the embankment, huge lanterns on bronze pedestals, burned gaseous and yellow in the murky night.

He thought about what the Spanish captain had said: "Wounds of our own . . ." *What are my wounds?* he asked himself. *How many have I got?* A long, loveless marriage that had ended in a bitter divorce, a few affairs that had ended badly, a lot of experience with the worst sort of people and the attendant law enforcer's disillusionment. A picture came into his mind, a network of scars, old and deep, crisscrossing his middle-aged torso. He shook his head;

he didn't like the image. He turned away from the water and started back toward the hotel.

Once again under the arcade, the window of a travel agency caught his eye. He halted and stared in. A poster showed a gondolier in silhouette against sparkling water and the dark outline of a great domed church. The words below were few and to the point: VENICE THE DREAM.

The next morning he returned and bought himself a ticket.

It was a morose autumnal Venice he had come to. The first afternoon the air turned chilly; after that he wore a raincoat when he walked. It was mid-October, near the end of the season, and there weren't many tourists. The Piazza San Marco was inhabited mostly by pigeons, and Caffè Florian was deserted, its waiters lonely sentinels guarding neat rows of empty seats.

He bought a guidebook, then set out to explore in a studious manner, intending to work his way through a list of churches, museums, bridges, palaces of cultural importance. But he soon realized that it was not great paintings of the Crucifixion that interested him; it was the lore of the old republic, her hardness, her cruelties. He understood, with a start, that it was her crimes he wanted to understand.

When he learned, for instance, that state enemies were once routinely executed by being drowned secretly in the middle of the night, he hastened to the Orphan Canal, where the drownings were alleged to have taken place. And he was equally fascinated by tales surrounding the feared Council of Ten and the even more greatly feared Three Inquisitors—tales of informers, night arrests, mysterious disappearances, undisclosed detentions, paid government assassins, official torturings, stranglings, knifings, poisonings, and beheadings, public and private, justified and capricious, the bodies often displayed without explanation between the "fatal pillars" in the Piazzetta. To live as a Venetian in the time of the republic, he understood, was to reside in a paranoid's nightmare. Stealth, vengeance, institutionalized terror—these, too, were among the traditions of La Serenissima. They were traditions he understood at least as well as the dignity of the churches and the grace of the bridges and canals.

As there was nothing to do at night, he went to an English-language bookstore, bought a copy of stories by Thomas Mann, and began to read *Death in Venice* after dinner in his room.

A dense and dreary tale, he thought, about a famous middle-aged German writer, hitherto tightly controlled, who finds his fate in Venice, intoxicated by a pale adolescent boy. The novel cut deeper than that, of course, was about form and formlessness, art and obsession, rationality and madness. Janek understood it, could savor its intricate design, but in the end he could not identify with its hero. Aschenbach, author of great books, and Janek, solver of a "great" case—both outsiders, lonely men, who had come to Venice on a quest. But while Aschenbach sought the abyss, Janek wanted only to crawl out of it, to be redeemed.

He noticed the woman several times before he really looked at her, and then, it seemed, he saw her everywhere, until, in his mind at least, their intersections became something of a joke.

She was a Northern European, most likely Austrian or Swiss, though possibly a German or a Dane. A stunning, stylish person, she looked to be in her late thirties. Very well put together, too: excellent figure, proud walk, handsome face, precision-cut blond hair. She wore exquisite clothes, well-cut slacks, elegant suede boots, and, over a salmon blouse, the finest, softest, blackest leather jacket he had ever seen. He liked the way she wore her silk scarf tied smartly at the side of her neck.

But it was far more than her style and grooming that caught his interest; it was, above all else, her eyes. Large soft gray-green eyes, sensitive, yearning—they reminded him of the eyes of the great French movie star of the forties Michele Morgan.

It became a game with him: Could he choose a church or museum at random, go there, and *not* run into her? There were other tourists trekking their way through Venice, but she seemed the only one on the same track as himself. How were they connected? Were their consciousnesses linked? Perhaps they should sit down and discuss it. But first she would have to recognize him and acknowledge the humor of their meetings.

For a while he was certain she didn't notice him, or else, he decided, she was the coolest woman in Venice. Then, while eating lunch alone in Harry's Bar, he saw her enter, pause, peruse the room, smile (or did he merely imagine that she did?) as she sighted him, then quickly turn away. He smiled back but was too late; she was on her way to a table at the opposite end. He watched to see if she was joining a companion, was relieved to see her sit down alone.

Relieved. What right had he to feel that way? The answer came to him almost at once. She was so damn attractive! Everything about her, her gestures, the way she moved . . . he knew he *had* to meet her. And the first step was to find out who she was.

In New York there would be no problem. He would simply follow her to her hotel, flash his shield at the clerk, and ask. But here in Venice he had no status, was but one of five thousand end-of-the-season stragglers in a centuries-long parade.

However, after three days of fortuitous encounters, he decided that he *would* follow her. A crazy idea, a little too close, perhaps, to Aschenbach's pursuit of the boy. But the notion appealed to him. He was a detective; he had the skills and also great curiosity. She certainly interested him more than any lifeless work of art. Let the tarted-up old whore of a city offer her meretricious charms to someone else. The lonely middle-aged detective from North America would track the live young beauty through her streets.

He picked her up outside Palazzo Ca' d'Oro. *How amazing,* he thought, *that I knew she'd come here!* He hung back, waiting, and then, as she wandered the galleries, began carefully to stalk her. She paused a long while before Mantegna's painting of St. Sebastian. Perhaps the naked, limp, pierced body of the executed saint excited her. Or else (and he hoped this was true) it aroused her compassion.

She boarded the No. 1 vaporetto. No difficulty following her onto the crowded ferry; he had only to linger among the workers to remain unseen. She disembarked at Pontile Sant' Angelo, and there he almost missed her; he nearly didn't make it off.

She began to walk down narrow alleyways and to cross little bridges, as if wandering irregularly without a plan. As he followed, he tried to stay a building's distance back. Once, when she stopped, he stopped as well. Then he watched as she consulted her map.

She entered an elegant women's store. Beautiful shoes and fine silk dresses were displayed in the window. She reappeared after fifteen minutes, and he was gratified that she carried no packages. Then she went into a tiny boutique that sold marbled papers and hand-bound notebooks. When she came out, she carried a shopping bag embellished with a golden lion.

Look at what I'm doing: making up a personality for her, just the way I would for a criminal!

He was tempted to stop right there, leave her alone, retreat. But it was too late. He was fascinated. The game was on, and now he must play it out.

Seeing that she was following a narrow street that would dead-end on the Grand Canal and thus force her to return and meet him face-to-face, he cleverly moved to a parallel alley, then walked beside her, invisible though only a few feet away. Trying to match his steps to the soft thud of her boots upon the stones, he could not deny to himself that he was thrilled.

She carried a camera, a viewfinder Leica, but he didn't see her use it until she paused before a tiny violin shop near the Fenice Theater. Then she stepped back onto a delicately scaled footbridge and carefully composed a shot. After she moved on, he stood where she had stood and saw what she had seen: three fiddles hanging in the shop doorway reflected in the canal beneath the shadow of the bridge. It would make a fine picture, he thought. And then: *Perhaps I am beginning to know her a little bit.*

She looked more at home when she reached the Piazza San Marco. She paused at its entrance, peered ahead, then crossed it with brisk, athletic strides. She paused again, to look up at the campanile, then moved rapidly into the Doges' Palace.

The Bridge of Straw; the Bridge of Sighs: he crossed them both close behind her, employing a small French-speaking group as his shield.

He followed her across the vast marble floor of the Sala del Maggior Consiglio and was surprised that she did not give even a glance to the huge Tintoretto on the wall.

Something was different about her. She seemed impatient, annoyed. Her forehead was creased, her stride anxious. She glanced at her watch. Did she have a date? Was she apprehensive about it? Was she meeting a man?

She backtracked to Santa Maria Formosa, then paused to study the stone head of a monster. Slowly he was learning more about her. Now, it seemed, she was interested in the grotesque.

Surely something was bothering her, for she abruptly turned again, and this time it was hopeless to avoid her. He walked straight past her, refusing to meet her eyes, circled, and deftly picked her up again as she headed rapidly back through the Piazzetta, then along the wide expanse that follows St. Mark's Canal.

Along the Riva degli Schiavoni, then, very briskly, tensely, across the Bridge of Wine and the Bridge of Piety to the open portion of the waterfront where old Venetians huddled on wooden benches trying to catch the faint heat cast by the brilliant October sun.

She was out of the labyrinth, in the open, and suddenly he knew why. *She's made me! Damn!* Too late now to retreat. A queasy feeling as he understood she was going to confront him. *Damn! Nothing I can do.* He would have to try to brave it out.

But when she finally turned on him, as he knew she would, she did not show an angry face. Rather, she smiled teasingly as she raised her camera and began to take his picture. Once, twice, then rapidly five more times, moving closer at each exposure, until, when she finally lowered the Leica, she was but three yards from his face.

"Do you speak English?" she asked with a German accent. He nodded. "I believe you're following me. You will please explain?"

She smiled as she waited for his response, and again he was struck by the beauty of her eyes. Also by her confidence. *She's got me, and she knows it. No choice. I'll have to own up.*

"I'm embarrassed. . . ." He grinned foolishly, feeling himself tongue-tied.

"American?" He nodded. "Do you know me? Have we met?" He shook his head. "I must interest you very much," she said, rolling her eyes in mock wonderment.

He grinned again, then caught himself. She was making him feel like a boy. "To tell the truth—"

"The truth! Yes, we must definitely have the truth!" she purred. "Because, you must know this, it is very rude to follow a woman through the streets. Adolescent Italian males do it, but a mature man and an American—that's quite unexpected. Frankly I would not have thought an American gentleman capable of such a thing."

She stared at him, levelly, waiting for his reply. And this time, he knew, she would wait until he gave her satisfaction.

"Yes," he admitted, "I was following you. I apologize. It was stupid of me and very rude. But please believe me, I intended no harm. I hope you won't call the police."

"Why should I want to do that?" she asked with a slight smirk. She was amused now, enjoying his discomfort.

Fine with me, he thought. *Keeps it between us. I'll take any humiliation so long as she doesn't bring in the cops.*

"You took my picture," he said. "If you felt harassed, then I understand you might want—"

"But I didn't feel harassed. I was flattered. You have a kind face. I knew you wouldn't bother me. If I ask you now, you will leave me alone. Correct?"

"That is certainly correct," he agreed.

She paused, then introduced herself. "My name is Dr. Daskai."

A doctor! He would never have guessed it. "Mine's Janek," he replied, again feeling dumb.

She offered her hand. He took it. They shook.

"And what do you do, Mr. Janek?"

"I'm a tourist—"

She shook her head; she would not accept evasions. "You know what I'm asking. In your professional life?"

He hesitated. "I'm a New York City detective."

"Do you have credentials?" He nodded. "May I see them?"

He showed her his ID and shield. She examined both carefully.

"A New York City lieutenant of detectives following me through the streets of Venice." She shook her head and rolled her eyes again. "I would *never* have imagined this."

"It was a bad mistake."

"Really?" She was skeptical. "Did you think I was someone else?"

"I was attracted to you, I wanted to meet you, but I was too shy to approach. We kept running into each other, and you didn't seem to notice."

"Oh, but you're wrong. I noticed," she said.

Janek stared down. "Look, I'm really embarrassed. First, because I followed you, which I had absolutely no right to do. And secondly, because, well . . . I'm supposed to be able to follow people without their knowing I am."

"In New York perhaps. Here you stand out."

"I understand that now."

"Well?" She stared at him.

"I guess I'm not as good a detective as I thought," he offered humbly. Perhaps there was still hope; he could see another smile growing on her face. "I realize under the circumstances what I'm about to ask will seem like a pretty shameless question."

"What question?"

"You have every right to refuse." She stared at him curiously. He paused, then took the plunge. "Would you let me buy you a drink?"

She reacted with mock horror. "Now he wants to offer me a drink!"

"You're right. Enough is enough. I'm sorry." He stepped back, ready to withdraw. "I won't follow you again. I promise. I feel like such a jerk—"

"Actually I am thirsty," she said.

Startled, he studied her face. She was smiling broadly now. *What does she think of me?* he wondered. *Attractive and shy? Or a lonely American buffoon?*

"I'm staying nearby, at the Danieli. The bar there seems very pleasant." She stared into his eyes. "Shall we try it? Of course, I insist on paying for myself."

Her first name was Monika. She was a psychiatrist. She lived just outside Hamburg and was a member of the medical school faculty there. She also had a specialized psychoanalytic practice—private patients she saw in the afternoons. She had written two books, one about the nature of rage, the other about narcissism and art. She was thirty-nine years old, widowed and childless. Her husband, an older man who had been first her teacher and then her mentor, had died of cancer the year before.

She didn't travel much; she didn't have the time. Her work was demanding, and she thrived on it. She had come to Venice on a private visit; she and her husband had taken their wedding trip here ten years before.

She had been hesitant about returning, afraid she would be haunted by memories, fearful she would slip back into the depression that had seized her after her husband had been buried and that had only begun to lift the last few months. So, in a certain sense, coming to Venice had been a test. Could she rediscover the city by herself, take pleasure in its beauty and art, or would it forever be tainted for her by nostalgia and regret?

He told her as much about himself as she had told him. And the longer they talked, the more he felt that there was nothing he would want to keep hidden. But then, on account of a few little things she let drop, he realized she knew more about him than he'd revealed.

"Yes," she admitted when he confronted her, "as soon as I saw your credentials, I knew who you were. I read a book, *Tödlicher*

Tausch it's called in German. I'm not sure what that would be in English. Maybe something like 'The Deadly Swap.' "

"*Switch,*" Janek said.

She nodded. "Well, anyway, I knew you must be the same Janek who solved that strange case in New York. The one with the switched heads. But I can tell by the way you're looking at me that that's the last thing you want to talk about."

He nodded, pleased she was so intuitive.

"Perhaps you came here to escape it," she added.

My God! he asked himself. *Does this woman have any imperfections?*

"So, in a sense," she continued, "we have both come here to escape our pasts. Can the brilliant fire that is Venice burn away our ghosts?" She smiled. "I know it doesn't work that way, and I believe you know it, too. Travel is probably the worst form of escape. People carry their baggage wherever they go. But still, it's a wonderful romantic illusion, the idea of going to a place where the colors are bright, the light brilliant, the art incandescent. But now I am ashamed. I'm talking too much. I think I've spent too many hours as prisoner of my patients, listening, always listening, and now I am feeling free and letting loose. Poor you"—she gently touched his hand—"to be *my* prisoner now, to have to hear me babble on. . . ."

He looked into her gray-green eyes, eyes so full of yearning. Slanting beams crossed the barroom, found her irises, entered them, and broke into a spectrum.

"I love listening to you," he said. Then he turned away.

"Why do you turn from me?" she asked softly.

"Forgive me," he said. "I'm blinded."

"Then we must move to another table." She began to rise.

"No, no," he said, touching her hand. "It's all right. It's not the light. It's something else."

"What?" she asked, intense now, curious.

"You," he said.

"Me?"

He nodded. "I'm blinded by the beauty of your eyes."

To hold her, kiss and touch her—that was like a dream. His true dream of Venice perhaps, though he hadn't known it when, for so many years, he had dreamed of coming to this city. The way she made love was subtle, but he did not feel clumsy with her as he sometimes did with women whom he thought of as elegant or fine. She made it seem very natural that they should lie together in her room—her wonderful room, No. 13, where, according to the plaque outside the door, the great French novelist George Sand had lived for a brief time in the winter of 1833 with her lover, poet Alfred de Musset.

"They parted disastrously," Monika whispered to him as they lay together afterward, lightly tangled. "Musset fell ill; then Sand ran off with his doctor." She caressed him fondly. "Musset never got over it. It was the defining trauma of his life."

They made love again, more tempestuously the second time, and then Janek could not quite believe what he was feeling. Something in him was being released. The heaviness was lifting; a wonderful new buoyancy was taking its place. Her steamy skin burned against his body. Their sweat ran together and formed a seal.

"I haven't done this since . . ." She turned to him, eyes glowing. "You're the first man I've been with since my husband died." Her fine eyes queried him. "It's been awhile for you, too, hasn't it?"

He nodded. "It feels good to make love again."

"Oh, yes. . . ." She showered kisses on his chest. "Frank, Frank. . . ." She made his name seem marvelous by pronouncing it in German. "It's very good. Very healthy. I think it must have been for this that I came to Venice." She licked his neck in long, even strokes. "But is this really happening?" She tenderly stroked his sex. "Yes, it is. And I *love* it. I'm so happy you followed me."

She looked up at him, her smile so bright, her eyes so brilliant—but this time he did not flinch, this time he drank in her light.

He took her to dinner at Antico Martini on the Campo San Fantin across from the Fenice Theater. There was only one other couple on the terrace, but they agreed they liked being in a nearly empty restaurant.

"Tonight Venice belongs just to us," she said.

He told her about himself, his marriage and divorce, his ambivalent affection for New York, how the Switch Case had changed his life, and how much he loved investigative work.

"You love it because you're good at it, isn't that right?" He nodded. "Tell me about it, Frank. What sort of detective are you?"

"Basically there're two kinds," he explained. "Scientists and artists. The scientists are puzzle solvers. They pore over evidence, figure out what's absent, then go after the missing piece. I'm probably more the artist type. I try to feel the case, identify with the perp, then generate the insight that will bring it all together. For me the best cases are the psychological ones, where to solve them you have to go inside a mind and touch the madness."

"You're really a psychologist," she said.

"In a way—but I have no training in it. I operate on instinct. And often what I do isn't very civilized, Monika. Underneath I'm still a street cop. And New York is one very tough town."

She nodded. "Will you forgive me if I ask you a personal question?"

"I think we've been pretty personal with each other so far."

She smiled. "You're famous. You've been the subject of a book and a movie. I ask you this because I realize it must be your choice: Why are you only a lieutenant?"

Her question amused him, but he gave her a serious answer. "I won't take a field command," he explained, "which is what an officer above lieutenant is obliged to do. If I stay a lieutenant—well, I keep thinking I'll be able to work cases until I retire."

"Tell me why you like them so much?"

"First, the problem, then the fun of the chase, the joy when I get the flash, figure out who did it and, most important, why. You see, once I know that, I can usually persuade the person to confess,

not just because I've got the goods on him but because my understanding of him usually makes him want to explain himself even
more. Then through his confession I relive the experience of the
crime. And once I've shared that, it's over."

"So you like confessions?"

He nodded. "Much better than building a case for trial. For me
when a crime is committed, a wound is opened . . . and I want to
be the one who closes it. An honest confession is the best kind of
closure I know."

She gazed at him. "Perhaps then you are something between a
psychologist and a priest."

He shook his head. "I can't absolve anybody. I haven't the right.
But I always try to grant criminals their humanity. To help them?
Partly. But I think it's really for myself. There's so much evil in
this world, Monika. Perhaps a billion varieties of evil. The kind
of work I do, and believe me it's very humble sometimes, puts me
in touch with evil every day. And strange as this may seem, I think
it's helped me gain a little wisdom. Though sometimes, I have to
admit, I don't feel all that wise. Like this afternoon, for instance—
following you around. That was very childish."

"Boyish." She corrected him. "I'm so glad you were boyish.
It was exciting to feel pursued." She met his eyes. "If you're not
a cross between a psychologist and a priest, then what exactly are
you, Frank?"

He shrugged. "Just a detective," he said.

They spent the night together in
her room. Early the next morning Janek moved out of his hotel
near the Giardino Papadopoli and into a single at the Danieli, just
down the hall from No. 13.

"Every morning I'll sneak back in and ruffle up my bedding,"
he told her.

She was amused. "That won't fool the chambermaids."

"I'm sure it won't, but I hope they'll appreciate my efforts."

"What do you want them to think? That you're discreet?"

Janek shook his head. "I want them to know I am protective of the German lady's reputation."

She laughed, then hugged him. "You're a very funny man."

Janek hired a speedboat to take them to Torcello, where they lunched on grilled fresh scampi, then explored the island's little lanes. In the Cathedral of Santa Maria Assunta they stood in awe before the apse, meeting the grave gaze of the Teotoca Madonna, whose cheeks are laced with mosaic tears.

To eat, make love, experience the beauty of Venice—these things became their enterprise. She had much to teach him about art, and he had much to teach her about the streets. On golden mornings they wandered the city, strolling along her white and ocher walls, upon her stone and marble alleys, across her rainbow-hued canals. They watched glass being blown. They sat in cafés and made up tales about the people who passed. They told each other the stories of their lives.

Then, late in the afternoon, when the sweet fragrance of autumnal decay mingled with the saline scent of the lagoon, the heady aroma aroused their lust and drew them back to No. 13 and to her bed. Here, as the sun painted the walls gold and pink, they kissed, grew intoxicated, rolled together, and explored each other with their tongues. They made love lazily until darkness fell. Then they slept for an hour in each other's arms, showered, and went out to dine.

Monika's husband, Franz Daskai, was thirty years older than she. A handsome, athletic man with leonine features and a full head of iron gray hair, he had been chief of psychiatry at the Hamburg hospital where she had served out her residency. One day he stopped to watch her play tennis on the staff court behind the residents' dormitory. A couple of days later he called her to his office to invite her to be his doubles partner in an informal interhospital tournament. She accepted; they battled fiercely and to everyone's amazement won the cup. A few months later, when she began to see patients, she asked him to be her supervising analyst. A year later they were married.

Franz, Monika told Janek, was a wise, sane man who was an exemplar to all his students. The men worshiped him, and the women adored him, perhaps because he was one of the few people in the profession who lived the kind of rational life that is the supposed goal of psychoanalysis.

Over their ten years together he had taught her much, but she believed his most memorable lesson was the eloquent way he defined the mission of a therapist. At some point in every patient's past, he believed, there occurs a character-distorting moment when an emotion and an experience, normally incompatible, come together and lock. Abuse and love, shame and pleasure—no matter how contradictory, the pieces engage so the person can survive his fear and rage. It then becomes the task of the therapist to locate this hidden lock, analyze its parts, then gently open it up to set the patient free.

"He taught me how to be a healer," Monika said. "That was his greatest gift. When, that first evening, you spoke of crimes as wounds and your role as detective-confessor—well, I thought, you and Franz would have liked each other. I think he would have understood you."

"And that's very important to you?" he asked.

"Yes," she said. "I believe it is."

As Monika was due back in Hamburg the following Monday, she and Janek planned to spend their final weekend together visiting some of the famous villas of Veneto. Instead of reveling further in the marvelous stage set that is Venice, they would seek composure on the mainland in Palladio's rational geometry.

But very early Saturday morning, even before the dawn, the phone rang in Monika's room. The call, surprisingly, was for Janek. He began to complain: Although the management no doubt knew he was sleeping in Dr. Daskai's room, it really had no right to ring him there. . . . Then he stopped. A familiar voice had come on the line. Immediately he felt a portent of woe.

"Frank, it's Kit. Tough job to track you down. But the Venice police are pretty good. Course, we had to kick some ass."

Something was wrong. "There's trouble, isn't there?"

"Yeah, Frank." Her tone was grave. "There is."

"Please don't stall. Just tell me, okay?"

"It's Jess."

His goddaughter. *Oh, God!* "What happened?"

"Stabbed, Frank. She was jogging in the park, and someone, we don't know who—"

"She's going to be all right?" But even as he asked, he knew the answer.

"Uh-uh, she's not. She's dead. I'm so sorry to be the one to have to tell you."

Something piercing like a silent scream burst across his brain.

". . . listening, Frank? Laura Dorance called, asked me to find you and let you know. She hopes you can come back. The funeral's tomorrow afternoon. What shall I tell her?"

"Tell her I'll be there," Janek said. Then he set down the phone, turned from Monika, faced the window, and wept.

"**J**esus! She was just a kid! Twenty years old! A junior in college!" They were in Janek's narrow room, Monika watching from the bed as, frantic and bitter, Janek paced and ranted while throwing his clothes into his bag.

Suddenly he stopped and turned to her.

"I can't believe it! I can't." He sat down beside her. She hugged him.

"I loved her, Monika. So much . . ."

In the lobby, after he had booked his flight, Janek gulped down three cappuccinos.

"Her father, Tim Foy—he and I were partners for five years. Then Tim transferred to narcotics, worked undercover, was found out, and assassinated. One morning he went out to his car, parked as usual in front of his house. He turned the key, and the car blew up—twenty pounds of dynamite. Jess, who was five at the time, was watching from the kitchen window. He waved to her; she waved back; then her whole world exploded before her eyes. According to Laura, she didn't start crying for a minute, just stared, confused, at the place where Tim's car had been. Tim, you see, was something of an amateur magician. Maybe Jess thought he was playing a trick. Some trick! They never found all the pieces of him. Her tears, God! They flowed and flowed. Later we learned her hearing got damaged, too. . . ."

They entered St. Mark's. The cathedral was deserted. The aroma of the incense was cloying and thick. Janek fell to his knees on the hard stones before the altar. Monika knelt beside him and held his hand as he prayed.

Afterward they did a tour of the piazza. It would be their final walk together in Venice.

"My wife and I never had children. So Jess was like my own daughter. When Laura was struggling, I was over at her place all the time, helping with Jess, baby-sitting, assisting with homework, telling stories. I even taught her how to play baseball in Flushing Park. That's when I realized she could be an athlete. She turned out to be a damn good one, too. She's on the Columbia College women's fencing team. Or, I should say, she was. . . ."

Monika held tightly to his hand.

Even after Laura Foy went to law school, met and married Stanton Dorance, and she and Jess moved into Dorance's big apartment on Park Avenue—even then Janek remained close to the girl.

"What a waste, Monika. A fine young life like that! What a terrible waste." He paused, then spoke quietly. "I don't think I could have loved my own child more."

He sat with Monika in the rear of the chartered speedboat, racing for the airport, knowing that now his life would be forever changed.

"I headed up the team that went after Tim Foy's killer. Today they won't let you work a case that's personal, but back then you could swing a deal or two. Anyway, it didn't take us long to find the guy who built and placed the bomb. A scrawny little character; I can't even remember his name. Anyway, we caught him, turned him, and he gave us the guy who ordered it done, a slimy, rat-faced drug dealer. He's serving a life sentence now." Janek squeezed her hand. "Sorry to make you listen to all this sordid stuff."

"Keep talking, Frank. I don't find it sordid." She touched his face, then gently kissed his cheek. "I want to stay with you as long as possible, stay close to you before you fly off."

"I wouldn't have had anyone to talk to if I hadn't found you."

"Well, we found each other, didn't we?"

Janek peered around. Venice was lost in mist behind. Ahead the lagoon was as still and flat and white as it had been the morning he arrived. The rising vapor carried the same faint sweet salt-marsh smell of decay.

"I wonder if I'll ever be able to come back here now. That call from Kit—I think I'll always associate it with Venice. The call . . . that broke my heart."

He didn't turn away from her this time, didn't mind now if she saw his tears. And when she mopped his cheeks with her fine silk scarf, he kissed her hand and whispered, "Thanks. . . ."

At the airport there was time to call Aaron Greenberg and arrange to be met in New York.

"Aaron and I work together," he told Monika in the coffee bar on the airport roof. "He knew Jess, too. He says the tabloids are full of it. Stanton, Jess's stepfather, is a big corporation lawyer. He and Laura—I feel so sorry for them. They say the worst thing that can happen to you is to lose a child. You never get over it, they say. . . ."

Monika accompanied him to the security gate. There he put down his bags so they could embrace.

"This can't be good-bye. I don't want to lose you."

"We're not going to lose each other. Don't even think that," she said.

"You've been the best thing to happen to me in years."

"I feel the same. We'll stay close. Somehow we'll manage to see each other, perhaps sooner than you think."

"I'll phone you tomorrow night."

The final call for his flight was announced. It was time to go. He hugged her as tight as he could. Then, just before he reached down for his bags, she handed him a package.

"I bought this for myself, before I met you." She smiled. "Now I want you to have it. Please take it, Frank."

On the plane, somewhere between Venice and Rome, he carefully unwrapped her gift. It was a fine antique Venetian wineglass, pure Renaissance in style, nothing fancy, no spirals or wavy bands of color, just a simple graceful transparent cone set upon an octagonal base.

As Janek held it to the window so the wondrous light of the Italian sky could play upon it and fill it up, he knew, by the way it reminded him of the clear, yearning beauty of Monika's eyes, that it was the choicest piece of glass he had seen in Venice.

3

Conversation with Mama

"Can you hear me, dear?"

"I can hear you, Mama."

"It's getting to be time again."

"Yes, Mama."

"Remember, it's not enough to feel the pain and then the fury. You've got to do something about it. Got to fix them good."

"I understand, Mama."

"He deserves it. Doesn't he?"

"Oh, he deserves it! He surely does deserve it!"

"So?"

"I'll use Tool again."

"What will you do to him?"

"The same as to the others."

"Let's hear you say it."

"Fix him. Shut him up forever."

"*Why*, child?"

"Because of what he did."

"And what was that?"

"Must I, Mama? Please!"

"You *must*! You know you *must*! Now tell me what he did."

"He was unkind."

"*Ha!*"

"*Very* unkind!"

"Don't make me laugh."

"Well, he *was.*"

"Of course, he *was,* you goose. But what did he *do*? Tell me!"

"*Insulted* me."

"Is that *all*?"

"*Hurt* me."

"Is that really all he did? Come on, child. Spill your guts."

"He *harmed* me."

"Can't say it, can you?"

"I can say it, Mama. I can say it all right. It hurts me to say it. But I *can.*"

"Then say it, for God's sakes. *Say it!*"

"He—"

"*What?*"

"Humiliated me."

"Don't whimper, child. Say it loud."

"*He humiliated me!*"

"Yep, that's what he did. So what're you going to do about it?"

"Pay him back."

"How?"

"Use Tool."

"Use Tool to do *what*?"

"Kill him."

"And?"

"Fix him!"

"And?"

"Shut him up!"

"For how long?"

"Forever."

"Say it again."

"Kill him and fix him and shut him up forever."

"There, that's the ticket. You got it, child. Yeah, you got it now."

Jess

On the Van Wyck Expressway, peering out of Aaron Greenberg's beaten-up Chevrolet, Janek felt malice in the air. Traffic was heavy. People sat rigid and angry in their cars. Cold rain pelted the asphalt through noxious yellow fog, while all around he could hear the biting sound of horns and, in the distance, competing sirens, perhaps a fire truck and an ambulance at odds.

He touched the window. Ice-cold. The wiper slapped back and forth. The city ahead, toward which they were moving at such erratic speed, could not yet be seen, but Janek could feel it, could feel its nasty breath, its rancor.

He turned back to Aaron, who sat straight in his seat, concentrating on the road. A short, taut, wiry man with weather-beaten skin, his eyes and smile were sweet. *My partner and best friend,* Janek thought. Kit would gladly have sent her car, but only Aaron, he knew, would come out to Kennedy Airport on such a day to meet him and bring him in.

"New York's got no gender."

Aaron peered ahead curiously. "What?"

"Venice is a 'she.' New York's an 'it,' " Janek said.

"Well, what do you expect, Frank? I mean, Venice is pretty. New York's not supposed to be."

Janek glanced at him. "You haven't told me anything."

Aaron continued to stare ahead. "Been waiting for you to ask."

"How bad was it?" He held his breath as he waited for the reply.

Aaron exhaled. "I don't know how to put it quite."

"Try." The floor pads in the car smelled wet and old.

"Worse than you think, Frank. Worse than you think."

They rode in silence for a time; then Janek asked Aaron to give it to him straight. Never mind the niceties. Just straight, like they were starting out on a case and Aaron was filling him in.

"All I got so far is what I heard around. The detective in charge didn't get back to me yet."

"What's his name?"

"Ray Boyce."

"Never heard of him."

"Neither have I."

"Well . . . ?"

Aaron winced. "She was done with an ice pick in Riverside Park, not far from her dorm room at Columbia. It was early evening. She went out jogging alone. That wasn't approved; but she did it a lot, and she wasn't the only one. Plenty of other kids run alone in the dark. I don't know where they think they're living. Nicetown, USA? Anyway, it was about seven. No witnesses. Nobody saw nothing. She never returned to her room. She didn't have a roommate, so she wasn't missed. In fact, well I don't know if I ought—"

"Don't try and spare me, Aaron."

Aaron nodded. "Understand, Frank, this is just what I heard.

Seems she spent a lot of nights away. She had boyfriends. Again, she wasn't the only one. Other kids—"

"Okay, I get the picture. Go on."

"Every morning, early, the Columbia men's crew goes running as a group. They found her and called her in. Apparently nothing was taken, not that she was carrying much. But she had a watch and a Walkman. If it was a mugger, that's what you'd expect him to take."

"So it wasn't a mugger?"

"Doesn't look like it."

"Who was it then? Pack of animals on a wilding, like the ones smashed up that stockbroker a couple years back?"

"Doesn't look like that either."

"What does it look like?"

"Take it easy, Frank. You're closing in too fast. I don't know what it looks like. Like I said, Boyce didn't get back to me yet."

"Check him out?"

Aaron nodded. "He's okay."

"So-so's what you mean."

Aaron shrugged. "They can't all be stars, Frank. Boyce got the call. So it's his."

Aaron was right, that's the way it worked, and it was a stinking system, too, because a good 20 percent of the detective force was barely so-so, and when it came to Janek's goddaughter, so-so wasn't going to be good enough.

He turned to the back of the car. Aaron had spread the tabloids across the rear seat. Janek's eyes flew across them. The headlines shrieked.

"If it wasn't a mugger or a pack on a rampage, who the hell was it?"

"Could have been a mugger," Aaron said. "He could have gotten spooked."

"Mugger with an ice pick? Where did they find it anyway?"

"What?"

"The pick."

"It was left embedded."

"Oh, Christ!" Janek moaned. Just hearing that made him hurt. "You know how I felt about her, Aaron."

Aaron nodded, then paused a moment before he spoke. "Tell you what I think, Frank, just based on what I heard. There wasn't any reason. It was just, you know, one of those lousy goddamn things. We get them all the time. You know—"

"Yeah. . . ." Janek knew all right. He knew all about them, though they weren't the kinds of cases he ever worked. A unique phenomenon of American cities, of which New York, on account of its population, had a greater share than anyplace else, they were the homicides that were rarely solved because there was nothing about them to solve. They had no point. They were the meaningless murders committed by madmen stalking people alone at night in public parks.

There was a TV news unit with a transmitting device on its roof parked across the street from the James O'Hara Funeral Home. Aaron stopped the car; Janek ducked out into the rain, then wound his way between the waiting limos, past the cameras at the door, and into the lobby. A stand on the far wall was stuffed with wet umbrellas. A dour man in a cutaway stepped forward and asked if he was there for the Wentworth funeral.

"The Foy," Janek said.

The man looked him over carefully. "You're the godfather?" Janek nodded. "They waited long as they could. They're about halfway through it now. West Chapel, up the stairs, second door on the right."

When he got there, Janek stood in the back and listened. An intense, frizzy-haired young man in ecclesiastical garments was speaking with bitter scorn of the horrors of New York.

". . . this Cultural Paradise, once so gracious, now choked with the downtrodden and the homeless. This Imperial City, once so elegant, now ridden with rape and murder. Just this past week a grandmother was dragged to her death by a purse snatcher at midday on Madison Avenue. And a brilliant young intern, with a great future before him, was shot at dusk outside New York Hospital because he refused to hand over his coat. And now our dear Jessica, beloved daughter of Laura, beloved stepdaughter of Stanton, and goddaughter of Frank, has been struck down . . . and we ask: What madness has been set loose in our city? Why must such a tragedy happen? For what reason? What cause? How can we allow it? What we can we say? What can we do? And our voices are mute, for we have no answers. . . ."

It was a long, narrow, overheated room, crowded mostly with younger people. Janek recognized a few: Jess's friends from high school and college, her cousins on Laura's side, and Stanton Dorance's two older sons, children from an earlier marriage. He also saw Tim Foy's mother, a thin veiled Irish woman in her sixties who now had lost both son and granddaughter to violence.

Ten or so well-dressed middle-aged men with well-trimmed hair sat together in a row. *Must be Stanton's law partners,* Janek thought. Laura and Stanton sat at the front in the bent, broken postures of the bereaved. There was an empty seat beside them. Janek waited until the minister paused, then crept forward to it. He hugged Laura, shook Stanton's hand, then settled back in time for the final words of the eulogy, which ended unexpectedly, not with a plea for reconciliation but on a shrill note of inexplicability and despair.

Afterward Laura grasped his arm. Even in grief she was a beautiful woman. "Thank God you made it, Frank. You know how she adored you. . . ." And then clinging to him, sobbing: "What am I going to do without her? I can't imagine. I just can't imagine. . . ."

Outside, Janek hustled Laura into the lead limo, while Stanton walked over to the waiting press, stood stoically in the rain and addressed their microphones: "Please, ladies and gentlemen, please give us some room for our grief. . . ."

In Queens, at the cemetery, just after they left the car, Stanton motioned Janek aside. Gravestones covered the bleak wet earth as far as the eye could see. Stanton's face, always strong, sometimes arrogant, looked weak and blotchy in the rain. His gestures, normally poised, were angular and abrupt.

"Find the animal who did this, Frank. Promise me you'll find him and bring him in."

Janek became aware then of a new wave of pain. It rose out of the center of his belly and spread across his chest. He thought: *Just think of yourself as a detective and then maybe a little of this hurt will go away.*

"I'll do my best, Stanton. But you know how these things go."

As Stanton stared at him outraged, Janek felt ashamed; what he'd said sounded so impotent. But then Stanton nodded. He understood. To live in New York was to understand all too well the vagaries of the criminal justice system and the cheap price of young human life.

When Janek met Aaron at 6:00 P.M. in the lobby of the Two-Six Precinct, he didn't have to ask for his opinion of Detective Boyce. Aaron offered it by seesawing his hands. "Tell you this, Frank, he ain't no Sherlock Holmes."

Aaron continued imparting his impression as they mounted the precinct house stairs. "He's pissed off. He denies it, but I can tell. Chief Kopta told him you're the godfather, so naturally he's going to extend you every courtesy. But see, for Boyce a front-page homicide like this is a chance to make a big impression. Then the famous Janek walks in. He's afraid of you, Frank, afraid you'll steal his case."

Janek's own first impression was that Boyce wasn't so much dumb as slow. He had a beer belly and not much hair. He'd combed a few thin brown wisps back carefully across his skull as if he thought they might cover his baldness and make him more attractive—but they didn't. The base of his face had a kind of squared-off look that reminded Janek of the bottom of a paper bag. But though his manner did not proclaim great brilliance, Janek recognized a predatory look. Aaron was right: This was a mediocre detective inflamed by a stroke of luck. The Jessica Foy case could be just the break he'd been waiting for for twenty years.

"I understand your special relationship to the victim, Lieutenant," Boyce began, "but let's not start off on the wrong foot. She's your goddaughter, but she's my case. Long as that's clear, we'll get along."

Jesus! Janek thought, but he kept his anger to himself. He knew that sooner or later a man who talked like that would blunder his way into Kit Kopta's bad graces.

"What do you really know about her?"

"Me?"

"You're her godfather, so I figured—"

This time Janek didn't bother to control his temper. "What the fuck, Boyce! I know a million things about her. What are you looking for me to say?"

"Know much about her social life?"

"What *about* her social life?" Now Boyce was wearing a cagey look, as if he had knowledge and it wasn't nice.

Aaron casually picked up Boyce's nameplate and tested it for strength. "Way you're acting, Ray, someone might think you're taunting the lieutenant here. Not a good idea, Ray. Why not just tell Janek what you got?"

Boyce shrugged. "I got a diary." He reached into his center drawer, pulled out a stenographer's notebook, and tossed it casually on the desk. "Read it, Janek. You may learn some things about her you didn't know." He headed for the door. "I'm going around the corner for coffee. Stick it back in the drawer when you're finished, okay?"

After Boyce left, Janek stared at the notebook, then cautiously reached for it. The sight of Jess's handwriting brought back memories of the sharp, funny postcards she'd send him whenever she traveled. He handed the notebook over to Aaron.

"Sure, I'll read it, Frank," Aaron said.

Janek found Boyce hunched over a chipped Formica table in the back section of a dingy coffee shop around the corner from the precinct house. During the day the place was frequented by detectives. Now Boyce was the only cop there. Boyce didn't look up as Janek approached, which gave Janek a chance to observe him. Boyce looked older and more tired than he had in his office. Janek felt a tinge of pity. *He has to wake up every morning and know he's Boyce,* he thought.

"Okay, Ray," he said, sitting down uninvited, "I know you resent me. You saw the miniseries and you thought it sucked. Maybe it did. Who the hell cares? Right now I'm hurting. I've lost someone I loved. So tell me what's on your mind. Who did this to her? Tell me what you think."

When Boyce finally looked up, Janek wasn't sure he'd cut into him very deep. But he knew he'd broken skin; Boyce was ready to show a human face.

"She was an honors student." Boyce waited for Janek to nod. "And a member of the women's fencing team." Janek nodded again. "She was tops, okay? Beautiful girl, full of life, popular, ace student, competitive athlete—what more could you ask? But there was a side that was unexpected. A strange unstable personal life. Boyfriends, but they weren't quite her style, she being so fastidious and all. Okay, last spring she takes up with a rich kid name of Greg Gale. And he introduces her into his crowd, where they dabble in highs—a little dope here, a mind game or two there, weird sex all the time. To get in with these kids, you have to be initiated. The initiation is you have sex blindfolded with one of them while the rest of the group watches the ceremony. Reading her diary, you get the impression she got off on it, like she wanted to roll a little in the dirt."

Janek nodded, but every word stung. Jess, blindfolded, having sex with a stranger before an audience—the image pierced his heart.

". . . but then, see, over the summer, she decides to straighten out. So early this fall, she starts going to a shrink. Then, about the same time, she breaks up with Gale. Pretty bitterly, too, it sounds like. No, I haven't talked to him. You're thinking: *Why the hell not? That's the first thing I'd do.* I got no answer for you, Janek, except that's not my way. Call me methodical. I like to lay the groundwork. I don't like going in asking questions till I have a pretty fair idea what the answers are going to be. A guy like Gale whose parents have bucks—I may get one crack at him before the family lawyer butts in. Understand what I'm saying?"

Janek nodded again. He understood very well.

"Thing is, Janek, people dabble in weird sex, maybe they dabble in murder, too. So this group she was going with is going to get looked at. They're going to get a very close look from me."

Janek sat back, shook his head. "I don't get it. I thought this was a random park murder."

"So did I at first. Now it turns out there're oddities."

"Like what?"

Boyce hesitated. "Something was done to her. Afterwards."

"What was done to her?"

Boyce looked uncomfortable. "Let's go back to my office. I'll show you the medical examiner's report and the photographs."

Janek declined. "Just tell me about it, Ray."

Again Boyce seemed hesitant. "She was glued."

"*Glued!* How?"

"Guy who killed her—maybe he had a little caulking gun. After she was dead, he pumped glue into her, into an intimate area, know what I mean? It's like he was trying to, you know—close off that part of her. . . ."

Close off! Janek felt sick to his stomach.

When they returned to Boyce's office, Aaron was waiting and Jess's notebook was back on the desk.

Janek gestured toward the notebook. "Do me a favor, Ray. I want the family protected. Make sure nothing in there gets leaked."

"Yeah," Boyce said, "but you know how it is. Stuff like that has a way of getting around."

"I'm asking you, don't *let* it get around."

"Sure, I'll do my best."

Aaron stared at Boyce fiercely, but Janek whispered, "Thanks." He'd used the same weak I'll-do-my-best-but-you-know-how-it-is just hours before with Stanton.

When they got back to Aaron's car, it had stopped raining. They compared notes as they drove downtown. Aaron confirmed that everything Boyce had said at the coffee shop was actually in the diary. There was one additional thing, probably not too significant: Lately Jess had been having bad dreams.

"This thing with the glue," Janek asked, "you didn't hear anything about it?"

Aaron shook his head. "Hard to keep something like that quiet, too. There isn't a reporter wouldn't kill to get hold of it."

"So maybe Boyce runs a tight ship."

"Isn't he a marvel! Thing is—can you trust him?"

"Hard to say. Like everyone else, he's out mostly for himself."

"Well, I'll tell you what I think, Frank. I think the guy's a schmuck," Aaron said.

Aaron stopped in front of Janek's building, a gray stone apartment house, formerly a tenement, with exterior fire escapes on West Eighty-seventh. Then he went around to the trunk, retrieved Janek's suitcase, and offered to carry it upstairs. Janek refused.

"Thanks, but you've done enough."

Aaron stood by the car awkwardly, as if he didn't want to leave Janek there alone. "I've been meaning to ask you, Frank. How was your trip?"

"It was going great till I got the call. I met someone. Someone terrific."

Aaron grinned. "That's grand, Frank. Congratulations. When do I get to meet her?"

"It's going to be complicated. She lives in Germany."

"Oh. . . ." There was nothing Aaron could say to that. "We'll talk tomorrow, okay?" Aaron put out his hand. Janek ignored it and embraced him.

"Thanks for sticking with me, Aaron. Thanks for everything."

"Don't worry, Frank. Whoever did this, we'll get him for sure."

Aaron spoke with such conviction that for a full minute Janek sustained belief. But then, as he stumbled into the gloom of his apartment, the notion faded fast.

It was a simply furnished place, mostly with pieces inherited from his parents, including the workbench from his father's accordion repair shop strewn with a half dozen accordions in various states of disrepair.

When Janek entered, he turned on a couple of lights, opened a window, placed his bag on his bed, then went into the bathroom to splash cold water on his face. Unfortunately he splashed too fast; the water, unused for two and a half weeks, ran a nasty rusty brown.

After he unpacked, he placed Monika's wineglass on a table near his living-room window so it would catch the morning light. Then he rewound his answering machine, sat down in his easy chair, and listened to his messages.

There were the usual utilitarian calls amidst the hang-ups. Shoes he'd left for repair were ready for pickup. A friend had Jets tickets if he was interested. His ex, Sarah, complained he hadn't bothered to inform her he was traveling. Then, as a familiar voice came on, Janek felt a chill.

"Hi. It's Jess. Please call me soon as you get back. There's something I want you to—can't explain it now. But it's important. Call me. Please. Okay?"

It was the last message on the tape. He rewound it and played it again. She sounded worried but still in control, as if she had something on her mind and was turning now, as she had all her life when something bothered her, to her godfather, whom she trusted above all other men.

He played her message a third time, striving to decipher each inflection. Then he played it a fourth, at high volume, listening acutely to the background noise. After that rendition he felt fairly confident that she hadn't called him hastily from a public phone. And that meant she probably hadn't called him in a panic. When he played it a fifth time, checking for subtext, he heard the same basic message he'd been hearing all along: This is Jess; I need your help.

He removed the cassette from the machine and stored it safely in a drawer.

It was only eight-thirty, but he was too exhausted to go out and eat. And it was too late now to call Monika—past two in the morning in Europe. He'd read an article that said the best cure for jet lag was to go to bed the moment you got home. But now, with Jess's message running through his brain, he knew sleep would be impossible.

He dialed Kit's home number. There was only half a ring before she picked up.

"I've been waiting for your call, Frank. Feeling lousy?"

"Of course."

"Understandable." She paused. "I spoke to Boyce this morning. Did you see him?"

"About half an hour ago. Maybe he's okay, I don't know yet." He hesitated. "Hate to ask for favors, Kit. You know I've been careful about that. I wasn't that keen about going to Europe. And I'm not all that anxious to be your special assistant or whatever you have in mind."

"Hey! Hold it right there!"

"Uh-uh, Kit—let me finish. People know we have a past. Or whatever they want to call it. Who cares, right? So we bend over backwards, and I'd probably bend further than you just so people wouldn't be tempted to say anything. You know how much I hate office politics and all that kind of crap. Well, this time I'm asking because I think what we got here is a set of special circumstances. I was the one headed the investigation on Tim Foy. So here you have someone just as close, in the same family, and it only seems right—know what I mean? Who'd complain? Nobody, except maybe Boyce, and you've got fifty cases you could assign him. And—"

"Stop it, Frank!" Her voice was sharp.

Janek shook his head. "What's the matter? Can't I even ask?"

"It's not going to happen, so you might as well forget it. No one's going on a case where they're personally involved."

"Oh, Kit, please, I don't need a lecture on department policy."

"Not department policy, Frank. *My* policy—it's the way I'm running the division."

"Jesus! You sound so fucking rigid."

"Is that what you think?"

"Maybe I'm out of line. I just feel—"

"Get some rest, Frank. You're not in condition to have a rational discussion. Cool down, and in a couple days come see me and we'll talk. Meantime, stay away from the case. I mean it. Stay away." Her voice softened. "You know I care about you. So trust me. Please. Now try and get some sleep."

But he couldn't sleep. Not after that. He took a shower, changed clothes, called Stanton, told him he was coming over. Then, downstairs, he hailed a cab and asked the driver to drop him at Park and Seventy-second.

The Dorances lived farther uptown, but Janek wanted to walk a few blocks before he saw them. The rain had stopped, but it was chilly, a raw, cold October night.

The entrance to Laura and Stanton's building was guarded by a doorman with an outsize regimental-style mustache. He wore a parody of a military greatcoat embellished with silver epaulets.

The small lobby, lined in mahogany, contained four plush leather club chairs with a rare Persian rug in the center. In the elevator Janek could smell a recently extinguished cigarette. The elevator man had been smoking contrary to regulations and now had hidden the butt, probably in a box concealed beneath his uniform.

Janek got off at the sixteenth floor. The landing was decorated in a Japanese motif. Even after Janek rang the bell, the elevator man waited until Stanton opened up.

It was a magnificent apartment, a duplex with a huge sunken living room, a full dining room, and four bedroom suites on the upper floor. Stanton, who was wearing a maroon smoking jacket with silk sash and satin lapels, ushered him into a small paneled library and offered him a drink.

"Where's Laura?" Janek asked.

"She's pretty tired, Frank. I thought—"

"I want to talk to her, too, Stanton. Please ask her to come down?"

Stanton nodded and disappeared. While Janek waited, he fixed himself a scotch. Then he looked around. One bookcase was devoted to family photographs, each mounted in a different style of frame, which collectively suggested what it meant to live a life of privilege.

His eyes were drawn to the pictures of Jess. There she was in pigtails at the summer camp she'd gone to in the Adirondacks, grinning at the camera. Another photo showed her older, mountain climbing in Switzerland, and a third showed her smiling broadly the day she graduated from her expensive private school. She was a handsome girl, tall and leggy, with high cheekbones, short honey-colored hair, and the confident eyes of an athlete. There were several photos of her fencing. One showed her holding up a trophy like an Olympic champion.

For some years Janek had observed the Dorance family with a sense of wonder at their numerous entitlements. Stanton's million-and-a-half-dollar duplex. His weekend place in Litchfield County. The winter vacations in the Caribbean, Christmas in Aspen, the month they spent on Martha's Vineyard in the summer. Laura had come a long way, and Janek was glad for her. He'd wanted nothing but the best for her and Jess. But he was still upset by Boyce's description of Jess's "social life." Laura had never mentioned difficulties. He had come now to find out why.

When Stanton reappeared with Laura, Janek stood to embrace her.

"You're still one gorgeous lady," he said.

"Oh, Frank. . . ." She hugged him again.

"Sorry to descend on you so late, but I've got some real problems."

"What kind of problems?" Stanton's hands trembled slightly as he poured himself a cognac.

Janek had been dreading this conversation from the moment he'd decided he needed it. Now the only thing to do was plunge ahead.

"You know what was done to her?" Laura looked toward Stanton. "I'm talking about the glue," Janek said. They both nodded. "This afternoon we spent an hour together driving to the cemetery, but neither of you mentioned that. I want to know why."

"We didn't want to upset you," Stanton said.

"Excuse me," said Janek, "but how could anything have made me feel worse? I'm asking you again: Why didn't you say anything?"

"We were told—" Laura started to speak, but Stanton interrupted.

"We were asked to keep that to ourselves. Chief Kopta told us not to get you excited, because she said you couldn't go on the case. I don't know how the Police Department works, Frank, but when the Chief of Detectives tells us not to talk about something, I don't see that we have a choice."

"Well, that's just fine, Stanton. But at the cemetery you made me promise to hunt down her killer."

"Yes. . . ."

Janek shook his head. "You can't have it both ways. Was that rhetoric or for real?"

"I meant it. Jesus, of course, I meant it."

"Good." Janek nodded. "Now let's see how far you're willing to go." He turned to Laura. "What do you know about a young man named Greg Gale?"

Laura looked confused. "Just that Jess was dating him. Then she broke it off."

"Ever meet him?"

"I think we saw him a couple of times," Stanton said. "Maybe for a minute or two when he came by to pick her up. Why do you ask? Is he mixed up in this?"

Janek ignored Stanton's question. He'd decided to concentrate on Laura. She was softer, more vulnerable, more likely to talk.

"Know anything about Gale's friends and how Jess was involved with them?"

"A little."

"Pretty fast bunch of kids from what I hear."

"Goddamn it, Frank!" Stanton smacked down his drink. "What're you trying to do? We just buried our daughter. Surely there's a better time."

"I'm a detective, Stanton. Good enough for you to ask for my help. But then you don't bother to tell me what was done to her or that she was moving with a fast bunch of kids who did drugs and played mind games and had group sex and I don't know what else. Better listen now: The girl was sexually mutilated. Doesn't take a genius to figure out she may have been killed by someone she knew. But you don't tell me anything, just leave me thinking she was a victim of a random park killer, and isn't that just awful!

Isn't New York a terrible place! Why do we all live in this hell-hole? Oh, dear! Oh, God! Oh, shit!" Janek steadied himself. "You've got two choices, Stanton. Tell me everything you know or withdraw your request. Because if you ever hold back anything from me again, I'm out of it. Forever. Understand?"

"Chief Kopta?"

"Never mind her. She's my problem, not yours."

Laura was crying now, softly into a handkerchief. Stanton stood beside her chair, one hand on her shoulder.

"All right, Frank. The hell with it! I don't know what we were thinking. Look, we didn't know exactly what was going on between Jess and Gale, but we got a few hints we didn't like. She was always boy-crazy. We assumed she, you know—fooled around. But we tried not to think too hard about it. What the kids do now, it isn't the same as in our day. If you're a parent, you can't do anything about it so you ignore it, maybe hope it goes away. I guess that's what we did."

Laura, obviously embarrassed, was staring at the rug. "Go on," Janek said. "Let's hear it all."

"There isn't much to tell. Early this fall, when Jess went back to school, she told us she wanted to break it off. We didn't question her. We just tried to be supportive. When she said she wanted to see a shrink, I told her to find a good one and not to worry about the fees. And that's just what she did. This Dr. Archer she started going to, a reputable woman, a clinical psychologist, seemed to help her a lot. As for not keeping you abreast of the details of her personal life, there were just some things we felt Jess wouldn't have wanted us to share."

Laura looked up. "She was a wonderful girl, Frank. But she wasn't perfect. No child is. She loved you very much, and she knew how much you adored her. More than anything she wanted your respect. I think she'd rather have died than disappoint you."

Janek shook his head. "Laura, Laura—she's gone now. We're way past the time when you have to worry about my being disappointed."

"Yes, Frank. I know. Of course. . . ."

They both looked as if they felt they'd been awful and stupid.

He didn't want to leave them feeling that way, so he decided to share the contents of their daughter's call.

"When I got home tonight, there was a message from Jess. She didn't leave the date or time, but it was the last call I got, so I know she made it no earlier than two days before she was killed. She sounded worried, said she wanted to talk to me, said it was important, urged me to call her as soon as I got back. What was it? What did she want? Think hard, because this is important. The girl's upset; then she's killed and mutilated. Maybe she felt she was in danger."

Laura stared at him. "I can't imagine."

"Could have been about her father," Stanton said.

Laura nodded. "It could." She turned to Janek. "A few weeks ago she started asking me questions about Tim. I was surprised. We'd barely talked about him in years. I thought, well, it probably came up in her therapy. I suggested she talk to you. I told her you knew Tim in a completely different way. She seemed pleased with that. She loved talking to you, Frank. So maybe that's why she called."

Janek thought about it. Did wanting to talk to him about Tim fit the tone of her message? Not likely.

"Well, maybe so," he said. He wound up the discussion, kissed Laura on the cheek, and started for the door. Stanton escorted him out to the hallway and stood beside him as he rang for the elevator.

"Well?"

"Well—what, Stanton?"

"I want you to promise me you'll hunt her killer down."

"I thought I already did."

"I want to hear you say it."

Janek looked at him. Stanton's eyes gleamed with a lust for vengeance.

"Yeah, I promise," Janek said. "I promise I'll hunt him to the ends of the earth. How's that?"

Stanton nodded. "Fine. That's fine, Frank. It feels good to hear you say the words."

The elevator arrived. Janek got in. The cigarette smoke was even more pungent than before.

"We'll stay in touch. Won't we?"

"Yeah, we'll stay in touch," Janek said to the closing door.

He was dreaming when, at six the following morning, his ringing telephone woke him up. As he groped for the receiver, he tried to recapture his dream, but the details were instantly lost to him, leaving him with nothing but a vague sense of dread.

It was Monika, and the fine clarity of her voice quickly drove away his demons.

"I was worried, Frank. You didn't call."

"Sorry. I got back too late. I figured you'd be asleep."

"I've been thinking about you, imagining what you've been going through. I wish I could be there with you now."

Wasn't she fabulous! Perhaps Venice had been more than a dream.

"I love the glass," he said.

"I hoped you would."

"I put it by my window. I want to look at it every day, to remind myself of Venice and how I met you there and what we found together." He pulled himself short. "Hey! I better shut up. This is getting sentimental."

"Don't be afraid of sentiment, Frank."

"No, Monika. But sometimes I'm wary." And then he poured out to her everything that was bothering him: the way Jess was stabbed, the gluing, the decadent boyfriend, and finally the diary.

"I couldn't bear to read it. I don't know why. First I thought it was her handwriting; then I realized I was afraid of what I'd have to read. Boyce almost leered when he offered it to me. I guess I didn't want . . . what? Disillusionment. Then, when he told me about her, that gang she was running with, having sex wearing a blindfold while the other kids watched . . . I don't know. I've seen a lot, maybe as bad as it gets, but I never connected Jess with anything sordid. Of course, it wasn't necessarily ugly. It all depends on how she approached it. She was a grown woman. She had every right to live her life. But still, I can't seem to come to grips with it. It's as if there was a part of her I didn't know."

Monika told him she thought that if he just looked at it in a certain way, he wouldn't feel so confused. As for Jess's secrecy, she assured him that that was not at all uncommon in a young person, especially with an older person the youngster loves.

"I think she knew that to you she would always seem a perfect little girl. And I think it's a sign of her love for you that she didn't want to disturb your illusion."

"Okay," he said, "that makes sense. But this sex thing—"

"Don't dwell on it, Frank. She sounds to me like a fairly normal young woman, fully entitled to her secrets, insecurities, struggles, her groping expressions of sexuality. No one is obliged to be a moral paragon. And there's so much in her diary that sounds positive. The fact that she broke off with the rotten boyfriend and started seeing a therapist is an excellent sign. And the fact that she tried to reach you when she felt she was in trouble—that alone should tell you how much you meant to her. I hope you don't love her any the less for what you've found out."

"Nothing in the world could make me love her less," Janek said. Then he started to choke. "God! I don't want to break down again."

"Please don't be embarrassed with me."

He smiled. "I just hate the cliché. You know: tough-New-York-cop-with-feelings."

"I never thought of you as tough."

"How did you think of me?"

"You were the big American I kept running into all the time, whom I lured into following me."

He smiled. She really was the best thing to happen to him in years.

There was a tremendous amount of mail waiting for him at the post office, so much that the clerk suggested he borrow a mail sack to carry it home. Junk mail, bills, magazines, and then, among the letters, one that didn't look right. He picked it out of the multitude and examined it carefully. It bore no return address. His name was handwritten in block letters on the envelope: "LIEUTENANT FRANK JANEK." The postmark, dated the day after Jess's killing, told him it had been mailed from Greenkill Prison. He ripped it open, read it quickly, then threw it down with disgust. The text, unsigned, was short and to the point: "JANEK, I SLEEP BETTER KNOWING YOUR GODDAUGHTER IS IN THE GROUND."

The road into Greenkill is as stark as the old red-brick buildings that comprise its campus. The complex looms upon a hill. Beneath its walls cows graze fields, a pastoral touch which, though meant to calm the inmates, only enrages them by mocking their confinement. Below the fields there is a moat, and below that interlocking rolls of razor wire. That October day, beneath stone gray clouds, Greenkill had a brooding presence. As Janek entered, he felt the screaming silence of the place and the stern essence of its gloom. But most of all, he felt the weight of unserved time.

He showed his badge, parked in the visitors' lot, then waited in the reception area until his visit was cleared by the warden's office. He checked his gun and ammo with the property clerk, was frisked by the gate guard, passed through the electronic barriers without setting off any alarms. Then he was escorted to a small plain attorney's room. Rusty Glickman, dressed in blue denim, was waiting for him in a cheap plastic chair set up before a battered wooden table.

"Pleasure, Janek," he said. But as he sat down, Janek responded only with a look.

It had been fifteen years since he'd last seen Glickman. Now he wasn't certain he'd recognize him if he passed him on the street. Glickman's tight black hair had mostly fallen out, replaced by a grayish fringe. His taut, lean body had gone to fat, and his breath stank of tobacco—not surprising since lung cancer, caused by excessive smoking of cigarettes, was the most frequent killer of lifers. But as Janek studied Glickman, he recognized the expression around his mouth. Even fifteen years of incarceration had not extinguished the sneer that said, "Whoever you may think you are, to me you're a total piece of shit."

"What brings you around? Social call? It's been what? Fifteen years?"

Again Janek didn't bother to answer. He reached into his pocket, pulled out the letter, and placed it flat on the table.

Glickman glanced at it. "So?"

"You wrote it."

"So what?"

"Why?"

Glickman shrugged. "Why not?" He smirked.

Janek slowly moved his head in close, deliberately invading Glickman's space.

"I know you're slime. But what could you possibly have against Tim Foy's daughter?"

"I got nothing against her. I didn't even remember he had a daughter till I read about her in the papers."

"So *why*?"

"You, the big shot detective from New York, got the balls to come up here and ask me that? I thought you were supposed to be smart, Janek." Glickman's voice was loaded with scorn. "I saw this shitty miniseries where this actor—what's his name, he's a lot better-looking than you—where he struts around making like he's so fucking brilliant. Lieutenant Frank Janek the character was called. What a pile of shit."

Janek stared at him. "Once a psychopath always a psychopath."

He stood. "I don't need your abuse." He moved toward the door to call the guard.

" 'Cause of you, I gotta spend the rest of my life in a rathole while you get to run around in New York playing Great Detective. You ask why I wrote you about the girl. I wrote so you'd come up here and I could look into your eyes and see your pain. That's all I wanted. Now I'm satisfied. I've seen it. It looks pretty good to me. I *like* seeing you in pain, Janek. Like I said, it's a real pleasure."

"Guard!" Janek shouted, then waited facing the door. No matter what Glickman said to him, he vowed not to react. But Glickman was on a roll. He had only a few more seconds and nothing to lose.

"You call me slime. You're the slime, Janek. You and your buddy—what's his name?—Foy. And his little cunt of a daughter, too. That's what she was, wasn't she? A little cunt, a slut, running around, twitching her horny little ass in the park. Know something? I'm *glad* she's dead!"

The guard had arrived, was working his key in the lock, but Janek didn't care. Even as he yielded to his anger, he knew he was making a mistake. *But fuck it!* he thought. He turned, raised his foot against the ledge of the table, and shoved as hard as he could, propelling the table straight toward Glickman, knocking him off his chair and onto the floor.

"See that!" Glickman shouted to the guard. "See what he did! Struck a prisoner! You saw it! *He struck a fucking prisoner!* That's grounds for a lawsuit! A big lawsuit! You're really fucked now, asshole! Probably cost you your fucking pension!"

Glickman was laughing, a sneering, bullying laughter, the kind you'd expect from a slimeball who'd order a bomb planted in another man's car. But Janek was already out the door. As he walked down the corridor, he could hear Glickman's laughter resound against the walls. By the time he reached the security gate he knew that he himself was now walking on a knife's edge of sanity.

That night, when he got back to New York, the craziness was really cooking in him. But being conscious of it and wanting to give it up were two different things. *I may be strung out,* he thought, *but I've still got control.*

Though emotionally exhausted, thoroughly jet-lagged, fatigued from his journey to Greenkill, he was nonetheless ready to do what Boyce was not: corner Greg Gale and squeeze him till he bled.

He called the number Aaron had provided and got a taped answer off a machine. He didn't like the sound of Gale's voice, a snotty prep school whine.

Angry but composed, Janek taxied to a block on West Ninety-eighth between Broadway and West End. He found Gale's building easily enough, a subdivided gray stone town house. He rang the buzzer to be sure Gale wasn't in, then walked over to the garage across the street. Yes, indeed, the night manager said, he knew young Mr. Gale. He kept kept his car there, but it wasn't there now. He'd taken it out earlier that evening. Janek tipped him in return for permission to wait in the office until young Mr. Gale returned. Then he settled back into a beaten-up swivel chair and tried to get some sleep.

Two hours later he felt a light touch on his shoulder. The manager, hovering, gestured toward the garage drive. A well-polished red Porsche was angled in the entrance, and a lean young male, dressed in a trench coat, was making his way across the street.

"Thanks," Janek whispered, then hurried out. He reached the vestibule of the town house just as Gale was unlocking the inner hallway door.

"Greg?"

Gale turned. He had light, wavy hair verging on blond and the smooth, symmetrical features of a secondary lead in a soap opera. The only striking thing about him was his pallor; he looked like the kind of person who ventured out only at night.

Janek flashed his shield.

"This must be about Jess."

Janek nodded. "Got time to talk?"

Gale glanced around. He seemed reluctant. Janek tried to make himself vulnerable. "Been waiting quite a while, Greg. Pretty cold out there." He rubbed his hands together as he spoke.

Gale nodded. "Well, okay. Shall we talk down here?"

"Up to you." Janek rubbed his hands again to emphasize the chill.

The young man shrugged. "Let's go upstairs." He grinned. "I gotta take a leak."

He was poised and he was handsome and the thought of Jess in his arms filled Janek with disgust. But he played along and smiled and followed Gale up the stairs, enjoying the thought of how the little jerk was shortly going to be sorry he'd invited him into his place.

Inside the apartment Gale excused himself, leaving Janek alone to look around. It seemed pretty lush for a college student, but then so did a red Porsche. There was black leather upholstered furniture, a sleek stereo, a top-grade TV with matching VCR, big collections of CD discs and videotapes, a shelf of mystery novels, and, most striking, a large photograph hanging over the fireplace. Beautifully framed, it showed a muscular naked black male posed on one knee before a standing young woman. Dressed in white equestrian garb, she peered down at the black with a disdainful, lascivious smile.

When Gale reappeared, Janek gestured toward the picture. "Interesting," he said.

Gale showed his teeth. "Like that, do you?"

"I didn't say I liked it. I said it was interesting."

"I took it."

"You're a photographer?"

"I fool around with it a little, yeah." Though the kid obviously wanted to sound self-deprecating, he came off as shallow and arrogant.

"Ever take any pictures of Jess?"

Gale ran his tongue across his lips. "A few. Want to see them?"

If they were anything like the kinky picture over the fireplace, Janek didn't think he did. He stared at Gale.

"I'll ask the questions, Greg. You'll answer them. Let's start off easy. What did you do to her in the park?"

"What?"

"You heard me."

"Hey! Are you for real? I want you out of here. *Now!*"

When Janek smiled, Gale looked confused. A slight vibrato in his upper lip showed that he was feeling fear.

"I know who you are. You're the detective she was always talking about."

Janek offered no response.

"Okay," Gale said, quickly adjusting his manner to eager-to-please, "you want answers. I don't know anything about the park. I didn't lay eyes on her the last seven weeks. We quarreled, and she kicked me out of her life. Naturally I feel real bad about what happened, but I don't know anything about it. That's all I'm going to say."

Real bad—shit! "Not good enough, Greggy boy."

"I want you to go."

Janek shook his head. "Not till I'm satisfied."

"Don't try to bully me, detective!"

"Think this is bullying?" Janek laughed.

They stared at each other. Then Gale made a move toward his phone. "I'm calling the police."

He picked up the receiver, but his trembling betrayed his fear. Janek walked over to him and casually held out his hand. Gale paused, then surrendered the receiver. Janek set it down. He lightly pushed Gale into a black wooden chair bearing Columbia University's coat of arms. He pulled up a matching chair and sat down close, so close he could see a quiver in the young man's eyes.

"All right," he said, "here's how it's going down. We're going to have a polite conversation in which I ask the questions and you give me truthful answers. The alternative is you get mad and try to punch me out. That's an attack on a law officer, felonious assault, which yields your basic five-year sentence. Not to mention the fact that then I'd have to hit you back, which would probably cost you your teeth. If I had a pretty face like yours, I don't think I'd like that very much. Your choice. I can handle it either way. See, I'm mad. My goddaughter was murdered. So basically I don't give a shit."

Gale lowered his eyes. "I told you—I don't know anything."

"Let's get more specific. Jess rejected you?" Gale nodded. "You resented her for that?"

"I don't know if I'd say 'resent.' I admit I was pretty upset. But—"

"Yeah, yeah—you don't know anything. Now tell me about the sex club?"

Gale screwed up his face to convey perplexity. "What are you talking about?"

Greggy's not too good an actor, Janek thought as he tutted and shook his finger. "No questions, just answers."

"I don't know anything about any sex club."

"Your little clique. The ones who watch while the new kid fucks blindfolded."

"You *know* about that?"

Janek reached forward and slapped Gale lightly across the face. "*I* ask. *You* answer. Last warning. Okay?"

"Okay, okay. But it's not a club. It's more like . . . a group of friends."

"How many 'friends'?"

"Nine or ten, depending on who wants in or out."

"Percentage of women?"

"Half and half."

"Who started it?"

"My idea originally."

"You recruit new people?"

"Sort of. But it isn't exactly—"

"You brought in Jess?"

"Yeah. But—"

"You planned to bring her into the group from the moment you started dating her. You weren't interested in her as a girlfriend. You just wanted another body, right?" Gale shook his head. "I want a straight answer."

"Well, maybe that is what I had in mind."

"Damn straight it was. From the start, right? But you never told her, did you? You waited till you thought she was ready. Then you proposed it, in a slippery kind of way like 'I know this great group of kids, they're really far-out, but I think you'll find them interesting.'"

Greg lowered his eyes, resigned. "Maybe that's what I did." Then he looked up. "But she was a big girl. And she went for it. Believe me, she enjoyed it. The moment I broached it to her, her eyes lit up. Probably hard for you to hear this, but Jess liked sex. I mean she *liked* it. And there's nothing wrong with that. We played safe, took precautions, used condoms. That's why we formed the group in the first place, so we could have some variety and still play safe. The whole idea was to make it fun. Not nasty like you're trying to make it seem."

"Did I call it nasty?"

"It's your tone. Your whole approach. You want to make me feel like a worm."

That much was true, but Janek wanted to define his own attitude. "I don't think sex is nasty. But I think someone who uses the guise of romantic involvement to entice a girl into that kind of thing is fairly low-grade slime."

Gale twisted in his chair. He couldn't take contempt. "That's pretty close to what she told me, too," he whispered.

Janek was grateful to hear that.

"She dumped on you?"

"I already told you."

"You must have resented her."

"I'm human. Wouldn't you?"

"Resented her so much you stalked her, stabbed her, and after you killed her, you attacked the part of her that mocked you the most, that mocked your manhood."

Gale jumped up. "What're you talking about? What part of her? Jesus!"

"The part you couldn't satisfy. The part that made you feel inadequate."

"I don't understand." He paused. "You mean, my cock? Is that what you're talking about?"

Janek smiled. "Not your lousy little cock, asshole. A part of her. *Jess!*"

Gale was still confused. "What part of her?"

"You tell me."

"Are you saying she was—that someone did something to her? God! I didn't know! It wasn't in the papers. Jesus!"

Gale sat back down, then began to sob. At first Janek was certain he was faking. But as the sobbing turned to gagging and then to heaving, he began to believe it was for real.

He helped Gale into the bathroom, then stood beside him as he fell to his knees and retched into the toilet.

"It's okay, son," he said. "Don't hold back. Let it out, let it out."

When finally Gale was finished and turned to him with a grateful smile, Janek knew he had broken through. The bond was forged. The interrogator had become the friend. And now the truth would emerge.

"I was crazy about her, Janek. I swear to you."

They were back in the living room in the university chairs, but Janek sat farther away this time. No need to sit close and apply more stress. All he had to do now was listen with sympathy as Gale, impelled to talk, regaled him with his story.

". . . you got it right, I recruited her. Just like I recruited the others. And it was always a kind of victory for me, too. I'd pick a girl out, walking across the quadrangle, or sitting alone in a lecture hall, or jogging, or laughing, or coming out of one of the dorms. I'd pick her because she looked good, had a great body, moved a certain way, had a well-packaged butt, her lips were sexy, or there was something, you know, about the way she laughed, her mouth, her tits, whatever. Then it became a game. Get her name. Get a date with her. Kiss her. Get her into the sack. After that it was usually pretty easy to lead them to the point where, you know, they thought it was *their* idea. Then came the victory part: putting the blindfold on them, leading them into the room, telling them to strip while everybody watched. We never told anyone who they were going to do it with. That was the game. Everyone liked it. Everyone wore the blindfold. The guys, too. Including me. That was the fun of it, to wear the blindfold, to strip and stand there until the selected person came forward, stood before you till you could hardly stand it anymore, then slowly reached forward and made contact. Fear and anticipation and the idea you were on display. Wondering who the person was, trying to guess, but preferring not to know because it was easier to let yourself go if you didn't. Plenty of time later to find out who and laugh about who you thought it was. To perform like that, be the object of so much attention—*I* loved it. Everybody did. Jess, too. You gotta believe me when I say this, Janek. She found it incredibly exciting.

"But, see, there was the problem, because when I watched her play with the others, a funny thing started to happen. It bothered me. I didn't like it. And I'd never felt like that before. So I said to her: 'Let's not do this anymore. Let's just go out as a couple.' She laughed, called me jealous, made fun of me 'cause I couldn't take it. 'You got me into this, Greggy,' she said. 'You created a monster. Now you'll have to live with it.'

"Over the summer we went separate ways. I had a half-ass job at my father's brokerage firm and was out in the Hamptons most weekends. Jess was with her folks up on Martha's Vineyard, so we didn't see each other at all. I called her a lot. She never called me. The few times I managed to catch her home she told me she didn't feel like talking. Then in August she went to Italy to some special fencing school. I wrote her, but she didn't answer. So okay, I figured when college started up again, we'd see each other and have a chance to talk. But come September she had a whole new attitude. Now all she wanted was to fence. She had ambitions, wanted to become an Olympic competitor. Her Italian coach had told her she had the potential for it but she'd have to give it everything she had. 'That's what I want,' she told me. 'I want to go all the way. I don't want to waste my energy anymore, dating people I don't care about or smoking pot and playing games with your chums.' 'Well, okay,' I said, 'that's fine. I'll go along with that. Let's start over, just the two of us.' But that didn't interest her either.

"We had a big fight. She told me she didn't care if she ever saw me again. She called me all kinds of stuff. 'Shallow.' 'Spoiled.' 'No backbone.' 'No integrity.' 'User.' 'Pimp.' And she was right. Maybe that's why it hurt so much. She saw through me clearer than anyone ever had. She saw me for what I really am, which is just what you're looking at now, Janek. Yeah, I think you see me pretty much the way she did. As a jerk. A zero." And with that he gave out with a forlorn little whelp and then a droopy self-pitying smile.

A nicely executed *mea culpa,* Janek thought, but he still had to be sure Gale hadn't gone after Jess in revenge.

"Okay, Greg. Pick yourself up. No law says you gotta be slime. That's a choice you don't have to make."

As Gale peered at him, searched his eyes for sympathy, suddenly Janek was sick of him. He was tired of people who made their confessions, then looked to him for solutions to their lives. What had he said to Monika that night in Venice? That he did what he did to gain wisdom, to comprehend the numerous varieties of human evil. But Greg Gale wasn't evil, at least not to a degree that mattered. He was smalltime-fuckedup-richkid-spoiled, and who gave a shit anyway? But somehow, some way this kid's life had touched Jess's, so no matter how sickening Janek found him, he still had to play out the string.

"You see yourself as decadent, but underneath you're pretty soft."

In return, as he expected, Gale gave him the warm, grateful, amazed look—the one Janek always got at this point in an interrogation—the look that said: "Thank you for understanding me so well."

"So you were hurt by her. She was a great kid, but she was capable of hurting. You don't decide to become an Olympic-class fencer if you haven't got some pretty hard stuff inside. In my experience women are tougher than men. Easy to forget that when they cry. But they can ream you out and backwards when they feel like it. Isn't that the truth?"

Still caught up by Janek's magical insights, Gale nodded solemnly.

"You were angry. It's okay, Greg. Admit it."

"Well, sure. Those things she said—"

"Made you feel like a worm. Pretty hard to take a beating like that without getting mad about it, wanting to hit the girl back."

Gale shrugged. "I didn't want to hit her. All I wanted was for us to, you know, hold each other."

"She rejected you, made you feel awful."

"Yeah. . . ." The spell was still holding; Gale was in a kind of dazed, suspended state.

"If she wouldn't go out with you, who would she go out with? You were jealous of what she did with the group. How about people you didn't know, sex you wouldn't be able to watch?"

"I didn't want to think about that."

"Of course not. You'd go crazy if you did. But how could you be sure? Unless there was some way to . . . close her off. Prevent anyone else from getting what you couldn't get. That's when you thought of it, right?"

He looked into Gale's eyes, but all he could see there was confusion. No anger, no rage, no word forming to come out or being throttled so it wouldn't. This boy didn't know anything about glue; of that Janek now was certain. Greg Gale hadn't stabbed Jess, and he hadn't mutilated her. He was lost in a reverie of his inadequacy as man, not in a fantasy of stabbing and gluing up a woman.

Janek stood. "I don't know what to say to you. You messed around with my goddaughter's head. I'd like to think you couldn't help yourself, but still, it's hard to forgive. I'm not going to try. I think you've been honest with me. I appreciate that. No need to get up. I'll let myself out."

But then, before he could turn, Gale stood up. He wanted to show Janek his photographs of Jess. Janek dreaded looking at them; he didn't want sordid images of her etched upon his mind. But he waited anyway while Gale dug the pictures out, and then he was surprised.

Gale's photos were not posed tableaux like the mistress/slave picture over the fireplace. Rather, they were superb black-and-white action shots of Jess fencing in tournaments, en garde, thrusting, making parries and ripostes and lunge attacks against her opponents.

He looked at them all carefully, admiring Gale's abilities as a

photographer. Then he came upon a shot of Jess so fine, so powerful, he could not tear his eyes away. Gale had caught her just at
the moment of a victory. Having scored, ripped off her mask, she
met the gaze of his camera with a great broad, beaming grin of
triumph.

Gale watched him as he examined this picture. "Like it?" he
asked. Janek nodded. "Take it. No, I mean it. I want you to have
it." And before Janek could protest, Gale placed the print in a
protective cover and presented it to him as a gift.

Clutching this image of Jess as he rode back to his apartment,
Janek knew, no matter what anyone said, that he would have to
find out who had killed her. The little girl he had nurtured had
grown into the magnificent woman in the photograph—and now
she was dead. The wound this time was not just upon society, nor
was it only upon Laura and Stanton. It was also upon himself, and
it would not be closed for him until he had hunted her killer down.

Oh, Jess, he thought. *Jess.*

That night, his second since his
return from Europe, Janek finally got a full ration of sleep. But it
was total exhaustion, not peace of mind, that closed his eyes. His
last thought, before falling off, was that Jess seemed to have been
at a crisis point at just the time she was killed. Was that significant
or merely a coincidence? He posed the question, then collapsed
into a spiral of fatigue.

It was Laura Dorance who set up
his appointment the following morning with Jess's shrink.

Janek arrived before the first-floor office entrance of a converted
two-story carriage house on East Eighty-first. He pressed the bell,
gave his name to a disembodied voice, and was buzzed in. He found
himself in a hall. Through an archway to his left there was a
sparsely furnished waiting room. He entered, took a seat, thumbed

through an old copy of *Psychology Today,* while a small radio, tuned at low volume to a classical station, yielded a gentle flow of Mozart.

At precisely eleven o'clock Dr. Beverly Archer appeared in the doorway. A very short, fortyish butterball of a woman, she welcomed Janek with a sympathetic smile. Warm and friendly eyes, slightly rouged cheeks, curly, dull reddish hair, she had the kind of bland features one often associates with people in the mental health field. But her voice gave her away; it was throaty, low-pitched, intense.

"Please come in, Lieutenant. I have forty minutes before my next appointment."

He followed her into a comfortable consultation room. A desk, two easy chairs, an analyst's couch, and bookcases filled with psychiatric texts. On one wall hung a reproduction of Van Gogh's sunflowers; on the other, a cluster of diplomas.

"Now what can I do for you?" Dr. Archer asked with a formal smile, after motioning him to one of the chairs.

"I'm sure Mrs. Dorance told you—"

"She said you were Jessica's godfather and that you're a New York City detective. But I must tell you from the start I'm most reluctant to discuss the contents of Jessica's sessions. Many people don't realize this, but the confidentiality of the therapist's office transcends even the patient's death."

Janek paused. The woman was more authoritative than he expected. He understood he would have to tread gently if he was going to get any information.

"Yeah, I've heard that, Dr. Archer, but her mother, her legal heir, has given consent."

Dr. Archer nodded. "So she told me. But you have to understand, there's a principle involved. If I make an exception, violate my pledge of confidentiality, then where do I draw the line?" She smiled. "My oath binds me to silence. Unless, of course, I learn that someone is about to commit an act of violence. And that, I'm afraid, is not the case here."

Oh, shit! A real hard-ass! "I notice you call her Jessica," he said.

"That was her name."

"We all called her Jess."

"So did I, Lieutenant. But I'm not speaking to her now. I'm speaking *about* her, and as you can probably tell, I'm feeling just a little uncomfortable doing that."

Dr. Archer, Janek noticed, pursed her lips into a little smile at the end of every sentence. It was a nervous habit, not unattractive or disconcerting, but he found it slowed him down.

"If it will make it any easier for you, Doctor, I already know a lot. We have her diary. We know about the sex group. I've already spoken with Greg Gale, and he's confirmed everything she wrote. If it's a question of protecting Jess's reputation, please believe that's foremost in my mind. I'm not going to repeat anything you tell me, and her diary won't be leaked. I guess what I'm saying is I hope you'll reconsider. My first priority, which I'm sure you share, is to find the person who killed her."

As he spoke, Dr. Archer nodded along. "Yes, yes, that's true, that's certainly true. And I shall certainly think the matter over." She paused, smiled. "Now why don't we start by talking a little about your own relationship with Jessica? I think that would help me to better understand your interest."

She was such a nice woman, so clearly attuned to listening, that even though Janek was not in the mood to unburden himself, he soon found himself speaking of his sense of loss. He spoke, too, of his discomfort with thoughts of Jess's sex life, his overreaction when Glickman called her names, and the tight control he had had to exert upon himself with Greg Gale the night before.

"It's as if suddenly I have to deal with a side of Jess I never thought about before." Janek realized he was speaking to this woman much as he had on the telephone to Monika.

Dr. Archer nodded. Indeed, she understood. But then she wondered if it was really necessary for Janek to deal with that side of Jess at all.

"I think it is," he said. "That's why I'm here. I need to know everything she did."

"Do you really need to, Lieutenant?"

"I think so. I'm surprised you'd even ask."

Dr. Archer settled back. "You're saying that to pursue her

killer, you must delve into every aspect of her character. I question whether that's true. My suggestion, and I make it with timidity and respect, is that you ask yourself why you're so disturbed by the intimate material you've so far uncovered. Is it Jessica you want to understand, or are you really seeking to understand yourself?"

Janek stared at her. It was an interesting suggestion, but he'd come for information, not therapy or analysis.

"What I'm saying," Dr. Archer continued, "and I emphasize I do so without making any kind of value judgment, is that you possibly were and perhaps still are overly involved with your goddaughter. Perhaps you had unconscious fantasies about her. Perhaps you longed for her in some way you don't fully understand. And now that she's been so tragically killed, you use that as an excuse to delve into the most intimate aspects of her life. I suppose what I'm really asking, Lieutenant, is whether you're the right person to be handling this investigation. I certainly don't presume to know the answer. I merely raise the question."

A maddening, if fascinating, forty minutes, Janek thought as he emerged, somewhat shaken, on the street. Dr. Archer could not be faulted. She had acted professionally and shown herself protective of her patient. But instead of behaving in a cooperative manner, as is normally the case when a doctor is questioned by a detective, she had smoothly, even tenderly turned the interview around, with the result that it was not the victim but the investigator who had become its subject.

He knew he would return, and he had no doubt he would eventually persuade her to cooperate. In the meantime, he was captivated by her insights. Was what she'd said true? Was Kit right? Was he, Janek, too personally involved? Did he *have* to know everything? And how would the psychologist react when she discovered that his investigation was unauthorized?

Arriving at Kit Kopta's office suite, on the nineteenth floor of the police building, Janek did not receive the usual warm reception. The crusty redheaded sergeant, who kept Kit's appointments and supervised her secretaries, treated him with a correct but cool distance. The chief, he was told, was busy in a meeting; he was to take a seat and wait. Janek sat and waited for nearly an hour, watching people come and go through the inner office doors. Finally the sergeant deigned to notice him again. "Okay, Lieutenant, the chief'll see you now," he said without bothering to meet Janek's eyes.

Kit was seated behind her desk in a no-nonsense posture. She watched him closely as he walked in.

Her scrutiny made him feel awkward. "Am I in trouble?" he asked.

"What makes you think so?"

"Making me wait an hour. I can read the undertones."

"Screw the undertones, Frank. You've been working the Foy case after I ordered you to stay away from it, even after I begged you as a friend. You went up to Greenkill and kicked a table at a convict? You've got to know how stupid that was! Then you intimidated some snotty college kid whose dad's got City Hall connections. A few minutes ago my sergeant got a complaint from Ray Boyce. What the hell are you doing seeing the girl's shrink without clearing it first?" She took a deep breath; clearly she was uncomfortable with her anger. "So to answer your question, yeah, Frank, you *are* in trouble. And not just with those other people. You're in trouble with me."

"What am I supposed to say?"

"Stop carrying on, Frank. *Stay away from this case.*"

"You're serious."

Kit flushed. "Damn right I am."

"Boyce is a mediocrity."

"He's a competent detective."

"He's too slow."

"A lot of people think you're way too fast."

Janek peered at her. "Are you telling me there isn't a chance you'll turn it over to me?"

"Not a chance in hell, Frank. If there ever was, there sure isn't now."

Janek nodded. He hadn't anticipated this, but he'd prepared for it nonetheless. He reached into his pocket, pulled out his badge, and slid it quietly across Kit's desk.

She stared at it as if it were a piece of stale cake. "Is that supposed to mean you resign?" Janek nodded. She shook her head. "Cut the drama, Frank. What the hell's the matter?"

"*What's the matter?* Laura and Stanton ask me to get the guy who killed their daughter. I tell them I'll do my best. Then it hits me I have to get him not just for them but for me. A girl I loved, a girl I helped bring up from the time she was a little kid, was savagely killed and mutilated. I'm an investigator. I know how to track down the kind of people who do such things. That's my trade. If you won't let me practice it as a police officer, I'm perfectly prepared to do it privately on my own."

She studied him. "You were always convincing, Frank." She paused. "Know who you sound like?"

"Who?"

"Sam Spade." She grinned and, when he didn't return her smile, reclined back in her chair, her sharp Greek eyes fixing him.

They stared at each other, two people who'd known each other for twenty years. Then Janek remembered that tough as Kit was, she was no rigid disciplinarian.

"Something you're not telling me," he said quietly.

She peered at him noncommittally.

"You're much too adamant, Kit. Why ask the Dorances not to tell me about the glue? There's more here than you don't want me working on a case because it's, quote, personal. Better level with me now. Sooner or later I'll find out anyway."

She stared across the room, as if weighing his suggestion. Then she focused on him again.

"You're right about Boyce. He's slow and mediocre. Two things you're not, Frank. If I put you on Foy, there'll be a serious investigation. And at this point that's not what we want."

Janek leaned forward. His heart was pounding. "Boyce's investigation isn't serious?"

Kit shrugged. "Boyce doesn't know it, of course. But his investigation's bound to be a sham." Janek started to rise. "Blow up at the end if you want to, Frank. But first hear me out." He sat back down. "We're fairly certain we know who killed Jess. We don't know his name, but we know his work. He's done the same thing before. The FBI's been tracking him for a year."

As she talked, Janek tried to concentrate. He didn't want to miss a word. But as hard as he tried, he couldn't shake off his fury. If he'd done as Kit had requested, played docile, stayed away from Glickman and Gale and Archer, he'd still be thinking about a random park killer.

She was talking now about a crack FBI team led by a specialist in serial murder cases, an inspector named Harry Sullivan. Sullivan believed the Jess Foy homicide fitted the pattern of his Happy Families killer, so named because several of the victims were apparently happy families killed together in their homes.

"They were all stabbed with ice picks. The stabbing's very specific. And the genitals of all the victims were glued," Kit said. "I mean *all* the victims, Frank. Men, women, and children. Obviously we're talking about a psycho. So far the FBI's kept it quiet. You know how these sex killers like publicity. Fortunately no reporter's put it together yet."

Janek could barely control himself. "You weren't going to tell me?"

"Of course, I was. After you cooled down. I didn't want you working on it, Frank. You were way too angry. You *should* be angry. But we both know an angry cop is usually not a very effective one."

He was angry all right. For him the worst thing in the world was to be unknowledgeable. He never expected that Kit would deliberately keep him in the dark.

But now she was speaking pensively, as if she were having second thoughts.

". . . okay, that's conventional wisdom. But sometimes anger can generate creativity. Maybe I was wrong." She looked at him. "I've known you a long time. You've never been one for the empty gesture. When you tell me you're willing to resign—well, I know you're serious. I can't put you over Boyce. Not now, not after what you've done. But I can probably assign you as liaison to Sullivan."

Janek frowned. "I run investigations. I don't do liaison."

"It's *their* investigation, Frank. You can only do what they'll allow."

"You know that's shit!"

"It doesn't have to be. And please don't give me the old line about how you hate the feds. Right now the case belongs to the FBI. If you want to work it, and I mean Happy Families, not just Jess, the only way is to work it with them."

"On what basis?"

"Why don't you go down to Quantico tomorrow, have a talk with Sullivan? If the two of you get along, I'm sure he'll find you a niche."

"And if we don't get along?"

Kit shrugged. "Boyce spins his wheels and Sullivan digs in. That's okay. We've had double investigations before. But a triple! Forget it, Frank. A triple's too arcane even for me."

"So it's take it or leave it—that's what you're saying?"

"Something like that." She paused. "I know you don't like it, but it's the best I can do."

He thought it over. "All right," he said. "I'll see Sullivan. But I want Aaron with me."

Kit gave that some thought, then agreed to it.

"So," she asked, "have we got a deal?"

They stood, shook hands; then she hugged him tight.

"I'm sorry, Frank. It was a close call. I did what I thought was best."

The morning he and Aaron flew down to D.C. the blue of the sky was so intense it made Janek's heart ache for Venice.

They rented a sporty Pontiac out of National Airport, then drove south for an hour until they reached the military base at Quantico; then they crossed through the reservation and entered the grounds of the FBI Academy. Here an oversize, rigorously designed glass and stone building was neatly set on a campus of perfectly manicured grass.

They were expected. The guard at the reception desk had their passes. While they waited for their escort, Aaron peered around the atrium.

"Sure all this is for law enforcement, Frank? Looks more like IBM."

Janek nodded. No crummy typewriters on rotten desks in roach- and rat-infested offices here. No drunks wandering in here off the street. This, he recognized, was law enforcement U.S. government style, practiced by men and women wearing dark suits and necklace badges working efficiently at computer stations. In this orderly temple of police science the windows were always washed and the floors were always shined and, when you needed something, you didn't have to beg; all you did was put through a requisition. Here, too, was the finest forensic crime lab in the world.

The Behavioral Science Unit, where Sullivan was headquartered, was a rabbit warren of windowless offices. When Janek and Aaron arrived, they were told Sullivan was in a meeting, but one of his staff assistants, a Nordic muscleman named Hansen whose shirt collar bit into his neck, had been delegated to take them on a tour.

Hansen led them down endless corridors, stopping from time to time to open a door and show them something dazzling: the director's paneled dining room; an Olympic-size swimming pool where agents were trained to swim while holding weapons; the world's largest, most efficient underground firing range.

After an hour of this Janek grew impatient.

"Look," he said to Hansen, "I don't mean to be rude, but I think we've seen enough."

"There's a lot more, Lieutenant," Hansen said. "Inspector Sullivan especially wanted you to see Hogan's Alley."

"What's that?"

"It's where we train police officers from all over the country in criminal apprehension."

"I think we can skip that," Janek said. "Please tell the inspector we've come a long way and now we're ready to work."

Hansen's face fell. He stared at Janek with unconcealed hurt, then dodged into a nearby office to use the phone. Janek watched from the corridor as, once connected, Hansen cupped his hand over the receiver.

"Probably telling Sullivan what uncouth louts we are," Aaron said.

Janek shook his head. He didn't like the setup. The tour had been laid on to intimidate. Sullivan wanted to soften them up, make them feel outclassed.

"All righty, Lieutenant," Hansen said, rejoining them in the corridor. "We're to go straight up to room two-oh-one."

Another march along endless windowed corridors, then up a stairs, around a corner, past hundreds of doors leading into hundreds of little offices until, finally, they reached the briefing room.

Sullivan was waiting for them. He was a stocky man about Janek's age, with an affable smile, beautifully coiffed iron gray hair, pink, well-shaven cheeks, and tiny, twinkling ice blue eyes. Though he spoke slowly with a slight drawl, this was no Ray Boyce. His gestures were sharp, his little eyes were quick, and he came off as shrewd and savvy.

But there was a cockiness about him that inspired in Janek a nearly instant dislike. He hadn't wanted to detest Sullivan. He'd come with the expectation that they would treat each other with respect. But the way the man stood, his back just a little too straight, his head angled upward, his chin stuck out just a little more than necessary, reminded Janek of a prison warden trying unsuccessfully to conceal his swagger.

He only hoped this first impression would be belied.

The briefing room was state-of-the-art with the latest in audio-visual aids. There was a polished white marble conference table with glasses, water pitcher, yellow legal pads, and sharpened pencils arranged like place settings for a banquet. Two tabbed briefing books, with Janek's and Aaron's names embossed on the covers, were centered perfectly before two deep upholstered swivel chairs with electronic gear built into the armrests. When Janek sat in his, he felt like a millionaire ready to deep-sea fish off the back of a yacht.

"Gentlemen," Sullivan announced, in a sonorous airline pilot's voice, "I thought the best approach would be to have members of my staff brief you on particular aspects of HF. Then, when you've got a handle on the cases, I'll rejoin you for the overview."

"HF—can you believe they call it that?" Aaron whispered.

Janek believed. The FBI was notorious for its abbreviations and acronyms. But he preferred HF to Happy Families, which smacked of a headline in one of the national tabloids: HAPPY FAMILIES KILLER STRIKES AGAIN.

The briefing that commenced, part lecture, part slide show, consisted of a procession of crisp, well-rehearsed young forensic analysts, each with his own area of expertise, doing his stint with pointer and easel, then yielding to the next.

They were shown detailed color slides of the five Happy Families crime scenes. People with stiffened limbs and ice picks protruding from their ears, eyes, and throats lay at odd angles in domestic settings. All were naked from the waist down, having been stripped in order to be glued. Janek found himself turning his head, then looking at the pictures obliquely with only one eye. He wasn't certain why he did this; it was a habit he'd acquired over the years. Perhaps, he thought, if only one eye were exposed, the gruesome images would be less deeply engraved upon his memory.

The agents used staccato tones to describe each set of victims along with details of the abuses each had suffered:

> *Miss Bertha Parce,* an elderly retired schoolteacher, found murdered in her bed in a single-room-occupancy hotel in Miami Beach, Florida
>
> *Cynthia Morse,* a wealthy divorcée, killed over Memorial Day weekend, with her two visiting grown daughters, in her luxury condominium in Seattle, Washington
>
> *James and Stuart MacDonald,* two aging playboy-type brothers, slain in their shared weekend house in Kent, Connecticut
>
> *The Robert Wexler family (husband, wife, three children)* killed in their suburban ranch-style home in Fort Worth, Texas
>
> *The Anthony Scotto family (husband, wife, and two teenage sons)* slaughtered in their Cape Cod-style home just outside Providence, Rhode Island

There was also a homeless man who didn't seem to fit the pattern, though he, too, had been stabbed and glued, then left in an alley in the Alphabet City section of Manhattan.

The presentation notably did not include anything about Jess. Janek wondered whether this was because the team was being considerate of his feelings or because it simply hadn't worked up that part of the briefing yet.

At exactly twelve-thirty a break was called, and Janek and Aaron were invited to join the analysts for a working lunch in the staff cafeteria. But as it turned out, the conversation there had little to do with the case. Rather, the agents solicited war stories from New York, for which they exchanged no personal revelations, only other war stories they'd heard from other visiting investigators.

Later, in the men's room, Aaron asked Janek what he thought was going on.

"They're looking to see if we're team players. Teamwork's what the FBI's all about."

Aaron laughed. "We're hotshots, ain't we, Frank?" Then, more seriously: "I feel out of place. Maybe it's the clothes. They all dress so nice. Even some of the ladies wear ties."

The afternoon session concluded the presentation of cases, after which their tour guide, Hansen, reappeared with another muscle-bound assistant to demonstrate the stabbing method. The men acted it out several times at normal speed and then in slow motion: a violent thrust with an ice pick from under the chin through the roof of the mouth, the ear hole, or the eye socket and then into the brain. The fact that the pick was always left embedded was, according to Hansen, "classic commando technique."

The star speaker of the afternoon was Dr. David Chun, brought in to explicate the killer profile. Janek had heard of him. The brilliant young Asian-American was not an FBI employee but a forensic psychiatrist on the faculty at Harvard Law School, who had testified at numerous high-profile criminal trials around the country. From the flattering way Sullivan introduced him, it was clear he considered Chun a major asset.

The moment the doctor began to speak, Janek understood why he was usually so successful with juries. He had the kind of deep, authoritative voice that compels attention and belief. But there was something canny, perhaps even vain in his presentation, that fitted with the subtle swagger Janek had observed in Sullivan and the entire HF team. The way these people behaved spoke of arrogant pride. They saw themselves as the best of the best. And they'd made it clear at lunch that if the two shaggy, scruffily dressed detectives from New York wanted in, they would have to prove they had the stuff.

Dr. Chun stated his belief that the organized crime scenes and ethnic background of the victims indicated a white male killer most likely in his late twenties or early thirties. Further, he believed the neatness of the gluing suggested excellent hand-eye coordination, as well as a certain protective concern for the victims' "bodily integrity."

"Various facts," he continued, "such as the forced entries, clean escapes, and the killer's ability to take on multiple victims, suggest a particularly confident individual, probably one with a high level of martial arts training. The stabbing technique raises the possibility of a military background. The psychopathology is sexual-sadistic; I would surmise that the killer possesses a large collection of sadomasochistic pornography. The gluings and lack of semen at the crime scenes speak of sexual fear indicative of a loner type. But the most striking characteristic is the killer's lack of gender differentiation."

The psychiatrist paused. Though his features remained composed, Janek picked up on something in his eyes. *It's almost as if he's afraid,* he thought as Chun continued in the same authoritative style.

"He glues up the genitals of men and women with equal thoroughness. Children, too, and, in the case of Fort Worth, even the family dog and cat. But beyond the genitals, all orifices seem to be fair game. With the Miami woman and the brothers in Connecticut we find mouths and anuses glued. In the case of Providence the wife's fingertips were glued together in a praying-type position. In the other cases fingers and toes were glued at random as if to create a webbed hand or foot effect. We call these variations subpatterns. They speak of something beyond conventional categories of sexual assault. In this case concepts such as straight and gay are useless, virtually irrelevant. We appear to be dealing with a man who engages in symbolic negation of any and all forms of human sexuality. One may surmise he has a disturbed relationship with a mother, who is possibly deceased. Finally, the killer is most likely sexually dysfunctional."

This time, when Dr. Chun paused, his breathing quickened, and he screwed up his eyes. When he resumed speaking, Janek was certain. *Something about this definitely frightens him,* he thought.

". . . there is one very unusual aspect. This killer chooses what we call difficult victims. With the exception of the homeless man and the young woman jogger in New York, the people he chose were not easy to get at, not easy at all. Most serial killers take an easy path, preying on hitchhikers and prostitutes. But not this one. He sets himself extremely tough challenges. From this we must infer intelligence, a capacity for careful planning, and a streak of competitiveness rarely demonstrated in this category of crimes."

After Chun was finished, he stared down at the floor, then raised his head as if he had something to add. He opened his mouth, then abruptly clamped it shut.

"Lieutenant Janek, Sergeant Greenberg—I thank you for your patience." Then he almost seemed to flee the room.

After Chun left, a full minute passed, during which Janek made out a short bit of conversation from the other side of the door. He strained to listen. It was between Sullivan and the psychiatrist. Chun sounded deeply upset:

". . . doesn't fit . . . diabolical . . ."

". . . overworked. Get some rest. We'll talk. . . ."

When Sullivan reentered the room, Janek was impressed by his sangfroid. He picked up the briefing just where Chun had left it off, dealing head-on with the issue of easy versus difficult.

"The homeless man was first and the Foy girl last," Sullivan began. "Both easy prey, both hit-and-run homicides committed outside at night in New York, and both glued quick and sloppy in the crotch. As you've heard, we find much more elaborate gluing when the killings are committed indoors. The killer goes in like a stabbing machine. But then he's careful, very, very careful with the glue. Squirts it in just right, makes sure everything's sealed up."

Sullivan paused for effect.

"All right, you know all that. We acknowledge the inconsistencies. In our discussions we've theorized a possible second killer, an outdoor killer, who murdered the homeless man and the jogger, as opposed to an indoor killer, who murdered the families. But the theory doesn't hold because there's another aspect to the signature. In all seven cases we find the weed."

Aaron shook his head. "You talking about pot?"

"Not pot, Sergeant. I'm talking about a literal weed. We didn't pick up on it at first. Then our forensic people noticed that there was always some wild plant left at the scene, a dandelion or a dried-up field daisy, a junk flower like you'd find in a vacant lot. This isn't a mystery novel. No rose or carnation or orchid here. Just a weed. A crummy weed." Sullivan turned to Janek. "There was a weed left near your goddaughter's body, too. . . ."

They finally did get to see Hogan's Alley. Sullivan insisted on it. Color-coded students (red T-shirts for FBI; blue for police) ran around what looked like a movie set playing cops and robbers. The inspector watched, extremely proud, but Janek found it tiresome. *These FBI people,* he thought, *live in a world of their own, where technology and profiling and games are ends in themselves.* Meantime, city detectives like Aaron and himself worked sleazy cases out of dirty offices. He had no doubt as to which of them had a better feel for the criminal mind.

Janek arranged to meet Sullivan that night at a D.C. restaurant, then drove Aaron back to National Airport.

"I want to get him alone," Janek explained. "Really piss him off."

"I thought we were supposed to make nice."

"You want to work with him?"

"Be pretty tough," Aaron admitted. "But I'll give it a shot if you want me to."

"Maybe it won't be necessary," Janek said.

He dropped Aaron off at the Pan Am Shuttle, then drove into D.C. Though it was only five o'clock, the sky was already darkening. Affluent-looking joggers were running all over the place, and the rush-hour traffic was starting to build. He parked his car in a garage at the Watergate complex, then set out to walk. After a while he felt himself drawn to a center of energy. It was the Vietnam War Memorial. He knew it from pictures but had always wanted to see it for himself.

When he arrived, he felt no disappointment. The wall was everything he'd imagined. And it evoked in him a strong feeling, a bittersweet nostalgia for his own tour out there when, in 1968, he'd worked narcotics with Army CID in Da Nang. But as he stood in the shadows with the other visitors, staring at the black granite while the last light slowly faded from the sky, he felt a strong, sad anger for the awful waste of that war and the young American lives that had been lost fighting it.

The restaurant Sullivan had chosen, small, elegant, and expensive, was situated on the lower level of the Watergate Hotel. Even as Janek entered, he felt Sullivan's intention. The inspector knew he wasn't wearing the right clothes for such a place, so again he was trying to make him feel uncomfortable.

Janek waited a full fifteen minutes before he realized that, too, was part of the plan. And then he found Sullivan pathetic. The manipulation was so unimaginative, an exact duplication of the method used that morning at the academy. Sullivan had proven himself to have a small-time bureaucrat's mentality. Such a man would solve a major case only by luck.

By the time the inspector did arrive, smiling, solicitous, excessive with profuse apologies, Janek had decided to play the first part of their dinner at his most collegial.

"Here's how we see it," Sullivan said, after coaching Janek patiently through the menu. "The five indoor family killings were very difficult to bring off. The two outdoor single killings were relatively easy. But in all seven cases we see the same thrust, same brand of ice pick, same basic mutilation of the genitals and the weed. So what we're thinking—"

Janek interrupted. "You're thinking the homeless man was for practice. After him the killer went after desired prey."

"You're good, Frank. I'm impressed. So tell me—what else do we think?"

"You think Jess Foy was for practice, too. You think the killer lives in New York because that's where he practices. You think when he wants to kill a family, he travels outside the city until he finds one that attracts him."

Sullivan grinned. "You've pretty much got it."

"So tell me," Janek said, "if he likes happy families so much and has so much positive experience with them, what does he need another round of practice for?"

Sullivan clicked his teeth. "Who the hell knows? These sociopaths have their own twisted logic. Some of it we understand; some we don't. Maybe the guy's losing his nerve. Maybe he's just sharpening his skills."

Janek was not charmed by that little witticism. And he wasn't sure which notion he disliked more: Jess as random victim or used as a practice target by a serial killer.

Sullivan sat back, his pink cheeks puffed out. "I feel something in all this, Frank. Something that goes beyond cases I've worked before. It's like, I don't know, it's a . . . Great Crime."

Janek stared at him. "What does that mean, Harry? A 'Great Crime'—what the hell is that?"

"Like that big case of yours. That Switched Heads thing. A great criminal conception. A killer playing a dangerous game, taunting us while he weaves his pattern. He sees himself as an artist. To catch him, we have to understand his art. In the end that'll tell us who he is. Decipher the pattern." Sullivan held up his hand. "Then he's ours." He shut his fist to simulate a trap.

"Any way you see me fitting into this?"

Sullivan smiled. "We stayed late, talked it over after you left. The boys think you could be a real asset."

"What about Aaron?"

"Not so clear. Don't misunderstand, Frank. I'm sure he's a terrific cop."

But with him on the team I'd have an ally, and you don't want that, Janek thought.

Sullivan leaned forward. He wanted to speak in confidence.

"I know it's tough. I know how cops feel. I know we're not the most popular guys around. But we've got the expertise, Frank. On a case like this we're the only game in town. Not just because we can coordinate on a national level but because we've been studying these guys, profiling them for years. After a while you get a feel for them. This one's tough, but I know there's a soft spot. There always is. With your help I think we can find it. I'd be truly honored, Frank, if you'd agree to join my team."

When the main courses arrived, they dropped discussion of the case. As they ate, Sullivan spoke casually of his ambition to write.

"It's what I've always wanted to do," he said. "Think about it—all the fiction writers out there who'd give their left ball for the kind of material we deal with every day." He took a bite from his plate. "Ever hear of Grey Scopetta?"

"No."

"A film director. Does these true crime things on TV. I figured with your miniseries and all you'd have heard of him."

"It wasn't *my* miniseries, Harry. I was just the police adviser."

Sullivan winked at him. "Don't be so modest." He gulped some wine. "Anyway, about Scopetta—he's been in touch with me about HF."

Janek put down his fork. "I thought the point was to keep it quiet."

"From reporters, sure. But the bureau likes filmmakers. Some way, we don't know how, Scopetta heard about the case and put through a request for a briefing. So we gave him one. Nothing like what you got. The smaller, simpler version. And nothing about the weed. Nobody knows about that, not even detectives in cities where the families were killed. Anyway, the two of us stayed in touch. So one day we're talking and he mentions I'm the guy maybe ought to write the script. I figured what the hell, why not give it a shot? So this past summer I flew out to L.A., took a crash course in screenwriting, one of those five-hundred-bucks-per-weekend seminar deals. Now in my free time, evenings and weekends, I've been writing away."

Again Sullivan lowered his voice.

"Look, this is the kind of case that when it's solved, there's sure to be a movie. So I figured why shouldn't I, the guy who's going to solve it, get a piece of the action? Somebody's gotta write it. Why not me? That way, soon as there's an indictment, the script's ready to go. Nothing wrong with what I'm doing; I checked with our ethics guys. I'm not showing my script to anyone. Just getting it ready, that's all. See, Scopetta explained it to me: Screenwriting is structure. So that's what I'm working on, the structure of the thing. And lately I've had this idea that working on the structure of the script is going to help me solve HF. Because HF's got a structure, too. Know what I mean? Solve it as a story and I may solve it as a case. Anyway, it's an idea. . . ."

Jesus, what an asshole! Janek thought.

With dessert, they resumed discussion of Happy Families. Having trusted Janek with his writing ambitions, Sullivan was finally ready to expose the most sensitive aspects of the case.

"Okay," Sullivan said, "you know what we've got. After a year of work, incredibly little. No prints. No fibers. No tissue cells. No DNA. The ice picks are common, sold all over the country, and the weeds are obviously untraceable. We believe the gluings were done with a standard caulking gun, the kind you can buy in any hardware store. He rams it into them, then shoots in potent animal glue. Now there was one thing we didn't get to in the briefing. Connections between the victims. Believe me, we searched for them. We have a powerful computer program designed to make that kind of search. So far all it's come up with is a city, Cleveland, which ties together only two of the families. The brothers in Connecticut were from there, and the old lady in Florida taught school there before she retired. Coincidence? Probably. If it was a small town in southern Ohio, I might feel different. A serial killer fixated on Cleveland—I just don't see a story line there. . . ."

Janek cleared his throat. *Time now to rattle him,* he thought. "Maybe it's not a serial case, Harry. Ever think of that?"

"You kidding? This is a classic. Of course it's a serial case."

"I'm not so sure."

Sullivan's pink cheeks began to redden. "What the hell're you talking about?"

Janek shrugged. "Call it a gut feeling."

Sullivan snorted. Then he turned sarcastic. "What else does your 'gut' tell you?"

"Now don't act offended, Harry."

"I *am* offended. You're questioning the premise of my investigation. What's bugging you?"

"No victimology."

Sullivan stared at him. Then he smiled. "Okay, you're good, you picked up on that. But see, even with the best software, the computer isn't perfect."

"Forget the computer. I'm talking about David Chun."

"David's upset about a couple things. But—"

"He talked about everything except what the killer found attractive, what he saw in his 'difficult victims' that made him decide to go after them. And that's the key, isn't it? If you've got that many victims and they don't tell you why they were attacked, well, then, what have you got? Far as I can see, nothing. Except"—he sneered—"'Happy Families.'"

"You're mocking that?"

"I don't mock homicide victims, Harry. But tell me, between the two of us, what was so goddamn happy about all those people?"

"Oh, come off it! That's just the name we use. . . ."

"Sure. That's how it started. Because you couldn't read the common element. But now it's like the name's defining the case. 'Happy Families'—how do you know they were happy? Because they lived in nice houses, nice neighborhoods, Dad coached Little

League, Mom baked apple pies, and kids were on the honor roll? Because their friends and neighbors told you they were? See, Harry, I never worked a case where I didn't hear the victims were just the greatest people, the finest, happiest people. And half the time it turned out they were just like everybody else, happy and unhappy, capable of hurting each other, even capable of killing each other if the stress got bad enough. I'm not saying your families *weren't* happy. I'm just asking how you *know* they were. Because I don't buy Happy Families. It's too vague. Show me a victim list of pretty blondes with hoop earrings or old ladies with hairy chins, then maybe I'll go along. But you don't have that. I think this goes deeper. I think these killings were victim-specific. I think there's an invisible thread connecting all these people and you and your team just haven't found it yet."

"After a year of work we haven't found it, the best serial killer team ever assembled. But *you're* going to find it? Great! Maybe you'll even find it tonight!"

Janek sat back. Sullivan's sarcasm didn't bother him. It only made him want to push the needle farther in.

"Know what I think, Harry? I think working out of Behavioral Science has got you overinvested in the serial killer idea. I think you're so wrapped up in that you can't see beyond it to anything else."

Now Sullivan was staring at him, trying to push him with a hard cop's stare. "Man, you've got some kind of balls," he whispered. "If I were you, I'd watch my step. Someone just might come along and cut 'em off. Know what I mean, Frank?"

Janek smiled. He'd forced Sullivan to resort to vulgar, tough guy talk. When a cop started talking about cutting off another cop's balls, he was aroused to a highly competitive state.

"I've heard about you," Sullivan continued, not bothering to conceal his bitterness. "I saw the way they played you on TV. This genius cop who didn't need a team, didn't need backup, didn't need nothing except his brain, which we're supposed to think is so powerful it should be registered as a dangerous weapon." Sullivan grinned. His cheeks were quivering. His little ice blue eyes were sparkling with envy. "So here we sit, end of our first day together. I lay my case out for you, a year's worth of work, and now you slip to me you got a theory of your own."

"Yeah, I guess that's about it," Janek agreed.

"I think it's a crock of shit."

"Maybe it is. But the question is, Harry, how're we going to find out?"

Sullivan glared at him. "Suppose you tell me, Frank."

"My suggestion is since you're so sure it's a serial case, you and your team continue working the way you are. Meantime, let Aaron and me follow up on my idea. We can set up a little two-man office in New York, in a precinct back room somewhere. Of course, we'll share what we find, but other than that, we'll stay out of your way."

Sullivan chewed on that for a moment. "Nice concept. Only trouble is . . . I don't see what's in it for me."

"Come on, Harry! There's plenty in it for you. You get the chance to compete."

"Compete?"

"FBI versus NYPD, you versus me. Whoever solves the case gets the glory: the book, the TV movie, the whole enchilada. Right now you've got the manpower and a year's head start. Pretty good odds." Janek smiled as he appealed to Sullivan's weakness. "You look like a sport, Harry. What do you say?"

"I'll have to think about it."

"Do that." Janek pushed away his coffee, tossed two fifty-dollar bills onto the table, and stood up. "That's for the dinner. I'm going to try and catch the last shuttle. Call me when you decide. But don't take too long, okay?"

New York was fogged in, so the late shuttle was diverted to Newark. Janek exited the airport terminal into a light and soothing swirl of softly falling rain. He shared a taxi into town with a businessman from Taiwan who admitted this was his first visit to the States.

As their cab approached the Lincoln Tunnel, the city was suddenly revealed, a million lights in the towers of midtown burning through the fog. It was a great romantic vision of Manhattan, and the Taiwanese gentleman peered at it, amazed. "You must be very strong to survive in a place like this," he muttered.

Janek nodded. *Yeah, you must be strong. And even then you may not survive.*

He dropped the visitor off at the Waldorf-Astoria, then asked the driver to take him through Central Park. There the fog clung strangely to the statues and hugged the glow of the sodium lamps.

When he finally got back to his apartment, he phoned Aaron at home, told him about his proposed competition with Sullivan. Aaron was surprised. On what basis, he wanted to know, had Janek come up with "victim-specific"?

"On no basis, except my feeling Chun had doubts and there was no way we could work under Sullivan. So I did the only thing that would shake the asshole up. Whatever he said, I said the opposite."

"But it *is* a serial case. I mean—isn't it, Frank?"

"Could be. I honestly don't know."

"Those guys seem so sure."

"Yeah, they're sure. But I wasn't bullshitting Sullivan. My true gut reaction is that they're all wrong." He paused. "Did you notice how bored they were? A year of grinding work, and they got nothing."

"Just a bunch of charts and a freaked-out psychiatrist. Still, if it *is* a serial deal . . ."

"Let me tell you something about serial deals, Aaron. When they're solved, *if* they *are* solved, it's usually because one night some hick town rookie pulls some guy over for a speeding ticket and happens to see a bloody knife on the seat. I say screw that."

"Fine, Frank. Fine. But where do we start—assuming Sullivan buys your deal and Chief Kopta approves?"

"We'll concentrate on Jess. She left me a worried message. Assume she knew she was in danger and was looking to me to help. If that's true, then the first question we've got to ask ourselves is: *What was Jess afraid of?*"

5

Mama Again

"**L**isten carefully, child."

"I'm listening, Mama."

"I'm concerned about Tool."

"Please don't be, Mama."

"But I'm *very* concerned. Unless a tool like that gets regular use, it can easily lose its edge. Preventative maintenance is so important, you know."

"I know, Mama. And I keep Tool in excellent condition. I work with it every day, keep it honed. I want it to stay sharp. And always be ready."

"Still, I'm concerned."

"Please, Mama—leave it to me."

"It needs supervision."

"I give it plenty of supervision."

"You know the problem with a tool like that? A tool like that can get out of hand, can start to have a mind of its own."

"No. . . . Do you really think so?"

"I *definitely* think so. You must watch Tool carefully, child, see it doesn't get any ideas or forget its place."

"I just don't believe—"

"Better listen to Mama. Mama knows best."

"Yes, Mama."

"A tool like that needs tending. A tool like that is dangerous. You create a tool like that and let it get away from you, you lose control. The whole point of a tool like that is it works *for* you, does *your* bidding. A tool like that goes into business for itself, you gotta think about getting rid of it."

"Yes, Mama. . . ."

6

The Fear

Ray Boyce was steaming, his forehead popping sweat. The long, thin wisps he kept carefully combed across his skull were mussed, and the squared-off bottom of his face was trembling like Jell-O.

"I don't get it," he griped.

Janek watched Kit recoil; it was as if the back of her big chief's chair were sucking on her spine. Janek looked around the office, a cavernous space that spoke of the high status of its occupant. The windows were huge. On the other side of the glass large snowflakes fell softly to Police Plaza below.

"I'm sweating out the case, doing a pretty decent job." Boyce mopped his forehead. "Least I thought I was." He spoke with a whine. "Meantime, Janek here does all this unauthorized bullshit. And for that he gets—*rewarded*?"

Boyce's question hung in the overheated air. Kit stared at him with faint disgust. Janek, sitting beside him in the other chair facing Kit's desk, felt sorry for him. The poor slob was going to mouth his way straight into trouble.

"I don't know I'd exactly call it a reward, Ray," Janek said gently.

Boyce didn't bother to look at him. He stared straight at Kit, waiting for her to render justice.

"It wasn't a reward," Kit said finally. "Detective Janek is a specialist in this type of crime. His insights will prove helpful in solving it. As for his unauthorized activity, I've put a letter of reprimand in his file. Want me to read it to you?"

Boyce shook his head. "That's Janek's business. All I care about is my role. Am I supervising Janek or the other way around? 'Cause if it is, I can tell you right now, I'm not going—"

"I'm the supervisor here. You and Janek will run parallel investigations. If either of you finds anything, you'll bring it to me."

"What about duplication?"

Oh-oh—don't push it, Ray.

"I'll worry about that," Kit said.

"Sure, you'll worry. But what about the people we're going to interview? Two detectives coming from different directions— that'll get everyone confused." He glanced at Janek. Then his voice turned bitter. "Of course, Janek here's such a famous investigator they'll probably fall all over themselves they'll be so flattered."

"That'll be enough, detective."

Boyce stared at her, nonplussed. "I may look dumb, Chief. But I can read the writing on the wall."

"What's that supposed to mean?" Kit's hoarse whisper should have cut straight to Boyce's ears. But the slob wasn't listening; he was too wrapped up in his self-pity.

"You don't want me in on this. You want Janek. I know why, too."

"Why?" Kit demanded.

"Because he's your . . . you know."

Oh, you poor hotheaded son of a bitch.

"My *what*?"

Boyce sputtered. "Your special friend's what I hear."

"Want a letter in *your* file, Boyce?"

"All I want is fair treatment!" But then something must have told Boyce he'd gone too far because suddenly he clamped his mouth. When he opened it again, his tone was different. "I respectfully ask permission to withdraw from the case," he whispered with restrained fury.

"Permission granted." Kit rose. "I've got work to do. Boyce, report to your precinct commander. Janek, stay. I've got a few choice words for you, detective."

She walked across her office to the window, stared out at the falling snow until Boyce had shut the door. When she turned to Janek, her eyes were glowing.

"You're really a prick."

Janek shrugged. "You're the one who told me to go down to Quantico."

"And you played Sullivan just right, didn't you? I should have known."

"I don't see the problem . . . now that Boyce has so graciously stepped aside."

"The problem, my friend, is he's going to talk. It doesn't do anything for my reputation to have a pissed-off detective saying Chief Kopta's not a straight shooter."

"Everyone knows you shoot straight."

"Yeah." She looked resigned. "Well, you did it, Frank. Set things up just the way you wanted them."

"So punish me for it. Put another letter in my file."

She shook her head. "I hope I won't be sorry about this."

"You won't be." Janek walked briskly to the door. "Sullivan's the one'll be sorry."

A̲aron had begged them space on the fourth floor of the Police Property Building in Greenwich Village between Fifth and University Place. The office was on the same floor as the narcotics storage room, past the detectives' lounge, down the hall, down three steps, up two, first door on the left. Aaron had borrowed two gray hard-rubber-top desks, two swivel chairs, a beaten-up filing cabinet, and an answering machine. When Janek appeared in the doorway, he was in the midst of sweeping out an accumulation of used styrofoam coffee cups, empty potato chip bags, and cigar ash from the last special squad to occupy the space.

"I see we're slumming," Janek said.

"It's okay, Frank." Aaron gestured toward a dustpan. Janek handed it to him. "Remember last spring when the President was here? Secret Service unit used this for a command post. That's why we got so many phones. Connected, too."

Janek looked at the phones, six five-button models, three on each desk. Then he sniffed the air. The room was overheated and much too dry. He turned to the ceiling; the fluorescent lights buzzed. He peered around, noticed a disgusting crust on the far wall, most likely pizza sauce, he hoped not blood. A radiator hissed out steam. He looked at Aaron, who nodded back, mutual acknowledgment that though their office was a shithouse, it was at least their own.

He helped Aaron sweep out the remainder of the junk, then returned the brooms and trash can to the cleaning closet. The corridor smelled of stale cigarette smoke. When he returned to the office, he noticed his rubber boots were leaking. He pulled them off and stared out the window. It had stopped snowing. On the street the buildup of perfect flakes was already turning gray.

He knew what he wanted to do: talk to everyone who'd had close contact with Jess, particularly the last few days of her life. He wanted to chart every hour of her final days: where she'd gone; what she'd done; the name of every person she'd spoken to.

He drew up a rough grid chart, showed it to Aaron, instructed him to get a police artist to paint it on their largest wall.

"And while he's in here with a brush," Janek said, pointing, "maybe he can do something about that crust."

He also assigned Aaron to talk to all the members of the Greg Gale group.

"Check them all out; get them alone; squeeze them hard. If you smell anything murderous or that smacks of a cult, let me know. But please keep the details of the fun and games to yourself. I'd just as soon not hear any more about Jess's sex life."

Aaron understood.

Janek had set himself another task. He taxied to La Guardia Airport, found a seat on the noon shuttle to Boston, then sat in the plane for an hour before it left the gate.

There were numerous announcements from the pilot: Air traffic was snarled up and down the eastern seaboard; half a foot of snow had fallen on Logan in Boston. Stewardesses prowled the cabin, offering tiny cellophane bags containing honey-roasted cashews. Then everyone was ordered off the plane. Then, suddenly, mysteriously, they all were ordered back on. And then, with undue haste it seemed to Janek, the plane revved up and took off with a roar.

When he reached Boston, it was nearly three o'clock. Janek took one look at the taxi line, found his way to the subway, transferred at Park Street, and fifty minutes later got off at Harvard Square. Some helpful students guided him to the Law School, an immensely long building, where numerous assistant DAs of his acquaintance had, in their student days, undergone excruciating torture.

Janek appeared in the doorway of Dr. David Chun's second-floor office just as the psychiatrist, already in his overcoat, was stuffing file folders into a briefcase.

Chun was not pleased to see him. "You should have called, Lieutenant. Unfortunately I can't talk to you now. I'm going home before the snow gets too deep."

"The snow stopped falling a couple hours ago, Doctor," Janek replied. "If you wait another hour, everything'll be shoveled out."

Chun stared at him. "You know better than to show up here without an appointment. Please tell me why didn't you call."

"I didn't think you'd see me. So I came up anyway, took a chance."

Chun sat down. "Why didn't you think I'd see you?"

Janek sat, too. He'd gotten the psychiatrist's attention. Now all he had to do was hold it.

"You were upset down in Quantico. I had the feeling you wished Sullivan had never involved you in the case. Something frightens you about it, something you don't want to discuss. I need to hear you discuss it, Doctor. That's why I came."

Chun studied him. "You're different from Sullivan. You're a listener."

"I try to be."

Chun thought a moment before he spoke. "Okay, Lieutenant, take a seat outside. I'll give my wife a call; then we'll talk."

When Chun came out, he was carrying his briefcase and still wearing his overcoat. *Uh-oh,* Janek thought, *he's changed his mind.* But Chun was no less anxious to talk; he just didn't want to do it in his office.

He guided Janek across Harvard Yard. Students were walking briskly on the freshly shoveled paths, and some freshmen were putting finishing touches on a snowman that bore a vague resemblance to Fidel Castro. Janek watched while a rosy-cheeked girl in a white ski parka stuck a piece of black wood into the effigy's mouth to simulate a cigar.

At Harvard Square the snow had turned to slush. A news dealer hawked hometown papers. Chun led Janek through the Coop, past counters displaying Harvard running shorts and T-shirts with amusing slogans, then out a rear door and across a narrow street.

As they entered the dark lounge called Casablanca, Janek was struck by a throaty torch song rendition of "As Time Goes By." The place, dominated by a huge blowup of Humphrey Bogart, was empty except for a few student couples. Janek glanced at the jukebox. It offered esoteric selections, old love songs from the forties and fifties, renditions by Dietrich and Piaf.

"Oh, yes, something *is* bothering me, Lieutenant," Dr. Chun said after they were seated and the doctor had ordered himself a double martini. "But you see, there's a strange thing about these serial cases. You work with them awhile, you're bound to go a little crazy. It's quite common to become depressed. Dealing with killers, talking to them, interviewing them—that can bring you down a lot sometimes."

He smiled, a crisp, neat little smile, then gulped from his glass. Waiting for the doctor to continue, Janek sipped some scotch.

"Those of us who do this kind of work are aware of that. Inspector Sullivan, too. He's a bright man, stubborn at times, but like yourself, he's a hunter, so for him there's always the challenge of the chase. Not for me. My job is to profile. And to do that, I have to go inside a killer's mind. I never had any trouble with that before. But this case is different. Please tell me, Lieutenant, if you will, why *you* think it's different."

"I never said it was different."

"But you believe it is or you wouldn't have come all this way."

The same small, neat smile again. Chun lifted a toothpick from the holder on the table, used it to stab his martini olive.

Janek nodded. "I found your presentation fascinating. A confident, organized, highly competitive killer, sexually dysfunctional and all of that. But I missed something important, an explanation of why the victims were chosen."

Chun popped the olive into his mouth. "You've seen the hole. You're a perceptive man." He cleared his throat. "People who are murdered by a serial killer are not chosen for death by accident. In a sense, for which we must remember never to blame them, the victims select themselves. By the way they look or dress or talk they become attractive to the killer. Sometimes they become stand-ins for a parent or another person who has played a significant role in the killer's life. When we first started to work on Happy Families, we assumed that one person in each family, most likely a female, was the target and that the others were killed out of collateral rage or simply because they were witnesses. Then we found the case of the two brothers. So the gender thing broke down right there. To put it in a nutshell, I have analyzed these victims very carefully, charting every observable trait. And I cannot come up with a single common element of attractiveness. Except, of course, the families."

"But everyone is a member of a family, Doctor. If that's the only

common element, why these particular families? For me the idea
of families doesn't pattern out."

Chun swallowed the remains of his martini. "You're right, of
course, and that, you see, is what frightens me so much about this
case. That's why I wish Sullivan had never brought me into it."
He screwed up his features the way he had in Quantico. "What I
feel here is . . . I don't know quite how to express it. It's as if there's
nothing here, nothing particular—do you follow what I'm saying?
It's as if this killer doesn't care about anything. As if nothing
attracts him. As if he only wants to kill. And as monstrous as a
serial killer always is, usually there's some little thing, some small
fascination with people no matter how twisted or perverse, that can
help us to understand him, maybe even to sympathize a little bit.
But here there's a void, a nothingness. I've never faced anything
quite like it. It scares me, the blankness of it, the nihilism, the
zeroness. Look at me, Lieutenant." Chun presented his face to
Janek. "Can you see how terrified I am? Because where there is
nothing, Lieutenant, no reason, no incentive, no caring, no human
bond, then there is nothing to understand." Dr. Chun grinned
helplessly. "There's just . . . nothing."

And with that the psychiatrist hung his head and stared discon-
solately into his empty glass.

$$\mathbf{T}$$hat night, back in New York,
the snow was swirling around the streetlamps, almost, it seemed
to Janek, like bugs on a summer's night. He phoned Aaron from
the airport, was surprised to learn that Jess's things were still in
her dorm room.

"The college wants the room back," Aaron told him. "They've
been bugging the Dorances to move her stuff out. But Boyce put
a seal on the door, then never got around to inspecting it. Course,
we already know what a dumb schmuck he is."

They met in midtown, rode up to the Columbia campus together, then separated at 114th Street, Aaron to continue his interviews with the Greg Gale group, Janek to check out Jess's room.

The dorm was a modern high rise. A moody female student with badly bitten nails and stringy, unwashed hair manned the lobby security desk alongside a grizzled campus cop. An oddly mismatched pair, they screened visitors and checked student IDs.

When Janek told the girl where he was going, she gave him a curious look.

"Kids've been getting pretty spooked around that room," she muttered.

While he waited for the elevator, Janek perused the dorm bulletin board. It was layered with notices that collectively demonstrated the richness (or perhaps, he thought, the poverty) of American college life: a lecture on Icelandic poetry; a rally for Palestinian rights; a black lesbian tea dance; a plea for information on faculty-student sexual harassment, anonymity promised to informants.

On the twelfth floor he paused before Jess's door. The corridor carried a blend of sounds issuing from adjoining rooms: students talking, laughing; TV shows; heavy metal rock; someone practicing a cello far down the hall. It was the sound of young Americans, and it filled Janek with a bitter pain. A week before, Jess had lived within this sound, had contributed to it. Now her silent room "spooked" the other kids.

The room he entered was small, a virtual monk's cell, containing a narrow bed covered with an Indian blanket, a pair of matching bookcases crammed with books, and a clean white Formica desk with a laptop computer centered on its top. A small CD player and a pair of earphones she probably used late at night lay on a little table beside her bed.

Janek sat down on the bed. He wanted to feel comfortable, but he couldn't. He glanced at the walls, which spoke so strongly of Jess. Almost every spare inch was covered with items from her edged weapons collection: fencing foils; rapiers; swords; daggers; knives. It was an odd hobby for a girl, but Jess had clung to it since she was twelve. She had fallen in love with the romance of swordplay from the day he had taken her to a repertory movie house to see José Ferrer in *Cyrano de Bergerac*.

"Thrust home, thrust home . . ." she had repeated afterward on the street, exuberant as she mimicked Cyrano's elegant lunge.

Restless on the bed, Janek moved to the bookcases, then knelt to inspect the titles. There were numerous volumes devoted to fencing and edged weapons and also martial arts, which Jess had taken up when she started college.

Janek remembered her words: "There's so much crime around there, Frank. All sorts of muggings and stuff. A lot of the kids are scared to walk alone, but I want to learn to take care of myself." He remembered the way she'd tossed her hair when she'd added: "I don't like walking around afraid."

He sat for a long time on the bed, waiting for something to happen. The walls, the books, swords and knives—he waited for them to speak, to tell him what had frightened her. When they stayed silent, he knew it was time to take the room apart.

He searched the dresser first. He wept as he touched her clothes: neatly folded pairs of jeans, sweaters, jerseys, shirts, underwear. Her workout clothes moved him most, perhaps, he thought, because they seemed so intimate; within these garments she had moved, run, perspired. He examined everything, turned out every pair of socks, patted down every T-shirt, all to no avail. Aside from a comb, some costume jewelry, a pack of condoms, and miscellaneous coins, he found nothing.

When he was finished with the dresser, he went to work on the closet, checking the dresses, placing them lovingly on the bed, then exploring the interior of every sneaker and shoe. Behind the shoes he found a set of chromed weights and, inexplicably, a bow and a quiver full of arrows. When he had the closet empty, he stepped into it and peered around. Just above the door he saw a piece of cardboard. It was taped to the wall.

He hesitated. Behind that cardboard she had hidden something. Did he have the right to intrude?

But his role now was not that of a respectful godfather; he was a detective investigating a murder. He reached up and pulled the cardboard free. Several photographs floated to the floor.

He stooped to pick them up. They were Polaroids. A series of four shots, they showed Jess and another girl, wearing fencing pantaloons but also unmasked and, mysteriously, bare to the waist, fighting with sabers like duelists.

At first he couldn't bear to look at them. The exposure of Jess's flesh, the way her pert young breasts were pointed, their tips so eager and erect . . . he felt obliged to avert his eyes.

What the hell was going on with her? What the hell did she think she was doing?

She was playing some weird sort of game, he decided—perhaps some species of charades. Whatever it was it had shamed her or she wouldn't have hidden the pictures. But it had also meant something important to her or she wouldn't have bothered to keep them.

He wondered who had taken the photographs. Their existence implied an observer. Then he remembered that Polaroid cameras contain self-timers, so the camera could have been mounted on a tripod and set to fire off automatically.

What are these pictures about? Do they have anything to do with her call?

As much as he hated the thought, he knew he had to examine them. Sweat broke out on his forehead as he held them closer, searching their backgrounds for clues. They had been taken in an all-white high-ceilinged room. No windows showed, but something about the slant of light made him think the pictures had been taken very early in the day.

The other girl had pale skin, short jet black hair, and icy blue eyes.

Who was she? What did she mean to Jess? Why on God's earth are they both bare-breasted? Were they posing, clowning around? Or were they really fighting?

From the intensity of their expressions they appeared to be duelists. In one shot, in a corner of the room, he could make out their discarded jackets.

Why were they fighting, risking disfigurement and injury? Were they settling some kind of grudge? Daring each other? Showing bravery? Exciting each other by the ritual of combat?

Janek sat at Jess's desk and held his fists to his head. First Greg Gale, now this. But the longer he thought about it, the more clearly he understood that Jess was no less enigmatic than other homicide victims he had investigated. So perhaps he shouldn't expect to understand her; perhaps, like every other human being, she would turn out to be unfathomable.

He took up his search again, combing through her notebooks. He checked her address book for coded telephone numbers. He pulled every book out of her bookcases and fanned its pages for hidden notes. He emptied her wastebasket, then searched each scrap for a revealing notation. When, at two in the morning, he finally left the dorm, a new security team was in place at the desk and he had to show his shield to get out.

He didn't sleep well that night. Images of Jess kept ricocheting in his mind. He recalled Dr. Archer's words: "Perhaps you had unconscious fantasies about her. Perhaps you longed for her in some way you don't fully understand. . . ."

Was that true? He had interviewed Jess's lover, handled her underwear, searched out her secret pictures. When he'd found the pack of condoms in her dresser, he'd tossed them casually aside. But inside, he hadn't reacted casually at all. The condoms spoke of sexuality; if she owned them, she used them. And now, as whenever he thought of her engaging in sex, he felt something he couldn't define: a quick flush of excitement, followed immediately by a hard, harsh throb of despair.

Had he desired her, and, detesting his desire, immediately repressed it? Perhaps Dr. Archer was right; perhaps he had forced his way into this investigation in order to stay close to Jess. Was he after her killer, or was he really chasing something inside himself, some perverse aspect of his character he had hitherto denied?

The question tormented him until, with the dawn, he got out of bed, went to his living room, sat in his easy chair, and stared at Monika's glass. Then memories flooded back, memories of their carnal afternoons in room 13 with the sea smell drifting to them from the lagoon. Longing for Monika, her body, and her touch, he knew that Dr. Archer was wrong. It was Monika he wanted, not Jess. Feeling confident this was true, he knew he could go on.

He and Aaron spent the entire first week of November talking to people, then using what they learned to fill in the grid on their office wall. As is usually the case with students, Jess's schedule was rigorously defined. She went to classes, worked out with the fencing team, studied, ate, slept. No one took attendance at Columbia, so there was no hard proof which classes she attended and which she cut, but by putting together the recollections of her friends, they were able to reconstruct a large portion of her final days.

There were other less typical things she did, and they charted these activities as well: her midmorning therapy sessions with Dr. Archer; her late-afternoon classes in martial arts at a dojo on upper Broadway; her long, lonely early-evening runs through Riverside Park. But still there were gaps, often hours long. And they had no way of knowing what she did at night; students in her dorm came and went as they pleased.

When Janek met Fran Dunning, he felt a familiar glow. She was the confidante he was looking for.

Jess's fencing coach, Sergei Simionov, pointed her out in the fencing hall at the Columbia gym. Janek recognized her at once; he had seen her at Jess's funeral and at the cemetery, too.

"They were teammates and best friends," Simionov said. He was a stout, mustachioed, barrel-chested Soviet émigré, a onetime Olympic medalist in saber. "Fran's the one you want to talk to," he said.

Janek stayed to watch the workout. Women athletes fascinated him. He liked their poise, the way they moved, their ease and comfort with their bodies. Fran Dunning, a thin, willowy blonde with pert features and puffed cheeks, moved across the exercise floor with the smooth, liquid mobility of a dancer.

He waited until the workout was over, then positioned himself outside the women's locker room. When Fran appeared, he introduced himself, then asked if she had time to talk. She was on her way to a biology lab, but she invited him to escort her as she walked across the campus.

"I know who you are," she said on the steps of the gym. "Jess talked about you a lot. I saw you at the funeral. I wanted to say hi, but you were busy with the Dorances. I didn't want to intrude."

Janek liked her. She had the same direct look-you-in-the-eyes manner as Jess. Taller, thinner, she carried herself the same way, too, back straight, head high in the confident manner of an athlete.

"I miss her a lot, still can't believe she's gone. You read about these things, but you never think they can happen to anyone you know."

"What do you mean by 'these things,' Fran?"

"Getting attacked, suddenly, for no reason. Running in the park, just enjoying yourself, thinking your thoughts. Then suddenly a man appears out of the dark."

"Could Jess have known her attacker?"

"The way I heard it, it was one of those psychos, maybe a mugger gone berserk." Fran stopped walking, looked at him. "Do you think she knew him?"

"I don't know yet," Janek said. "Did you see much of her the last few days before it happened?"

Fran nodded. "The Sunday before. We spent the whole day together."

She and Jess saw each other daily at fencing practice and also spent time together on weekends. That particular Sunday was the last day of the Custom Knives Show, so they joined up in the morning, took the subway down to Grand Central, then walked over to the Hotel Roosevelt, where the show was being held.

"Jess got me started with knives. She had this great collection, mostly historical pieces, Italian stilettos, a couple of Japanese tantos, an Indonesian kris, a terrific French rapier. When I saw her stuff, I knew I wanted to collect, too. She was very generous with advice, and she steered me to the good dealers. That's how we became friends. On the fencing team we were rivals. We kidded each other about one of us switching to saber so we wouldn't have to compete. The joke, of course, was that neither of us was willing to switch."

American-made custom knives were Jess's most recent passion. And as with the historical daggers and swords, she was the one who took the lead, learning to differentiate the work of the leading makers, then introducing Fran Dunning to the field.

"The knives some of those men make are remarkable," Fran said. "They're like art objects, but still, you can use them. Hunting knives, bowies, fighting knives—Jess thought knifemaking was one of the few crafts at which Americans excel."

The knife show was held on the mezzanine floor of the hotel. The main room was a large hall, filled with long exhibition tables arranged along aisles, occupied by hundreds of knifemakers from all over the country who had brought their wares to sell. At first Jess and Fran explored together; then they split up so each girl could look at the knives that most interested her. When Fran rejoined Jess, she sensed her friend was upset.

"I asked her if something was the matter," Fran told Janek as they crossed in front of Butler Library. "She shook her head, said it wasn't anything. I went along. What else could I do? But I didn't believe her. As I'm sure you know, Jess was not a moody type of girl. But something must have gotten to her because she started out so exuberant, but when we met up at the door, she was downcast, almost sullen."

"What did you do after the show?"

"Took the subway uptown, worked out for an hour with foils in the gym, then showered and went out to eat at a Chinese restaurant on Broadway and a Hundred and Nineteenth."

"Anything unusual happen?"

"Nothing I can think of."

"Did either of you buy a knife?"

Fran nodded. "Jess did. A real beauty, a switchblade with an ivory handle. It wasn't legal. The man who made it was very cautious about showing it to us." She smiled. "Jess told me you'd give her hell if you ever found out she bought it."

A switchblade—why on earth?

"I didn't find it when I searched her dorm room," Janek said.

"Maybe she dropped it off at her mother's. If I knew Jess, she probably hid it someplace."

Janek thought about hiding places. "Something I want to ask you."

Fran peered at him. "I'll help you as best I can."

"First, close your eyes." Fran obeyed. "Now think of two women fencing. Imagine them topless, both of them."

"Uh-huh. . . ."

"Think about it. Does the image remind you of anything?"

Fran shook her head. But Janek felt something tentative in her denial.

"Does it embarrass you?"

Fran blushed. "It *is* kind of wild."

She's not a very good liar, Janek thought.

"I found photos of Jess and another girl fencing like that. They were hidden in Jess's closet."

He stared at Fran, waiting for her to respond. When she looked away, he stopped walking and gently touched her cheek.

"Please understand," he said. "I need to know everything."

"Yeah. . . ." Fran took a deep breath. When she spoke again, her voice was agitated and her delivery faster than before. "There's a painting by a French artist, Émile Bayard. It's called *An Affair of Honor.* Jess found it in one of her books about dueling. It shows two topless women fighting with rapiers while three other women look on. Jess was intrigued by it—I don't know why. She was equally intrigued by a whole slew of stories she dug up on women duelists. She told me she wanted to write a paper about them for some feminist-oriented European history course she was taking."

"But there's more to it, isn't there, Fran? Did she ask you to fence topless with her?"

Fran nodded. "I didn't want to. For one thing it's dangerous.

For another . . . I just didn't like the idea. So I told her: 'I'm a jock, but I'm not that butch.' I think she understood."

"Did you take her proposal as a sexual overture?"

Fran shook her head. "If Jess was inclined that way, she never showed it. No, I think it was just something she wanted to do. Fencing, fighting—those were things she loved. In some way, I guess, the image turned her on. And once she got it into her head, she wanted to act it out."

Janek showed Fran the Polaroids. Fran could not identify the other girl, nor did she recognize the room where the pictures had been taken.

"I wonder if it's a fencing salon at the Ruspoli Academy in Italy. Fran was there last summer. It's certainly not any practice room we use around here."

"A final question," Janek said. "Did Jess do or say anything that Sunday, anything at all, that made you think she might be afraid."

Fran shook her head. "I don't think Jess was afraid of anything. That's why she was such a terrific fencer. I remember something she said to me once: 'I'll take life any way it comes.' I think if she saw someone running toward her with an ice pick, she'd have put up a terrific fight. She knew karate. She could disarm a man twice her weight. So whoever killed her must have come at her from behind, and the only reason she didn't hear him coming was that she had her Walkman turned up at the time."

Aaron's interviews convinced him that none of the members of the Greg Gale crowd had harbored any ill will toward Jess.

"They're not murderous types, Frank. Just your standard spoiled, overeducated, decadent, attractive young people with a hunger for dope and thrills. Actually they don't do that much drugs. Mostly pot, occasionally a little coke. To them the sex group's good clean fun, not a cult they'd kill to protect."

Aaron had looked into former boyfriends, too. Except for Gale they all seemed to be jocks.

"Maybe not the brightest guys, but most of them fairly decent. She didn't like pretentious or overstudious types."

Simionov, the fencing coach, had told Janek pretty much the same thing: "She talked straight and she fenced straight and she liked straight-talking people. If she'd lived, who knows how far she might have gone? Bronze medal, maybe even silver." The coach had shaken his head with grief. "She had everything: talent, will, strength and speed, and as fierce a fighting spirit as I ever encountered in a woman. Who knows? With a little luck she might have gone all the way."

Fran Dunning phoned Janek two days after their walk.

"You said I should call you if I remembered anything."

Good girl! "What do you remember?"

"Something Jess said at the Chinese restaurant. It's probably not important, but I thought I should tell you anyway. She said she might have to stop seeing her shrink."

Interesting. "Did she say why?"

"No. But I'm sure the reason wasn't financial because she once told me her stepfather was paying the fees. I wouldn't remember her mentioning it except the week before she'd been very positive about her therapist."

"Try and recall her exact words, Fran? Did she say she might have to stop or that she wanted to quit?"

"I don't remember exactly. But I had the feeling that she was disgusted about something, that whatever it was, it was gnawing at her, and that if she stopped seeing her therapist, it would be at her initiative." Fran paused. "I could be wrong, Lieutenant, but that's what I thought at the time."

Janek thanked Fran and reminded her to call him again if she remembered anything more. When he put down the phone, he thought about what she'd said. Jess's comment could have been a casual remark, but still he was glad he knew about it. He'd been looking for an excuse to see Dr. Archer again. This time, he resolved, he would limit the discussion to her former patient.

The therapist had set their appointment for 5:00 P.M. As before, she appeared at the door of her waiting room precisely on the hour.

"Nice to see you again, Lieutenant. You have fifty minutes," she announced with a sympathetic smile.

As Janek followed her into the consulting room, he noticed that her curly red hair was dyed.

"Now, how may I help you?" Dr. Archer began smiling again after they were seated in opposing chairs.

"Jess tried to get in touch with me two days before she was killed. Any idea why?"

Archer shook her head. "I have no idea, and I can't imagine why you'd ask me that."

"Her father and I were partners once. Laura Dorance thinks Jess might have wanted to ask me about him. Did she talk about him much in here?"

The psychologist looked pained. "As I told you before, Lieutenant, even though Jessica has passed away, I don't feel I can properly discuss her therapy."

"Look, Dr. Archer, I'm conducting a criminal investigation. Right now I need your help. If you refuse to give it to me, then I'm faced with a problem. I can write you off as an unhelpful witness or I can seek a court order to compel you to respond." The therapist was staring at him. Janek smiled to soften his threat. "I certainly hope that won't be necessary."

Dr. Archer sat very still. The office was silent except for the muted sound of classical music issuing from the waiting-room radio. After waiting futilely for her to speak, Janek decided to take her silence as acquiescence.

"Laura tells me Jess began asking questions about her dad about the time she started seeing you. Laura assumed his name came up in therapy."

"His name did come up," Dr. Archer affirmed.

"Just his name? Or his character?"

The therapist tightened her lips. "I am truly mystified," she said. "Why are you asking me about this?"

"Please, Dr. Archer, I'm not your patient. I'm here to ask questions, not answer them."

She turned away, irritated. "And you expect me to respond without the right to ask questions of my own—is that how it goes, Lieutenant?"

Janek turned conciliatory. "Can't we try and work this out?"

Archer turned back to him, then folded her hands neatly on her lap. "I shall try to help you as best I can," she whispered, then clamped her mouth shut.

He found the next half hour trying. Archer kept her word, answered all his questions clearly, sometimes even exhaustively. But she made no effort to be pleasant. Rather, she replied to him in terse sentences while gazing at him as though she regarded him as a torturer.

Tim Foy: Yes, he was discussed; in therapy a patient's parents always are. Jessica had described watching her father get into his car and then seeing it explode. Her father's death had been the traumatic event of her early years, yet her long-term response to it had been surprisingly positive. Seeing him die had hardened her will. She was determined never to become a victim. She developed an aggressive personality that she channeled healthily into sports. All of that was entirely to her credit.

Bad dreams: Yes, Jessica had been having them lately. Nothing unusual about that. A patient often feels a requirement to bring dream material to her analyst, especially in the early stages of therapy. The content of her dreams varied, but they were typical college-age stress fantasies: facing an exam while blacking out all knowledge of the subject; finding herself naked in a room in which everyone else is dressed; letting her teammates down by stumbling during a fencing match and thus losing a tournament to a rival school.

Sex: Jessica had the normal longings of a woman her age with no indications of lesbianism beyond normal parameters. Again much to her credit, her initial exhilaration at the anonymous sex to which Greg Gale had introduced her gave way fairly quickly to feelings of inner emptiness and ennui.

The topless fencing episode: That could be viewed in a sexual context, although Dr. Archer saw it somewhat differently. Jessica had brought it up at their first session. It was her "presenting symptom." She was disturbed about it. She felt that by staging the scene with the other girl, a British fencer she had befriended at the Ruspoli School in Italy, she had done something forbidden, possibly even evil.

"The imagery of the Bayard painting embedded itself in Jessica's mind," Archer explained. "She was fascinated by the seminudity of it, the notion of women exposing their bared flesh to a steel sword. She equated it with the stripped-down costuming of male boxers. To fight bare meant to duel seriously, even to the death. We spent several sessions working through her troubled feelings about it, especially her guilt over having talked the English girl into trying it. In my analysis I tried to focus on the underlying meaning of the scene. What we came up with (and I emphasize we did this together) was that Jessica's strong attraction to fencing and to martial arts was based on her romantic notion of heroism. I called it the gladiator's syndrome, the idea that the highest, most noble way of life is the way of the warrior who regularly offers his body to injury or death for the delectation of the public. The gladiator's sacrifice is for the benefit of those who watch him. By engaging in dangerous fights, he fulfills the innermost needs of his audience, channeling its bloodlust into sport, stylizing its collective aggression into art. At the same time he, or she, in the case of Jessica, surrounds herself with an aura of glamour. It's close to the Japanese samurai ideal, but with the added component of exhibitionism. It's a hard, short life of intense experience—perilous, painful, and, ultimately, self-sacrificial."

It was a brilliant analysis, and Janek was dazzled by it. He was also impressed at the way Archer seemed to come alive. But the change in her demeanor made him uneasy. The voice she used to explain the fencing episode was different from her voice when answering his other queries. It was more vital, authoritative, indicative of an inner power and confidence that didn't fit with her earlier pettiness. Now he felt he was listening to another person altogether, a strong, dynamic temperament hiding behind a bland, nondescript façade. But even before, he realized, Archer's eyes had betrayed her. Her relentless gaze should have warned him he was dealing with an extraordinary individual, far more passionate, forceful, and intelligent than her insipid professional manner and constricted body language would suggest.

But then another transformation, which Janek found equally surprising, took place. When he mentioned the Polaroids he'd found in Jess's closet, he saw an immediate pinching up of the eyes, followed by a grimace of anger. The reaction was fleeting, covered up almost instantly by a patient nodding of the head. But Janek was certain about what he'd seen: Jess had not told Archer about the pictures, and for that the therapist now felt betrayed.

"I take it you didn't know about them," he asked.

Archer shrugged the omission off. "A patient will almost always hold something back." Her tone connoted superior wisdom. "A little shield against the therapist, a small corner of privacy to be preserved."

"Do the photographs surprise you?"

"Not the photographs so much as the way Jessica hid them. I have to admit that surprises me a bit."

"Why?"

Archer raised an eyebrow. "You found them, didn't you?"

Janek squinted. "You're not suggesting she expected me to search her room?"

"Of course not, Lieutenant. But she didn't hide them all that well. A good hiding place is an irrevocable hiding place, one that stays secret even after the hider's death."

"So what does that tell you?"

When Archer began to speak, Janek recognized the same authoritative voice she'd used while analyzing the fencing incident.

"It tells me Jessica wasn't all that ashamed about partaking in the scene. I know from what she told me how difficult it was for her to set it up. I know she proposed the idea to a teammate here in New York and, to her embarrassment, was rebuffed. Still, she needed a confederate, in this case the English girl, and so she took a chance. By merely broaching such a bizarre idea, she risked exposing herself to the other girl's ridicule."

"But this time the other girl went along."

"She did. And I think that that, ultimately, is what got Jessica so upset. Not that the English girl went along, but the *way* she went along, as if she took it as a seduction on Jessica's part and regarded it as a forbidden act."

"But there's still something I don't understand, Doctor. You say Jess was troubled by the incident. If she was, why didn't she destroy the photographs?"

Archer paused to reflect. "Difficult to say. Perhaps for the same reason people often hesitate to destroy documentation even when it contains material that's painful for them to see or read. Jessica staged the duel. She had a large emotional investment in it. To destroy the photographs of the scene she'd worked so hard to set up would be to deny herself any chance to contemplate it in the future and perhaps even to revel in what she'd done."

Janek smiled. "You're a fascinating woman, Doctor. It's very interesting to talk to you."

The therapist smiled demurely, then glanced at her watch. "Which brings us," she said, "to the end of the session. Your fifty minutes are nearly up."

"A final question." Archer motioned for Janek to ask it. "I have it from one of Jess's closest friends, who spoke to her just days before she died, that she was thinking about quitting therapy."

"And you want to know what I think about that?" Archer looked past him toward the opposite wall. "In this business we're used to sudden changes in a patient's feelings. In the therapeutic relationship the therapist often comes to represent important figures in the patient's life—parent, sibling, lover—toward whom the patient then acts out. So, you see, when a patient contemplates leaving her therapist, it's only a natural by-product of the process."

"So I shouldn't make too much of it?"

"You may make of it whatever you like," the psychologist replied, rising.

On their way to the door she turned to him again. "Have you given any thought to what I said last time?"

Janek nodded. "I thought about it."

"And dismissed it out of hand?"

"Not at all. But after I thought about it awhile, I decided you were wrong."

Archer grinned. "You work in a most dangerous and stressful field, Lieutenant. There's bound to be some distortion in your view of things."

Janek smiled. "Think I could use some therapy, Doctor?"

Her grin widened. "We can all use therapy, Lieutenant. In your case I'd say it certainly wouldn't hurt."

They both chuckled over that. Then at the door Janek thanked her for her time. "I hope we can talk again."

The therapist nodded. "Anytime, Lieutenant. Just give me a call. I shall always try to fit you in."

That evening Janek took a long walk. Leaving his apartment at six o'clock, when the rush-hour traffic was just at its crest, he headed up Broadway to merge with the throngs still surging out of the subways. On his route he passed stores offering high- and low-fashion garments; markets offering sturgeon and pastrami; Chinese, Turkish, Lebanese, and Ethiopian restaurants; bars catering to gays and transvestites; panhandlers; dope dealers; homeless people living in cardboard boxes; old people sitting on benches; and aggressive young people on the make. By the time he reached the Columbia University campus, he felt he had confronted a cross section of the human condition.

At 114th Street he turned into Riverside Park. Although it was a chilly November night, the joggers were out in force. He didn't see many lone runners; press and TV coverage about Jess was still in the public mind. But as he walked farther uptown, the number dwindled off, until, north of the Columbia Presbyterian Medical Center, there were none at all.

It was a basic principle of his trade that the first step in any investigation was to go to the crime scene and get a feeling for the place. Since he and Aaron had taken over the case from Boyce, he had been putting such a visit off. Now, approaching the spot where Jess's body had been dragged off the jogging path, he felt his heartbeat quicken.

The streetlamps were on, but in the long, narrow strip of parkland the foliage was dense and the shadows were deep. Despite the darkness, it didn't take him long to find the spot. Orange-tipped police stakes caught the ambient light cast by cars racing above on Riverside Drive. And then he was surprised. There were a good dozen bunches of flowers, mostly dried up but all the more poignant for being so, arranged along the bottom row of stones of an old retaining wall just behind the site. Stubs of candles were set there, too, in little hardened pools of melted wax. People had heard that a fine young woman had died in this place; they had been moved, had come and left tangible evidence of their caring. So now in the underbrush, amidst the jettisoned Coke cans and discarded sandwich wrappers, a small shrine had been erected at the Scene of Suffering. It would last until the first heavy snow.

The glue: Janek was obsessed by it. The ice picks were bad enough; they didn't reflect the caring of a knife, the quick dispatch of a bullet, the hatred of a poison. Leaving the picks embedded was bad, too. You didn't bother to use something fine to take your victim's life; you used a throwaway. Like eating your dinner off a paper plate or drinking your wine from a styrofoam cup, it was a way of showing your contempt.

But the glue was worse; the glue was truly awful.

Janek had investigated many homicides in which victims had been bound. He'd seen handcuffs and rope burns and even barbed wire cutting into flesh. He'd seen his share of mutilations, too: cuts, slices, and, in the Switch Case, actual dismemberment, decapitation. But glue was different. Glue was made of animal wastes, old bones and hooves boiled down to a viscous jelly. Glue was what you used to stick pieces of wood together, not to bind the parts of a human being. Glue said: "I don't desecrate by cutting; I'm not a psychotic acting out my rage." Glue said: "I'm cool, patient. I go about my chosen task the way an undertaker goes about his. I'm neat and careful and whistle a merry tune as I seal up people's body cavities."

Janek thought he hated this killer more than any killer he had ever sought, not only because the man had taken the life of a person he had loved but also because he had done so with such dehumanizing scorn.

He was watching the late-evening news, trying to concentrate on an awful story about a ten-year-old boy set on fire because he refused to buy crack from a school bully, when his telephone rang. It was Monika calling with wonderful news. She would be coming through New York in three weeks' time, en route to a psychiatrists' conference in San Francisco.

"I hope you're planning to stay awhile," Janek said.

"Can I take that as an invitation?"

"You bet you can! How much time can you give me?"

"Two or three days. Maybe a couple more on my way home."

That wasn't very much, but it was better than nothing. "How about a couple of years?" he asked.

Monika laughed. "Why don't you come out to San Francisco with me?"

"Sure. And take a little room down the hall so the chambermaids won't get any funny ideas."

As they talked, he picked up the glass she'd given him, angled it so it caught the light.

"Maybe I ought to join you in Frisco," he said. "I've been spending so much time with shrinks lately I'm sure I'd feel right at home."

Monika was intrigued by his account of his meeting with Dr. Chun but was skeptical about something Dr. Archer had said.

"It's true," she told him, "that a patient who wants to leave therapy can be acting out against an analyst who reminds her of a difficult figure in her life. But your goddaughter wasn't in treatment long enough to develop that kind of strong transference relationship."

"How long would it take?" Janek asked.

"Several months at least."

"Can you think of any other reason why Jess may have wanted to quit?"

"There could have been a lot of reasons. Anxiety caused by her therapy or a personal dislike for her therapist. I lost a patient once because he saw me unexpectedly in a nightclub."

"What was so bad about that?"

"Normally nothing. But this man idealized me. When he saw me dancing with my husband in a sexy environment, he was thrown into such turmoil he couldn't relate to me any longer as his analyst."

"You say he saw you. Did you see him, too?"

"Yes, our eyes met," she said.

"How did you react?"

"I smiled at him."

"Ever occur to you he might have followed you to the nightclub?"

She laughed. "I never thought of that."

"It could make all the difference," he said. "To me the question is did he quit therapy because he saw you or because you saw him?"

"And therein," Monika said, laughing, "must lie the difference between a detective and an analyst."

Later he asked her if she thought Archer had deliberately misled him.

"I have no way of knowing," she said, "but her acting-out explanation strikes me as glib."

"Well, suppose Jess ran into her unexpectedly at the knife show? Something happened there that changed her mood. But why would seeing Archer shake her up?"

"How did Jess feel about knives?"

"She was passionate about them."

"Well, then, that could have been it," Monika said. "Suddenly there was her analyst infringing on her territory. But it's all conjecture, isn't it?"

"It always is," Janek agreed.

The next morning, over breakfast with Aaron at a Greek coffee shop around the corner from the Police Property Building, Janek described Dr. Archer.

"Tiny woman, built like a butterball, kindly smile, bland, self-effacing voice, a little fussy, a little too precise about time. But when I stoke her up, she turns difficult. Doesn't want to answer questions, wants to ask them. The end of our first interview she tried to turn things around, make me think I was probing because I had 'unconscious sexual fantasies' about Jess. Second time I put on some stress, and suddenly I started picking up on her anger. She's good at concealing, but the rage shows through, which tells me how strong it must be inside. She gives me a plausible but phony explanation as to why Jess may have wanted to quit on her, a lot of brilliant but tortured analysis about the fencing incident, and some strange stuff about a good hiding place being an irrevocable hiding place—whatever the hell that means. I don't know what the bottom line is on her, Aaron, but something about her isn't right."

Aaron picked up a jelly roll. "She's weird, Frank. Ever meet a shrink who wasn't? You don't think she's the Happy Families killer, do you?"

He shook his head. "How could she be? But still . . . I don't see Jess relating to a person like that."

Aaron put down his cup. "I know what you're thinking."

"What am I thinking?"

"That maybe the feds didn't conceal their case all that well. Maybe it leaked out. This guy Chun—he's a shrink. So maybe he spilled to another shrink, and Archer heard about it through the grapevine and did a copycat job on Jess."

Janek smiled. "Swear to God, Aaron—I never thought of that. But now that you bring it up . . ."

Aaron nodded. "Yeah, Frank—I'll check the little lady out."

Laura Dorance couldn't remember who referred Jess to Dr. Archer. "I think it was one of her friends," she said.

But when Janek called around, none of Jess's friends would admit to having made the referral.

That night, as he walked home from the subway, he noticed an unshaven man in a seedy suit lingering near the front door of his building. As he approached, the man stared at him.

"Janek?"

Janek stared back. "Who's asking?"

The man unclenched his hand. He'd been holding an old newspaper clipping. He showed it to Janek. It was a picture taken at the time of the Switch trial. *Oh-oh*, Janek thought.

"It's you, isn't it?" The man's breath stank of cabbage. There was dandruff on his shoulders.

"So what?" Janek said.

"You guys work long hours. I've been waiting here since five."

As the man put his hand into his pocket, Janek tensed, reached beneath his jacket, gripped the handle of his Colt. But when he saw the paper with the blue legal backing, he relaxed and let go of his gun.

"I am serving you, Lieutenant," the man said, offering Janek the document.

Janek snapped it out of his hand. One look told him what it was. He stared at the man with disgust.

"Great business you're in."

"Hey, don't take it out on me, fella! Just doing my job."

Janek brushed by him and entered his building. Inside his apartment he sat down and read the document. It was a notice that a lawsuit had been filed by the firm of Streep & Holster on behalf of its client, one Clarence "Rusty" Glickman, wherein Glickman alleged unlawful assault resulting in severe physical and psychological injury, for which he demanded a jury trial and one million dollars' damages.

Janek didn't sleep well that night. Something—something he'd seen that could be important—nagged at him. Unable to recall what it was, he flopped from side to side in torment.

At two in the morning he remembered and sat up: *The arrows! I forgot to look inside the quiver!*

The next morning he phoned Laura and asked her if she'd saved it.

"A bow and arrow set—I don't remember anything like that."

"It was in her dorm-room closet."

"I never saw it. I couldn't even bear to go up to her room. When you called and told us it was all right to move out her stuff, Stanton went up there to collect her swords. He's put them out on consignment with a dealer. We decided to give away the rest of her things. Stanton phoned the Salvation Army. They sent over a truck."

"Do you happen to know if Stanton turned up an ivory-handled switchblade knife?"

Laura asked him to hold while she checked Stanton's list. A minute later she was back.

"Lots of knives but no switchblade. Sorry, Frank."

The Salvation Army sorted its pickups at its general warehouse in Brooklyn. Once inside the building, bulk donations were broken up. Toys went to one floor, furniture to another, clothing to a third, etc. Items such as archery equipment, unsuitable for general sale, were relegated to a special area.

By the time Janek found a friendly sergeant willing to help him, the bulk of Jess's stuff had long been sorted and shipped back out of the building, distributed to various sales outlets in and around the city.

"But there's still a chance on the bow and arrows," Sergeant Hunter told him as he led Janek rapidly down a long corridor lit by naked bulbs past cages filled with donations. The whole place smelled like a dry cleaning establishment. The sergeant's dog, an overweight dachshund named Clarence, scampered ahead. Hunter, dragging one foot behind him, strove mightily to keep up.

"We've got rooms here filled with anything you'd ever need," Hunter said. The sergeant had bloodshot eyes, wild hair, and a ragged gray-streaked beard. "We've got a room of shoes, a room of crutches, a room of old dentist's equipment. We got pots and pans, lawn mower parts, old chemistry and Erector sets." Hunter rattled off other types of items processed at the warehouse: pinball machines; waffle irons; bathroom scales. "Would you believe we've even got a cage here filled with discarded artificial limbs? Strange maybe, but think about it. A guy loses his leg, say, in the war, and the vet hospital fits him out with a spare. Then he dies. So what does his widow do? Bury it with him is one possibility. Another is she calls us up. 'Can't stand looking at it,' she cries. 'Get it out of here.' And we take it, the way we take darn near anything. 'For every pot there's a top'—that's what my mother used to say."

The weapons room was not a cage. It had a solid door. "Don't want just anyone nosing around in here," Hunter said, working a key inside the outsize padlock while Clarence, the dachshund, dribbled saliva over Janek's shoes.

There were no actual guns inside the weapons room, though there were plenty of toy models and realistic replicas. The array of other weaponry was fascinating, ranging from the kinds of sticks with nail points used to clean up parks to a huge wooden sword with the word "Excalibur" burned into its blade. In between there was a hoard of tomahawks and African-style spears, assorted clubs, maces, cudgels, blackjacks and shillelaghs, sundry bomb and mine casings, numerous darts, slingshots, catapults, boomerangs, brass knuckles sets, and, in one corner, a homemade guillotine.

The archery equipment was positioned against one wall. Gazing at the crossbows, longbows, competition bows, and myriad quivers filled with arrows all bunched together in a vertical pile, Janek wondered how he'd manage to recognize the equipment that had belonged to Jess. He'd barely glanced at the bow when he'd discovered it in her closet and tossed it with the quiver into the pile of clothing on her bed.

But there was one important thing he did remember about it: The gear had seemed almost new. Scanning the bows before him, he reached for the one that appeared the least scuffed up. He pulled it out and examined it. The name DIANA was scrawled in blue grease pencil on the inside curve just above the handle. The handwriting didn't resemble Jess's, but the bow had an elegant feel to it that made him think it was the right one. He set it aside and knelt to examine the quivers.

He rejected ones made of wood or hide. The one he'd held that night had been aluminum. There were three of these, all relatively unsoiled. He took all three and emptied them out onto the floor, being careful to keep the arrows of each in separate piles. Then, with Hunter standing behind him and the dog, Clarence, sputtering through slobbering chops, he inspected each arrow, many of which were tipped with extremely sharp points, and, when he had done that, the interior of each quiver. Finding nothing, he turned the quivers over. On the bottom of the first he found DIANA written in the same blue cursive script. He stuffed its arrows back inside.

"This is it," he said, looking up at Hunter.

The sergeant shook his head, incredulous. "Got to congratulate you. All the years I worked in this dump, you're the first guy came around looking for something he gave away and ended up finding it." He pointed to his dog, vigorously wagging its tail. "See, even Clarence is amazed."

Diana: It was only later on the Brooklyn Bridge, driving back to Manhattan, that Janek thought of Diana, the huntress, twin sister to Apollo, virgin goddess of the moon, usually depicted holding a bow.

What difference did the archery stuff make anyway? he asked himself. And the moment he asked the answer came to him like a blow. It was not that he'd forgotten to look inside the quiver that had kept him up the night before. It was the word connection between Jess's possessing a bow and arrow and the name of her therapist: *Archer.*

"Oh, she *is* a piece of work is Dr. Beverly Archer," Aaron said, shaking his head.

He read to Janek from his notes, compiled after five days of investigation and surveillance, as they sat together in their office, the grid on the wall nearly filled in now with the activities of Jess's final days.

"You've been to her house, Frank. You know the routine. No receptionist. Patients ring and get buzzed in. Two doors to her office, one to the waiting room, the other opening directly to the front hall. That way nobody sees anybody, conventional practice in therapeutic circles. But maybe there's more to it here. Maybe this one doesn't want people to notice something not so conventional, from what I understand. Get this: All her patients are young women."

"No guys?"

"Just females."

"Interesting," Janek said. "Tell me more."

"She owns the building, lives in the apartment upstairs, rents the basement to a young woman, a librarian. I'd say the good doctor leads a tight, constricted life. All day long she sees patients. First appointment eight in the morning, last six at night. They all go in looking anxious and come out looking kind of dazed. Know what I mean, Frank? Glassy-eyed, smiling, but the smile's the shit-eating kind, like they're all wrapped up in themselves, their dear little egos so nicely massaged and all. Whatever she does to them in there, they all look like they feel better afterwards. Then, when the last one leaves, she waits a few minutes, comes out to do her errands. Usual stuff around the neighborhood—shoemaker, dry cleaner, grocery store, that kind of crap. And that's it. She's out for maybe half an hour; then she's back inside. Lights go off downstairs. Lights come on upstairs. Nine-thirty or ten, upstairs lights go off, too. And there she is, locked in, snug as a bug in a rug. No social life, no dates, no friends I can find out about. Her work is her life. It's girls all day long. Except for two other interesting little things she does."

Janek knew how fond Aaron was of turning reports into sagas. He used all the tricks of the tale-teller's trade: asides; digressions; embellishments; authorial opinions. Best of all, he liked to evoke questions. So Janek asked him one: "What two other interesting little things does she do?"

Aaron smiled. "Tuesday nights she teaches a class in 'Problems of the Adolescent and Postadolescent Female' at the Eisenberg Psychoanalytic Institute in Chelsea. I checked the place out; it's a reputable institution, no quack joint. They train laypeople, mostly Ph.D.'s, who want to be professional analytic-oriented therapists."

"And the second thing?"

"That's the goody. Thursday mornings she's picked up by a car service, then driven out to a hospital called Carlisle in Derby, Connecticut. She's a one-day-a-week consultant out there. It's a special kind of hospital, Frank—a hospital for the criminally insane." Aaron tongued his lips to show how much he relished this juicy bit of information.

"So, an austere life devoted to work. That can be a rewarding way to live," Janek observed.

"So I hear, though I haven't tried it myself. But you were right, Frank. There *is* something about her. Maybe it's the expression on her face when she doesn't think anyone's looking. Lonely, desperate, tense, maybe even—"

"What?"

"I don't know." Aaron shrugged. "Angry. . . ."

He handed Janek her curriculum vitae and a photocopy of a professional paper she'd written for *The Review of Psychology.*

"I can't make head or tail out of it. Maybe you'll have better luck," he said.

Janek glanced at the CV. The first line in the personal background section sent a clarifying wave crashing across his brain: "Place of birth: Cleveland, Ohio, 5/6/50."

That night Janek read Archer's paper. He found it intelligent, coherent, and unusually compelling. In it she described three female patients: "Alice," "Wilma," and "Ginny." All three were in their early twenties, and each was tormented by an obsessive fixation upon what Archer called a "shaming incident," a traumatizing event in the girl's past that had inspired great shame and humiliation.

The patient Alice, a blond athlete from an affluent suburban family, could not go an hour without remembering in vivid detail the gloating expression on her younger sister's face while she, Alice, then ten years old, had been severely spanked by their mother for an act the younger sister had actually committed.

Alice was so obsessed with that injustice and the shame aroused by the witnessed punishment that she could barely function as a college student, often losing all concentration, once even in the middle of a final exam.

After describing the crippling effect of this memory, Archer went on to describe the treatment she had devised. This consisted of provoking the girl into emotionally reliving the shaming experience in all its humiliating aspects, but with the novel difference that in the reenactment the outcome for Alice was triumphant. This time, under Archer's guidance, Alice was able to "reread" the expression on her sister's face. This time it was not gloating that she saw but shame and deep remorse. Thus, by rewriting the script, encouraging Alice to devise a new ending in which she would emerge victorious, Archer had managed to vitiate the destructive power of the memory and even to assist Alice in increasing her sense of personal confidence and self-respect.

After describing two similar cases, Archer held out hope for patients traumatized by early shame. Though a successful treatment could not be guaranteed, the therapist was encouraged to be as creative as possible in devising ways wherein the patient could work through the insult to her ego.

"Above all else," Archer wrote in the conclusion of her paper, "we therapists must never underestimate the debilitating effects and the haunting power of early shaming incidents. Often patients will carry the burden of such incidents as baggage through their lives, baggage, moreover, that possesses the surrealistic quality of becoming increasingly heavy as the patient ages. Eventually, unless a cure is effected, the load may become so heavy that the patient will suffer terrifying stress or even break down totally beneath its crushing weight."

Aaron, wearing one of his Hawaiian shirts, stood at the far end of the office, nursing himself from a mug of coffee. It was early the following morning. A cold rain, which had fallen overnight, had frozen on the ground, creating sufficient ice to turn the sidewalks into bobsled tracks.

"Tell me about it, Frank," Aaron urged. "Let's see what you got."

Janek, perched on the corner of his desk, spread his arms. "I've got nothing, absolutely nothing. You know that."

"So tell me about nothing. Worst I can do is laugh in your face."

"It involves a number of leaps," Janek said.

Aaron bit off the end of a jelly roll. "Go ahead," he said. "Leap."

Janek nodded. He stood and began to pace. "Two days before she was killed Jess tried to get in touch with me. Something was troubling her. About the same time she told her best friend she wanted to quit seeing her shrink." He turned to Aaron. "Leap number one: It was the shrink she wanted to talk to me about."

"Could be," Aaron said, biting off the center section of his roll. "I'll buy that. Go on."

Janek resumed pacing. "Jess was never involved with archery, but she had an unused archery set in her closet. Her shrink's name is Archer. Leap number two: The archery set's somehow connected to the shrink."

"Farfetched but . . ." Aaron made a wave motion with his hand. "Interesting," he conceded. "So far I got nothing to laugh at."

Janek nodded. "Try this. When Sullivan put his high-powered FBI computer to work on the Happy Families crimes, the only victim connection it came up with was that two of the people were from Cleveland. Now it turns out Archer's from Cleveland, too."

"So?"

"It starts to add up. I think Archer's involved. I think she did something or she knows something she's not telling. I think she found out Jess saw or suspected something about her and—"

"You think she's the Happy Families killer?"

Janek shrugged. "Well, I wouldn't go that far. Not yet."

Aaron gulped down the rest of his roll. "Now you've done it, Frank. That's a real stretch. Wanna know what I think?" Janek nodded. "It doesn't jell."

"Of course, it doesn't jell."

"So let's talk about it."

"It's impossible. I'm the first to admit that. This tiny fat lady, forty years old—she couldn't possibly break into all those houses, murder all those people. She doesn't have the strength to be a stabbing machine. She may have the hatred, but she doesn't have the guts. The Cleveland connection—that's meaningless, too, because, among other things, only two of the victims are tied together that way. Then there're other dangles, like why would she want to glue their genitals, and what's the meaning of the weeds, and what could Jess have possibly seen, and how could tubby little Archer get in and out so fast, so clean, never seen by anyone, slick without a trace. And I guess the biggest dangle is how could a trained psychologist with a full practice and a respectable career, who consults a day a week at a hospital for the criminally insane— how could such a person possibly be an insane killer herself? She's a healer, right? She specializes in helping young women trauma- tized by 'shaming events,' right?" Janek paused. "So it's impossi- ble—right?"

Aaron grinned. "Sure, it's impossible." He looked into Janek's eyes. "But we know what we gotta do, we gotta satisfy ourselves." Aaron stretched. "The only way I can think to do that is check out the Cleveland-connected victims, see if either of them ever crossed paths with Archer. Another thing—Jess was Archer's patient, so I'll want to check if any of the other victims ever had her as a therapist. If it turns out even one of them did"—he grinned again—"then we'll really have something."

Janek nodded. "That's what I hoped you'd say. Why don't you get right on it? And while you're at it, make a low-level request to Sullivan's people for copies of the victim files. Not just the Cleveland pair, but all of them."

Aaron nodded. "I'll ask for the crime scene photos, too."

"To throw them off?"

"Partly," Aaron admitted. "And also because I think you ought to focus on the weeds. The weeds are a message. You're good at reading messages." He looked at Janek. "What else have you got to do?"

Janek smiled. "Nothing too important. I thought I'd try and put in a penetration agent, that's all."

Early that afternoon Janek at- tended women's fencing practice. He found something tangy and enticing about the aroma of female sweat that wafted across the gym. Later he waited for Fran Dunning outside the women's locker room. When she appeared, her hair was still wet from her shower. Again he escorted her across campus to her afternoon biology lab.

"I'd like to take you up on your offer to help," Janek said. "I need some information on Jess's shrink."

"I already told you everything I know."

"Of course, you have. But I wonder if you'd consider doing more."

"What?"

"Going to Dr. Archer as a patient for a while. All you'd have to do is call her up, tell her you were Jess's friend, that you've been deeply troubled since she was killed and you feel you could use some help. I'm sure she'd give you an appointment. Of course, we'd reimburse you for your fees."

Fran turned to him, her eyes curious. "You think her shrink had something to do with it?"

Janek shook his head. "I'm not going to lie to you, Fran. I don't know the answer to that. What I *do* know is there's something there I have to explore. I'm not asking you to do anything more than see this woman a couple of times, then fill me in."

He could tell by the flush on her cheeks that the idea attracted her. But she was also wavering, perhaps not certain she could bring it off.

"No spying, no snooping, no playing detective," he warned sternly. "You go in as Fran Dunning, with real feelings and real distress. If she asks about me, and I doubt she will, you can tell her all about our interview. The only thing you musn't tell her about is this conversation we're having now."

"What do you want to know exactly?"

"How she acts, her manner with you, her feelings, if she reveals them, toward Jess. I've been in the waiting and consulting rooms, but I haven't seen any other parts of the house. So you might want to ask to use the bathroom, then let me know if you notice anything interesting on the way."

"What would you consider interesting?" He could see excitement in her eyes.

"Whatever strikes you. Believe me, Fran, if I thought there was any danger, I wouldn't ask you to get involved. This is a voluntary mission. If you don't want to do it, I'll understand."

"Oh, I *want* to do it," she said. "When do I start?"

Janek smiled, then handed her a piece of paper. "Here's Dr. Archer's number. You might want to give her a call this afternoon."

The next day Sullivan called.

"How you doing, Frank?"

"Fine. You?"

"Grand, just grand." Sullivan paused. "Understand you want to see some of our material?"

"Problem with that?"

"No problem. But I'm curious. Haven't heard a peep out of you since you started up there."

"Been busy getting organized, setting up an office, all that. NYPD's a little different from the FBI. We're the poor cousins, remember, Harry?"

Sullivan chuckled in response, a little roll of heh-heh-hehs. When the chuckling finally died away, he got to the point. "Actually I called you about something else."

"What was that?"

"Your surreptitious little trip up to Harvard Law School."

"I wouldn't call it surreptitious."

"Call it whatever you like. Chun has withdrawn as consultant on HF."

"So?"

"What the hell did you say to him?"

"What're you talking about?"

Sullivan's voice hardened up. "Don't bullshit me. You go up there, next thing I know he quits."

Janek laughed. "Don't be an asshole, Harry. Chun was uncomfortable with the case. Anyone could see he was."

During the ensuing pause Janek imagined Sullivan's mouth tightening to a line. But when Sullivan spoke again, his voice had turned cool and businesslike.

"We're pouching off the stuff you asked for. You'll get it by the end of the day."

"Damn gracious of you."

"Either of us finds out anything, we share it, right?"

"That was the deal."

"Well, good luck, Frank." And before Janek could wish him the same, Sullivan clicked off.

He spent the next three days studying the crime scene photographs.

When they arrived, he and Aaron tacked them up at eye level in neat, even rows on the office walls. Then, while Aaron worked the phones, trying to track down connections between the two Cleveland victims and Beverly Archer, Janek stood before each photograph, staring at it, trying to enter into it before moving on to the next.

He found this work extremely trying. He could not sustain it for more than a quarter hour at a time. When he felt he had sufficient command of his morning or afternoon quota of brutal images, he would leave the office to take long walks through Greenwich Village.

Sometimes he would wander as far as the Hudson River piers across from the strip of gay leather bars on West Street or, in the other direction, beyond Tompkins Square Park into the network of cross streets known as Alphabet City. And always on these walks, amidst these squalid surroundings, he would try to imagine the killings taking place. He did this with all the homicides except for one; he still could not bear to imagine what had happened to Jess.

The trick was to take the still pictures and turn them into movies. Horror movies, splatter movies—those were what he projected to himself. But hard as he tried he could not see tiny Beverly Archer performing a starring role. The intensity, the rage were there—of that he was nearly certain—but not the movements or the staging. He simply could not see her rushing into rooms, surprising people, thrusting at them with ice picks, then working on their fallen bodies with glue. Like most people in this world, Janek thought, the little shrink killed people in her dreams. But could she actually draw their blood? Could little Beverly wield the pick?

It's getting interesting," Aaron said.

Janek had just returned from one of his walks. The moment he came through the door he could feel a certain cocky confidence in the room.

"Tie-in with Archer?"

"A very nice one." Aaron grinned. "Old Bertha Parce, the retired schoolteacher in Miami—seems she taught forty years at Ashley-Burnett, a snazzy private girls' school in Shaker Heights. And guess who happened to attend Ashley-Burnett during that same period?"

"Little Beverly Archer."

"You got it, Frank."

Janek sat down. He needed a few moments to think through the implications.

"So now it's not just Cleveland; it's a small exclusive school *in* Cleveland," he said. "Jess's shrink, Bertha Parce's student—" He looked up at Aaron. "It's almost too good to be true."

Aaron nodded. "I like it. It's starting to come together. But we're going to need a hell of a lot more. The subtle telephone approach can take me only so far. You know what I want to do, Frank: go out to Cleveland and make a real investigation into the lady's past."

Janek shook his head. "Too early. Expose our theory, and we run the risk of it getting back to her, plus we could screw ourselves permanently with Sullivan. Which wouldn't matter if we turn out to be right. But if we're not . . ."

"So what do you want me to do?"

"Keep plugging on the Connecticut brothers, the MacDonalds. Match them with Archer and you win a ticket to Cleveland."

"And if I can't match them?"

Janek shrugged. "We'll have to take another approach."

There was something about the weeds, a way they were connected, that haunted him on his walks. It was something that he'd seen but that hadn't registered yet, a binding metaphor that remained just beyond his grasp. He found that the harder he struggled to dig it out of himself, the stronger his resistance to giving it up.

Exhausted after three days of endless reruns of his self-made murder movies, he decided to try to free-associate. He remembered the moment the process began. He was walking in an area of old coffee and cheese warehouses on Desbrosses Street when, strangely, he detected the aroma of dead flowers in the air.

The weeds: No question that Aaron was right; the ugly dour little plants contained a message. But what was it? What did they say?

They had been left so they would be easily found; that could account for the fact that Sullivan's people didn't notice them at first. Left in plain sight, they were perhaps too obvious.

When, after four killings, Sullivan's team finally *did* notice them, the weeds from the earlier cases had long since been swept away. But research revealed that they'd been there as well, their presence validated by photographs taken by local investigators.

Once focused on the weeds, Sullivan's forensic experts were relentless. They carefully collected the scruffy little specimens, then sent them to the FBI lab for analysis. Alas, no secret writings were discovered inside, nor were any poisons or stains found upon their surfaces. So if the weeds did not conceal a message, then they must *be* the message. But again Janek wondered: What did they say?

Not orchids or roses or carnations, Sullivan had told them in Quantico, meaning, Janek supposed, not the noble flowers left by mystery-story killers. But if the weeds were, in fact, ignoble, could they then be taken as ironic comment on those elegant, glamorous fictional murderers?

That was one possibility.

Another was that the killer saw himself (or herself if it was Archer) as unglamorous, ignoble, homely. And with that thought the binding metaphor sprang suddenly into Janek's brain.

He mulled over his idea for a moment, then stopped on a street corner, stood still, and closed his eyes. Carefully he recalled the various crime scene photos in which the weeds appeared. Slowly at first, then faster and faster, he forced the pictures to flash successively on a screen inside his brain. Yes, the metaphor was pretty, but would it hold? He would have to go back to the office and examine the pictures again.

His heart was racing as he entered the Police Property Building, tore up the stairs, then down the hall. With sweat breaking out on his forehead, he rushed past Aaron to confront the pictures on the walls.

As he looked at each one in turn, the metaphor locked more firmly into place. But still there was ambiguity: The killings had taken place indoors, inside rooms each of which had four walls.

It was time now, he knew, to look closely at the pictures of Jess. And when he did, the metaphor was validated. Up in Riverside Park the weeds had been left leaning against the same little stone wall where he had seen the remnants of candles and flowers left by mourners.

Exhilarated, he turned to Aaron, who, phone in hand, was gazing at him skeptically from his desk.

"It's the weeds," he said. "They're always placed beside a wall."

"So?" Aaron asked, waiting for the punch line.

"That's it," Janek said.

"What?"

"The meaning."

"Meaning? If you don't mind, Frank, please tell me what you're talking about?"

"It's how she sees herself, Aaron. It's her message, her calling card."

"So how *does* she see herself?" Aaron asked impatiently.

Janek turned to stare out the window. "As a shy and homely girl without a partner at the dance. As a wallflower," he added mournfully.

Later, when they pulled out the seven pictures and lined them up together, it was so clear Aaron wondered aloud how Sullivan's people could possibly have failed to see it.

"It was their own word 'weeds' that threw them off," Janek said. "They locked themselves in with that. If they'd started out calling them flowers, degraded, ragged flowers, they probably would have figured it out."

But still, he knew, it was the placement near Jess that really was the clincher. And perhaps, too, before one could read the message, one would need to have a certain sort of woman in mind—a woman who could be considered a wallflower at the dance of life.

Janek met Fran Dunning at a coffeehouse around the corner from her dorm. It was one of those sixties-type places, with little marble tables, uncomfortable European café chairs, and a lone, slow, and very spacey waitress.

Fran had had three sessions with Beverly Archer. She found her a highly professional and compassionate shrink.

"She's really nice," Fran said, "the way she makes you feel so comfortable and all. It was kind of intimidating to walk in there, not knowing what to expect. But then I started talking about Jess, and I could see she was moved." Fran paused. "There were tears in her eyes, Lieutenant. She cared for Jess; I know she did."

Fine, thought Janek. *It works better if Fran likes her.*

Fran hadn't seen much of the house. The lavatory was on the first floor, off the therapy room. On her way to it she'd passed through a small office containing a couple of locked filing cabinets

and a framed poster for a Botero exhibition. She'd also noticed a
burglar alarm system, keypad and siren, inside the coat closet off
the front hall.

"Did you mention the knife show?" Janek asked.

"Not yet." Fran paused. "Want me to?"

Janek shook his head. "You've done enough, Fran. No need to
see her again. Thanks for all your help."

Fran stared at him, concerned. "I wish you'd tell me what this
is about, Lieutenant. I just can't believe Dr. Archer had anything
to do with, you know . . ."

Janek nodded. He knew he had to give her a reason. "It's not
a question of whether she had anything to do with it. It's more a
matter of whether she knows something and is holding back.
Whenever I ask her about Jess, she talks about patient-therapist
confidentiality and how it applies even after death. I find that
strange, don't you?"

"I guess so. I never thought about it actually." Suddenly the
robust girl athlete seemed terribly fragile. Her smile was weak; her
eyes were confused. Janek patted her reassuringly on the hand.

Aaron wanted to bust into
Archer's house.

"Just for a look-see, Frank. Me, alone, on a Tuesday night, when
she's teaching her class downtown. I'll slip in and out. She'll never
know I was there. You won't either, 'cause I won't tell you about
it."

"What good will that do?"

"If I see something, I'll say I'm strongly convinced there's
evidence in her house. Then we'll figure out a way to get at it
legally. That way at least we'll *know.*"

Janek was familiar with the technique and its rationale: the
illegal break-in or wiretap to assure yourself that you weren't
wasting your time, that there was a real case to be made. He had
never employed it and was contemptuous of detectives who did. It
wasn't just the illegality, though that was bad enough. It was the

chain of deceit that followed, that led inevitably to perjury in court. It would be one thing to acquiesce if Aaron wanted to go in for a look, another to state later under oath that he hadn't known anything about it.

Aaron understood. "That's what I thought you'd say. But if there was a way, Frank—a way that was, say, a little less direct, what would you think about that?"

Sounds like shading. But he felt he ought to hear Aaron out. Then, as he listened and began to feel seduced, he understood why Kit Kopta didn't like to assign detectives to cases in which they were emotionally involved.

They were in Aaron's car driving up Third Avenue. It was past midnight. They had long since passed Ninety-sixth Street, the infamous DMZ, and were now deep into the huge Hispanic neighborhood of upper Manhattan, where the store signs were in Spanish, the streets were crowded, bodegas sold live chickens, and pharmacists' wives told fortunes.

"In all my years with Safes and Lofts," Aaron was saying, "Leo Titus was the slickest burglar I ever met. Charming guy. I know you'll like him."

"I thought I wasn't going to meet him."

"Yeah. Sorry. I forgot. Anyway, if you did meet him, you'd like him. How's that?"

"Irrelevant," Janek said.

They passed a battered-looking storefront gym. It wasn't like a yuppie health club in midtown. Up here a gym was a real, sweaty, sour-smelling place where slick-haired Latino boys with names like Pedro and Paco slugged hard at leather bags and skipped rope with exquisite poise deep into the night.

Aaron was still talking about his favorite burglar: "Leo's got this corny MO, but it always seems to work. First he makes a point of going into the house legally in daylight. Comes on as a telephone or Con Ed repairman: 'Hey, lady, gas leak around the corner, gotta get into your basement,' or 'Line trouble, lady—gotta inspect.'

He's got nice company credentials, and he's got his girlfriend working as backup. If anyone asks questions, he gives them her number. She's waiting on the other end to verify."

"Yeah, slick," Janek agreed.

"On the first go-around he sees if there's anything worth taking, figures out how he's going to get in, and neutralizes the alarms."

"What's he looking for?"

"Not the crap the addicts take. No computers or VCRs. Leo goes for the good stuff: money; gold; jewels; bearer bonds. He likes stamp and coin collections but won't bother much with art. Too cumbersome, he says, hard to sell. He likes stuff he can stick into his pockets."

"I doubt Archer's got anything he'd be interested in."

"You may be surprised, Frank. Anyway, it doesn't matter. Leo'll find something, and we'll take it from there."

It was a complicated scheme, devious and tempting, which was why Janek had agreed to go uptown and take a look at Leo Titus. But he didn't think he'd end up going for it. *I'm much too true blue a cop for this,* he thought.

Aaron pulled into a space on the east side of Third, center of the block between 112th and 113th streets. He cut the engine and pointed toward a bar. A narrow red neon sign flashed BAD BOY. "We're meeting in there," he said.

"Gay bar, isn't it?"

Aaron nodded. "One of the esoteric ones. Whites cruising Latinos and blacks."

"I thought you said this guy had a girlfriend."

"Yeah, he does. But he's kind of a swish sometimes, too. Goes home occasionally with guys. He's gotten into some nice Park Avenue apartments that way."

"Shit!"

"Hey, Frank! This isn't about sexual preference."

"You know I don't care about that. But you make him sound, I don't know—undependable."

Aaron clamped his jaws. "Leo's highly dependable." He glanced at his watch. "Time I went in. I'll talk with him a few minutes, then bring him out and parade him up and down the block. He'll know someone's looking him over but won't know who. All I want is for you to get a feel for the guy. Watch his moves, see what you think."

Janek nodded. "Yeah."

As he waited, he asked himself what the hell he thought he was doing sitting low in a car in this none-too-elegant neighborhood, implicating himself in this thoroughly illegal maneuver. And the answer, he knew, was that he was at a point where he didn't care about legalities one way or the other. All he cared about was finding Jess's killer.

When Aaron walked out the door of Bad Boy Bar with Leo Titus in tow, Janek strained forward to peer. Aaron slouched in his usual manner, but Leo, a small, suave, coffee-colored man with neatly cropped hair and a debonair mustache, stepped forward with a stylish gait. And then, as they made their promenade down to the corner and back, Janek had to smile. It was impossible to dislike Leo. The lithe cat burglar moved with the bold grace of Fred Astaire. He almost seemed to prance.

"What do you have on the guy?" Janek asked as Aaron drove them back downtown. It was past 2:00 A.M. The street life of Spanish Harlem gave way to the cold, silent, empty residential cross streets of Manhattan's Upper East Side.

Aaron glanced at him quizzically. "Huh?"

"He's not going to do this for charity, is he?"

"Charity?" Aaron shook his head. "Not Leo."

"So?"

"He owes me a favor, Frank. Let's just leave it at that."

Janek nodded. He knew better than to pry into the intricacies of a detective's relationship with an informant. Such alliances could be built upon almost anything from real affection and respect to manipulation and fear. This time, Janek suspected, it wasn't Leo who owed Aaron a favor; rather, it was Aaron who was about to incur an enormous debt.

"Here's the plan," Aaron said. "Tuesday night, soon as Archer leaves for her class at Eisenberg, we pull up to her place and wait. We're running a surveillance. After a while we happen to notice a black man with a briefcase enter the house. We sit tight. For all we know Archer gave him the key."

Janek nodded. "Go on."

"After a while the dude comes out. And now we notice instead of a briefcase he's carrying this overstuffed satchel. We look at each other. 'Hey,' we say, 'maybe a robbery was committed in there.' So, having probable cause, we step out of our car and grab the guy. Leo's scared. He's done two tours in Attica, and he doesn't want to go up for a third. He starts to bargain. Is there any way he can get himself out of this mess? We don't take bribes, we're not that kind, but we're very interested in what he may have seen that could tie Doc Archer to the Happy Families crimes. Well, seems with all his snooping around Leo came across some pretty interesting evidence. So he trades what he saw for a walkaway deal on the robbery. And on the basis of that, valid information from an informant, we get a warrant, go in legally, and impound whatever he saw."

"Suppose Leo doesn't see anything?"

"Then he exits with an empty satchel. The satchel's the signal: If it's bulging with stuff, he's seen something, we move in on him and make the deal. Otherwise no harm done. He just walks away."

Aaron looked at Janek. "What do you think?"

Janek stared ahead. "We never had this conversation."

Aaron shook his head. "That's right, Frank. We never talked about any of this."

Tuesday, December 1. All day Janek asked himself if he wasn't making an enormous mistake. Twenty-five years in law enforcement and he'd never done a deal like this. *Suppose Leo* does *find something,* he asked himself, *and they go in after it, and then Archer gets a smart lawyer who finds Leo's entry just a wee bit coincidental. The lawyer goes to the D.A., who opens Leo up with the threat of a perjury charge. Leo quickly gives up Aaron, but Aaron hangs tough.* Could he, Janek, live with himself if Aaron got in trouble for helping him out? No way! He'd turn himself in with the result that the doctrine of "poisoned fruit" would prevail, the evidence against Archer would be tainted and quashed, Archer would get away with murder, and he, Janek, could end up doing a year in the penitentiary.

Would it be worth it? Not if it went down that way, it wouldn't be.

But there was another scenario, far more succulent. With one bold stroke he might solve a case that could otherwise require years of orthodox investigation.

That, he was ashamed to admit, was a possibility he could not resist.

At seven that evening, fifteen minutes after Archer's last patient left her house, Beverly Archer herself emerged, bundled in a shapeless gray goose down coat.

It was teeth-chattering weather. Janek and Aaron watched shivering from their parking spot as Beverly seemed almost to be swept by the wind down to the corner of Eighty-first and Second, then attempted to flag down a cab.

Several passed her by. Perhaps they didn't like the look of the short, dumpy lady thrashing at the air with her arms. But then a large Checker glided to a halt, Archer hopped in, the cab took off downtown, and, a few seconds later, after Janek stepped out of the car, Aaron waved to him and took off after the cab.

For thirty minutes Janek waited on the corner, collar up, arms clutched to his chest, trying to avert his face from the wintry wind. "Knives-in-the-cheeks" was what he called the relentless, driven icy air that ripped into the sides of his face.

He was shaking when Aaron finally returned. He stumbled back into the car, then immediately began rubbing his hands while Aaron pulled into a fire hydrant zone directly across the street from Archer's house.

"Sorry I took so long. I thought I should follow her all the way just in case she forgot something and came back."

"She could still come back."

"Harder now. Class started at seven-thirty. Which gives us a good hour and a half." He glanced at his watch. "Leo should be turning up. I talked to him this afternoon. Yesterday morning he did his utility man routine. No problems. The alarm system's disarmed." Aaron grinned at Janek. "Don't worry, Frank. No paper trail. I called him from a booth."

But Janek was nervous. *Still got time to cancel this madness,* he thought. He was about to call the whole deal off when Aaron gestured toward the corner. Leo Titus was crossing Third Avenue. "Good old Leo," Aaron whispered.

Later Janek would wonder if the reason he didn't cancel then was that he didn't want to cause Aaron to lose face.

Leo didn't even glance at them as he approached the house. And then Janek had to admire the man's cool. Leo walked straight up to Archer's front door, paused briefly, and two seconds later he was in, the door was closed again, and even someone watching would have no reason to suspect that a burglar had just entered the house.

"Guy's got moves," Aaron marveled.

Fifty minutes passed before Janek became uneasy. Then, when he asked Aaron if Leo wasn't due out pretty soon, Aaron responded with patronizing patience as if Janek were a rookie in need of a steadying hand.

"Keep the faith, Frank. This is our one crack at her. It's gotta be a thorough search. Leo's good. He knows how to look for stuff, and he knows how much time he's got left. Don't worry. If there's something in there, he'll find it."

But that wasn't what Janek was worried about.

Twenty minutes later Aaron, too, started showing signs of nervousness.

"Class breaks at nine. Takes her a minimum of fifteen minutes to get home. Point of fact, she usually hangs around a while answering questions, stuff like that. So we're safe for another half hour at least."

"Does Leo think he's got till nine-ten?"

Aaron exploded. "I'm not stupid, Frank! I told him nine max. He's got fifteen more minutes. He'll make it. Trust me—he'll be out of there in time."

At eight fifty-five they turned to each other. "Should have wired him up," Aaron said.

But Aaron knew there was no way they could have wired Leo, though it would have been nice to listen to him as he worked. If they wired him and something went wrong, their role would be exposed.

At nine Aaron smashed his fist against the steering wheel. "That son of a bitch better not try a double cross."

"*Could* he?" Janek asked.

"If he found something really valuable—I don't know." Aaron paused. "I can't imagine it. Anyway, we would have seen him come out." He paused. "Unless there's some way he found to sneak out through the back." He hit the wheel again. "But he wouldn't. He wouldn't dare! He knows I'd come after him. I'd never rest!"

Ten minutes later Aaron announced he was going in no matter the risk to the case. Janek gently put his hand on Aaron's arm.

"Yeah, you're right, someone has to go in. But this is my case. If it's going to get screwed up, I'll do the screwing."

"You can't go in there, Frank. You're a lieutenant, for Christ sakes!"

"I'll say I saw a thief enter and followed him in hot pursuit."

"Jesus!"

"They'll believe me."

"Leo's my boy. I feel . . . awful."

"Could be it's not his fault. Maybe he ran into whatever." Janek picked up a radio. "No talking unless you see Archer. Then just one squawk."

It was only on the doorstep of Archer's house that he wondered how he was going to get inside. He wasn't one of those detectives who excelled at opening locks. But when he took hold of the doorknob, turned it, and pushed, he was not surprised to find the door opening easily. Somehow he expected it to open, as if he had dreamed of the very sound it would make, as if everything that had happened and would happen on this night was familiar to him in some mysterious way.

The door, of course, was taped. Perhaps Aaron had told him Leo always taped his doors while describing the burglar's technique. Janek closed the door softly behind him, then stood very still. The hallway was dark except for a residual glow from the street that filtered in through the narrow leaded windows on either side of the portal.

The coat closet door was open. Janek glanced inside. A tiny bulb on the burglar alarm keyboard burned red to show that the system was armed up.

But Leo had neutralized it the day before. There was no danger; motion detectors would not set off the siren. Janek listened but heard nothing. Then he thought he felt vibrations, a faint thump on the floor above. He glanced at his watch. Nine-eleven. He had four minutes to find Leo and get out. He headed for the stairs.

They were carpeted. He could barely hear his own footsteps as he crept up to the landing. He paused to listen again. This was the mysterious residential portion of the house he had been thinking about for a week. Janek waited until his eyes adjusted to the darkness, then continued to the second floor. Nine-twelve. Three more minutes. He noticed a reddish glow from an open doorway down the hall.

He passed a closed door, probably a closet, then a door that was partially open. A glimpse of floor tiles suggested a bathroom. He paused.

"Leo," he whispered. When he heard nothing, he whispered the burglar's name again and again heard no response.

He crept farther up the hall to the open doorway where he'd

seen the glow. He stood there and peered into a cavernous high-ceilinged room strangely filled, like a photographer's darkroom, with dim red light.

It was a bedroom, but unlike any bedroom he had ever seen except perhaps in a movie. An enormous four-poster stood free, a foot or so from one of the walls. Opposite the bed there was a wide niche which once may have contained a fireplace. In this niche hung a full-length life-size oil portrait of a woman. A light extending from the wall above the painting shed red light upon its surface.

Janek stared at the picture, his eyes riveted to its dominating imagery. The woman depicted wore a low-cut silk scarlet dress and held a microphone in her hand. Posed before a dark velour curtain held open by a gilded rope, she appeared to be singing in a smoky ambience. But what was most striking about her was the halo of thick, glossy red curls that surrounded her head, her hard-edged alabaster white features, and the equally pale, lustrous exposed flesh of her upper bosoms, which swelled within the clinging silk of her dress. The woman made a striking figure, at once carnal and statuesque, sensual and unobtainable. And although the painter had worked in a standard academic style, he had caught something vibrant and alive in his subject, a moment when she projected herself, bursting with life-force, to the viewer.

But even as Janek was awed by the powerful image before him, his head began to whirl with a kaleidoscopic array of other images in the room. Below the portrait, arranged upon an odd piece of furniture set within the niche, he saw a number of anomalous objects he could not make out clearly in the red light. Something about them was important. He wanted to decipher them, and was about to move closer to do so, when his eyes, drawn around the room, fastened onto the curled figure of a man lying on the floor at the foot of the bed in a puddle of dark liquid.

Leo!

The moment it registered on him that Leo Titus was lying there, probably dead in a pool of his own blood, the radio strapped to his belt began to squawk. A second later he heard Aaron's voice.

"Shit, Frank! She's coming now, fast!"

Gotta get out of here!

Hearing a sound behind, Janek turned in time to see a short, slim, bald-headed figure, dressed top to bottom in black, ice pick in hand, poised in the doorway to the room. A second later the figure, weapon raised, was rushing at him through the reddish gloom.

Janek feinted to the left. At the same time he reached for the Colt strapped to his ankle. Too late. Before he could crouch, his attacker was upon him, plunging down the weapon.

He knew he'd been hit. No pain, but he could feel the steel strike the bone of his shoulder and then his right arm hanging limp. His only chance now, he knew, was to get to his gun with his left hand. He knelt and struggled for it even as he saw his assailant step back two paces, produce a second ice pick, raise it, and thrust at him again.

He ripped the Colt from its holster and, hand trembling, fired at the advancing figure. The pain was coming upon him now, a great wave of pain that filled his head with delirium. He fired a second time, directly into his adversary's body. And in that same split second, when he saw the body blasted back across the room and knew for certain that it was a woman, the pain smashed into him; he felt a wave of nausea and understood that on her second foray she had stabbed him in the throat.

He could feel the blood gushing out of him. And then, as his legs collapsed slowly, he was seized with the certainty that he was going to die.

He came to in an ambulance. He knew it was an ambulance because there was a white-coated medic leaning over him, working on his throat, a siren was blasting directly above, and Aaron was crouching by his head, whispering encouragement.

"Hang in there, Frank. Just a block from Lenox Hill Emergency."

"Aaron . . ."

"Frank?" Aaron's face was above him now, slightly blurry but recognizable.

"It was Archer, wasn't it?"

Aaron shook his head. "Wasn't her. But don't worry." Aaron smiled. "You got her. You blew the little bitch away."

"Then who?" But before Aaron could reply, Janek felt himself sinking back into a pit of pain. "Tell Monika—"

Oh-oh—I'm passing out.

When he woke again, he was on his back, naked beneath a sheet, being wheeled rapidly down a tiled basement corridor. Kit Kopta was by his side.

"Kit . . ."

"Right here, Frank."

"Who?"

"Don't worry about that now. You're going to be all right. The surgeons'll fix you up."

Surgeons. . . . Christ, it hurt!

Perhaps he dreamed it, though later he would tell people he woke up terrified during the operation, felt the heat of the lights on his face, saw the surgeons and nurses in their pea green smocks and masks, felt the probe of their instruments as they worked on his shoulder and his throat. And then seeing something in their eyes that told him he had a chance to live, he resigned himself and slipped back into a fuzzy chemical-induced sleep.

Kit was beside him when he came to in the recovery room. He could feel the tight grip of her hand.

"You're going to be okay, Frank. I've got some good news for you, too. Aaron got hold of Monika. She's flying in tonight."

"Great . . ." he murmured.

"Your arm should be all right. A week here, a week at home, and that should do it. As for your throat—well, another quarter inch and she'd have waxed you. She didn't, thank God!"

"Who *was* she?" His voice sounded strange to him, raw, hoarse, a mere whimper that sent pulses of pain shooting through his brain. He tried to sit. *"Who?"* he demanded.

"Take it easy, Frank. Lie back. She was the girl downstairs, the one who rented the basement apartment. She'd been Archer's patient in Connecticut."

Connecticut! What the hell was going on?

"But was she . . . the one? You know. Was she—?"

Kit was nodding. "Sure looks that way. I just got off the phone with Aaron. They went through her apartment, found ticket stubs, ice picks, caulking guns, glue. Sullivan's shitting in his pants. Because you solved it, Frank. You did it, you brilliant son of a bitch! You solved Happy Families!"

"Archer, she—"

Kit shook her head. "She didn't know anything. That's what she says. The girl was fixated on her, and . . ."

He felt his eyes starting to close. He struggled but couldn't keep them open. Kit's voice was distant now, as if in the back of a deep cave. "Rest, Frank. We'll talk later. Aaron'll be here soon. He'll explain. . . ."

When he woke nauseated and agitated in a darkened room, there was a moment of clarity. "You solved it." Had Kit actually said that?

Was it possible?

How could he have solved it?

How?

7

Wallflower

Diana Proctor, braced like a West Point plebe, stood rigid in the garden just outside the window. Back arched, eyes forward, head straight, chin down—in this exaggerated posture her nose was but inches from the glass.

Beverly Archer, sitting in the consulting room, glanced at her and smiled. The rain, running down Diana's young and ardent face, streaked her cheeks like tears. The girl's hair, cut close and butch, hung limp like wet black yarn. Her gray T-shirt, bearing the word TRAINING in small block military letters, clung sopping to her rib cage and chest.

What a sight! You'd think the poor thing would have to move, but there she stood still as stone just as she'd been ordered. She was shivering; no surprise, since she'd been standing out there for nearly forty minutes and still had twenty more to go. Rain or shine, a sentence was a sentence; an hour had been decreed, and an hour would be served. A fat little alarm clock, standing on tiny feet, was perched upon the windowsill. Diana's eyes were fastened to its taunting face, her features frozen, locked. That, too, had been ordered. If the eyes were permitted to drift, the strings of control would weaken. In a matter of this kind control was everything. Obedience and control.

To Beverly the glass between them, transparent yet impenetrable, symbolized their relationship: intimately bound yet separate and apart. Here she sat within, sheltered and warm, flipping casually through a magazine, while Diana stood less than a foot away, braving the elements as she performed her penance. The polarity was perfect, Beverly thought, and best of all, Mama would approve.

She remembered: Mama zippering her into an oversize snowsuit, then pulling the collar up above her head so her face was encased as well. "Better be good, Bev, or I'll zip you up forever. . . ."

She glanced again at Diana. Poor girl! But Diana craved hard discipline, reveled in it. It was discipline that had made her strong, that would make of her a perfect steely tool. With a person like Diana, discipline was the only way. Break her; control her; then build her up again. Take the raw killer rage and forge it to your need. Train her; teach her obedience; then she will serve you and Mama, too. Then she will be better than a bullet, better even than a knife.

She remembered: "Learn to be an archer, Bev," Mama said. "Find your arrow, sharpen it up, string it to your bow, and let it fly. It'll travel far and true, hit your targets again and again. . . ."

Beverly rose from the black Eames chair, set down her magazine, and moved to the window. She stared straight at Diana, trying to distract her, make her eyes flicker a moment from the clock. Not a blink. Good girl! Beverly was proud. Perhaps Diana's nipples twitched a little against the drenched gray cotton of her shirt, but her eyes, disks of sky blue ice, held firm.

Twenty minutes later Diana, trembling, stood before Beverly in the office. Her skin, so very pale, glistened with rain and sweat.

"Tonight you learned something," Beverly said. The girl nodded. "What?"

"That I can do it," Diana whispered, still shaking with chill.

"Do what? Go on, girl—speak." Beverly intentionally tightened her lips to make her mouth appear authoritative.

"That I can do as I'm told."

"And that's important. Why?"

"Because there'll come a time—"

"Maybe soon."

"—soon, when you'll order me—"

"To perform a mission."

"Yes. And then I must perform it exactly as you tell me."

"Without deviation."

"Without any deviation. And then I must return, stand before you as I'm standing now, and report to you everything I did."

"Everything, accurately, in scrupulous detail."

"In the most scrupulous detail," Diana affirmed.

"And so your task tonight—?"

"Was to show I can obey you without questioning, that I'm capable of doing what you tell me, exactly—"

"And correctly."

"Yes."

"To serve me and obey."

Diana nodded. "Serve and obey."

The girl drew in her breath. When she spoke again, she lowered her eyes, as was her habit whenever she uttered an opinion of her own. "I believe tonight I have shown you I can," she offered hesitantly.

Beverly smiled, rose, stood before Diana, patted the girl gently on the head. "Yes, my dear. We're coming along nicely now." She toyed a little with Diana's stringy, dripping hair. "Down to your room now, off with those nasty garments, towel your hair, put on something nice and clean, then join me in the bedroom for a cup of tea."

At Beverly's gesture of dismissal, Diana raised her eyes, gleaming with incipient tears. "Thank you, Doctor," the girl whispered, then, quick as a cat, scooted from the room.

Afterward Beverly stood alone in the office, thinking about the next phase of Diana's training, the next degree of obedience she would instill. The control must be remote, she thought. *Following orders with me hovering about is easy. Total submission beyond my sight—that will be something else.*

She had always believed that the concept came to her on a certain rainy afternoon when she was fifteen years old, came just after a crack of lightning revealed the inky blackness that lay beyond the fine, tight gray fabric of the sky.

A romantic fantasy most likely, although perhaps it really had come to her then, at least in some rudimentary form. She knew well from her studies of human psychology that life-changing ideas often seem to strike like bolts delivered from above.

But it was not as if she were actually seeking some means of reprisal at the time. Nor was she worrying over one or another slight the way she so often did. Quite the contrary. So perhaps it was because she *wasn't* trying to figure out a way to squash her enemies that a method of revenge came to her, heaven-sent if you will, and then, of course, it was so perfect, so beautiful she had no choice but to devote the remainder of her life to seeing if it was actually possible to bring it off.

Get someone else to get them for you. There it was in a nutshell, so to speak, and, like so many great notions, startlingly simple once you thought of it.

But there was a special element to this particular notion, the craft and cunning of it that always made her smile. The thin, tight, knowing, masking, taunting smile that said she knew something the others didn't and was harboring a plan that would see them all in hell. No matter what you do to me, the smile said, no matter what you say, what insults you heap, what humiliations you force me to endure, in the end I'll get you back, and now, even as you torment me, I know exactly how I'm going to do it, too. Yes, that's what her thin, tight, knowing, masking, taunting smile said.

Mama knew. "Be an archer," she said. "Find an arrow; string it to your bow."

Mama, of course, had been playing with words, making a pun out of their name. What Mama meant was, go for the weak spot, which had always been Mama's way. But Beverly thought her own approach was far more cunning. *Find someone else to do your dirty work. Get yourself a human tool.*

It took her years to find Tool, and when she finally did, the moment she laid eyes on it was one of the most ecstatic of her life.

There she is! she said to herself. *That's her! I can see it now, can see her doing all the things I've been dreaming of. Yes, no question, that's her, I know it, she's the one!*

Then she peered at the girl a second time to make sure she was right.

It wouldn't do to pick out the wrong person just because so many years had passed and she'd grown impatient to settle up her scores. She'd waited this long; another year, even another decade wouldn't matter if Tool was right. But on second look, and third! and fourth!, she was still convinced the girl was perfect. The tool she'd been looking for had been delivered. Beverly felt her head surge with power the way she imagined the cockhead of some prehistoric man had once swelled with potency when he stared at a rock and realized for the first time that he could use it to crush a rival's skull.

It had been a gray day, the kind of sad, warm, unbearably humid day when the sky's the color of old pewter and the air's so close your brain feels soggy and your joints begin to ache. The kind of day when you don't feel like meeting new people because even the sight of the ones you already know drives you up the wall. You want to scream, that's the kind of day it was, but you don't, don't show even a smidgen of your pain because you're a professional, a shrink, a clinical psychologist, certified and sane and socialized and analyzed, so you just smile your thin, tight, masking smile and go in to meet the new patient.

There she sits, tense, coiled, twenty years old, five feet two inches tall, 110 beautifully conditioned pounds, hair black like a witch's, eyes so hard and blue they make you think of ice. And yet there's something vulnerable about her, too, a visible yearning, a need, and you grasp at once she's got a craving you can satisfy.

She's a murderess.

"Another little murderess, Bev," Carl Drucker tells you as he hands you the file. Carl pretends to hold the folder as if it were too hot to handle, and his sheepdog's eyes twinkle when he enunciates "murderess." Carl always feigns amusement over the most dangerous patients, but he doesn't fool you. He's scared of them, so frightened he'd surely wet his pants if he had to be with one of them alone. Poor Carl. For all his training, evil still confuses him. He knows in his brain that there's no such thing, there's only antisocial behavior, but he doesn't really know it the way you do, deep down in your gut.

"Seems our new Missy Perfect chopped up mommy and granny, little sissy, too. The old story, Bev. Strict family. Religious nuts. Wouldn't let the girls watch TV, let alone go out on dates. Mommy was stupid. Granny ruled with the strap. So one day Missy broke, took the old wood ax, and chopped 'em up."

Another twinkle from Carl. *Better watch it, Carl. Don't want to end up on my list, do you?*

"Why the sister?" you ask. *As if you didn't know!*

"Oh, Bev—why's the grass green? Jeez, you've been around. Sissy was *there*. She probably ragged her. 'Diana's gonna get it, Diana's gonna get it, neah, neah, neah!' So, while you're chopping the authority figures, you might as well chop up the taunting little bitch, too. But it's interesting, come to think of it, there weren't any men around?" Carl, stroking his wimpy mustache, assumes his Great Psychiatrist pose. "She went for the ladies, split their heads, then gave 'em each a couple of chops between the legs. Split, split, split. She's a little sickie, I can tell you. Sue Farber tried talking to her, couldn't even get close. We thought you'd do okay with her, though. More your type, Bev. Wanna give it a shot?"

Sure. Why not? It's what you do for a living, work with disturbed young females all day long, and you know the offenders aren't that much different from the nice polite college kids either. The bottom line is usually pretty much the same, a snake ball jangle of angry sexual confusion working its way out through eating disorders and, in this case, good old matricide.

"You'll take a look?" You nod. Carl's eyes twinkle. "That's my girl. Diana Proctor's her name." He strokes his wimpy mustache. "Good luck, Bev. And don't take any sharp instruments in there with you. Heh-heh-heh."

Poor Carl. He knows they're all incurable. He knows he's running a warehouse for psychotics and the state's rehabilitation policy is so much crap. Hell, you're lucky if you can get one of them to construct a coherent "feelie" in the OT shop, let alone relate to you on a therapeutic basis. But Carl doesn't care. He's beyond all that. He's a proper civil servant now. Maybe there was a time when he wanted to save the world, effect great cures, write up great cases, apply psychiatric theory to social problems, reform penology, rehabilitate irreversibles. But he gave up on all that long ago. He thinks you've given up on it, too, doesn't know that you're here looking for a tool and that in about five minutes you're going to find yourself one in young Diana Proctor, murderess.

How did she know? Even now she couldn't tell you, though Diana had been in continuous training with her for more than a year, and there'd been five years of weekly therapy sessions before that, before she could get her out of Carlisle and under full-time supervision.

It was the whole gestalt, she often told herself, recalling the moment of their first encounter, so clear in her mind it could have taken place within the hour instead of years before.

It was her need; she reeked of it, she told herself. *I could smell*

her hunger the way you smell bread in a bakeshop. She'll be my tool.
And so now she has become. . . .

It was one of those mysterious encounters that take place once
in a lifetime if a person is lucky, like finding your dreamboat sitting
beside you on a tour bus or like accidentally pressing the shutter
of your camera at the very moment a prominent politician is
assassinated.

Of course, it wasn't *that* accidental. She'd been working at the
hospital all those years just waiting for the right tool to come along.
Diana was perfect. The hard part would be to get her out.

*S*hhhh. Here she comes now. Up
the stairs on tippy-toe, just like a little lynx. She pauses in the
bedroom doorway, silhouettes herself the way you trained her
against the light of the hall. An elegant black form against a warm
yellow rectangle, waiting, waiting for your order.

"Come in, my dear. Feeling better?"

The little thing nods as she scampers toward you. The tail ends
of her wet hair, slicked straight back, comb lines visible, cling
seductively to her sinewy little neck. She sits down on her stool
and helps herself to a cup of tea. You watch her as she blows on
the hot liquid, smile at the sight of her pink little tongue as it darts
out between her lips to test the temperature.

"I'm going to reward you for your very good obedience, Diana.
Tomorrow at dusk you'll enter Central Park, dressed in black,
dressed to kill. You'll carry two holstered ice picks strapped to
your arms and several bulletin board-type pins, you know the kind,
with the little colored knobs on the ends."

The lynx nods eagerly.

"The first part of your mission will be to pick out a person on
one of the paths. Your target should be alone, big, male. A jogger
would be fine, but a walker or an ordinary tourist will do as well.
Stalk him for at least fifteen minutes. Make sure he's the one you
want to hit. Then, when you see an opportunity, execute an attack.

Don't kill him; just stab him with one of the pins. A quick jab in his rump will do the trick. But remember, it won't count unless it makes him squeal. Approach from the back; stick him; then retreat and lose yourself in the woods. Move rapidly toward the West Side. Go to some stores; hang out awhile; then take a bus back. Don't come home on foot. So, girl—think you can do all that?"

The little lynx smiles. "Piece of cake."

"Is it now? I guarantee it won't be so easy. A hundred things can go wrong. Pick on an off-duty cop and you're in trouble. He'll shoot you if you don't run fast enough. Or what if your target shouts for help and there happens to be a good Samaritan around the bend? See, you have to think of everything, analyze the mission. Tell me, what are your most important decisions?"

Lynx gazes up at you. Her ice blue eyes burn with predatory lust. "Choosing the target," she whispers. "And deciding when to prick him."

Smart girl! Sometimes you're so proud of her you want to kiss her all over. But instead you stroke her head, pet her the way Mama used to stroke and pet you, offering affection in exchange for loyalty and obedience. What the tool needs is tough love, not sex; sex she can provide for herself.

"Okay, go on back down to your room now, lie on your bed, close your eyes, and think the whole thing through. Remember, he's got to squeal. You'll take my little tape recorder with you, so you can bring me back some proof. Wear rubber gloves, of course, and leave the pin in. That'll slow him down in case he's the pursuing type. He'll have to pull it out first, and by then you'll be gone in a puff of smoke. So, tomorrow night?"

"Please, yes, Doctor," the little tool begs.

The plan was to make Carl think it was his idea, that recommending Diana for release had never crossed your mind. Sure, you'd done wonders with the little murderess, vacuuming out her brain, servicing and reinstalling her

superego, instilling remorse for her evil acts and a strong desire
for redemption. You'd even made her into a leader in the wards,
a girl the others turned to for settlement of minor disputes. And
she'd become virtually indispensable in the hospital library, not to
mention earning straight A's in her extension courses in library
science. The little murderess has proved herself reliable, trust-
worthy, contrite, but no, Carl, it has never ever occurred to you she
should be released.

"Jeez, Bev. . . ." Carl turns away, starts stroking his pointy little
beard. The wimpy mustache wasn't enough; this year he sees
himself as Freud. "I mean, what're we doing here if we're not
preparing them for release? Isn't our purpose to save their broken
little souls?"

"Yes, of course. . . ." You furrow your brow. What a hoot, but
you have to appear sincere. "Don't forget, Diana committed three
murders, Carl. She axed her own mother. The public won't stand
for it if all she's got to do is spend five years in cushy old Carlisle."

"Think so, Bev? I'm not so sure myself."

You can't believe it! He's actually thought the whole thing
through!

". . . those kinds of objections, you know, don't come from the
public. It's the survivors who usually put up the stink. They write
the judge. They lost their loved ones, and the killer's got to pay."
Carl twinkles. "But here," he says, "we've got a unique situation.
There *are* no survivors. There aren't any cousins, aunts, anyone
who cared for any of them or even gave a rusty shit. Diana finished
off her whole family. So what I anticipate is a quiet hearing in the
judge's chambers with a sympathetic prosecutor going along. Let's
go to the wall for her, Bev, and, while we're at it, show the state
we can do what they pay us for. Diana's barely twenty-five. I hate
to lose her, but she's entitled to a future. I talked to her this
morning. She refers to the 'old me who did that very bad thing'
and how, though she knows that 'old me' was definitely her, and
wouldn't dream of not taking responsibility for her actions, she
feels emotionally disassociated from the person she used to be and
thoroughly incapable of doing what she knows she did. Thanks to

you, Bev, she's practically cured! And I thought I'd never see the day. Anyway, you know that people who kill close family members are almost never dangerous to anybody else."

Ha! That's what you think, twerp!

Carl turns slowly toward you again, places his hands ceremoniously on his desk. "Look, she's your case. Whatever you decide I'll back you up. But think about this: If you don't want to take on responsibility for initiating a release, and believe me, I can understand why you might not, I'll be happy, with your consent, to take that upon myself. Believe me, Bev, every shrink on staff will join the cause."

Carl's eyes dance merrily in their sockets.

Remember what she was like that first time? Young Murderess Ready to Strike. She had the killer eyes, the kind you'd seen so often in sociopaths, the fear and hatred raging to get out. Those kinds of eyes tell you there's no compassion, no identification with another human's pain. You have those very eyes yourself sometimes but never show them to the world. They're turned inward, and over the years you've worked up a mask so you can play the healer and make the troubled girlies think you care about their wearisome anorexia or tedious bulimia attacks.

She, Diana, Tool-to-be, had the true killer's glow and, fairly rare in combination with that, a deep, deep need to submit. She was a storm trooper waiting impatiently for orders, a gladiator frothing at the mouth to fight. She craved authority, a coach, a savior, and as she met your eyes, she knew you would be the one to give structure to her rage, focus it down until it became a pure blue torch point of fire.

How could you both tell so much from just a glance? Because you'd been looking for each other all your lives. You'd been rummaging for years in prisons and mental hospitals, searching always for a certain look, and Diana had been seeking you, too,

even though she didn't know she had. So when you walked into
that little room, she saw in you the governess of her dreams, and
you saw in her a fine young ward who would help you balance up
all your old accounts.

It was, as they say, love at first blush.

"They're calling you little murderess around the hospital,"
you told her, speaking passionately and looking straight into the
little murderess's killer eyes. "They're frightened of you. They
think you're dangerous. They say I'm a fool to sit down in here
with you alone. But I am *not* afraid, Diana. I know you won't
harm me. I understand why you did what you did, and I'm going
to say this to you now, before you even speak a word: You were
right to kill them, and you oughtn't to be feeling any guilt over
it. None! None at all! They abused you and by doing so brought
everything that happened upon themselves. Mother, grandmother, sister—are you supposed to bear unendurable suffering
just because it comes from your blood relations? Everyone's got
murderous feelings toward family members, but few have got the
guts to take up an ax and pay them back. You're different. You
have got the guts. So whatever happens between us now, Diana,
I want you to know how much I respect you for your bravery."

Having made your passionate personal statement, you assumed a cooler, more professional demeanor. "Now listen carefully, we're going to be working together. I'm going to be your
doctor and help make you well. After I prove to you that what
you did was right, we're going to take a good hard look together
at who you are and what you ought to be. You have a whole
lifetime ahead of you, Diana. In a few years, when you're ready,
I'll get you released, and then I'll show you how to realize your
potential. I'm going to help you first by building you up, making
you feel strong and confident. Now tell me—what do you feel
about what I've just said? Tell me your true feelings. I want to
hear."

The girl started to sob almost at once. You hugged her to you
and urged her to weep on.

"It's okay. Let it out. Cry it all out of yourself. Clean yourself out with the tears, Diana. You'll feel better afterwards, I promise. . . ."

In the end, after the weeping gave way to sporadic little moans and sobs, she spoke the golden words you'd been waiting for: "I feel at last . . ."

"Go on, my dear."

"I've met—"

"Yes. Tell me, who've you met?"

"Finally someone—"

"Yes, go on."

"—who understands me. Really does."

"You believe that?"

"Oh, yes." She nodded shyly. "I do."

You immediately hugged her to you again, then gently rocked her in your arms. "That's right, Diana. You have, you have, sweet girl."

And it was true! You did understand her! You truly, truly did!

The method was to envelop her in an alternate reality, a fictive world of your own creation existing parallel to the so-called real world, yet which to an outside observer would appear the same. To Diana, however, confined within your web, every so-called normal value would be subverted. Purposes, motives, principles, matters of morality and personal honor—in your alternate world such things would not have the same meanings as they did outside.

She's down there now in her dank little hole of a room in the basement, dreaming through her mission. She's imagining the feeling of popping the pin into the posterior of some unsuspecting man, the way it'll sink so nicely into his cushy ass. And then his yelp, squeal, cry, little chirp of pain, and how she'll record it as she runs by and how the pitch'll change because she'll be in motion. You smile to yourself: The exercise, if questioned, could be construed as a practical demonstration of the Doppler effect.

You went to watch her work out at her dojo at Broadway and 110th, a big hot, humid room on the second floor above a supermarket, where you were greeted by the deep-throated cries of zealous young fighters and the tangy aroma of their bodies at work.

Diana was in the first line with the best of them, energetically slashing at the air with her strong young arms. You loved the way Tool threw fast kicks and punches in unison with the others, mostly giant males. She looked so right among them, cute, too, in her white canvas gi jacket, white pants, and black obi. But you'd seen the backs of her hands after a workout, raw from hundreds of knuckle push-ups ordered by her instructor, and occasional marks, too, across her back from hits delivered with a bamboo stick, penalties for poorly executed exercises or that obscure and thus endlessly punishable offense of the dojo, insufficient respect.

There was another girl in the class that afternoon who caught your interest, reminding you of someone from your past. She had blond hair cut into a wedge, beautifully tanned skin, and a smile that lit up her entire face as she punched and kicked the air. You watched her carefully during combat exercises. She easily overpowered her opponents. She was taller than Diana, though just as perfectly proportioned, and her eyes were entirely different. While Diana had cold killer's eyes, this girl's eyes blazed clear gray like a warrior's. And while Diana had been trained to sneak attack her targets from behind, this girl was the sort to approach hers from the front in fair, refereed competitions.

That evening, as you ministered to Diana's bleeding knuckles, you asked her the other girl's name.

"Oh, you must mean Jess," Diana said. "Sensei says she's the best fighter in the class."

Remember Bertha Parce, Mama? That old mean bag of a bitch English teacher at Ashley-Burnett? Yes, that one, who enjoyed making fun of certain selected kids in front of all the others. Remember the time I told you about when she read a story of mine aloud to the entire class? The story I wrote about you, Mama, the true one about your opening night at the Fairmount Club Lounge, when Millie and I hid in back of the curtain behind the orchestra and you belted out those great Porter tunes, "You're the Top," "I Get a Kick Out of You," "I've Got You Under My Skin," and the crowd went wild. "More! More!" they shouted, and you grinned and belted out a couple more: "Let's Do It," "So in Love," and, as your final encore, "Another Op'nin; Another Show." Even then they clapped and howled and begged for more. God! Do you remember?

I wrote my story about that night, and everything I felt during it, the way my heart brimmed with pride in you, Mama, standing out there in your glittering sequin-trimmed crimson strapless, knocking all those fancy folks for a loop. And then how you brought me and Millie out. "I want you all to meet my two girls," you announced. "It's way past their bedtimes, but they wanted to be here to see if their old ma could really sing." And the crowd went berserk again! I remember one fat old man in particular, with slicked-back gray hair, who stood and clapped until the rest of them followed suit. And then some bosomy lady yelled, "Bravo! Bravo!" and you glowed, Mama, you positively lit up electric in the smoky, booze-scented dark of the lounge.

That's what I wrote about, and the grip of little Millie's hand in mine, and the swelling up I felt inside, the warmth of my pride in people knowing I was your daughter. I wrote, too, about how, late that night back home, you came into my room to tuck me in and how you smelled, the faint scent of perfume on your skin, the remnants of powder on your cheeks, and the glow on you still, the glow that comes from being applauded, and the aliveness of you, the pulsing energy, the power I felt when you reached down and grasped me in your arms. I wrote about how I fell asleep remembering the applause, listening to it echo, and how, just before I slept, I whispered four words to myself. I think you know them, Mama. "A star is born" is what I whispered. And I wrote how I smiled then and fell asleep and how I thought that was the happiest, proudest, most sublime night of my entire life, Mama, and I wrote about it that way, too, trying to capture the special quality of its magic.

A week later I was positively thrilled when Miss Parce announced she was going to read my story out loud in class. Except she had barely read a couple of paragraphs when I realized what she was trying to do. She read it in this mean, sarcastic way, and soon, sure enough, she had the other girls tittering, smirking, glancing at one another, and rolling eyes. And then, caught up in the spirit of the thing, she broadened her satiric attack, making funny little faces while relentlessly decimating my story, assassinating my every line, until finally all my words lay shattered and broken on the floor.

When she was finished, when there was nothing left of what I wrote except the sporadic tittering in the back of the room, she looked straight at me, eyes glowing, and said: "Tell us one thing please, Beverly: Is there a single line in this entire tale in which there resides one tiny particle of truth?"

I stared back at her uncomprehending, too stupefied to reply. The classroom went silent. You could hear a pin drop, as they say.

"Well, *dear?*" she asked, and, when I still didn't answer: "What's the matter? Cat got your tongue?"

She stared cold stone hard at me, her black pupils tightened down to points. And then she smirked. I wanted to speak. I wanted to cry out, beg her to stop staring at me. But I couldn't; I was too humiliated. And still, the mean old witch would not relent. She kept staring, and then her mouth turned cruel, and she dabbed her tongue to her lips like a snake readying to strike and said: "I've heard your mother actually does sing in nightclubs. Is that correct, my dear?"

I must have nodded faintly, for she went on.

"Well, I must say that is a *unique* occupation for a mother. And I'm sure she does very well at it, too. But Beverly"—and here her voice turned false-friendly—"there are things we write about when the assignment is 'Describe a sublime moment in your life' and there are things we don't write about, we don't even mention in polite conversation. I would have hoped you understood that."

With that the old witch wrote a great big *F* in red ink across the front page of my story, then daintily placed it facedown on her desk.

The girls in back had gone quiet again. And at just that moment (and she could have timed it so perfectly only by design) the bell rang to announce the end of class. The others shuffled out of the room in mortified silence, leaving me and the bitch alone. I began to cry. Miss Parce smiled at me and, in the phony manner of a wise, friendly teacher, said: "Now, now, my dear, no need to weep, I'm sure. . . ."

As I sat there choking on my tears, I knew, Mama, that I would pay her back one day. Yes, Mama, I knew I would live to see her dead, mutilated, too, if I could manage it. But most important— dead! dead! dead!

Listening to the tape Diana brought back from Central Park, feeling her excitement rise at the sound of Diana's running feet, Tool's "uh!" as she plunged in the pin, the delicious squeal of the jogger victim, his "yeeeeeow!" as he was stuck, then his curses receding in the distance as Diana's feet hit dirt when she dodged off the running path and into the woods, Beverly knew she would always want Diana to bring back something from her missions.

It was only later, upon her realization that the quick kills Diana would be making would preclude the possibility of recording her quarries' cries of pain, that she evolved the notion of trophies. She wanted always to have something, some object taken from the Scenes of Bloodletting, to touch, caress, and hold. It would give immediacy to Diana's reports, and perhaps most important, it could be offered up to Mama on the wall.

Mama told her: "Truly now, dear, in your training of Diana, you've found your true vocation. I think at heart you were always a behaviorist hiding in an analytic therapist's cloak. Rewards and punishments, increasingly complex tests of obedience—these are the only ways to dominate and compel. Certainly the progress you've made with the lynx proves the efficacy of your approach. My God, Bev, take a look, will you, at the incredible little tool you have wrought!"

The vigorous training workouts—long, slow, loping jogs along the bridle paths of Central Park; short, sharp wind sprints along the East River esplanade; huffing and puffing calisthenic sessions on the cold basement floor of the house: sweaty muscle building on the Nautilus machines at the Eighty-sixth Street Health Club; harsh, exhausting martial arts training at the West Side dojo; the special intensive ten-day commando course in Boulder, Colorado; endurance exercises; obedience tests; ice pick attack drills performed against straw dummies in your holiest of holies, your bedchamber—all were carefully designed to build strength and speed, refine coordination, increase response time, restore vigor in the face of fatigue, and, most important, inspire a yearning to kill. Once the craving was instilled, the obsession would build, and once the obsession was implanted, the command to execute would be ardently obeyed. "It's all in the preparation," Mama told you. "The long, hard months of training will pay off," she said, "in the swift split seconds of attack." But since the kills will be so very swift, you and Tool must receive gratification some other way. Perhaps through slow rituals performed afterward upon the cadavers, rituals of vengeance by which your rage will be satiated and the humiliations you endured will be many times repaid. "Remember, Bev," Mama said, "it's not sufficient to settle your old accounts at par value. Too many years have passed; the interest has built up and by now far exceeds the original charges entered in your ledger."

Diana Proctor stands poised in a corner of the cellar, sleek and slinky in her black cotton bodysuit. Two specially designed holsters, each containing an ice pick, are strapped to her forearms. Across the room a scrawny tiger cat, abducted from the street, prowls around a plastic dish of kitty tuna bits.

Beverly studies the human lynx, breathing slowly, deeply, awaiting her order. Finally Beverly decides it's time.

"Kill it," she orders.

Diana doesn't move. Beverly approaches the girl, then slaps her hard, smack!, across her face.

Diana, eyes front, lips trembling, receives the blow as her due. Beverly watches as the pale skin of the lynx's cheek turns pink, then red from the impact. Both understand the meaning of this chastisement. Delay and/or squeamishness will not be tolerated.

"Kill! Kill the cat!" Beverly whispers her command, and this time an admonished Diana instantly obeys.

In a single, beautiful, scything balletic motion the tool executes the little creature. Afterward they both stare down at its rigid body, neck up, ice pick thrust through the throat deep into its tiny brain.

"Clean up the mess; deposit it in a trash can on the avenue; then report to me in my bedroom," Beverly orders. "I have a choice new punishment in mind for you, my dear. One that will, I'm sure, instill a greater eagerness to obey."

Diana, braced, nods acceptance of this directive. As Beverly turns, she smiles quietly to herself. The little lynx can't wait. She loves correction. She'll be lubricating like crazy by the time she mounts the stairs.

$\mathbf{Y}$ou told Tool to befriend the girl named Jess, the lovely, strong, brave gladiator at the dojo. You had in mind a kind of recruitment but naturally never mentioned your intentions.

$\mathbf{A}$fter Tool flew down to Florida, slew Bertha Parce, and brought back your trophy, a hair curler found in a funny bright blue plastic box beside the old schoolmarm's bed, you quizzed her endlessly about the gluing of the bitch's vagina, what it felt like to slather in the gooey stuff, then squeeze the labia majora shut.

"Did she smell down there?" you inquired, grinning. "Like a rotten old fish, I bet," you added, pinching your nostrils with disgust.

Your delighted interest in the aromatic dimension most definitely spurred Diana on. She described everything, as she'd been trained to do, in the most exhaustive detail. And you relished every word, for that was the bliss—the imagining of it, the reconstruction, the obsessive staging and restaging of the execution. Your re-creations, fueled by Diana's reportage, gave you more pleasure, you were certain, than anything you might have felt had you gone down there and done the wonderful deed yourself. Your imagination, embellishing powerfully upon the details Diana provided, could create scenes far more intense than what had actually taken place.

$\mathbf{I}$t was so funny, Mama, when Carl went through the file and kept pulling out the reports I'd planted so carefully, ingeniously, and diligently through the years, flatly written case file summaries which contained no evaluations, no recommendations, and certainly no self-congratulation.

They purported to be simple factual accounts of Diana Proctor's treatment, and Carl kept quoting them to me, saying things like "Just listen to what you wrote, Bev!" and "Jeez, Bev, listen to this!" and "God's sakes, Bev, can't you see the forest for the trees?" He was using them, see, to try to convince me the little murderess had recovered and was ready for release. And I kept resisting: "I'm not sure, Carl"; "I might have overstated that, Carl"; "But don't forget, she killed them, Carl—killed them, then split their crotches with an ax!"

I toyed with him until I got him riled. I was acting like a hard-ass, he said, a tough bitch shrink, the kind he hated, and he was genuinely surprised since when he'd hired me, it was for my humanity, not my clinical skills or my degrees. What happened to my compassion anyway, he wanted to know, and had it occurred to me I might have spent too many years playing shrink-goddess to my patients, in the process losing sight of them as vulnerable human beings? At the very least I owed Diana the benefit of a doubt. I'd brought her along this far; why the hell couldn't I see she was ready to go the distance? And I just stared at him, Mama, until he started to rave: What kind of a person was I? Had I become one of those neurotic power-tripping shrinks who refuse to let a patient go because they can't bear to relinquish their control?

See, Mama, he was using my own words to make his case, and the longer I refused to buy it, the stronger became his conviction he was right. In the end, when I finally relented, his investment in Diana's "rehabilitation" exceeded anything I could have worked up with a direct appeal. I hornswoggled the little twerp, and he never knew it. I'm telling you, Mama, it was so damn funny to watch him fall so easily into the trap that took me the better part of five years to lay. Like taking candy from a baby. It was just, I don't know . . . hysterical.

There was another little trap I laid, not for Carl but for Diana. Call it my safety valve, Mama. I laid it . . . just in case.

The trap consisted of creating a traceable path between Diana and the signature, a path that would not run through me. So I instructed her to tell Carl, Sue Farber, the librarian, and a couple of her cronies among the patients that she was a sort of "wallflower type," and that was why she didn't like going to hospital dances. None of them would think anything of it, unless, of course, they were questioned about it later on. Then they'd all remember, wouldn't they? You bet they would!

I also had her sign a note to me with a droopy flower leaning against a wall, a note I could plant without comment in her file. The best part of it was the way I persuaded Diana that the devalued flower she'd leave at each gluing would, in fact, be *her* signature.

A neat little double trap, if I do say so, for although she would only be the tool, she would *think* she was the artist!

Beverly Archer, wearing a prim navy blue wool skirt and freshly ironed white blouse, sits in a chair in her bedroom facing the full-length life-size oil painting of her mother on the wall. Diana Proctor squats on the floor between Beverly's legs, also facing the portrait. The girl wears jeans but is bare above the waist.

"You know why we're facing Mama?" Beverly asks. "You do, don't you?"

Diana shakes her head. "I'm not sure," she whispers.

Beverly, tightening her grip by pressing her knees together, feels the girl shudder. *The little lynx is afraid,* she thinks. *As well she might be, considering she's about to get it.*

"We're facing Mama because we want Mama to *see,"* Beverly explains patiently. "Isn't that right, my dear? I mean we *do* want that, don't we?" Beverly squeezes her again. "Well?"

"I guess so," Diana responds.

"Guess! Well, I assure you we most definitely *do* want her to see. We want Mama to witness your correction." Beverly pauses. "You know why you're going to receive correction, don't you?"

"I think so," the girl mutters.

"Tell me?"

"Because I hesitated."

"You did, and now you're going to be punished for it."

Beverly does not feel unkindly toward Tool. On the contrary, she feels quite maternal toward her. But the tool has erred and must be disciplined. The principle of unquestioning obedience must be reinforced.

"You know I don't like to hit you, Diana. You know how much it hurts me," Beverly says.

"I know," the girl concedes in a whisper.

"Especially as I understand what you went through as a child, the beatings you took from your grandmother. You know how much I despise brutality."

"Yes, I know that, Doctor."

"So you must concede that when I strike you, there has to be a very good reason?" The girl nods. "What you did before down in the cellar, hesitating, standing there petrified, not even acknowledging my order, was deserving of the good, hard slap you got, wasn't it?"

Beverly feels another wave surge through Diana. "Yes, I deserved it. I know I did."

"Well, what I'm going to do to you now is not like that slap at all. It's important for you to understand the difference. I slapped you to shock you into action. The purpose was to sting and stun, make you aware of your responsibility to obey. The correction you will receive now has an entirely different objective. It's to remind you of your status vis-à-vis myself. What is that status, Diana?"

"You're the doctor and I'm the patient," Diana says as if by rote.

"Correct. And who is in charge in a doctor-patient relationship?"

"Doctor is always in charge."

"Completely, in charge of everything?"

"Everything."

"And patient's role is—go on, girl, fill in the blank spaces?"

"Her role is to obey Doctor."

"*Always.*"

"Always."

"No matter what Doctor prescribes."

"No matter what."

"And so if Doctor says, 'Kill the cat,' then patient must kill the cat, correct?"

Diana nods. "Patient must immediately kill the cat."

"Easy to forget sometimes, when the assigned task is disagreeable. Nobody wants to stab a helpless creature and make a bloody mess on the floor. We both understand that. But there are many disagreeable tasks to be performed in this life. Mama taught me that, and now I'm teaching you."

"Yes, thank you, Doctor."

"Good. Now we shall proceed with the correction."

Beverly grabs hold of Diana's hair, pulls her head back so her face is pointed up at the portrait. "Look up at Mama, straight into her eyes. Keep your eyes fastened to hers. Don't look down again until I tell you."

Beverly reaches to the little round marble-top table beside her chair and extracts a pair of stainless steel scissors. Feeling Diana tense between her knees, Beverly freezes with the shears as if posing for a photograph. She looks up at Mama, smiles, and nods, then, taking up a big handful of Diana's glossy black hair, abruptly snips it off.

Diana, finally comprehending the nature of her chastisement, moans while Beverly looks down at the hair lying inky black in her hand. It is beautiful luxuriant hair, thick and soft, the little lynx's protective fur. And it's going to come off now, all of it, every single strand, until Diana's head is as smooth as a billiard ball.

Snip! Snap! Snip! Snap! The hair falls fast beneath the scissors. Beverly can feel the sweat on Diana's neck as she holds the girl's head steady, can hear the sobs that rack the poor lynx's body, too. Every so often, out of kindness, she reaches around to Diana's face to wipe away the tears. But still, she cuts, relentlessly.

"Now, now, my dear," she comforts.

Tool, for all her distress, is behaving well. Even as she weeps copiously for her loss, her eyes remain riveted to Mama's. Good little tool, brave little tool, but the hardest part is yet to come.

Diana's head, now topped by a mop of ragged black, still must be clipped and shaved.

Beverly, finished with the scissors, takes up a small electric clippers, turns them on, applies the clipper head to Diana's skull. Buzz, buzz, buzz, she mows the hair straight off the top the way she's seen it done in films about marine recruits, slowly, inexorably shaming the girl caught tight between her knees.

More tears now, great rivers of them, as Beverly takes up a shaving brush, dips it into a bowl of warm water, stirs it around in a cup of soap, then applies the rich lather to Diana's head. Swish, swish, swish, she shaves the head clean with a razor. And all the while she whispers: "Now, now, little darling. Now, now. . . ."

Diana's hair is everywhere, on the floor, on Beverly's skirt, sticking to the girl's bare moist torso, front and back. Her pale shoulders and breasts are decorated with little flecks of black, and her skull gleams white like alabaster.

Beverly cradles the girl's head in her arms, tenderly petting the back of her neck. After granting permission for Diana to lower her eyes from Mama's, Beverly urges her to turn and sob upon her lap.

"There, there," Beverly says, gently caressing the well-shaved skull. "There, there, my little precious. It was difficult, I know, but it wasn't as bad as that. And I have a lovely black wig all ready for you, to cover you up when you go out."

Diana stares up at Beverly, her eyes large, beseeching. "You're not going to let me—?"

"No, my dear. Every few days we'll be shaving you clean again. I'm afraid you won't be allowed to grow another full head of hair until you've completed all your missions."

"Oh, Doctor!" The girl's red, teary eyes are filled with pathos. Beverly, slightly touched, knows she must not relent.

"Think of yourself as a Ninja warrior. They shave their skulls to symbolize their commitment."

"I so love my hair long."

Yes, long like a witch's. "And so do I," Beverly assures the girl. "Which is why we shall be saving all the trims. I have a lovely rosewood box to keep them in. Some evenings we'll get them out, feel them, and remind ourselves of the glorious mane you had and will someday have again."

"Yes, thank you, Doctor," Diana says gratefully, hugging Beverly around her waist.

Beverly hesitates. There is more correction to be administered, and she wants to assure herself now that the little lynx can take it. It won't do to push the girl too far; the purpose is to humble her, not to wound or break her spirit. There is also something about this additional correction that causes Beverly to pause. She wonders whether she'll be able to inflict it without trembling a little bit herself. Shaving Diana's head was one thing, but the other more intimate area . . .

Beverly looks up to the portrait, asks Mama what to do. The answer comes back immediately.

"Make the little bitch shave her own pubes," Mama says. "Have her lie on her back on the bathroom floor, spread her legs before the mirror and scrape herself. Stand behind her, watch her as she does it, and smile as you do. The correction will be more forceful and the submission more complete if she's required to do it under supervision."

"Thank you, Mama. You're so clever about these things."

Beverly Archer leans down and whispers into Diana's ear: "Come with me, dear, into the bathroom. There's still a little more hair to be removed. . . ."

Bertha Parce, Cynthia Morse, Jimmy and Stu MacDonald, Bobby Wexler, Laura Gabelli—I got six of them, Mama, six so far. Cindy was best, I think. Tool did a first-class job on her. Not only glued her up tight but her daughters, too, who (their bad luck!) stayed over with her in Seattle for Memorial Day. Tool also glued Cindy's hands together so I could imagine her begging me for mercy and, while she was at it, webbed her feet as well.

Remember Cindy, Mama? Remember what she did? I could never ever forgive her for it. My best friend, the one I trusted more than anyone else, whose declarations of sisterhood I naïvely believed. The roommate to whom I confided my secret yearnings, passions, fears. And then, after all of that, to have her turn on me so cruelly.

You probably guessed it. We were lovers. I'll never forget those wintry nights at Bennington when we pleasured each other, then slept together warm in each other's arms. I'm not ashamed of having loved her, Mama. There should never be shame where love's involved. And I *did* love her; that is why her betrayal was so calamitous, why it did a hell of a lot more than just sting me to the quick.

God! Remember what a wreck I was when I came down from Bennington, told you I wasn't going back, that nothing would ever ever make me return? And the way I cried, days of weeping it seems like now, and you were worried because I wouldn't eat and barely got out of bed.

"Bev's having a little breakdown," I overheard you tell Lisa Walters. But it was a major breakdown I was having, Mama, and it was that lousy traitor bitch who brought it on. What she did was unforgivable. And I never did forgive her for it. No, I never did.

What I still can't understand is *why* she turned. I never did anything to her except love her. So . . . maybe that was it. She couldn't take my love. It was too powerful, too consuming. Fearing it, she betrayed my trust.

A year after it happened I wrote her a letter. "Please," I begged, "all I want to know is why. Please just tell me why?" She didn't answer. I should have known. So there I was, humiliated again. And then I vowed that one day she'd beg something from me, beg me not to glue her.

She was an ice goddess, was Miss Cynthia Morse, with her thick blond hair, parted to the side, so she could throw it back whenever it fell into her eyes, fling her head and throw it back like the fine Thoroughbred mare she knew she was. Her skin tanned more beautifully under the sun than any human's skin should be allowed to, her eyes were clear and gray, and she had a wonderful smile that made her whole face light up like a sunrise. I don't think I'll ever forget the touch of her, the satiny feel of her flesh, the fresh salty flavor of it, and the smell. Her small but perfect breasts cupped in my hands, the feel of her ribs through the skin of her flanks. She was a knockout beauty and I was plain, she was popular and I was disliked, she was gregarious and I was a loner, but still, she chose me to be her friend.

I was proud of that. I believed I was envied for it. Anyone in the whole college would have been happy to be Cindy's roommate, but she had chosen me. "You'll keep me honest, Bev," she told me one afternoon, spring of freshman year, when we took a long walk together across the meadows and she broached her proposal that we room together in the fall. "I can talk to you. You're always there to listen. Know what I think you should be? A shrink. Ever think of it, Bev? I know you'd be good at it. You're so giving, you know. Such a good listener. And you have such good intuitions about people, too."

Oh, I was giving all right! I gave her everything I had. Friendship, affection, love, later my passion. That was my undoing.

"This it, Cin?"

"Oh, yes, Bev. Down there, yes. There. That's the place. *Yes! Right there! Oh!* Do me, Bev. Please do me there again. Oh, yes, yes, your mouth feels *so good.* . . ."

And I did. I reveled in it. Before I knew what she was up to, I would actually beg to be allowed to taste her. That's how stars-in-my-eyes stricken I was. Well, ha!, she's the one begging now!

There were nights, I remember, January and February nights, when we'd put a Mozart horn concerto on the stereo, then lie together in her bed in the dark of our room, watching the snow falling gently outside.

"This is great, isn't it, Bev?" she said, hugging me. "This is the way it should be. Just the two of us together like this, together and forever. I truly wish our lives could go on like this forever. Don't you, Bev? Don't you?"

One night I asked her if she thought a day would come when we'd each have a man in our lives.

"Men! Oh, Bev, sometimes you're just so screwy. I haven't seen any *men* around here. Have you? All I've seen are boys, and I don't mean just the kids, I mean the whole damn male faculty, too. Men!

Ha! Who needs 'em? I sure don't. On a night like this, what could a man do for me that you can't do?" Cindy paused, stretched. "Hey, wanna go down under the covers? Feel like it, huh? It's so nice when you're down there taking care of me. Helps me to sleep, you know. Hey! What're you doing? Oooo! I *like* that. You never did *that* before. Where'd you learn *that*? You've got great moves, kid. No boy I ever went out with knew how to do *that*. Oh! Yeah! Yes!"

For two months I loved her, passionately, feverishly. She didn't reciprocate, just had me do special things to her, things she let me know she liked by the way she wiggled and moaned and swooned. And I was glad to do them, although I believe now some part of me must have known I was being used. But even if I'd realized it at the time, I wouldn't have cared. The bliss, you see, was all mine. Her needs became my obsession; her secret chambers became my pleasure domes. All day long in my various classes I'd think about servicing her at night. I was totally enraptured by her, enthralled, enslaved, possessed. Cynthia Morse, blond Thoroughbred mare— she became my world.

Looking back now, I can see it all coming and wonder at my blindness to what was going on. She needed me that winter, but as soon as spring came, she was ready to cast me aside.

That in itself could be understood. In this life, as you so often remind me, Mama, people use one another all the time. "It's all this use," you say, "that makes the world go around." But use is one thing, betrayal another. Cindy betrayed my love for her, betrayed it in a vulgar way. Use can be forgiven but not betrayal. You taught me, Mama: *Betrayal must be avenged.*

I had gone down to Cambridge for the weekend to do some research at Widener Library. My intention was to spend the night in Millie's Harvard dorm room, work the following day, then return to Bennington on Sunday night. But when I got to Millie's, I found I wasn't welcome. She and her roommates had male guests; there'd clearly be no room for me unless I slept on the floor. In any event there'd be no privacy.

I was furious. I'd told Millie I was coming, and she'd promised she'd save me space. We got into a fight, which led to my walking out in a snit. Steaming with anger, I decided to hell with research, I'd return immediately to Vermont.

Back in Bennington, tired and depressed, I taxied to my dorm from the bus stop. Our room was empty. Cindy wasn't there. Feeling needy for her friendship, I decided to search her out.

I found her finally, or rather should say I heard her, for it was her unique effervescent laughter that told me where she was. In a room on the floor below, belonging to Gretchen Hawes and Karen Tate, well-known campus lesbians, close buddies of Cindy's but not, I'm afraid, of mine.

I don't know what made me hesitate before I knocked. Perhaps I was curious about what was inspiring so much giggling inside, afraid, too, that my depressed mood might bring the others down. I certainly didn't want to intrude and put a damper on their fun. So I stood outside the door and listened. And then I understood: They were talking about me.

"She's too much, Cin. *Too much,*" said Gretchen.

"Well, I think she's very sweet," I heard Cindy reply.

"You *would.* Seeing as how you've been on the receiving end." Laughter.

"Sick, sick, sick," said Karen. They all broke up.

"Play us some more. Come on, Cin. More!"

Much giggling again, and then I couldn't believe what I heard. My own voice, on tape, begging Cindy to let me love her: "Please, Cin. I know just what you need. Please—let me do it. I can make you smile, you know I can. *Please.*"

The blood rose, boiling, to my face. I felt as if the top of my head were about to explode. My voice! Begging to be allowed to pleasure her! And she recorded it! And was playing it now for *them*!

"Hey, I've got an idea, Cin." Gretchen tittered. "Bring the little mouse down here one night. Share some of that 'please, please, please' with us, okay?"

"I've got some special places she can do." Karen snickered. "So long as she *begs* for it." And then: "Sick, sick, sick!"

I wanted to scream. Don't know why I didn't. I wanted to curl up, die right there on the floor. But instead I took hold of the doorknob and shoved the door open. The three of them were sprawled out on their stomachs on top of Karen's bed, the little tape player in the center.

Six eyes met mine, laughing, defiant eyes. And then, when they realized I'd been listening, those six eyes turned mean.

"Snooping, Bev?" Gretchen sneered.

But I ignored her. I stared straight at Cindy. "You recorded me?"

She shrugged, then smiled sheepishly. "Yeah, well, I guess I did."

"How does it feel to be a rat?" I spat the words, then reached to the tape player and ripped out the cassette.

"Hey, watch it!" said Karen. "You can screw up the machine. We were just having a little fun. God!"

But I kept my eyes on Cindy and let her have it. "Is this your idea of fun?"

"Get off your high horse, honeybunch," said Gretchen Hawes. "Eavesdropping at the door is like reading other people's mail. Do that, and you deserve what you get."

I met their eyes with as much contempt as I could summon, then, bursting into tears, ran back to our room and flung myself onto my bed. "How could she? How could she? How could she?" I screamed into the pillow. I wept and wept and wept.

Cindy turned up an hour later. She'd been drinking. I could smell the booze on her the minute she walked in. I pretended to be asleep. She was noisy as she undressed. It was clear she wanted to disturb me. Finally she spoke: "Stop faking, Bev. I know you're wide-awake."

"How *could* you do that to me?" I asked. "How *could* you?"

"You kind of let yourself in for it if you know what I mean," she said.

I sat up in bed. *"Let myself in for it?"*

"Sure. The way you've been slinking around all winter, trying to get into my pants all the time. I mean, now and then it's fun, but when I asked you to be my roommate, I didn't know I'd be taking the, you know, lezzy route."

"But it was *you!*"

"Uh-uh, Bev. Was you started it. I never put the make on you. I wouldn't want to." She snickered. "You don't turn me on."

I stared at her. This was my Best Friend! "I turned you on plenty as I remember," I whispered bitterly.

"Work your tongue around long enough you'll get a reaction. I'm just flesh and blood, you know."

"So you never cared for me? Is that what you're saying?"

"Frankly I like guys, but I try to understand other points of view. You know the saying 'Different strokes for different folks'? Right?"

I rushed at her then, attacked her with flailing arms and nails. I wanted to scratch out her eyes. Being bigger and stronger, she overpowered me easily. Finally, when I was exhausted, pinned to the floor, she looked down on me and smiled her unforgettable smile.

"Let's not make such a big deal out of this, huh? There're still a couple months till the end of the term. Let's try and get along, Bev. I'm sorry about playing the tape for those guys. I really am."

Sorry about playing the tape! What about recording it? What else besides playing it did she have in mind when she taped me when I was most vulnerable?

It all had been a setup, that much was clear; I'd loved her as best I could, but to her I'd been little more than a pest.

The next day I packed up my stuff. She came into the room just as I was finishing.

"Leaving, huh?"

"What did you expect?"

She shrugged. "Well, it was nice while it lasted, Bev. It's too bad you had to sneak back early on the weekend."

Sneak back! The girl was incredible.

"You hurt me, Cin. Hurt me a lot."

"If I did, I'm sorry, I really am. I'm sure you'll get over it. When you do, I hope we can be friends." She shrugged again and left the room.

Twenty years ago, and I never did get over it, Mama. And I

never loved anyone carnally again. I'd learned the risks the hard way and didn't like them. Cindy was the last lover I ever had.

That whole spring was miserable, that whole summer, too, not to mention the whole rest of my life. But as they say, you live and learn. And there was one good thing that came out of our relationship: Cindy steered me to my profession. On her advice I became a psychologist.

By the following autumn, tired of suffering, I decided to concentrate on my anger. And then I began to have fantasies, delicious fantasies of Cindy begging me not to hurt her the way she'd hurt me.

In response I shrugged and smiled and told her not to make such a big thing about it. I was going to kill her; that's all I was going to do. After all, she was only flesh and blood; isn't that what she'd said? And after she was dead, I was going to seal her up with glue. No big deal, right, Cin? Different strokes for different folks, right? Huh? *Right?*

I'm looking now at the trophy Tool brought back from Seattle. The yearbook of our Bennington class. Nice book, though I'm not in it. Nice picture of Cindy as she was then, tossing back her head to flick away the long blond hair that always used to fall across her face. Reminds me a little of someone I've seen recently, same eyes, hair, same warming, radiant smile.

Carl's bedazzled reaction when you broach taking the tool into your house: "Sometimes you surprise me, Bev."

"I don't know what's so surprising, Carl. Diana's my patient, she's my responsibility, and since I've got an unrented basement apartment available, and she's going to be coming to me four days a week for therapy anyway . . . well, it just seems natural to throw in a little housing, too."

"Sort of like a halfway house for her. That what you have in mind?"

"Now that you mention it—sure, why not?"

His little eyes dance a jig. "And you were so against her being released."

"Never against it, Carl. Hesitant about proposing it, that's all." You shrug. "I guess you could call me conservative when it comes to murderesses."

He strokes his beard, becoming grayer and more pointy by the month.

"What about a job?"

"There're a lot of possibilities right in the neighborhood— museums, institutes, archives. She's a trained librarian. She'll have no trouble finding a position."

"Small-town Connecticut girl—think she can hack it in the city?"

You put your hands on your hips. "I'm from Cleveland, Carl. I can hack it, so why not her?"

He fondles his beard again. "Want to know what I think? I think you're one superduper human being. How's that?"

You stare at him incredulously. "Well, thank you, Carl. I believe that's the first real compliment I've ever had from you. And we've worked together a lot of years."

"We have, Bev. And pardon me for not being one of those bosses effusive with the praise. But when I say something like that, I mean every word of it. I think you're an incredibly talented shrink and a terrific person, too."

Flattered and stunned, you shake your head. "I'm going to treasure what you're saying, Carl. It really means a lot."

When you first noticed the tall blond girl in Diana's martial arts class, you knew she reminded you of someone, though you couldn't put your finger on exactly whom. It was only later, after you asked Diana to get to know the girl and cultivate a friendship, that it struck you whom she reminded you of. Cindy Morse, of course.

Then you couldn't wait to get your hands on her. But you were patient. Patience, you might say, is your middle name. And Diana was clever about it, too, building the friendship slowly, exactly as you'd ordered.

You'll never forget the evening Diana reported that she and Jess Foy had gone out for coffee after class. As you'd instructed, Diana told Jess she worked part-time at the New York Society Library and confided, too, in a most casual way, that she was in intensive therapy with a female shrink. Jess, in turn, informed Diana that she was a student at Columbia, where she was also on the women's varsity fencing team. She herself had never gone to a therapist, she said, although there were times when she was sorely tempted, what with the pressures of college and all. The girls chatted about karate, gossiped about the sensei, and exchanged tales of their initial embarrassment at having to change clothes in the unisex dojo locker room. But then, giggling, each admitted to the other that she now deliberately took no special pains to conceal herself when undressing.

"Let the novice hard-ons drool, that's my motto," Jess told Diana.

Diana reported how much she liked her new friend and was pleased at your instruction to nurture the relationship and make it grow.

Beverly Archer and Diana Proctor both were aware that the stakes were high and that for each of them, in separate as well as connected ways, it would be a night of destiny. Depending on the outcome, Beverly would learn whether the course she had embarked upon obsessively so many years before would finally lead to the attainment of her goals. For Diana the night would prove whether her murderous passions, once raging and incoherent, now disciplined and honed, could be applied to the completion of Beverly's design.

As the day ended, the strain between the women, always apparent on account of the extreme polarity of their roles, seemed to increase with the inexorable withering of the light. Beverly was more snappish than usual; Diana, quieter and more withdrawn. As night settled in, there was a palpable tension in the second-floor bedroom, where they waited, silent, before the large portrait of Beverly's mother in the niche.

Beverly had turned on the red lamps so that the chamber was curiously illuminated, suffused with crimson light redolent of blood. She wore the same scarlet dress as was depicted in the portrait, a dress that had once belonged to her mother and that she'd had altered to fit her shorter, plumper frame. But there was something anomalous about her in that particular costume, designed to be worn by a featured singer in a nightclub. And since Beverly had refused to have it dry-cleaned, it still reeked faintly of tobacco, alcohol, and sweat, the signature aroma of her mother's professional milieu.

Diana Proctor, dressed in the costume of a night killer, full-length black bodysuit, black sneakers, tight-fitting close-cropped black wig, black latex gloves, had two ice picks fitted into leather holsters strapped to the insides of her forearms. In a small waist sack, suspended from her belt, rested a caulking gun loaded up with glue and, wrapped carefully in tissue paper, a withered field daisy collected that morning from Central Park.

An hour later Diana, in a loose denim jacket that concealed the ice picks, sat alone at the end of a subway car on a sparsely filled downtown express. The train hurtled through the tunnels, swaying and moaning, wheels grinding against the tracks. To a neutral observer Diana might have appeared drugged and in a daze. In fact, she was visualizing, a process taught to her by her therapist in preparation for the important act she was on her way to perform.

She got off her train at Union Square, took the exit stairs that led directly to the park above. Once outside she sniffed the night air, clean and cool, then made her way east along Fourteenth. It was a quiet weekday evening; traffic was sparse, and there were few pedestrians. As Diana approached Second Avenue, she began to look around. She was searching for a quarry, not a stray cat or dog, not even a jogger to prick in the butt with a pin. Tonight she was stalking something bigger. She was looking for a human she could kill.

Unbeknownst to Diana, Beverly Archer was close by. While

Diana had waited uptown for her express, Beverly had left her house, hailed a cab, then ordered the driver to speed south to East Fourteenth and Second. Now she stood in a phone booth, phone in hand as if making a call, waiting for Diana to appear. She saw the girl, springy and taut, ready to strike, moving rapidly toward her. Though tense herself, Beverly was filled with pride. The girl approaching was a weapon she had forged, a tool trained to kill on command. On *her* command.

Diana, unaware of Beverly, continued east on Fourteenth. On First Avenue she turned south, and then after two blocks, east again on Twelfth.

After ten minutes of walking she entered the so-called Alphabet City section of Manhattan, where the avenues are lettered A, B, C, and D. This was a neighborhood of broken-down tenements and vacant buildings turned into crack houses. Here, behind the garbage cans in the alleys, one could find occasional homeless persons sleeping curled in messes of tattered blankets.

After exploring this area for a quarter of an hour, Diana located three possible quarries. Her first choice was an old man, sleeping and wheezing noisily, his body curled just inside the back doorway of an abandoned store. He had covered himself with a long piece of cardboard. His cheeks bore a grayish stubble, and locks of iron gray hair surrounded his ears.

Diana stood poised, staring down at him, thinking out how best to proceed. She had rehearsed the procedure numerous times, both with Doctor and alone, and it was certainly not as if she had never attacked live people before. But still, she hesitated. This man meant nothing to her. He had never abused her. He had no meaning in her life.

"It will be a cold kill," Doctor had explained, "the most difficult kind to bring off. Yet because it will be cold, it will be an excellent test. If you have trouble with the coldness, you can always warm it up. Just imagine your target is a person who has shamed you, hurt you in a way no apology can repair. Put a little bit of your mother into him if you like, your grandmother and sister, too. Remember, Diana, you're well practiced with the picks. It's not the killing but the gluing that's going to draw upon your strength."

Diana stared down at the sleeping man, wheezing and sputtering in the night. But it wasn't thoughts of members of her own family that fired her up to strike. It was the elegantly coiffed redheaded singer in the scarlet dress on Doctor's wall who thought up all the awful punishments. Yes, it was *Mama* lying there beneath the cardboard. *Mama* who deserved to die!

In a series of moves as quick and balletic as the ones she'd used on numerous dummies, Diana Proctor attacked the old man's throat. A moment later the belabored wheezing stopped.

Off now with the cardboard cover. A series of quick flicks with the utility knife and the encrusted trousers were cut loose. The fly zipper was already open. Diana pulled off the shoes, wrapped in filthy towels, then placed a heel in her victim's crotch and hauled the torn-up trousers down.

Doctor had been most specific about the way she wanted her enemies desexed. Female organs were to be filled and pinched shut, male organs glued back between the legs. Using her black-sneakered foot to pull down the stained underdrawers, Diana exposed her quarry's blue and flaccid genitals to the air. Then she pulled out her caulking gun and set to work. When she was finished, she unwrapped the withered field daisy and lovingly placed it in the doorway beside the building wall.

Beverly waited for Diana in an all-night bookstore on Third Avenue near Twelfth. Browsing titles on a table of Specials & Bargains, she glanced up every so often at the large plate glass window facing the street. Diana had to pass by here after she had completed her mission; it was on her prescribed route home.

A few minutes past midnight Beverly caught sight of the lynx, elegant in her black garb, approaching from down the avenue. Beverly hurried out of the shop to intercept her. Was that a killer's glow she saw on the little murderess's face?

For Diana this meeting was unexpected. Surprised, perhaps even frightened, she asked Doctor if she had done something wrong. Beverly, instead of answering, placed both hands on Diana's arms, then ran them along the girl's sleeves. Feeling only one pick beneath Diana's jacket, she expressed her pleasure with a grin.

"Problems?" she asked. Diana shook her head. "Bring a trophy back for Mama?"

Diana nodded, reached into her pocket, handed Beverly a carefully folded piece of paper, an advertising flyer for a fortune-teller resident in the neighborhood.

"He wasn't carrying much," she explained.

Beverly, pleased with the flyer, understood. "It's not the monetary value of the trophy that's important to Mama, dear. It's the way it speaks of the victim's mentality."

Alone in a taxi, on her way uptown, Beverly trembled with exhilaration. Tool worked; it could settle old accounts. Soon there would be fulfillment of a long-held cunning dream.

Diana, riding home in a deserted subway car, felt the same dizzy exhaustion she had felt years before when she killed the female members of her family. *It's hard and exacting work, but it has its pleasures,* she reminded herself, as the train swayed side to side, hurtling through the tunnels.

An hour later, having bathed and changed, Diana presented herself at Beverly's bedroom door, ready to report every detail of her outing. Beverly sat in her usual chair, the portrait of her mother looming above. She beckoned the girl into the room. Diana stood at stiff attention, and the debriefing ceremony began.

At one point in the recitation, when Beverly inquired whether Tool found it necessary to conjure up an actual character in her life in order to bring herself to kill the homeless man, Diana raised her eyes for a moment to the face on the painting. Smiling knowingly to herself, she answered respectfully: "I took your advice, Doctor. I thought of Mother."

You were very pleased with Tool for the way she recruited Jessica. And Jessica herself made a particularly lovely patient. If only you could harness *her* energy, you wished, as she droned on about seeing her father die in an exploding car. If only you could send *her* on missions, you yearned, as she explained how for years she couldn't bear to look out a window when someone was about to drive away.

There was a special quality she had, one unfortunately that Tool lacked. It was the quality of seeming untamed, perhaps even being untamable. You knew you'd have to use drugs if you were ever to train her to do your bidding. The very notion of channeling her aggression, disciplining it so it could serve your purpose, definitely excited you. You had some delicious daydreams about that during several of her sessions, in which you imagined her being broken by degrees. Undoubtedly she stimulated such fantasies because she was so strong and competitive. Whenever you saw her, you got the kind of charge you imagine a horse trainer gets when confronted with a powerful Thoroughbred filly. Yes, it would be a real pleasure to make a champion out of this one, to teach her to kill for you on command. And it was her very inaccessibility on that level, the fact that you knew you could never make her into a tool, that fueled your "what if?" fantasies and made seeing her in sessions such a pleasure.

Two women, Beverly Archer and Diana Proctor, stand toe to toe inches apart. Both are short, just a little more than five feet tall, but while Beverly is middle-aged and pudgy, Diana is young, lean, superbly conditioned, and extremely strong. Beverly's arms are flabby; Diana's are roped with muscle.

Yet it is the weaker older woman who dominates the stronger, younger one. By the force of her intellect and the power of her dream she had made Diana her slave. And behind Beverly there stands always the life-size portrait of Victoria Archer, pushing, goading her daughter to forge Diana into the tool of her vengeance.

The room where they stand is an oversize bedchamber situated on the second floor of Beverly Archer's Manhattan house. The painting of Victoria Archer takes up a large niche opposite the bed. It is illuminated with a reddish glow similar to one cast by the spotlight at the notorious Fairmount Club Lounge in Cleveland, Ohio, scene of Victoria Archer's greatest triumphs as a singer. During her nightclub singing career, red was Victoria's trademark color; she had naturally red hair, always wore a crimson dress, her entrances were keyed with a red spot, and pink light played upon her face while she sang. But her daughter's trademark color is different. She is just now in the process of explaining the difference to Diana.

"You are my knight," she tells the girl, "and as such, you must wear your lady's colors."

"What are your colors?" Diana asks humbly.

Beverly glances up at the image of her mother, then back to Diana. "Black, all black, black on black," she responds.

Diana Proctor, wearing outdoor clothing purchased out of a catalog from L. L. Bean and a nondescript light brown wig, proceeds as instructed to Grand Central Station in New York City, boards a noon train, then sits quietly with her backpack at her feet until, an hour and forty minutes later, the train pulls into New Haven, Connecticut.

At a storefront near the railroad station, she rents a standard-size Chevrolet for a two-day period, telling the friendly clerk she intends to drive into Vermont to view the magnificent autumn foliage that has been well reported in the newspapers and on TV. She will most likely spend the night in a motel up there, she says, and then, getting an early start, return the car late the following morning in time to catch her 1:00 P.M. train back to Providence, where she is a graduate student at the Rhode Island School of Design.

It's a cool Sunday afternoon in mid-October. As Diana drives her rented car into the Connecticut countryside, the sun glitters, and the sky, an intense shade of blue, makes a brilliant backdrop for the foliage now nearly at its peak. The passing woodlands, clusters of maple, oak, and ash, are russet and gold. Fallen leaves, in a multitude of hues, coat the lawns of homes, and trees, arching overhead, cause the sunlight to dapple the worn macadam roads.

Diana's route, as traced by Beverly Archer on an Automobile Club map, takes her through the picturesque towns of Woodbury, Roxbury, and Washington Depot. She refills her gas tank at a Shell station in New Preston, then continues west, along the edge of Lake Waramaug, finally arriving at the town of Kent, Connecticut, a little past 4:00 P.M.

Here she parks in a shopping center lot, takes a stroll, stops at a coffee shop, where she devours an egg salad sandwich and a large glass of Coke. After eating, she returns to her vehicle, hitches on her backpack, then proceeds to hike her way out of town. Shortly after crossing the Route 341 bridge, she passes the campus of the Kent School, an exclusive preparatory boarding school bordering the Housatonic River. Within an hour she arrives on foot at the main entrance to Macedonia Brook State Park.

It is 6:00 P.M. when Diana enters the park, relieves herself at one of the portable toilets set up near the entrance, then quickly follows a trail heading north directly into the woods. Since the sign at the entrance instructs hikers that the park closes officially at sunset, Diana wishes to disappear into its wilderness as quickly as possible.

Twenty minutes of rapid walking bring her to a small stone bridge that spans Macedonia Brook. But instead of crossing it, she consults her compass, turns off the trail, and begins to follow the water on a vector south through uncleared brush. Once she is certain she is alone, invisible to other hikers who might still be lingering on the trails behind, she unloads her backpack, takes a long sip of water from her canteen, then proceeds to strip off her brightly colored hiking gear and wig and change into her all-black executioner's garments. When she is fully dressed for the work she has come to perform, she hoists her pack up again, then follows the roaring brook back to the southern edge of the park.

Here, abutting the wilderness, sits a nicely renovated white clapboard farmhouse. Only a hedge of bushes, a wire deer fence, and an old stone wall separate this residential weekend retreat from the parkland. In a place she carefully selected at the height of summer two months before, Diana takes off her pack, then sits upon it. She will wait at least four hours before moving closer to her prey.

As darkness falls, the lights in the house come on, first in the kitchen, then on the front porch, then in the living and dining rooms. From time to time the forms of two men can be seen passing by uncovered windows or silhouetted against the translucent curtains that protect the rooms on the upper floor.

As evening wears on, cooking smells, including the aroma of roasted lamb, reach Diana from the house. Sounds reach her too: conversation; laughter; recorded music; television news. She waits patiently until the smells and sounds subside, until the downstairs and finally the bedroom lights go off. Then she stands, stretches, and carefully straps two holstered ice picks to her forearms, and her usual glue and wallflower pack around her waist.

The moon, showing a three-quarters face, illuminates the woods. Diana climbs over the ruined stone wall that separates the park from the property belonging to the house. Using a pliers, she separates a portion of the deer fence from a tree, slips in, makes her way through the hedge, then emerges finally onto cleared land.

Crossing the lawn, she resembles an apparition, her black clothing blending with the shadows cast by the trees, her shaven head, reflecting moonlight, shining amidst the darkness all around. In the forest behind an owl hoots. The only other sound is of rushing water, a tributary of Macedonia Brook that crosses the property to cascade over a small waterfall on the far side of the house.

Diana has no difficulty entering the premises. On her reconnaissance visit over the summer she discovered a ground-floor lavatory window with a broken lock. Lynxlike she pulls herself through this opening, then drops silently to the tile floor inside. The owners, brothers, own no pets. This night, she is grateful, she will not have to kill any dogs.

A muttony aroma, which she smelled earlier outside, still permeates the interior. Passing through the kitchen, she notices an empty wine bottle on the counter. She presses her hand against the front of the dishwasher, feeling a familiar warmth. Then, pausing at the kitchen window, she stares out across the lawn. She can see the hedge she passed through on her way in, but the woods behind are lost in darkness.

The first step of the old stairs creaks when she places her foot upon it. It will not be possible, she understands, to ascend and make her kills silently one at a time. She hesitates. Unfortunately there is always an unexpected complication. This time it's the bedrooms. The house is old, eccentrically built and renovated, and thus difficult for her to map out in her mind. She tries to visualize where the bedrooms will be in relation to the top of the stairs. On the basis of observations made earlier from the woods outside, she comes up with a reasonable guess.

Still standing on the first step, she works out a strategy. She will rush up, execute the brother in the bedroom on the left, then wait for the other brother to come into the first one's room to see what the commotion is about. Doctor will want to know about this, and myriad details more: what it felt like to rush up the stairs; how many steps it took to reach the bedroom from the landing; the position of the first brother in his bed; a description of his night-clothes; whether his window was open; the smell of him; the sounds he makes (if any) as he dies; how he looks when he's stripped for gluing; the exact size and shape of his genitals; the feel and weight of them in her gloved hands.

Diana, coiling to attack, prepares herself to take mental photographs of all that will transpire. She has proposed to Doctor several times that she bring along a camera to document details. But Doctor wants no part of mechanical documentation. "*You* are my camera," Doctor has said. "It's your point of view, the killer's view, that interests me. Not that of a neutral machine."

The sound of a cough from the second floor. Diana freezes on the first step. Perhaps one or both of the brothers are still awake. But no difference—she has killed awake people before.

Suddenly she leaps, taking the stairs two at a time, bounds off them onto the springy pine floor of the landing, twirls martial arts-style, then barges through the half-open doorway to her left. A blubbery middle-aged man, lying naked in his bed, is in the process of raising himself up as she bursts in.

"Who the hell—?"

She notes the explosion of fear in his eyes as she punches at him with her fist, violently knocking back his head with the blow. Before he can recover, she thrusts her first ice pick up through the exposed portion of his throat, then shoves it with all her force deep into the soft tissue of his brain.

She hears a sound, turns, sees the second brother standing in the doorway. Their eyes meet for a moment, and then he flees. She is at his heels as he rushes into a bathroom, then desperately attempts to shut her out. She aims her foot at one of the door panels, kicks full force, splintering the wood. The man, middle-aged, paunchy, balding, backs up against the toilet. He stares at her and at her ice pick, terrified. She stops all motion, meets his gaze.

"You must be Stu MacDonald," she says softly.

The man shakes his head. "I'm Jimmy. That was Stu in the other room."

Diana shrugs. "Doesn't matter. He's gotten his. Your turn now."

"What do you want? What are you going to do?" Jimmy Mac-Donald whimpers hoarsely. "Please, miss, there's money in the house. Art objects. A valuable coin collection. I'll give you all of it if you'll go away, spare—"

Diana shakes her head. "No mercy tonight," she intones.

Jimmy nods. "Yes, I see that. No mercy. . . ." He tries to speak calmly in the hope that by so doing, he will gain himself several extra seconds of life. "Could you at least tell me why, miss? Why you want to hurt us?"

"Doctor."

"Doctor? Who's the doctor?" Jimmy becomes angry. He screws up his eyes. "What the hell kind of doctor are you talking about?"

"Dr. Beverly Archer."

At first Jimmy's eyes cloud with confusion. Then a small flicker of remembrance ignites somewhere deep within.

"Bev Archer? But that was so long ago. Must be twenty-five years. Surely she doesn't still think . . . because it wasn't us, you know. It was set up. She ought to talk to her—" Jimmy shakes his head. "Bev can't still be angry over that."

Oh, she's angry!

Diana feigns an attack with her second pick, then waits for Jimmy to raise his hands in a posture of defense. When he does, she punches at him through the opening, hitting him hard in the center of his stomach. As he chokes and doubles over, she stabs him through the window of his right eye, then thrusts her pick deep into the mushy substance within his skull.

The killing done, Diana calmly switches on lights in order to examine her handiwork. Jimmy lies on his side, ruby red blood pulsing from his eye socket across the white tiles and into the grout lines of the bathroom floor. In the bedroom Stu MacDonald lies sprawled out on his back, half on, half off his bed. Diana takes mental pictures of their positions, for she knows the kinds of questions Doctor will ask.

Both killings together have taken her a total of ninety-seven seconds. Not bad, she thinks, for such a complicated house. Moreover, she has engaged for the first time in actual dialogue with a quarry, a unique experience she is eager to share. Even as she prepares the brothers for gluing, she imagines the keen expression that will transfix Doctor's face when she describes the confusion slowly giving way to recognition in Jimmy MacDonald's frightened eyes.

An hour later, having glued up both brothers and collected two new trophies of her hunt, Diana drives one of their vehicles, a gray Jeep Wagoneer, back into the town of Kent. When she emerges from the Jeep, she is wearing the same nondescript light brown wig and L. L. Bean hiking clothes she wore earlier in the day. She transfers her backpack into her rental car parked in the shopping center lot, then, careful to observe all traffic regulations, drives back across the Route 341 bridge, continuing this time into New York State and on to a preselected spot far off the main road where she can park safely, curl up, and get some sleep.

The next morning, on her way back to New Haven, Diana decides to make a brief side trip. She does so in full knowledge that should she confess this unauthorized detour to Doctor, she will be severely punished.

Nonetheless, passing so close to Derby, Connecticut, she feels the need to look again at Carlisle Hospital. The place means much to her. Having been incarcerated there on account of the ax murders of her mother, grandmother, and sister, she spent five relatively happy years in intensive therapy before a judge signed an order for her release.

Departing from her designated route, she follows the side road that leads to the institution, then stops her car a hundred feet from the main gate, turns off the ignition, and stares in through the sturdy wire fencing that surrounds the grounds.

Far in the distance, between the red-brick main treatment building and the gray cinder-block residence known as A, she makes out a small group of young men and women playing touch football in a field. They are much too far away to recognize, a good thing, too, since she knows well the awkwardness of meetings between former patients and patients still confined.

As she watches, a man exits the door of the main treatment building and walks to a second building, which houses the manual therapy shop. Diana recognizes this person on account of his stride. He is chief psychiatrist Dr. Carl Drucker, a gentle man with merry eyes and a funny, pointed beard who, in her last months at Carlisle, assured her she was cured.

Now something bittersweet wells up within Diana as she remembers Dr. Drucker's kindness and watches the young people in the distance at their play. She thinks nostalgically of the years she spent in this institution, happy, lighthearted years. And although she acknowledges the enormous debt of gratitude she owes to Doctor for her release, there is a side of her that wishes she were still locked up inside.

Tears well in her eyes as she recalls her life here, how she was permitted to wear her hair long, to roam freely about the grounds, to meet, talk, perform, and make friends without having always to ask permission in advance. Now in the city every moment of her existence is regulated, bounded by Doctor's demands to perform missions and bring back trophies of her kills. *Am I free now?* she asks herself. She doesn't know the answer. But peering through the locked gates of Carlisle, she fondly remembers carefree days within.

There is but an hour of light left after a warm October day, an Indian summer day in Manhattan. Two young women, one short and dark, the other tall and blond, stand on a bluff in Riverside Park overlooking the Hudson River. Although both wear workout clothes, tank tops and running shorts, the taller woman's garments are brightly colored, while the shorter one's are totally black.

The short dark-haired girl is holding a bow. She has notched an arrow in its string and is demonstrating the pull to her taller friend. Very slowly she pulls the arrow back. At full extension she holds it poised for flight. She stands this way for what seems an eternity, both hands steady, the bow not moving, and then, very slowly, she raises the bow upward in an arc so that the arrow is pointed directly at the sun. Again she holds her position. Then, suddenly, she lets the arrow fly. For a moment it shows black against the dark orange solar disk. Then it disappears from sight.

The taller woman nods. She is impressed. The shorter one offers her the bow and aluminum quiver filled with arrows. The tall girl, accepting, promises to practice diligently. The shorter one assures her taller friend that she need not return the equipment until she has mastered the technique.

Remember the MacDonald brothers, Mama, Jimmy and Stu, those tall, strapping, handsome all-around fellas at Caxton Academy when I was at Ashley-Burnett? So many of the girls had crushes on them. In those days they were the type you were supposed to swoon over and adore. Stu played football, Jimmy basketball, and they both were great dancers. Broad shoulders and even broader smiles. Hunks of what the girls called U.S. Prime Grade A Beef.

There was something marvelously shallow about them, too. Oddly that may have been their most attractive feature. They weren't tormented intellectuals or overly mature and thus awkward among their peers. They weren't emotionally skewered by a bizarre home life, or artistically gifted, or unpredictable in any way. The MacDonald boys acted their age. They were interested in sports and cars and girls and not terribly much else. Easy going, fun-loving playboy types, who, like all red-blooded guys back then, were always looking to get laid. But if a girl turned them down, they didn't get too upset about it. Men and women, boys and girls—to them relations between the sexes was a game of flirt, conquest, and submit. Sometimes you won, other times you didn't; but win or lose, you knew there'd always be another round. What I'm getting at, Mama, is that with the MacDonalds what you saw was what you got: two normal white bread all-American boys, the kind who, when they grew up, would run businesses or sell stocks and help keep our nation strong.

Except what I saw was *not* what I finally got. Because there was a dark side to the MacDonalds, a side they hid so you wouldn't see it, except maybe sometimes when they were drinking or smoking grass, and then there was a little bit of blackness showing, enough so that if you were an astute observer, you'd catch a glimpse of the smallness, the meanness, the part that would always take advantage, the cheap crooks crouching behind the cardboard pasteups we used to call (ha!) gentlemen.

Remember, Mama: I was fifteen years old. There was a dance that winter over Christmas. I didn't want to go, but you said I must because the parents of the kids giving it had put my name on the list as a favor.

I hated dances, first, because I was such a maladroit dancer and, second, because I was so rarely asked onto the floor. I was too plain for the Cleveland boys. Something about me, withdrawn and worried, put them off. I wasn't sexy. I didn't have your looks or charm or poise. I was clumsy and mousy and too smart for my own good. I hadn't yet learned the craft of pretense . . . of which I am a master now.

And so I went. You gave me little choice. You bought me a dress, not particularly flattering or attractive, and you arranged a ride for me with someone else's father. Studying me while I waited, amused at my anguish, you asked why I was looking so damn tragic since it was just a dance. I really wasn't going to be burned at the stake, you said. I might even enjoy it if I tried a little bit. "Come on, Bev—let's see you smile," you said. "And try not to be a wallflower, okay?"

I remember riding downtown silent in a car filled with giggly, overexcited girls, off to some dark, stuffy club on Euclid Avenue, where there were rows of old oil paintings on dark wood-paneled walls and the air smelled of dead cigars. I followed the others up a grand staircase and into a ballroom, where an orchestra was playing the smarmy, sentimental standards of the day. There were kids buzzing around, parents smiling, a bar for soft drinks, and couples dancing on the floor.

Well, Mama, just as I'd foreseen, I stood by the wall with the dozen or so other wallflowers, unattractive girls, girls with acne on their faces, girls who were merely shy—stood with them, a stupid, turd-eating grin on my face, looking hopeful, eager, waiting, waiting for what I knew would never come.

On the other side of the room stood our counterparts, the stag line: unattractive, shy, acne-faced boys who didn't dance well and acted silly around females. We wallflowers eyed the stags and the stags eyed us and no one came over, and thus the evening wore tediously on.

But there was something afoot that night. The MacDonald brothers had cooked up a private little scheme, something no wallflower had ever experienced or even hoped for in her dreams. They'd decided between themselves that they would romance one of us clinging to the wall. And for some reason, I've never managed to fathom why, they settled upon me. Me, Mama! They chose me to be their Cinderella.

They began their courtship early in the evening. First Jimmy and then Stu came over and asked me to dance. No one watching could believe it. Dreamboat Caxton boys, the kind a girl would kill for at Ashley-Burnett, offering themselves to mousy little Beverly Archer, twirling her off to dance in strong, authoritative arms.

They were good dancers, so agile and slick they made me feel like a princess at a ball. Around, around I danced with them, first Jimmy, then Stu, then Jimmy, then Stu again, around and around and around.

Those MacDonalds knew how to charm a girl, knew how to talk and to seduce. After they warmed me up, got me all sweaty and excited, they led me off to an anteroom, and there Stu produced a slim silver cigarette case filled with lovingly rolled, thickly packed joints. He lit one and took a deep drag, passed it on to Jimmy, who also inhaled and then passed the joint to me.

It was good stuff, as I recall. But I wasn't used to it, and very soon it had me flying higher than a kite. Then back to the ballroom for more whirling and twirling, each of them romancing me, working me over, and I got high on it, it was a dream come true, a dream I didn't even know I'd had: drab, little, brainy Bev Archer getting her first taste of what it felt like to be desired.

Oh, yes, Mama, those boys made no bones about their cravings. They lusted for me; they made that clear enough. They even whispered provocative little endearments as we danced.

Jimmy: "You're really special, Bev. I've had my eyes on you since September. I just couldn't get up the nerve to do anything about it till now. There's something of your mom in you, isn't there? Stu and I've been down to the Fairmount Club Lounge and heard her sing. One very sexy lady, your mom."

Stu: "We both knew as soon as we saw you. Jimmy nudged me. 'She's as sexy as her mom. Probably as talented, too.' Hey, it doesn't upset you to hear me use that word, does it, Bev? 'Cause it's true. I mean you *are* sexy . . . if you don't mind my saying so."

Mind? Of course, I didn't mind. I loved it, adored it, was intoxicated by the thought. Sexy was what *you* were, Mama, and it was the one thing I was certain I was not. I had never felt sexy, wasn't sure I'd even know the feeling if I did. But then, as it turned out, I *did* know. Because while they were talking to me, I began to feel aroused.

Thinking back on it now, I don't think it was those particular boys that got me going so much as the general situation I found myself in: being high; being told I was sexy; being attended to as

if I *were* sexy; being competed for and treated so openly as an
object of desire.

I had no doubt they both hungered for me. They made it man-
ifest, pressing themselves against me as we danced, making sure
I was aware of their rigidity, showing me the hard bodily proof
of their lust. But I'm sure now it wasn't their stiff cocks that
excited me. Male organs have never done much for me one way
or the other. It was the aura of their excitement, the evidence of
their craving. I certainly didn't feel I wanted to be screwed by
them, but most assuredly I enjoyed the fact that they pined to
screw me.

There was a part of me, too, that knew sooner or later one or
the other of them was going to make his move. But I wasn't
thinking about that very much; I was too excited by the here and
now of it all. Still, I wasn't naïve. I was your daughter; I knew
about sex; I'd met your lovers. And the girls my age at Ashley-
Burnett gossiped about little else but boys, what they liked to do
and how a girl could handle them if she kept her wits about her.
So on a mental level I pretty much knew what to expect. But having
no practical experience and no psychological training, I badly
underestimated my predicament.

It was around midnight (the dance was scheduled to end at 1:00
A.M.) that they first broached the notion of driving me home.

"We've got a car," Jimmy said. "We can easily drop you off.
Anyway, aren't you getting tired of this crappy dance? Let's leave
now, stop off for a nightcap at this dive we know. The bartender's
a good guy. He'll serve us without making us show ID. What do
you say?" And when I hesitated: "Not scared to go to a bar, are
you, Bev—you who used to hang around with your mom at the
Fairmount Club Lounge?"

Actually I was thrilled with the idea of going to a bar in the
company of two handsome tuxedo-clad boys. So I sought out the
girl whose father had driven me downtown, told her I'd arranged
another ride, and enjoyed the obvious envy in her eyes when she
warned me to watch out, I could get a bad reputation hanging
around with the MacDonalds.

A bad reputation! At that moment I couldn't think of anything
I wanted more!

We never did stop off at any dive, of course, if such a place did
actually exist, which I doubt. Once we were in the car (Stu at the
wheel, me and Jimmy in the back) the slim silver cigarette case
emerged again. Jimmy and I shared a joint and then started in on
a second. Meanwhile, Stu drove us to a deserted overlook above
the Cuyahoga River, parked, got out, came around to the back, and
sat down on my other side.

There I was, Mama, boxed in between them. And then the fun
began. Stu deep kissed me. That was okay; I'd been looking
forward to a real kiss like that. But then Jimmy kissed me that way,
too, and that was kind of strange. I mean, there I was sandwiched
between two brothers, both of whom were trying to make out with
me at once.

"Hey, please! One at a time," I said, or some such nonsense.
That only encouraged them. Next thing I knew they both were
simultaneously trying to undress me or at least gain access to my
top.

"Down, boys!" I said, in the haughty way an Ashley-Burnett girl
might address a pair of obstreperous guys. And when that didn't
stop them: "Enough! Jimmy, Stu! Come on, let's all go home."

"Uh-uh, Bev," I remember Jimmy saying as he leered. "Get into
a car with a couple of horny brothers, you gotta take the conse-
quences. Right, Stu?"

There was a lot of giggling then, I remember, mild attempts on
my part to push them off, equally lighthearted attempts on theirs
to unclasp my bra. We were in a kind of three-way wrestling match,
laughing, having fun, and I confess I enjoyed the struggle, doubt-
less because I figured it wouldn't continue very long. Stu and
Jimmy were decent, well-brought-up young men. Sooner or later,
when they realized I wasn't going to play, they'd give it up, we'd
stop off for the promised nightcap, and then they'd take me home.

That, Mama, was conventional dating wisdom as it was promul-
gated amongst the student body in the corridors and locker rooms
of the Ashley-Burnett School for Girls. But wise though it might
have been, it began to dawn on me some minutes into the struggle

that in this case it was not going to apply. Then I panicked. I was
scared, Mama, real scared. I began to struggle, struggle hard, and
then, as can happen in close quarters like the back of a car,
somebody got hurt.

It was Stu. Struggling with them both, I managed to stick my
elbow in his eye. He got mad. "Watch it, bitch." Then he slapped
me, not full force, of course, but hard enough to make me scream.

Jimmy cupped his hand hard over my mouth.

"Why'd you hit her, Stu?"

"Bitch poked me in the eye."

"We weren't 'sposed to hit her."

"Who cares what we were 'sposed to do. Let's do what we want.
Yeah?"

At that Stu ripped down the entire front of my dress. And then
the real combat began. Even through the haze of pot I knew I was
in trouble and tried seriously to fight my way out of the car. Jimmy
took hold of my arms and held them tight behind my back. Then
Stu pulled off my bra and grabbed hold of my breasts. When I
screamed, Jimmy cupped my mouth again. This time I bit his hand.

"Fuck!" He was furious. He grabbed hold of my hair and
yanked it back. "Bite me again, I'll clobber you, too."

I screamed at them to let me go, and when they didn't, I began
to beg. But by then they were all fired up. I'm sure all my struggling had turned them on. They'd reached the point where they
wouldn't let me loose until I gave them something in return.

"Think we danced with you all night 'cause you're so attractive?" Stu sneered. He answered his own query. "Only reason you
trot a wallflower is to get her to put out later on."

Then they really started to work me over, Mama. They grabbed
at me and grasped at me and taunted me for my ugliness. They
laughed when I started to cry. "Bet she's wet down there, too," one
of them said.

The struggle went on for a good ten minutes. They laughed and
hooted and talked about me in the third person as if I didn't have
ears or couldn't understand.

"Look at the way she twists. Like a snake. What she needs is
a good fucking, yeah?"

"Let's rip her panties off and fingerfuck both her holes."

"Better, let's strip her and throw her out of the car. Make her hitch home bare-ass."

"Yeah!"

And then, almost suddenly, it was over. The sneering and abuse petered out; the dark threats and rough grabs gave way to laughter and a lighter touch. There we were again, three kids squeezed together in the back of a car, the guys smiling, telling the girl to calm herself, the girl whimpering and shaking, then gingerly accepting the offered handkerchief to wipe away her tears. Stu got back in the driver's seat, drove us back to Shaker Heights. Half an hour later I was let off in front of my house with a "Good night, Bev. See you around, kid." I heard their laughter as they drove away.

What they did to me that night wasn't a "date rape," Mama, but I think it was worse in a way than any rape I ever heard about in my practice. Instead of raping me, they abused me; that, I've always thought, may have been their plan from the start.

I can just imagine the dialogue: "Hey, Stu, let's have some fun. Tonight, at this crappy dance we gotta go to, let's pick out one of the wallflowers, a real ugly-duckling type, know what I mean? Then dance her around, make her think she's got us all hot for her body. Then see if we can get her to do something really raunchy like suck us both off at once, maybe even take it up the ass."

"Sure, great. But what if she doesn't want to?"

"She will. She'll be so grateful she'll do anything."

"And if she isn't?"

"Screw it, bro. We'll dump on her. Give her something to remember us by. What do you say?"

In the end, Mama, it wasn't my body that was violated; it was my ego, my very soul. They shamed me, broke me down, made me cry and beg. They degraded me nearly as much as one human can degrade another, except, since there were two of them that night, my degradation was doubled.

You weren't there when I got home. You were still down at the lounge, having a drink with your cronies after your final set. But even if you'd been home, I don't know what I would have told you.

I was just so embarrassed, so humiliated, so incredulous about what had happened. I doubt I could have talked about it to you or anyone else.

I tiptoed up the stairs. Millie was sound asleep. In our bathroom, I stripped off all my clothes and stared woefully at myself in the mirror.

It was Cinderella who stared back at me, Mama, Cinderella after her moment of triumph at the ball, transformed after midnight back into her drab and lonely self. But I was different inside, in a way that didn't show for several years. That night a killer was born. This wallflower, I promised myself, will one day have her revenge. And a few months later, on a miserable cold and rainy day, when I was sitting in the window seat on our landing and saw something in the sky, a flash of lightning and then a glimpse of black, I smiled as I grasped the process by which my vengeance would one day be wreaked.

The flashes of pain, the hurts, the shames! Wallflower, wallflower, wallflower! I'd show them what a wallflower could do! I'd leave a flower by their walls! Oh, yes, I would, Mama! Oh, yes, I would!

Bobby Wexler and Laura Gabelli, they got theirs, Mama: Bobby and his new brood out in Fort Worth; Laura, her hubby and children up in Providence.

Bobby was executed, of course, for the way he treated me that summer between junior and senior years at Ashley-Burnett, when you were singing at the Cavendish and he thought, since he was already sticking his repulsive member into you, it might be fun to take out your daughter and stick it into her as well. Naturally he didn't succeed. I *swear*, Mama, I *never* tried to compete with you. All your men were Private Property as far as I was concerned. But I know you had your doubts when Bobby went around telling everyone I'd put out. The little shit! When I rejected his advances, he went into a pout and then, out of wounded vanity, tried to stir up mother-daughter trouble. He wanted to come between us, Mama, and he almost succeeded, too. It's for that I gave the asshole his due. I just hope he likes the way I had him glued. He won't be getting any more erections now!

Laura got hers for gabbing. After I transferred down to Tufts, the little bitch tried to put the make on me and, when she got slapped down, went around telling everyone on campus "Bev had a big love affair that went sour with her roommate up at Bennington." She told all her lesbian pals they'd do well to stay away from me as I was very bad news. So how do you like your new glued-up pussy, Laura? Bet your husband likes it, too, heh! heh!

Probably the best parts of these executions, Mama, were the trophies Tool brought back for you. From Bobby's house a beaten-up paperback copy of some crappy self-help book (as if he could ever help *him*self!) and from Laura's that funny old eggbeater, evidence of her newfound "domesticity" no doubt.

Yes, the first six were all on account of sexual humiliations. Even old Bertha Parce when you think of it—her attack on me was but a disguised attack on *your* sexuality. And the gluing of their genitalia seemed appropriate to such offenses. As for the family members unfortunate enough to be present at the times of execution, their organs were also glued so as to terminate the bloodlines, so to speak.

But now there are other pages in the ledger. Names of people who shamed me in other ways, like arrogant Professor Gaitenburg at Western Reserve, who mocked me during my orals, or Dr. Wendell Greer, the gynecologist, who tried to feel me up on his examination table. Ruth Kendricks, Geraldine Pearson, Pat Tinder and Walter Kinsolving, Rachel Spargo, Linda Nash, Richard Duggan and Violet Kraus. Oh, Mama, I could give you a list a hundred names long. There were so many of them, so very many, and there's not nearly enough time left in this life to take care of them all.

It must have been something in my eyes that set her off, the way I looked at Jessica. Maybe she identifies Jessica with her sister whom she loved and killed. "I had to kill her to save her from Granny," she told me once, back at Carlisle. Or maybe she identifies me with Granny, the ogress who ruled her life. Whatever weird connections she's made, the damage now is done. Poor Tool is bewildered, angry, hurt. But she's just going to have to control herself. Mama was right. Once a tool starts getting a mind of its own, things can go bad very fast.

The fight takes place in a small all-white room on the third floor above the dojo, a room reserved for private contests among the sensei's students. Afternoon light, pouring in through the high windows that face upper Broadway, makes the hard bleached oak floor shine.

The room is empty except for the two young female combatants, one blond and tall, the other black-haired and short. Dressed in gi jackets and pants, breathing heavily, they stand several feet apart in postures of confrontation, faces creased with rage and pain. An aura of aggression edged with danger envelops them. A faint aroma of perspiration perfumes the air.

Both women know this room well. They have fought matches here many times. It was here, too, that, giggling, they stripped to the waist several months before and amicably dueled with sabers with only a borrowed Polaroid camera to witness their carefully orchestrated contest.

Their fight today is different. A new element, a clear intent on the part of the shorter combatant to hurt and seriously vanquish the taller, has become evident only moments before. Now the two young women, chests heaving from their last contact, appraise each other. The stare of the short one, Diana, is hard and cold; the stare of the taller, Jess, is injured and perplexed. Then, like rival warriors about to engage in a final clash, their eyes meet and lock.

205

"I think we should stop awhile, cool down," Jess suggests. But she does not relax her fighting stance.

Diana shakes her head.

"You really want to go for it then?"

Diana gives her answer, a rush attack.

The women collide, brutally punch and kick at each other. Grunts of effort and sharp cries of pain resound off the walls. The smell of sweat turns pungent as, for a full twenty seconds they stand close, in nearly intimate contact, raining and blocking blows. Flesh is bruised. Blood spurts. Knuckles become raw and burn. Finally, exhausted from the struggle, the two fall back to try to control their labored breathing, each trying hard, too, not to show how badly she's been hurt.

Finally Jess speaks: "This isn't sport, you know."

Diana squints. "For me it is."

"If we continue like this, one of us'll be killed."

"That's what a real fight's about," Diana replies.

Still in her fighting stance, Diana suddenly reaches up and pulls at her hair. A moment later she casts a wig down upon the floor, then grins as she reveals her closely shaven skull.

Jess stares at Diana, trying to decipher the meaning of this gesture. Now she sees something in her opponent's icy blue eyes, a murderous look, savage, almost feral, that she never noticed before, even though the two have been friends for months. Suddenly Jess makes a decision. Turning her back on Diana, she strides across the room, opens the door, and exits without a word.

Diana, relaxing her stance, smiles knowingly. To leave a fight, turn one's back on an opponent without making the obligatory bow, is to deliver an unpardonable insult. *And it will not be pardoned,* she thinks.

My mistake, Mama, was to forget how passionate she could be. Her deeply submissive attachment made me forget that this was a girl who killed her mother, grandmother, and sister with an ax, then split all three of their bodies straight up from the crotch.

That she might be jealous if I gave special attention to a patient—well, I should have thought of that and taken steps. But things got out of hand. I remember your words: "If a tool goes into business for itself, you gotta think about getting rid of it."

And that, sadly, Mama, is what I may have to do.

It is 8:00 P.M. A chilly evening in New York. Diana's nostrils quiver as they catch the smell of rotted leaves, a late-autumn smell rising from the dark, wet parkland below. Cold rain fell in the afternoon; now there are puddles on Riverside Drive.

Diana, jogging downtown, does not avoid these puddles. Rather, she runs straight through them. At this hour the drive is nearly deserted. On either side, graceful streetlamps burn sulfurous in the night.

Across the dark canopy of wet bushes and trees Diana catches sight of the Hudson River, its surface gleaming black like roiling oil. Beside the river, streams of cars, headlights streaking, speed along the West Side Highway.

Diana cannot hear these cars; they are too far away. All she can hear is the steady *pat-pat-pat* of her feet upon the wet pavement and a light buzzing sound inside her brain.

Her quarry, unaware she is being tracked, also jogs, but two hundred feet ahead and a hundred feet below amidst the trees. Every so often Diana catches sight of her, a tall, thin light-haired woman dressed in a dark track suit, loping along a path that winds and turns through the narrow park. Diana is on a collision course with this woman. The point of intersection is a mile ahead. She feels an excitement different in quality from what she felt when carrying out missions for Doctor. This time it is her own enemy she is after, an opponent she knows well from numerous encounters. She also knows that this quarry is most likely armed, a fact that enhances the thrill of the hunt. Diana intends to strike first, hard and fast from behind. The battle should be over before it is even joined. That is the method she was taught.

Although it is cold, Diana is lightly dressed. She wears a thin black long-sleeved T-shirt and black nylon running shorts. She also wears a nylon waist sack loaded with paraphernalia for her kill: her weapon, an ice pick, which she will strap on to her forearm when she is ready; a caulking gun filled with glue to mark and desecrate her victim; and a shriveled flower plucked earlier from Doctor's garden, which she will leave as her signature beside a little wall she discovered near the killing site.

She has calculated everything. Only a half mile now to the place she carefully picked out. She increases her speed from a jogger's pace to a fast flat-out run. She bears right at the fork where the sidewalk that borders the drive meets a paved path that descends into the park. Once among the trees, she pulls out her weapon and fits it into the sheath strapped to her arm. She is now on an intersecting vector with her quarry, whom she sees clearly jogging a hundred yards ahead.

What luck! Jess is wearing a Walkman; she will not be able to hear Diana's steps. Diana looks around; no one else is on the path. She and Jess are alone in this narrow strip of park. Ahead, the great illuminated tower of Riverside Church soars into the night sky. Beyond a faint glow is cast by the city's lights.

A light rain begins to fall. Diana shivers slightly but runs on. She notices that Jess has begun to pick up her pace. Diana speeds up even more. *Pat-pat-pat* go her feet. She feels her heartbeat quicken as her ears find the sound of Jess's steps. *Pit-pat pit-pat pit-pat.* Jess is but a hundred feet ahead. Impossible now to stop. The rhythm is set. The momentum of attack is carrying her along. Diana pulls her pick from its sheath, holds it underhand as she swings her arms. Fifty feet now. Thirty. Twenty-five. Jess is almost within her reach. In a burst of speed Diana overtakes her. And then, in a single violent motion, she raises her right arm and with full force plunges the pick sideways so that it enters Jess's brain directly through the ear.

Jess, stabbed, falls upon the path, and as she does, the buzzing inside Diana's head suddenly stops. Feeling hot, feverish with victory, Diana grabs hold of Jess's feet and drags her body into the thick, wet brush on the right. She pulls her through the fallen leaves to within a few feet of the ruined wall, then lets go of her, stands back, and stares down at her face.

At one time Jess was her friend, but when she, too, became Doctor's patient, Diana's liking of her turned to hate. Now that hate is purged. Her rival is but dead meat on the ground. Diana kneels to untie the string that secures Jess's sweatpants, then pulls them down to the girl's ankles. She grins when she sees the switchblade knife strapped against Jess's side. An opponent's weapon—what a fine trophy that will make!

As Diana uncaps her caulking gun and sets to work with the glue, her only regret is that now that her onetime friend is dead, she will never be able to give back the archery set she borrowed the week before.

She's down there in the basement now, brooding over her unauthorized kill. All right, you made her into a killing machine, so you've got to expect a certain amount of carryover. She's human after all. But to leave the wallflower signature and use the glue, methods reserved for *your* tormentors—that was crazy, that means she's out of control.

She can't even explain why she did it. A fit of jealousy? But it was Tool who got Jessica to come see you in the first place. Tool recruited her. She was Jessica's friend. She knew what therapy was. What did she expect? That you'd treat Jessica differently? That you wouldn't take her into your office and listen to her for an hour three times a week?

No, it had to be something more. This past autumn, when Jessica asked for the name of her shrink, Tool was quick to send her on. Remember the way she beamed when she told you to expect the call?

What about their actual relationship? How much do you really know? Could they have been more than gym buddies? Could they have been lovers?

Be rational about this; don't let the stress generate fantasies. The truth is you still don't know what they did all those times they went off together after martial arts class. Come to think of it, isn't it strange Jessica never mentioned Tool except the first time she called?

"Diana Proctor gave me your name. We take a martial arts class together on the West Side. I'm looking for a good therapist. I'd like to come in and talk about it if that's all right."

Yes, of course, it was "all right." You were extremely interested in treating someone who looked so much like Cynthia Morse. And this girl was so much nicer without any evident cruel streak. She was a decent, direct sort of person, but with Cindy's great looks, smile, and appeal.

So what were you after with her anyway? Looking to seduce her? Don't be absurd! Those days are long gone, and anyway, the girl was young enough to be your daughter. But admit it, she attracted you. She was just your type. And just about the same age as Cindy was then, before she turned on you and earned herself a place in the ledger.

No, there's got to be more to this than meets the eye. Tool and Jessica must have had some kind of emotional connection that, when it snapped, generated rage in Tool and set her off.

Remember the little encounter at the knife show? Running into Jessica with Tool in tow didn't strike you as being all that important at the time. But suppose Jessica, seeing her shrink unexpectedly in the company of another patient who happened to be her friend, got curious, decided to trail you for a while, and then saw something she didn't like.

Wait a minute! Remember the famous "English girl" she met in Italy, the one who fenced topless with her? The truth is you've had only her word on that. You never saw the photographs, didn't even know about them until Janek brought them up. Why didn't she tell you about them? Could she have been afraid you'd ask to see them? She couldn't allow that because if she did, you'd recognize the other girl. Suppose the alleged "English girl" was a subterfuge? Suppose Jessica didn't want to tell you she'd actually played the topless fencing scene with Diana? If that's true, then they definitely *did* have something going, perhaps not overtly sexual, but certainly sexualized. And if that's the case, then there was enough unresolved energy to unleash Tool and cause her to explode.

But go back a moment, think about that knife show. What could Jessica have seen you and Tool do that might cause her to mention to a friend that she was thinking of quitting therapy?

You might have spoken harshly to Tool or petted her. You do that unconsciously sometimes, out of some twisted maternalism no doubt. If you'd had your wits about you, you'd never have gone to that damn knife show in the first place. It was Tool's idea. She said she wasn't enjoying using crude store-bought ice picks all the time, she wanted a fine weapon, something she wouldn't have to leave behind, something really sharp with a ritualistic flavor to it, and since there was a knife show in town, would you attend it with her, take a look, see if anything caught your eye?

So there it is. Tool set the whole thing up. She knew Jessica would attend the show, probably even knew which day. She enticed you into taking her there because she wanted Jessica to see her with you, and she probably did something there that you didn't even notice, like taking your arm, squeezing it—anything to provoke Jessica and force her out of therapy.

This is terrible! It means Tool's been using you! It means you've lost control of her, created a Frankenstein's monster just as Mama said.

Calm down! Look at the implications. Janek's got the photographs. If Tool *was* the other fencer and he should see her entering the basement apartment, he'll recognize her at once. He already suspects you. He's not all that great at hiding what he feels. Or, more likely, he's deliberately letting his suspicions show in the hope you'll get spooked and tip your hand.

The main thing now is to keep Janek from seeing Tool.

But there's something even more important, which is to get to the bottom of Tool and Jessica's relationship. Tool has to tell you whether she was the "English girl." Once you're certain about that, you can take the necessary countermeasures.

So the thing to do is get Tool up here in front of Mama. Mama always intimidates her. If you can get her up here naked in front of Mama, Mama'll make her talk.

It is night. The scene is a shadowy and cavernous bedchamber dimly lit with soft reddish light. At one end a large four-poster oak bed stands free of the walls. At the other, three female figures are arranged in frozen postures as if posing for a *tableau vivant.* From the expressions on the faces of these players, a spectator might well feel that a question hangs upon the air. But not one of the figures moves or speaks. The question, if there was one, remains unanswered.

The first figure, young, muscular, firm-fleshed, stands at stiff attention. She is naked, her head and body totally shaved, a fine gloss of perspiration coating her like a dew. The soft red light that paints her exposed skin emphasizes the blush generated from within. Her eyes, too, are red, as if from weeping.

The second figure, older, shorter, plump, sits opposite the first in a high-backed chair. She is dressed in a too-tight strapless crimson gown which can barely contain her bodice. Her eyes are narrowed as she stares with cold reproach at the younger woman's face. But the younger woman does not return the seated woman's gaze.

Rather, her eyes engage the eyes of a third woman, actually a painted image hanging on the wall just above the seated woman's chair. This woman, the one in the picture, wears the same crimson gown as the live woman below, but the garment suits her better. While the breasts of the seated woman are constricted by her gown, the bosoms of the painted woman fill hers perfectly. There is a curious resemblance between the seated woman and the painted one that must haunt a spectator. It is as if each one's face, in a completely different way, is a caricature of the other's.

But perhaps what would seem most strange would be the power-

ful force field of emotions that appears to exist among these players. A spectator would know that the three are bound to one
another in some inexorable and yet tragic way, bound so tightly
and forcefully that anything outside their triangle, any person or
event, would have no meaning to them at all.

"**S**he says she did it because Jes-
sica wouldn't return her bow! What do you think, Mama? Hours
of punitive bracing and she comes up with that."

"The bow we gave—"

"Right, Mama, the bow we presented to her when she came back
from commando school in Colorado. Remember, she was first in
her class out there, and we thought she ought to be rewarded for
doing so well, especially as most of the other students were males.
Besides, she'd told us her martial arts instructor had suggested she
take up archery to hone her concentration. So we mail-ordered an
excellent target bow and set of arrows and laid them out for her
on the bed so she'd see them first thing when she reported in after
her trip."

"But wasn't there another connection?"

"Of course, Mama! Do you think I'm such a bad analyst I didn't
understand what was going on?"

"Gosh, Bev, you're touchy today. I don't think you're a bad
analyst at all."

"Forgive me, Mama. I thought you were implying that I wasn't
aware of the play on words. Because, of course, I was. Diana
wanted a bow so she could play archer, or should I say 'Archer'?
She liked being the patient but also wanted to play at being Doctor
or at least try out the authority role for a while. If she had a bow
in her hands, she'd be a kind of Archer, with real potency, too,
as a bow can be an extremely powerful weapon."

"You were always a wonderful analyst, Bev. You have your
deficiencies. Who doesn't? But you've always been good at your
job."

"What deficiencies?"

"Oh, please, let's not get into that."

"I think we should get into it. I've known for some time you've found me deficient. Now's as good a time as any to clear the air. I'm waiting, Mama. Tell me where you find me wanting. I can take your criticism. God knows, I've taken it all my life."

"You're sure you want to hear it?"

"I'm sure."

"Okay, but just remember you asked for it. So don't complain."

"I won't."

"Let's start with this wallflower business."

"Is that what it is? A 'business'?"

"You know what I mean."

"I'm not sure I do. I happen to be a wallflower."

"No, dear, that's what you made yourself into. No one's born a wallflower. A wallflower creates herself. Something in you likes being a wallflower, so you have Tool leave those flowers beside the walls, as if—"

"As if *what,* damn it, Mama?"

"There, see, you're getting angry. You were always so touchy, Bev. You could never take the slightest bit of criticism."

"Never mind that! Just tell me how I've made myself into a wallflower, since that seems to be what you think."

"It's not just what I think, dear. It's the truth. And having Tool leave those homely, withered flowers by the bodies only reinforces your negative self-image. Which, frankly, you could remedy if you'd just find yourself somebody who . . . you know."

"Somebody to screw me. That's what you mean, isn't it?"

"I knew this dialogue was going to turn unpleasant, Bev. I think it would be better if we stop talking."

"Certainly, Mama, if that's the way you want it . . ."

There's a difference, Mama, a big difference between us. It's important for you to understand the difference and why, as much as I might like, I cannot be like you. For one thing, I don't have your looks. I know, I'm not really *bad*-looking. And I certainly don't feel sorry for myself. In this world, as I so often remind my patients, you've got to play the hand you're dealt. But you're beautiful, Mama. Just look at yourself, your eyes, complexion, bones, the marvelous planes of your face. There were those who called you the most beautiful woman in Cleveland. You played the part, too. Grand. Mysterious. Elusive. Even cruel at times. Not really cruel in the sense of mean or small, but cruel in the way that a great woman projects cruelty, becoming, as the poet said, a Lady of Pain. Mystical. Unfathomable. My nurturer and my nemesis.

It was you who taught me the lines:

> *Cold eyelids that hide like a jewel*
> *Hard eyes that grow soft for an hour;*
> *The heavy white limbs, and the cruel*
> *Red mouth like a venomous flower.*

Sometimes when I'm lying in bed, I look up at you and think: *How could I, little me, be the child of such magnificence?* I know I shouldn't run myself down. I am who I am and, as such, am as valuable as any other human on this earth. But it hasn't always been easy being your daughter. I never had your stature, your beauty, your compelling personality. I had to find my own way to power, and the way I found, the way of concealment and craft, is not nearly as attractive as yours. While you played torch singer to Cleveland, bewitching your audiences with songs, I took a less flamboyant route, studying the permutations of the human mind, then working within the interstices to create unique effects. And while your color was and always will be red, color of flames, mine is and always shall be black, color of night.

There were times, Mama, when you hurt me deeply. I never told you this before. I know you never meant to hurt me; I know that whatever you did, it was always with my own best interests at heart. But there're still times when I feel the pain, and then I wonder: *Is it worth it to keep on living, to try to make my way in this pitiless, indifferent world?* I do my best. I work hard with my patients, pretending always to listen to them with sympathy. I try hard not to seem like one of those small, tight-lipped therapists who listen and listen and give nothing back in return. But there's so little I *can* give, Mama, to assuage so much cruelty, torment, so many hurts and humiliations and intractable problems in other women's lives. Who can solve them all? Who can bind up all the wounds? Who can assuage the hurts and blunt the cruelties and tell the wounded ones there is hope and time will heal. It's hard, too, to listen all the time, always to care about *them,* absorb myself in *them,* focus my attention on *their* difficulties, when I have so many of my own. I haven't wanted to think always of the past, obsess over the old hurts and wounds, but it's been hard not to, the pain's been so real, and, Mama, it's always there.

I was left with no choice, it seems, but to try to wipe it out with acts of retributive justice. The only other option for me was to allow the awful pain to strangle me, choke me to death with its poisonous vines.

You know your silent treatment's killing me. Do I deserve it, do I really? I'm very sorry, truly *very, very sorry* I was insolent. But I never denied my overriding love for you. So there really wasn't anything for you to get so offended about.

Will you please answer me, Mama? Have you forgotten the trophies I had Tool bring back for you! The offerings I made to you? The years I spent listening to your sob stories? I practically did your goddamn wash for you! Have you forgotten that?

Go ahead, ignore me. Just don't forget—I'm an analyst. I know you're hiding something, and I have a pretty good idea what it is. I want you to confess to me. That's right, Mama, I want the truth. Tell me the truth, and I'll forgive you for it. Because I know you did something, Mama. *I know you did.*

Think back. Remember that last little exchange with Jimmy MacDonald just before Tool stabbed him in the eye? You don't remember? Then I'll refresh your memory. Jimmy said: ". . . it wasn't us, you know. It was set up. She ought to talk to her—" And then he stopped.

Her *what*? Her *mother*? Could *that* have been the person Jimmy was referring to? Was he thinking of *you,* Mama?

Since you don't deny it, since you refuse to say anything . . .

well, I'll have to draw my own conclusions, won't I? Yes, I'll just have to draw my own conclusions, hurtful though they may be. . . .

*S*hhhh. We have to whisper now. We don't want Tool to hear us. If she hears, she may decide to attack us first. We're going to have to get rid of her. That much is clear. And to do that, we're going to have to set her up so well that there'll be no doubt she was always acting on her own. That won't be hard. All the receipts from her various trips, the paper trail as they call it, have been safely preserved on our orders in her room. And Carl Drucker will gladly testify that we resisted when he first broached release. The most important thing is to make sure the little lynx hasn't kept a diary or anything that can directly tie us to the crimes. Of course, we *are* tied to them indirectly: It was her insane obsession with us that pushed her to kill these various figures from our past. That's easily documented. All the information she needed was available in our personal files, to which she had ready access by virtue of living in the basement of our house. The plan is foolproof. Even if the cops suspect our influence, all the evidence will point to Tool alone. But we mustn't forget to move the trophies. They mustn't be in front of the portrait; rather, they have to be hidden away in various corners and drawers. The paper trail should nail her nicely, as will the wallflower trap we laid so carefully at Carlisle. We'll have to do it quickly. It will take all our courage, and we'll have only one chance to get it right. The staging must conform to the provocation: Tool tried to kill us; we struck back at her in self-defense. After all, she's a confessed killer. All we ever wanted was to help her adjust. She attacked us, her therapist and mother surrogate, just the way she attacked her own mother, with an ax. We managed to kill her only because she slipped. Another second and her ax would have split our skull. We defended ourself; we had no choice. It was either her or us.

Too bad, of course, but now that we gather she killed all those other fine people, whole families of them, it seems, and by so doing replicated her original crime against her own family—well, we can't help wondering if perhaps she's not better off dead. This may seem odd, coming as it does from a healer, but we truly believe there are times a person is truly better off in the grave than living possessed by the kind of demons that ravaged poor young Diana Proctor's tormented soul.

*W*here are you, Mama? I need
you now, need you so much! Why are you so silent?
Talk to me. Please, talk to me! Pleeeeeease!

8

The Trophies

Janek repositioned himself against the soft white beach towel Monika had arranged upon the cushions of the chaise. It was not a tan he was after but heat. He wanted the sun to strike the center of his chest, wanted its dry hotness to enter his bared body and to spread. Anything to drive away the chill within that made him tremble even now in the middle of this hot, windless December afternoon on the Isla de Cozumel.

The terrace where he lay exposed, naked except for a pair of green jungle-motif trunks Monika had bought for him at the airport, was just a few rock steps down from their *caseta*, perched sixty feet above the beach. From where Janek lay he could see nothing except a line of palms clinging to the curving shore and a vast expanse of blue divided cleanly by the horizon. Below the line was placid cyan sea, above it serene azure sky, and not a whitecap or a cloud marred these seamless surfaces.

He turned to look at Monika. She lay topless on a matching chaise a few feet away, her oversize sunglasses perched on her nose, a German-language paperback open and face down on her belly. At first Janek thought she'd fallen off to sleep, but then he saw a smile spread slowly across her face.

"How're you doing?" he asked.

"Feeling dreamy," she said. "I love it here. How about you?"

"I'm definitely feeling warmer."

"Well, you should. You need more sunscreen." She rose, spread lotion onto her hands, came to him, and, standing behind, began to apply it slowly and evenly to his chest.

He gazed up at her. "That's sexy."

"It's meant to be." She brushed her fingers lightly across his nipples. "You're a very sexy man."

"Thanks for saying that," Janek said, "but I don't feel very appetizing. Pale, middle-aged, scarred . . ."

She spread the lotion very carefully over the wounds on his shoulder and his throat.

"You look good, Frank. A few days down here and you'll start feeling good, too. It may take time, but sooner or later your mind will catch up with your body."

He glanced up at her again, then turned away, feeling tears rising involuntarily to his eyes. This had been happening regularly since the stabbing, and he hated himself for not being able to control it. He was glad he was wearing sunglasses; he didn't like to expose his vulnerability. But when he remembered that Monika had been with him in Venice when Kit had called and told him Jess was dead, he knew it was absurd to feel embarrassed with her. He pulled his glasses off.

"Either I feel cold and start to shake or else I tear up," he said, turning so she could see his eyes. "It's not because of pain or sadness, and certainly not remorse. I don't know why the hell it happens, Monika; but I don't like it, and I want it to stop."

The police psychiatrist had told him the tears and shakes were delayed manifestations of stress. But there was a feeling that came with them, which he couldn't quite define. Monika wanted him to let her help him explore it, but he felt he wasn't ready yet, that he had no words with which to express it. It was something dark that he had glimpsed which had entered his mind and gotten lost in the canyons of his brain and which now he feared because it made him feel cold or caused the tears to rise.

She made herself a place to sit beside him, then gently kissed his eyelids dry. Then she took his glasses and set them back on his face, carefully arranging the temples behind his ears.

"I never killed a woman before. Never even shot at one."

"You know gender isn't the issue, Frank."

"A woman. It feels strange."

"You're chivalrous."

He smiled. "I've only rarely been accused of that."

"Oh, Frank . . ." She took his face between her palms. "To kill a person even in self-defense—I understand how difficult it must be to live with that. And I know that no matter what Kit and Aaron say—that you had no choice, that surely she would have killed you if you hadn't killed her, that she was a sociopath, a murderer—I know none of that means anything so long as you're haunted. That's why we're here, to rest, talk, perhaps reorder all those terrible events. In the meantime, remember you're not tainted by your deed, not soiled by it in any way. But you are changed on account of it. So now your task is to come to terms with this new Frank that you are, to understand him and come to love him again."

He took her hand. "Thanks for saying that."

"I like being your lover-shrink. You know I do. Still, when the demons are within, only you can chase them out." She paused. "I love you. Please remember that."

He brought her hand to his lips. "I won't forget."

They had come into his room during the week he was in the hospital, first Aaron, then Kit, then Aaron again, then Aaron and Kit together. On each visit they told him the story, rotating the puzzle so he could examine it from every side. But no matter how many different ways they told it, it always came out the same. The basic story, well constructed because they were excellent detectives, seemed to him wrong and incomplete. He listened to them, nodded, asked questions, and took in their answers, but in the end he told them that good as their story was, he was not going to buy it.

The facts were simple enough. The woman he had killed was named Diana Proctor. She was a librarian who paid a nominal rent to inhabit the basement apartment in Beverly Archer's house. Six years before, in Danbury, Connecticut, she had murdered three members of her family with an ax. Having been declared mentally incompetent, she'd been committed to Carlisle Hospital for the Criminally Insane, where, after five years of intensive treatment under Beverly's supervision, the entire hospital staff, led by its director, Dr. Carl Drucker, determined that she had made a full recovery and lobbied vigorously for her release.

On this matter of the release there was an important point. Hospital records showed, and Dr. Drucker verified, that Beverly Archer had not been in favor of setting Diana Proctor free. Diana wasn't ready yet, she had written; perhaps a few more years of therapy were indicated. But the rest of the staff was convinced of her recovery, so in the end Beverly reluctantly went along.

The girl seemed to function well in the city. She obtained a part-time job at the New York Society Library on East Seventy-ninth Street, where co-workers described her as congenial and her work as exemplary. She lived quietly in Dr. Archer's basement, undergoing sessions four times a week. She also joined the West Side Academy of Karate at Broadway and 110th Street, where she became an accomplished martial artist. It was there that she met Jess Foy.

Other students at the academy described them as friends. And it was Diana who referred Jess to Archer when Jess asked her to recommend a therapist. In addition, it turned out that Diana was the so-called English girl in the fencing photograph Janek had found taped to the wall of Jess's closet. She was the owner, too, of the bow and arrows Janek had tracked down through the Salvation Army. Mr. Yukio Katsakura, the sensei at the academy, described a violent match the two girls had fought in a private upstairs room the week that Jess was stabbed. The reason he hadn't mentioned this to Aaron, when he was interviewed early in the investigation, was that when he inquired about it, both women had smiled gaily and shrugged it off. Katsakura had assumed they'd just gotten carried away, a not infrequent occurrence among young, well-motivated fighters.

One could only speculate as to why Diana had killed Jess. Possibly she became jealous of her friend, who was a superior athlete and martial artist and who she may have believed was favored by their therapist. Beverly herself theorized that Diana had made erotic overtures to Jess and, upon being rebuffed, had acted out her fury. But whatever Diana's rationale, the murderous act was part of the same insanity that had led her to slaughter her relatives one horrible Sunday morning six years before.

It was the Archer connection to three of the other victim clusters (Bertha Parce; Cynthia Morse & family; the MacDonald brothers) that struck Janek as the story's most peculiar feature. As best the detectives were able to reconstruct, Diana became so obsessed with her therapist that when Beverly was asleep, Diana rummaged through her papers and came up with these victims' names. Then, out of some strange, twisted, perhaps jealousy-driven madness, she methodically located them, flew to where they lived, executed them, and glued their genitals, always leaving her wallflower signature behind.

There was no question that Diana thought of herself as a wallflower. She had described herself that way several times to friends at Carlisle. Carl Drucker turned over a note from Diana signed "Wallflower" which police handwriting analysts verified was in the girl's hand. Moreover, a huge trove of evidence was found in Diana's room: airline ticket receipts, motel receipts, car rental receipts, caulking guns, glue, ice picks, and, most important, a hit list bearing the names of all the Wallflower victims. Kit said the evidence was so convincing that had Diana survived her encounter with Janek, she would easily have been convicted of murder.

Which still left several other killings to be explained: the homeless man, the two non-Archer-connected Happy Families, Leo Titus, and the attack against Janek on the final night.

The homeless man, according to Kit and Aaron's theory, was a practice shot in preparation for the later homicides. Diana, it seemed, was quite rigorous in her preparation. In addition to karate training, she worked out regularly at a local health club and two summers before had taken a ten-day course in commando tactics at a shadowy survivalist school in Colorado, where she learned the ice pick technique.

(Aaron found the receipt in Diana's desk. Beverly had no knowledge of the foray; Diana had simply told her she was going white water rafting on her vacation.)

In any event, it seemed consistent with such rigor that Diana would first try out her newly acquired skills on a relatively defenseless target in New York before venturing to distant cities in search of whole families to execute.

As for what exactly had attracted Diana to the two non-Archer-connected victim clusters (the Robert Wexler family in Fort Worth and the Anthony Scotto family in Providence)—that, said Aaron and Kit, would probably never be known. Beverly Archer had her own theory—namely, that the very image of a family stirred up tremendous murderous aggression inside Diana, similar to the aggression that had exploded on the morning she killed her own core family with the ax.

The stabbing of the cat burglar Leo Titus was easier to explain. By intruding into Beverly's house, he posed a threat of invasion to which Diana's hair-trigger mentality could only respond with an attack. Janek, of course, was another invader and thus had to be killed like the first. In her interview Beverly stated her belief that had Janek not succeeded in stopping Diana, she herself would have become a victim the moment she reentered her house. An extra irony of the affair was that the Archer-connected Wallflower victims (Parce, Morse, and the MacDonalds) were minor figures in Beverly's past, people with whom she'd been out of touch for years. She hadn't even known any of them were dead until Aaron showed her the FBI's victim list.

The shrink seemed to have suffered something close to a nervous breakdown as a result of the discovery that her "best patient" had in fact not been cured at all but had, even while in intensive therapy, committed a series of horrible murders against these past players in her life. Beverly's suffering over her therapeutic catastrophe was demonstrated to Janek on the videotape of her interview with Aaron.

While still in the hospital, Janek viewed this tape several times. In it the psychologist seemed truly shattered. The tight, withdrawn quality she'd displayed in her interviews with him was replaced in Aaron's interview by tearful eruptions of agony and remorse. Her cool half-smile was supplanted by haggard, tormented eyes, making for a portrait of a woman in despair. But after rerunning and studying the tape, Janek decided her performance was feigned. No matter her broken appearance and the apparent sincerity of her grief, he did not believe a word of it.

The result was that no matter how many times Aaron and Kit told him their story and no matter how much evidence they carted into his hospital room to prove it, Janek insisted it was not complete. If, as all the evidence showed, Diana Proctor had physically committed the murders, then, Janek maintained, by some method he could not describe Beverly Archer had put Diana up to it.

"You're usually right about these things," Kit said. "But how can you be so sure?"

"I feel it," Janek replied. "I don't care how many times Diana described herself as a wallflower or signed her name that way. For me Beverly Archer is the only wallflower in the case. The flowers left beside the walls at the murder scenes were her signatures, not Diana's."

On their first day in Yucatán, Janek and Monika settled into their rented *caseta,* then lay out on their terrace in the sun. When it grew dark, they drove into Cozumel, looking for a place to eat. They explored for a while, finally settling on a quiet thatch-roofed restaurant on the beach where the wine was good and the fish was fresh and well prepared.

Afterward they took another walk through the town, passing various bars and clubs, pausing occasionally to listen to laughter or music playing within. Then Monika drove them back to their little blue and white house, where the garden was filled with orchids and hibiscus and the terrace overlooked the sea. Here they sat out as they had in the afternoon, staring across the water at a magnificent tropical moon, which reminded them of the moon that had lit their way not two months before in Venice.

"It happens every night around this time," Janek said. "I start feeling chilled and then afraid."

"Of the dream?" He nodded. "I can give you a pill," Monika said. "It will help you sleep and probably stop you from dreaming. But I don't recommend it."

"Why not?"

"I think it's good for you to dream, Frank. Even if the dream is bad. If you can dream it through, the power of the dream will weaken, and then you'll be released."

Janek thought about that awhile. When he spoke again, his voice was hushed and steady.

"I can't see all the details. I see the redness over everything. The glow like a kind of rust. And I see the picture, so big, looming there: the handsome face; the glossy red curls; the sparkling eyes; the cruel, sensual mouth. And then I see this slim, little, bald woman charging at me like a fiend. She sticks me. I feel the pain. The room begins to spin. And then I see other things, objects, but I'm whirling so fast I can't tell you what they are. I want to see them clearly, Monika. I think that's why I dream about them. To see them again, hoping this time they'll register. Because they're important. I know they are." He sat back, shrugged. "I have no idea why."

That night, when the nightmare came and he began to shake, he felt her arms wrap his chest. The nightmare passed. He got up, shuffled to the bathroom, poured himself a glass of water, and drank it off. Back in bed, in her arms again, her breasts warm points against his back, he felt better, less haunted, not so cold.

"**I**'ve got an idea," he whispered to her in the morning.

"What?"

"It's nice here. I like it. But I want us to go back to New York."

"We just arrived, Frank."

"I know. But there's something I want to do. The photos Aaron showed me weren't enough. I should have insisted on seeing the room again for myself. What do you say we fly up there this morning, spend twenty-four hours, then fly back? I know it'll be expensive, but I'll pay for the tickets. I think seeing the room in daylight will help."

She shook her head. "I don't think so, Frank. I don't think that will help you at all."

"Look, I'm not a child. Whatever's there—I can take it."

She smiled. "Of course, you can. But there isn't anything there. You'll be wasting your time."

"But—"

"Please, listen to me. Right now you're recovering from two major physical wounds and a great deal of psychic stress. In a few brief seconds, perhaps the most intense of your life, many things converged on you—sounds, sights, revelations. You saw things. You were attacked. You defended yourself, hit back at your attacker. Your mind suffered overload. Time and space were fore-shortened and condensed. Some memories were etched, and others, perhaps the most important, were lost in the trauma of shooting that woman and being stabbed. No wonder you keep reliving those moments. The key to your nightmare, to your chills and tears, lies someplace within. Not in the actual room, as you might see it in daylight if we flew back up to New York today, but in the room as you *experienced* it that night, the room as it *seemed* to you then. I told you that if you can re-create the vision that haunts you, it won't disturb you anymore. I believe that's true. It will become just another memory. The bad dream will . . . disappear."

He rolled onto his back. "Fine," he said. "Now how am I going to do all that?"

"After breakfast I'll drive down to the village. I'm going to buy you paper and a set of crayons."

"Oh, Monika, please. . . ."

"I'm serious, Frank. I want you to draw."

"Draw what?"

"The sea. The house. The garden. Whatever you like. Draw me if you want, or I'll bring a mirror out to the terrace and you can try to draw yourself. And if other images happen to come to you, then you'll draw them, too. You see, to draw a thing is to master it. I believe soon you'll be able to see those objects you cannot remember now. When you see them, you must try to draw them even if the images are only partial. Draw them and you'll control them. And then the dream will lose its power."

Aaron had brought photographs of Beverly's bedroom to the hospital. They had pored over them together. Everything was as he remembered it . . . almost. Leo Titus lay dead on the floor at the foot of the bed. Diana Proctor lay dead where she'd fallen after Janek's bullets had blasted her back. The light in the room was dim and red, and the painting was in the niche. But the portrait seemed smaller in the photos, less intense, the manner of its display less compelling to the eye. Everything looked the same, yet the cumulative effect was different. It was as if Janek's mind had played a trick on him, distorting the actual scene, which in the police photos appeared relatively normal, into something threatening and grotesque.

And still, there were things missing from the photos, those strange and inappropriate objects which haunted his dreams. Where were they? The room had been searched, and nothing out of the ordinary had been found. When Aaron asked Janek to describe the objects, he shook his head, for he could not.

"I just know they were there," he said.

The dream was always the same: a cavernous bedroom; reddish light; a huge oil painting of a woman; strange, not clearly seen objects arranged symmetrically before the portrait. He looked to his left: A body was curled on the floor. He looked to his right: A black-clothed virago with shaven skull rushed at him out of the gloom. At the very instant in his dream when he felt the ice pick slice into his flesh and hit his bone, he was possessed by the feeling that he had entered into something more than a stranger's bedroom, that he had entered into a secret chamber inside a madwoman's mind.

When he awoke from the dream, his thought was always the same: It was Beverly Archer's madness, not Diana Proctor's, that had been displayed.

He had other visitors over his two weeks in the hospital and his week of recuperation in his apartment. Laura and Stanton, attentive and concerned, arrived with two magnificent bouquets. Later Stanton came alone to tell him in a bitter whisper that he was glad Janek had killed the girl.

"A trial would have been awful, Frank. All that stuff about Jess—we don't even like to think about it." Stanton paused. "You gave us closure. We'll always be grateful for that. If you ever need anything, any kind of help, I want you to think of us and call."

After Stanton left, Janek had a feeling that he probably wouldn't be seeing much of the Dorances anymore. The three of them had shared Jess, but now that she was gone, there was nothing to bring them together again except the all-too-painful memory of her promise.

Sullivan also paid him a visit. He brought no flowers but was respectful and solicitous. If he was envious of Janek's resolution of his case, he succeeded in concealing it.

When Janek asked if anyone on his team harbored doubts that Diana Proctor had been the HF killer, Sullivan gazed at him mystified.

"Gee, Frank, why do you ask that?"

"No particular reason," Janek said.

"You think we're the kind of people who'd resist a case solution because an outsider got to it first? I'm offended. Whatever you may think of us, I promise you we're not that small."

Janek let it go. Sullivan, like any good FBI man, was interested in forensic evidence, not psychological speculation. But then Janek became aware that Sullivan was not visiting him merely to wish him well. He had his own agenda, which, after the pleasantries, he wasted no time bringing up.

"I was talking last night to Grey Scopetta, my film director friend."

"Yeah, I remember you mentioning him," Janek said.

"We both feel there could be a terrific miniseries here. What we're hoping is you'll give us a release so we can pitch the idea to a network."

Janek smiled graciously. "You don't need a release from me, Harry. Just don't use my name, okay?"

"But we have to use your name, Frank. You'll be the star." Sullivan stood and began to pace the little room. "Think of it. Two miniseries! You'll be the most famous detective in the country!"

"I've tasted fame, Harry, and as they say, it's vastly overrated."

"You're not serious." Sullivan paused. "Are you, Frank?"

Janek nodded. "I don't want to be portrayed in any more movies. But that shouldn't stop you guys. The case is in the public record. We all know police work isn't about stars; it's about teamwork. As team leader you can rightfully think of yourself as the leading man."

As Sullivan shook his head, Janek noticed something desperate in his eyes.

"What's the matter?"

The inspector sat, then twisted in his seat. "Tell you the truth, now that it's wrapped up, HF, or Wallflower I guess we should call it now, isn't all that dramatic from a story point of view. As Grey says, who cares about some nutty, bald girl who killed people because she was hung up on her shrink? But he feels there could be a very strong story if we structured the whole thing around you. Put you right in the center of it. Your character arc could make it work."

"Character arc?"

"You know what I mean."

"No," said Janek, "I don't think I do."

"The way you change as the case develops. You go in one sort of guy and come out another."

Janek was quiet. He didn't like the sound of that. It was too close to the truth. The notion of having his soul exposed to millions of people filled him with a special kind of dread.

Sullivan was still pitching. "Try this. Cynical world-weary NYPD detective gets personally involved when his goddaughter's murdered. Grief-stricken, he goes after the killer with a vengeance, cuts through all the bureaucratic horseshit, finds the murderess, and shoots her dead. I mean, that's a real *story*, one a network will buy."

Janek looked at Sullivan sharply. "For me it wasn't a story, Harry. It was a murder case just, like all the others."

"Yeah, sure, I know you say that. But—"

"Forget it."

Sullivan lowered his head. When he spoke again, his tone was meek. "I hope you'll reconsider, Frank. Maybe later, when you're feeling your old self again . . ."

Janek waited until Sullivan raised his head and then met his eyes straight on. "Don't hope for that, Harry. It's not going to happen."

At first when he looked at the crayons Monika bought him, thirty pristine pastel crayons neatly organized by color in an elegant compartmentalized wooden box, he felt loath to touch them lest he violate their perfect order. But after he sat down on the chaise, propped the large spiral-bound pad of paper against his knees, and ran his fingers across the surface of a sheet, it seemed to cry out for color.

His first sketches were tentative and sloppy. But still there was a satisfaction in using his hands to try to reproduce the purity of the terrace view. And the longer he drew, the more he enjoyed it. It was a technique worthy of being mastered. He thought of the combination of intensity and patience exhibited by his father when he sat at his bench working on broken accordions in the little repair shop he'd operated on Carmine Street. *Perhaps,* he thought, *if I imitate the way Dad used to squint at the exposed insides of old accordions, I'll manage to get the swing of it.*

Monika, careful not to disturb him, busied herself inside the house, preparing food she'd bought in town. Then she went out to swim and jog along the beach. When she returned two hours later, he showed her his latest sketch of the view. The sea and sky, divided horizontally by the horizon, were a simple study in blues. She liked it, and so did he.

"I'm pleased," she said. "You're enjoying yourself."

"Yeah, I am," he admitted.

She kissed his shoulder and went back inside the house. At midday she brought out a tray of tortillas, guacamole, and beer. They ate and laughed, then retired to their bedroom to make love and then to nap.

At three, well oiled with sunscreen, he returned to the terrace for another round of drawing. But this time, instead of portraying the view, he tried to sketch his dream.

He tore off several sheets before he was satisfied with the general design. When he finally felt he'd gotten it right, he began to fill it in.

"It really does look like a nightmare," Monika said when she came out onto the terrace with her book.

Janek stopped drawing. "I don't have the hand for this."

"No one expects you to draw like an artist, Frank. Just try to make it schematic."

"This is pretty much it," he said. He pointed to a small table set before the portrait. "I think the objects were here."

"Well, that's something, isn't it?"

"What do you mean?"

"You never mentioned a table before."

Janek nodded. She was right; he hadn't mentioned it because he hadn't remembered it.

"Well, they had to be set out on something, didn't they?"

Monika smiled. "Keep drawing, Frank. Sooner or later you'll work it out."

By the end of the afternoon he had not resolved the objects in terms of their shapes, but he had positioned them, indicated by X's, in a straight line on the table.

He showed the sketch to Monika. She studied it. "The arrangement's strange," she said. "Maybe that's important."

"What do you mean?"

She shook her head. "The way everything is lined up, the table, the painting, the niche. It's hieratic, almost like the apse of a church. The table could be the altar. And the objects—"

He leaned toward her. "Yes?"

"They're equally spaced, symmetrically set out. Almost like relics. Or offerings . . ."

"Offerings to the portrait?"

She thought about that. "Perhaps. But I think it goes deeper. Suppose, instead of the portrait, there was something else in that niche, a sculpture or a painting of Christ on the cross. You wouldn't say the gold chalices on the altar were offerings to the painting. You'd say they were offerings to Jesus or to God."

Janek sat up. "That's it!" he said. "What I saw were offerings to the woman in the picture."

"Who is she?"

"Beverly told Aaron it was a portrait of her mother, who died a few years ago." He paused, then pointed to the table in the sketch. "I don't think there was a table here. I think I saw something else. Something like a table, but with a different shape beneath. I'll try and draw it."

He turned over a page of his pad, then started feverishly to draw. She stood behind him as he tried out a shape, crossed it out, tried another and still another.

"In the police photos there wasn't anything beneath the picture. Aaron thinks it took him about two minutes to reach me after he heard my shot. Beverly got to the bedroom just after I fell. If there was something there, she'd have had time to move it."

He drew an oval, then drew a rectangle over it.

"If she moved it, it couldn't have been very big," Monika said.

"I think it was big. But maybe it was lighter than it looked."

"Where could she have hidden it?"

He shrugged, drew a bookcase, then redrew it so its bottom half stuck out. "It could have been portable, on wheels, or something like a card table that folds up." He drew an angry slash across the page. "Shit, I don't know!"

Monika, behind him, massaged his shoulders. "Let it go for now, Frank. You've done enough today."

"It's so maddening. I can almost see it. But not quite."

"Of course, it's maddening. Like forgetting someone's name even when you can see his face."

"Exactly!"

"What do you do when that happens?"

"Rack my brains till I come up with his name."

"If that doesn't work?"

"I forget about it awhile."

"Then?"

"It usually comes to me later when I'm thinking about something else or doing something strange like eating peas."

"When you're *consciously* thinking about something else. Meantime, the subconscious part of your brain is processing the problem. You can let the same thing happen here, let your subconscious take over and do the work. Eventually the solution will come, probably sometime tonight."

"Then what?"

"Then on to the next problem. You see, the wonderful thing about drawing an encrypted dream is that it gives you a chance to break down a big riddle into smaller and more manageable parts. What you want to do is get the table right, then go on to the objects."

He gazed at her. "Anyone ever tell you you're terrific?"

"Oh, all the time," she said. "My patients are always telling me that."

"You're kidding!"

She smiled. "Shrinks are used to hearing endearments. But when I hear them from you, Frank, I know they're real."

That night they ate dinner in the house, then drove down to the village to walk. A Mexican boy with gleaming teeth approached them on the street. He showed them a tray of handmade silver jewelry. When Monika showed interest in a pair of earrings, Janek bought them for her. The boy held out a cracked piece of mirror so she could look at herself as she put them on.

Later they stopped outside a modest bar that fronted on the beach. There was a light breeze that made the palms sway and churned up the smooth surface of the Gulf. Someone was playing a piano inside. "Looks like a decent saloon," Janek said.

The place was half filled. The high season wouldn't begin until Christmas. Janek and Monika took a table between the bar and the pianist, a young black woman with a red scarf tied around her head. She was playing the kind of restful dinner music that doesn't require much attention.

Janek grinned. "I'm glad we could have this week together." He paused. "Do you really have to fly home on Christmas?"

"I wish I didn't," she said. "But I have patients waiting and an early class the following day."

He looked at her. "I usually spend my holidays alone."

She leaned across the table and kissed him. "Not this year."

When the waiter brought their margaritas, Monika asked him in Spanish about the pianist. The waiter said she was a gringo. "But a nice one," he added.

Janek turned to look at the piano.

"I wonder . . ."

"What?"

"That table I drew, the table that wasn't a table—I wonder if it could have been a piano." He took a sip from his drink. "I don't see how it could have been. A piano's much too big. Hard to hide a piano even if it's on wheels." He took another sip. "Still, it had that piano shape, like a little upright, you know, with the objects arranged on the top just below the bottom edge of the painting."

He summoned the waiter, borrowed a ballpoint, made a quick sketch on his cocktail napkin. He turned it so Monika could see. "Something like that," he said.

She stared at the sketch. "Didn't you tell me the portrait seemed bigger in the dream than in Aaron's photographs?" Janek nodded. "We know the portrait didn't change. It's the same one you saw. But suppose there was a piece of furniture just under it, something that because of its scale made the picture seem bigger than it was."

Janek nodded. "Take that piece of furniture away, and the portrait would appear smaller. It's still life-size, but in the dream it looms over everything." He thought a moment. "Suppose it wasn't a real piano. Suppose it was a miniature or a model. That would be enough to confuse the scale, at least at a quick glance. And if it was a miniature piano, she could have hidden it."

"Hidden the relics, too, dispersed them around the room."

"Yes . . . the relics." Janek finished off his drink. "I like that word. Relics offered up to the image of her mother in the little chapel she constructed in her bedroom niche. Consecrated relics, you could say, or sanctified ones. Perhaps more than relics. Perhaps trophies, trophies of acts committed in her mother's honor. Mementos of sacrifices. Tributes offered in thanks or to appease."

He looked at Monika, nodded. "You were right this afternoon when you used the word 'hieratic.' That bedroom was a fucking shrine."

That night he didn't dream about the whole room, only about the portrait. In his dream the woman's face came alive, her eyes blinked open, and her mouth opened and shut mechanically like a doll's. He woke up drenched in sweat.

In the morning he gulped his coffee, then hurried out to the terrace to draw. He sketched the painting and an underscale piano beneath it and then made X's on the piano's top. How many trophies had there been? He drew various quantities. When that didn't work, he took another approach. There had been seventeen Wallflower killings in all. He drew seventeen X's on top of the piano. Too crowded. But there had been only seven victim clusters. When he drew seven X's, the design looked right.

He turned the page, started to draw on another sheet. He drew basic geometric shapes: cubes; boxes; cylinders; spheres. Then he started to put them together. The work possessed him. Soon he forgot where he was. He tried various combinations of shapes, filling a dozen sheets by noon. Then, exhausted, he pushed back the pad and tried to look at his sketches objectively.

He believed he had successfully rendered three of the relics, or trophies as he thought of them now. One was a small book, another a large book, and the third a piece of paper with printing on it. Assigning them to the first, third, and fourth positions, he drew them into his master drawing, replacing the first, third, and fourth X's on top of the piano. Examining his master drawing again, he was pleased. The three trophies looked right, in their correct positions, too. He put down his pad and sat back exhausted. He had worked five hours straight.

That afternoon, after making love, he and Monika followed steps, cut from stone outcroppings, straight down from their little house to the beach. It was only when he was in the water and tasted its saltiness that he realized his eyes hadn't teared up in the twenty-four hours since he'd started working with the crayons.

At the end of the afternoon, back on their terrace, relaxing with margaritas in their hands, he showed Monika what he'd accomplished in the morning.

"Two books and a piece of paper. All rectangular and more or less flat," she commented. "You're doing fine, Frank, going about it methodically, working from abstract shapes. So far so good. But if you get stuck, you might want to give up control of your crayon, let it loose on the paper. It's a method I sometimes use to get patients to free-associate. You'd be amazed at the powerful material that spews out. Of course, if you do let yourself go, doodle or draw at random, it won't be the crayon that's guiding your hand; it'll be your subconscious."

They drove down to Cozumel for dinner, choosing the same quiet fish joint they'd enjoyed their first night on the island. As they ate, Monika asked him what bothered him most about Kit and Aaron's explanation of the Wallflower crimes.

"Too neat," he said. "Real life isn't like that. Real life, as you know, is very complicated, with all sorts of twists and turns, trails that split off and dead-end or tail back. But this Diana Proctor story comes out slick, almost like a novel. Whenever I see a structure like that, I ask myself, 'Who's the writer here?' "

"Why do you call it slick?"

"First, the way it was revealed. Right after the shoot-out, Aaron goes down to the basement. There he finds this incredibly complete paper trail in almost perfect secretarial order that accounts for each and every ice pick and Wallflower homicide. Diana flies into Seattle; the ticket stubs are there. She rents a car at the airport, returns it the following morning; the receipt is neatly stapled to the ticket stubs. Aaron asks the Seattle cops to check the mileage between the airport and Cynthia Morse's condominium; the answer that comes back is exactly half the distance that shows up on Diana's car rental slip. That's the kind of perfection you don't usually find in real life."

"She was a librarian. Librarians are organized."

"Sure, but this is better than organized. Every time she went out she knew exactly where to go, never got lost, never made a slip. A killer working on her own, even a highly organized one, can't be that precise. But if she was working with someone else, war-gaming her missions, then such superb execution might be possible."

"So it's the perfection that bothers you?"

"And all the papers that back it up."

"But Beverly couldn't know you'd go into her house and fight it out with Diana."

"Of course not. And she also couldn't know how it would end up if we did. I could have injured Diana, in which case she'd have been available for questioning, and then Beverly's role, if she played one, would probably have come out."

"What are you saying, Frank?"

"That Beverly might have been planning to get rid of Diana, leaving the whole neat paper trail so we'd pin everything on the girl. By a fluke I got to Diana first. But that's speculation. There're other things that bother me, too."

"What?"

"Why did Diana shave her head and body and go around in a wig? We're supposed to believe she was some sort of austere self-styled ninja. It's possible. But maybe there's another explanation. Maybe the shaving was part of a system of control."

"Beverly's control?"

He nodded. "Then there're the victims. I've got a whole lot of problems with them. We can account for the homeless man, and we know Diana had some sort of relationship with Jess. But what about the three victim clusters connected to Beverly Archer? If Diana was operating on her own, how did she come up with those particular people? Did she choose them at random from the hundreds of names she found in Beverly's papers, or was there a reason she chose those particular three? Then you have to ask yourself how Beverly could have been so blind to what Diana was doing. Sullivan's people came up with a couple of cases where a serial killer committed murders while in treatment with a shrink.

But this is different. Beverly was an experienced therapist who knew her patient very well. She'd been treating the girl for six years straight, had her living in her basement, was seeing her four times a week. You're a psychiatrist, Monika. Can you imagine being that familiar with a patient without sensing something bad was going on?"

Monika thought about it. "Patients can be very deceptive. But you're right—it's extremely difficult to imagine that. I also wonder how someone as young as Diana could become so expert at subterfuge."

"That's why I think Beverly was a collaborator, even the brains behind the whole series. The problem, of course, is to prove it. To do that, I have to know why, what she was up to, what her game was all about."

"What do you think it was about?"

"You read Beverly's paper on shaming incidents. She seemed to specialize in patients traumatized by shaming events in their pasts. Doesn't an obsession like that usually come from within?"

"It can, certainly. Shrinks who concentrate on homosexuals often are homosexual. Shrinks who specialize in sadomasochism tend to be haunted by that type of fantasy."

"Well, suppose Beverly was as traumatized by shaming incidents as any of her patients? Suppose, to rid herself of her obsession, she decided that the people who had humiliated her should be killed? Suppose she recruited Diana in Carlisle, created a dependency, then arranged for the girl's release so she could send her out on missions of revenge? The targets would be her old tormentors, even as far back as her childhood."

"I thought Aaron said Beverly hadn't been in favor of Diana's release."

Janek nodded. "There's another thing that's slick. It's like it was all a setup from the start. Beverly carefully laid down a paper trail at the hospital that would throw police suspicions off, then laid down a second paper trail in Diana's room in the basement that would cinch the story the girl was acting on her own."

"You're talking about something extremely fiendish, a conspiracy that goes back years."

"Yeah." He grinned. "And now there's another character. The mother in the portrait, the one behind the piano altar, who gets trophies offered up to her of the people Beverly had Diana kill."

Early the next morning, a Sunday, Janek hurried out to the terrace to draw. When his abstract geometric shapes didn't join into anything recognizable, he changed his approach and, employing Monika's method, freed his crayon from conscious control and let it loose upon the paper.

At first he scribbled numerous spirals. When Monika looked in on him, she muttered something about double helixes and human chromosomes.

He played with vertical spirals, then horizontal ones, then cylinders with spiral decorations. One of the last set looked right, but when he couldn't make it coherent, he turned to Monika for help.

"Which position is this one for?" she asked.

"Number two."

"The second killing?" He nodded. "That was the old school-teacher in Florida."

"Bertha Parce."

"Did you see pictures of her?"

"About twenty slides."

"Anything strike you?"

"Just that she was a withered old lady living in a crowded single room in some horrible old folks' hotel on South Beach, Miami."

"Was she stabbed in her room?"

He nodded. "She was asleep."

"Anything else strike you?"

"Just the wallflower. I remember the FBI briefing officer pointing it out. It was sort of leaning in the corner of the room."

"Anything else?"

Janek closed his eyes, trying to recall the photographs he'd pinned to his office walls in New York. "There was a lot of junk around, old lady's stuff." He hesitated. "Come to think of it . . ." He began to draw again, this time imposing his will upon the crayon. "I'm on to something. . . ." He continued to draw and in three minutes rendered an object that fitted perfectly in position two. "That's it. Yeah, I'm sure it is." He turned his master sketch so she could see it.

"What is it?" she asked.

"A hair curler. Old Bertha Parce had a whole mess of them on the table beside her bed." He picked up a blue crayon, began to fill the curler in. "The one I saw in Beverly's apartment was made of light blue plastic," he explained.

I't took him until the end of the day to render the sixth trophy. The problem, which he only discovered late in the afternoon, was that it consisted of two objects rather than one. And that made sense when he remembered that the fifth victim cluster had consisted of two men, brothers named MacDonald, who shared a weekend house in northwestern Connecticut.

In the end he drew two sticks side by side. But they weren't just ordinary sticks. There was something unique about them, portions that stuck out. Remembering Monika's questions from the morning, he began to ask similar questions of himself. What was in the crime scene pictures? Was there anything he'd seen in them that might resemble sticks?

One of the brothers, he remembered, has been stabbed in his bed. The other, whose palms had borne defensive wounds, had put up a struggle in the bathroom.

Janek left the terrace, went inside the house, phoned Aaron at his home in Brooklyn.

"Hi," he said when Aaron answered. "Good thing I caught you."

Janek asked Aaron if he'd be willing to go into the office, even though it was a Sunday, and take a look at some of the pictures pinned up on their walls.

"Jesus, Frank," Aaron said. "I thought you went down there to rest."

"I am resting," Janek said. "I've been lying out on the terrace with a view of the sea, taking in the rays."

"But you're still thinking about it?"

"Doing more than that. Monika's got me working with crayons."

"Jesus!"

"I want you to look at the Bertha Parce pictures and see if you can tell if any of the hair curlers beside her bed are missing. Then check out the pictures at the MacDonald house. See if you notice anything missing there."

Aaron agreed to drive into Manhattan, check the photographs, and call him back. The call came an hour and a half later.

"Yeah, Frank, there's a box of old lady's hair curlers just like you remembered. But it's partially closed, so I can't tell if the set's complete."

"What about the brothers?"

"I'm standing in front of the shots right now. I don't see anything in the bedroom. It's minimal, neat and clean, not like the old lady's place. But it looks like they shared the bath. I see two of everything—hairbrushes, razors—you know, the kind of stuff guys use."

Something in Aaron's voice told Janek he was holding back.

"You *do* see something, don't you?"

"Jesus, Frank! Even from Mexico you can read my mind."

"What is it?"

"No toothbrushes. Could they be the odd-shaped sticks you're talking about?"

Janek turned to Monika. "Toothbrushes. A pair of toothbrushes, lined up side by side."

"Sounds like you're getting excited," Aaron said.

"I'll be a lot more excited when I get this whole thing figured out."

"Still think Beverly was behind it?"

"I *know* she was. We're going to prove it, too."

He asked Aaron to spend the next few days working on the two non-Archer-connected victim clusters, the Wexler family in Texas and the Scottos in Providence. Aaron was to check by phone with people who knew them—survivors, friends, colleagues at work.

And he was to be sure to inquire about both husbands and wives since they didn't know which family members were the intended targets.

"What am I inquiring about?" Aaron asked.

"What do you think?"

"A Beverly Archer connection."

"Of course, because if you find one, we'll know she lied to you. If she *did* know those people, just one member in each family, that's enough to go to Kit for authorization to reopen the case."

"What authorization do I have to do this?"

"You're wrapping up loose ends."

"Maybe I should check out Diana, too, see if there's a connection to her."

"Sure, go ahead," Janek said casually. "But you won't find anything. Beverly's the one."

The next morning he drew and drew but couldn't get anywhere with trophy number five. One thing he knew: It wasn't a simple shape like a toothbrush, a hair curler, or a book. It was an elaborate object, larger than the others, something with parts that stuck out all over.

"Some of the parts are like the hair curler," he told Monika as they climbed down to the beach. "It's got wheels and a handle. It's mostly metal, but I think the handle's made of wood. I even think there're gears on it." He paused. "What the hell could it be?"

They made an encampment at the bottom of the rocks. She spread her beach towel on the sand, then lay down on her back. "If it's got moving parts, it must be some kind of machine," she said.

"Yeah . . ." He looked at her. She was wearing a brilliant white bikini that contrasted with her lightly tanned skin. "Pretend for a moment you're Diana Proctor. You've been sent up to Providence to kill a person and bring back a trophy of your kill. What kind of trophy are you going to take?"

Monika raised her head. "I won't know what I'm going to take until I see it. It'll be a spontaneous decision."

Janek lay back and stared up at the sky. "Whatever it is, you're bringing it back to Beverly to put up on the piano altar for Mama. Won't you make a point of bringing back something you know will please your shrink? It can't be valuable. It can't be something that will be missed. And it certainly can't be an object that can be traced back to the people you've just killed. It's always something humble, like a hair curler, or a couple of toothbrushes, a piece of paper, a book. Something the victims have touched. Something almost . . . intimate, don't you think?" He turned to look at Monika. She was gazing past him. "Forgive me," he said, "I'm thinking out loud. I know it's tiresome. I'm sorry to go on and on."

She stood. "It's okay, Frank. You told me you were a worrier." She looked out at the water. "I'm going to swim. Want to come?"

He shook his head. "I'll just lie here and worry."

She smiled, then started for the water. He watched as she ran across the beach, then high-stepped into the waves. When she was out far enough, she turned, threw him a kiss, and plunged. He watched her swim for a while, then lay back, closed his eyes, and tried to free his mind of the fifth trophy for a while.

Think about something else, he told himself. *Or better yet, don't think about anything at all. Just lie here and feel the sun. Breathe in the mellow aroma of the sea. Let the sweet winds of this tropical paradise caress your tough old urban hide.*

He must have drifted off. The next thing he knew droplets of water were dancing on his chest. He opened his eyes. Monika was leaning over him, vigorously drying her hair.

"Good swim?"

"Terrific." She spread out her towel. "I was bobbing around out there, trying to think what's made of metal, has wheels and gears and a wooden handle, and has parts that look like hair curlers. I came up with something." She lay down. "It's what you call a real long shot."

He leaned toward her eagerly. "What've you got?"

She grinned. "How does an old-fashioned eggbeater grab you?"

A piece of paper with printing for the homeless man. A hair curler for Bertha Parce. A small book, probably a much-read paperback for the Wexler family. An oversize book for Cynthia Morse. A pair of neatly arranged tooth-brushes for the MacDonalds. An eggbeater for the Scottos. That left only position seven, the last trophy position, the Jessica Foy position, marked with an X.

He couldn't bring himself to try to draw that trophy. He couldn't even bear to think about it. Or did he resist, as Monika suggested, because to render it would make the scene in the bedroom clear and then he would no longer be haunted by his dream?

When he asked her to explain that, she said people often resist giving up a source of pain.

"Imagine how you'd feel without it, Frank? What would it be like *not* to be tormented?"

"I'd love it."

"You think so? I'm not so sure."

"Why wouldn't I love that? I don't understand."

She sat down on his chaise, placed her hand upon his knee. "Physically you're fine. Your body's mended. But your mind is wounded still. Like anybody who's spent years living dangerously, you've become addicted to stress. If you saw the seventh trophy, the puzzle would be solved and the stress would be relieved." She spoke kindly. "Maybe you're not yet ready for that. I think maybe you need to suffer awhile longer. Don't you?"

He stared down at the water, then slowly turned back to her. His eyes, she saw, were filled with tears.

They had leased the house for five days, intending to spend their last two on the mainland in Yucatán, where Monika wanted to visit some of the great Mayan ruins. So on the fifth day they flew from the Isla de Cozumel to

Mérida, where they checked into a low all-white Moorish-style hotel set amidst a tranquil park of pools, flowering jacarandas, and palms.

The next morning they rented a car and went exploring. They had prepared for this visit by reading about the Mayans, enough so that they would know the purposes of the structures and the basic meaning of the art that they would see. But they were far less interested in archaeology than in viscerally experiencing the sites.

On the weed-choked field before the great pyramid at Chichén Itzá, Monika admitted to being deeply intrigued by the ancient Mayan cult of cruelty. Janek was attentive as she spoke. She made a stunning figure, he thought, dressed in white cotton slacks and a white polo shirt, her old Leica hanging casually from her shoulder, her face framed by the silver earrings he had bought for her in Cozumel.

"Human sacrifices," she said, "priests in bejeweled robes excising hearts from naked living persons on a high altar before multitudes of witnesses—it was an atavistic culture, Frank, obsessed by astrology, magical beasts, worship of the sun, sacrifices to gods who demanded blood." She paused. "In my profession we speak of the subconscious as if it were a kind of jungle like the one around us here. Dark, dank, overgrown, filled with snakes, reptiles, and other threatening creatures, a place where the most elemental drives, to dominate, rape, avenge, and kill, thrive without constraint. Well, here we have a place cut out of such a jungle where ancient men created a great civilization. And what did they do? They didn't suppress their animal drives. Rather, they organized them, turned them into a religion of cosmic symbols and dramatic ceremonies." She paused again. "Perhaps they were a little like the Venetians in that regard. Remember their carnival costumes and winged horses and the churches everywhere we turned?"

He loved listening to her. She was the most brilliant woman he'd ever been involved with. And the things she said found a responsive chord. He believed she was right, that there was as much cruelty in the masterpiece that was Venice as in this ancient capital

of Mayan culture. A different kind of cruelty perhaps, more refined, less direct, but in the end nearly as ruthless and as bloody.

He borrowed her camera, took a picture of her. Looking through
the lens, he saw a beautiful woman poised against sunstruck stone
ruins with dense green jungle foliage behind. Perhaps, he kidded
her, she might want to use his picture to represent herself on the
back of her next book.

"You know," he said, "the gorgeous and brainy German shrink
visiting the cradle of high barbarism in Central America."

Later, as they explored the site, strode along its walls, among
its steles, gazing at the sculptures incised into the stones—grotesque human figures in elaborate headdresses, mouths grimacing,
eyes bulging, frozen in postures that suggested the commission of
violent acts—Janek asked Monika if these images were not expressions of the evil that had always fascinated him and that, he so
often claimed, he struggled in his work to comprehend.

The answer she gave surprised him a little bit: "Perhaps it isn't
merely the mystery of evil that intrigues you, Frank. Perhaps it's
something bigger, the mystery of the human mind."

"I think you know what the sev-
enth trophy is," she told him that evening.

They were back in Mérida, sipping tequila by the hotel pool
beside an open thatch-roofed garden bar. Janek looked around.
There were two other couples and a black-haired Mexican bartender with Indian features gazing at the setting sun. On the tables
were tiny hurricane lamps. The candles flickered in the dying light.

"If I know what it is, I sure can't see it now," he said. "What
makes you think I know?"

"The trophy taken from Jess should be the easiest one for you
to figure out."

"Because she was jogging?" Monika nodded. "She had a watch
and the keys to her room on a leather thong around her neck. She
was wearing a Walkman. All those things were found." He heard
his voice break. It still disturbed him to talk about Jess this way,

as a homicide victim instead of a person he had loved. "What else could she have been carrying?"

Monika shook her head. Her expression was compassionate. "I think you know," she said quietly.

Later in their room, as they lay naked together on their bed while the ceiling fan revolved slowly overhead, he broached the subject again.

"You think you know what it is, don't you?"

She looked at him. "I could venture a guess."

"But you won't tell me?" She shook her head. "Why not?"

"It's better for you to tell me, Frank," she said in a whisper.

In the morning he was angry. He spoke harshly while they dressed.

"I'm not in therapy. This isn't about me. It's a fucking murder case. Why won't you help?"

She turned to him. She spoke calmly. She was buckling her belt. "Why must I tell you what you already know?"

"Damn it, Monika! Don't speak to me in riddles!"

She stood still and faced him. Her eyes were sad. "Of course this is about you, Frank," she said gently. "It's your dream, your vision. Why don't you just close your eyes and look inside yourself? It's there. All you have to do is look."

After breakfast they went out to the hotel pool for an early swim. He watched her as she breast-stroked back and forth. *Who am I kidding?* he asked himself. *I loved Jess. I ought to know what Diana took from her.* But what was missing? He couldn't think of anything. What would Jess carry when she went out jogging? *Maybe there was no seventh trophy,* he thought.

It came to him on the plane that afternoon, shortly after they had taken off for New York. They were crossing the Gulf of Mexico, still and green below. He peered out the window, and then he saw it in the pattern of the reefs.

He turned to Monika beside him. "It was a knife."

She nodded. "I think so, too."

"That switchblade she bought at the knife show, the one Fran Dunning said had an ivory handle. I'm sure that's what I saw."

She squeezed his hand. "Feel better now?"

He leaned toward her, kissed her. "Thanks. You were right, I must have known what it was. Why did I fight it?"

"I think it hurt you to see her knife sitting there. Your hurt blinded you, and then you couldn't see the other trophies either."

"But why did it hurt so much?"

"Because it was hers. And possibly because of something else. If she was carrying a knife, she could have put up a fight. But she didn't get the chance. She was attacked from behind. The thought of that still makes you furious. Your fury may have blinded you as well."

It was a dazzling New York that greeted them, cold but brilliant, a city of sparkling granite and shimmering glass. As they taxied into Manhattan, Janek was struck by the difference between this arrival and his arrival from Venice eight weeks before. That day he and Aaron had driven though a damp and noxious fog that matched the sorrow and confusion in his soul. Today, with Monika, the air was clear. And now, too, he knew what he was up against.

They settled into Janek's apartment, then at dusk went out to walk. Upper Broadway was filled with Christmas shoppers. On Fifth Avenue all the stores were jammed. Santas with scraggly beards stood on corners rattling pails. At Rockefeller Center skat-

ers glided across the ice, while above the golden statue of Prome-
theus, Christmas lights blazed upon an enormous spruce.

They ate in a little Czech restaurant on West Twelfth Street. The
owner, who had known Janek's father, embraced him when they
walked in. After dinner they strolled through Greenwich Village.
There were crowds of young people out on the streets, many
walking briskly on their way to parties while others, grasping bags
choked with gifts, attempted to flag down cabs. Foursomes stood
on corners making jokes, waiting for traffic lights to change. A
drunken old man, in a tweed suit and bow tie, stumbled past them
mouthing the lyrics to "Hark! The Herald Angels Sing."

"I love this energy," Monika said. "New York's a fascinating
town."

"It's no Venice, but it takes a bum rap," Janek said. "It's a cruel
place, but it can be wonderful, too."

She nodded. "I've often wondered what it would be like to live
here. I've been offered a visiting professorship of psychiatry. Last
month the Albert Einstein College of Medicine approached me
again. Perhaps I should accept, move here for a year." She looked
at him. "A year of living dangerously."

"We could get to know each other pretty well over a year," he
said.

She smiled, took his arm. "I wish I didn't have to go back so
soon. But sadly I do."

Later that night, at his apart-
ment, he asked if she'd be willing to take a look at Beverly Archer.

"Just to observe her," he said. "She'll never know."

Monika thought about it, then agreed. "I'm not a forensic psychiatrist. I doubt I'll see anything. But I confess—I'm very curious."

Janek phoned Aaron, asked if he could set it up. Aaron thought
he could. Beverly's schedule was so rigid, he said, there shouldn't
be any difficulty arranging a covert surveillance. They'd park on

Second Avenue down the block from her house and wait for her to come out after her last appointment. When she started on her round of errands, Monika could follow her and observe.

$\mathbf{T}$he plan worked. At exactly six fifty-five the following evening Beverly appeared. When she went into a dry cleaning shop, Monika got out of the car and followed. Sitting with Aaron, waiting for her to return, Janek started feeling nervous.

"This reminds me of one very bad night."

Aaron reassured him. "I know it's spooky, Frank, but your girl's terrific. Don't worry. Beverly's met her match."

When Monika returned, she was shivering. Janek took her hands, rubbed them to restore warmth. She seemed disturbed. "Let's go get something to drink," she said.

Aaron drove down Second to a cop hangout near East Seventy-first. The place was filled, cops full of holiday bluster toasting one another with mugs of beer. Janek and Aaron nodded to acquaintances; then the three of them squeezed into a booth.

"A strange woman," Monika reported after the waiter had brought her tea. "A lot of people in my field are. The profession's always attracted troubled individuals. They often make gifted therapists."

"So she's just another weirdo shrink, is that what you're saying?" Aaron asked.

Monika shook her head. "More than that. She functions, of course, very well from what you've told me. But I felt I was observing an extremely high-strung person, very tense, very tightly controlled. The way she moves, dresses, smiles at the sales clerks, tilts her head, tightens up her lips—it's as if there's a NO CONTACT! DON'T TOUCH ME! sign hanging on her back. Still, for all her smiles I could feel the rage coming off her. Sexual rage, too. She truly hates males. It shows every time she deals with one."

Aaron glanced at Janek. "Could she have done what Frank says?"

"Sent the girl out to kill her old enemies? I can't tell that from looking at her. But in theory, yes, it's possible."

"But by using a surrogate killer," Janek asked, "didn't she give up the pleasures of killing the old enemies herself?"

"Not necessarily. The pleasures might have been even greater for her. She'd have the satisfaction of knowing she had done them in fiendishly, and I think it would have been very exciting for her to hear Diana describe the glue mutilations, too. That would have been the best part of it, perhaps the only erotic excitement she's capable of having."

Monika went on to analyze the paradox in a person such as Beverly, who, though ostensibly asexual, could still take an intense sexual interest in her victims.

"The brain is more flexible than people think," she explained. "It can do a kind of somersault. What seems disgusting can suddenly become appetizing; what's repulsive can suddenly become erotic. In a flash a person can become addicted to the very thing he or she previously hated. It's a way to survive in the world, to turn pain into pleasure, to take the worst, most painful scenarios of one's childhood and, by controlling them, rewrite the script so that in the new final act there is victory rather than defeat."

"Beverly's victories are the executions, right? Executions of the people who humiliated her in the past?"

"Again, we're talking theory, Frank. After only fifteen minutes of observation I can't tell you this woman did what you think. But yes, she *could* have done it, and if she did, I don't think her victories would have been just the executions. To me the neuterings are far more important. Killing an old enemy is one thing. Doing something to his body is quite another. Attacking the genitals, the seat of your enemy's sexuality, is the ultimate revenge. To have another person do it for you and then describe it is a way of distancing yourself while still enjoying your old tormentor's degradation. It's like hearing about something bad that has befallen a rival. You didn't do it, you didn't dirty your hands, but you have the satisfaction of knowing that the person has been dealt a devastating blow. We have a special word for that in German. *Schadenfreude.* It means taking joy in another's pain. If you're right, I think *Schadenfreude* may be what Beverly Archer is all about."

"Okay," said Aaron. "That makes sense. But could she have gotten Diana to kill and glue all those people? We know the girl killed her mother, grandmother, and sister. But except for Jess, the others all seem to have been perfect strangers."

"It's not that difficult for one person to gain control over another's mind," Monika said. "Behavioral methods, hypnosis, rote training, rewards and punishments, plain old-fashioned domination—there are many ways. The basic method is simple: get someone dependent and susceptible in your power; then circumscribe her world so that your commands have the power of laws. You see it all the time in cults, prisons, terrorist groups, pathological personal relationships. In Nazi Germany you saw it on the extraordinary scale of an entire nation. There's a part in all of us that responds to force and craves to be controlled. We want to be led, commanded, told what to do. If it weren't for that particular trait, human society probably wouldn't work. But what is extremely difficult is to force someone to perform an act completely contrary to his moral nature. Here, however, you have a girl, still young and malleable, who had not only killed people before but afterwards attacked their sexual organs. The distance from ax to ice pick, from chopping at genitals to imprisoning them with glue, is not all that great. So, to answer your question, yes, everything Frank has theorized is absolutely possible. But whether it happened or not . . . I'm not the one to say."

Late in the afternoon on Christmas Eve, Janek went down to Police Plaza to see Kit Kopta. This time the crusty red-haired sergeant who ran her office greeted him with warmth.

"How's the shoulder, detective? The throat?" And before Janek could answer: "That was one close call. Too bad you had to wax the girl. Luck of the draw, I guess. Anyway, Merry Christmas!"

Kit rose when he came in. "You look grand, Frank. I don't think I've ever seen you with a tan."

"Well, it was a great trip."

She smiled. "I can just imagine the two of you snuggling on some Mexican beach. What I'd give for a little vacation."

"Why don't you take one? God knows you deserve it."

She laughed. "Sure. Check into a Club Med. Have a three-day affair with a gorgeous Nordic ice god, the kind with a stomach so hard you can use it for a washboard. Make an ass out of myself trying to stuff my body into a bikini. Hang out at the bar, pay for drinks with little doodads off my necklace, and wish to hell I was back here in good old tit-freezing New York, where at least I don't have to act jolly or pretend I'm having a good time."

Janek shook his head. "Are you always like this on Christmas Eve?"

"It's not as if I had a nice husband to go home to." She smiled. "I'll probably end the evening curling up with a bottle. But I'm not bitter. Maybe a little ironic, that's all." She sat down behind her desk, turned serious. "Now what's all this about you wanting to reopen the case?"

It took Janek twenty minutes to lay out his theory of the Wall-flower crimes. Kit didn't interrupt him or nod encouragement; she just gazed steadily into his eyes. When he finally finished, she asked him what exactly he wanted her to authorize.

"An investigation."

"What sort of investigation?"

He squinted at her. Her tone seemed hard. "What's the matter? My theory too farfetched?"

She stood, walked over to the window, stared down at Police Plaza. "Sure, it's farfetched. You know it is. But so is the theory you were too smart to swallow, the one Sullivan and his people seem to have bought whole hog."

"So what's the problem?"

She turned to face him. Her thick black hair framed her little face. "The problem is if you hadn't nearly gotten killed that night, I'd have put IA on your ass."

"What're you talking about?"

She glared at him. "You and Aaron and your phony story that you just happened to be watching when this burglar let himself into Archer's house—do you really think I bought that crap? Don't insult me, please!"

Janek stared at the rug. He'd made a point of forgetting that extralegal maneuver. Now, reminded of it, he felt ashamed.

"It was a look-and-see operation, wasn't it?" she continued. "Not the most subtle one I ever heard about either. I figure the black kid was Aaron's snitch from the time he worked Safes and Lofts."

Janek spread his arms. "It was my idea. It was wrong. I'm sorry I did it."

"Still, it worked for you. Got you inside, got you a quick look at some stuff, and now you've built a pretty theory around it. Fine. Maybe you're right. Maybe this Beverly Archer is the evil, manipulative murderess you say. Anything's possible, Frank. But you'll never get her for it, not if you're going to carry on like that."

"I'm not going to carry on like that. I won't do anything like that again."

She looked at him, rolled her eyes, and returned to her desk.

They spent the next ten minutes bargaining. He wanted to go to Providence and send Aaron out to Texas to look for Archer connections among the two "unconnected" families. Then he wanted another three weeks of travel for them both to try to discover what incidents may have occurred between Beverly and Bertha Parce, Cynthia Morse, and the MacDonalds. Then he wanted at least ten days in Cleveland, digging out everything there was to be found on the woman. Plus whatever additional travel and per diems might be necessary depending on the information all these interviews produced.

Kit stared at him, her large brown eyes sparkling beneath her Grecian brows.

"Basically you're asking for unlimited backing on a theory neither of us has the nerve to broach to the FBI."

"You always said my instincts were good, Kit. Here's a chance to back me up."

"Sure, back you up. Then you get impatient and pull another Leo Titus because your goddaughter was a victim. No thanks, Frank. Forget it."

"I gave you my word. Want me to give it to you in writing?"

She laughed. "Then I'd really have to fire you, wouldn't I? Your written promise would be a confession you broke your oath."

"Shit!" He stood up, angry. "She did it. I know she did. I'm going to nail her, Kit, no matter how long it takes."

Kit studied him. When she spoke again, he could tell by her tone that she'd made a decision.

"Even if you're right, and you just might be, it's the toughest kind of case to make. Suppose you prove Archer was totally fucked over by every single person Diana Proctor killed? So what? You're talking mind murders, Frank. You've got no witnesses, no one you can turn. Diana, your coconspirator, is already dead. It's a dead-end case. You know it is."

Janek tried to interrupt, but Kit motioned him to keep quiet until she was finished.

"I'm telling you the facts of life. No DA will take on a case like that unless you bring him a full confession. How the hell are you going get one? I talked to the woman myself. She's a stone-cold hard-ass. She knows she's out of it; she knows there's no evidence. If you're right and she was behind it, then one of the main reasons she operated the way she did was to insulate herself from a criminal prosecution. So now, tell me, why should she confess?"

He shook his head. "I don't know yet. But she will."

"Going to *make* her, Frank? Going to beat it out of her?"

"Of course not."

"Then how?"

"Underneath the smile she's totally crazed. A crazy person can be broken."

"And you're the man to break her, right?"

"I'll sure give it my best shot," he snapped.

Kit grinned. "Fine. That's fine. I'll go along with that. But unlimited backing . . ." She shook her head. "Between you and Aaron I'll give you three weeks' worth of travel. Split it up any way you like. Plus you can keep your office till the end of January. After that bring me what you've got and we'll reevaluate the case together. But you better bring me something good. Otherwise both of you are going to be reassigned."

It wasn't what he wanted, but he knew it was all he was going to get. After he accepted her offer, she escorted him to the door. Just before she opened it, she lightly touched the scar tissue on his throat.

"I would have been very sorry if something had happened to you, my friend."

He turned to her, kissed her cheek. "You talk tough, Kit, but you're still a pussycat."

She smiled. "I'm glad you found someone, Frank. I liked what I saw of her, especially the way she shot over here when we called to tell her you'd been cut." She stood before him, took hold of both his hands, stared up into his face. "Listen to me. Don't poison the fruit," she warned quietly. "If Archer did it, I want you to nail her. But with a straight nail. Hear me, Frank? Make damn sure that nail goes in her straight. . . ."

When he left Police Plaza, the sky was dark, but the city seemed strangely void of rancor. *It's the holidays,* he thought. But then he remembered: Christmas was the season when New Yorkers turned their rage against themselves. It was the season of suicides.

He found a liquor store open on Nassau Street, went in, bought a chilled bottle of champagne, carried it home on the subway in a paper bag. Monika was waiting for him. They drank it out of the goblet she'd given him in Venice. The wine tasted very good, they agreed. If anything, the ancient glass enhanced it.

He told her about his interview with Kit, the deal they'd made, the pressure he was under now to develop sufficient proof to keep his investigation alive.

"I'm not going to be able to do the kind of deep background work I like," he said. "That'll take months, and we don't have months. No support team either. Just Aaron and me."

"Then you'll have to focus your search," she said.

He nodded. "Any ideas?"

She thought about it. "The lady in the picture, the mother up there on the wall—I'd look to her first. Look to the past, Frank. Try to reconstruct the family history. The secret is always there. . . ."

Later, after they had made love, they clung to each other in the dark. He was filled with passionate adoration for his stylish, brilliant, nurturing German psychoanalyst.

"I love you," he told her in the middle of the night. "I love you more than anyone I've ever known. Has anyone ever said that to you before, Monika? Has anyone ever loved you so much?"

9

The Gauntlet

On Christmas morning he cooked breakfast for Monika, then taxied with her out to Kennedy Airport. After she had checked in, they went to the Lufthansa waiting lounge and exchanged gifts. He presented her with a framed vintage Berenice Abbott photograph of the New York skyline.

"A little remembrance of New York," he said. "I hope this'll make you want to come back."

She held the picture to her chest. "It's beautiful. I love it. But if I come back, it'll be because of you."

Even as he opened her gift, a heavy blue envelope tied with golden ribbon, she apologized for its modest value. He was delighted with what he found inside, a picture she'd snapped of him surreptitiously in Mexico while he lay out on their terrace in his bathing trunks trying to draw the trophies.

"You really helped me. You know that?"

She smiled. "It was for my own benefit. It's hard to sleep next to a guy who's having bad dreams all the time."

"You!" He embraced her. "What am I going to do without you?"

"You'll do fine. Promise me you'll visit soon."

"As soon as this case is finished," he promised.

He waited until her plane took off, then walked slowly back though the nearly empty terminal to catch a bus to Manhattan. There was a certain poignancy, he thought, in the tawdry, commercial Christmas decorations placed sporadically about the airline lobby.

$\mathbf{T}$he next morning he drove out to the airport again, this time to La Guardia to see Aaron off for Cleveland. In front of the terminal Aaron briefed him on the peculiar traits of his car, which he was leaving in Janek's trusted hands.

"She drinks oil the way my ex drank booze, so it's best to check whenever you gas her up. And remember, don't stick your finger in the little hole where the cigarette lighter used to be."

"Yeah, yeah, very funny. Call me when you find something, okay?"

Aaron looked at him. "This is a big one, right?"

Janek nodded. "I thought Sullivan was a real asshole when he called it a great crime. Now I think maybe he was right."

"Don't worry, Frank, I won't blow it. If there's anything out in Cleveland, I'll find it for you."

$\mathbf{T}$hat afternoon, back in the city, Janek waited until it was exactly ten to three. Then he dialed Beverly Archer's number. "Pick it up, butterball," he whispered.

"I know you just finished with a patient. So pick up the goddamn phone."

She answered on the sixth ring.

"It's Janek," he said. "I need to talk. How about tomorrow morning?"

There was a long pause at the other end. "All right." Beverly's voice was steady. "I have a cancellation at eleven."

When he set down the receiver, he looked at his hands. No shaking, no trembling.

I just might bring this off, he thought.

W hen she showed herself at the waiting-room door, she looked exactly as she had the last time they'd talked. Gone were the distraught features and agonized grimaces of Aaron's videotaped interview. She was once again the cool and proper professional, the superior, unflappable clinical psychologist.

"Lieutenant." She smiled her thin-lipped smile.

"Doctor." Janek smiled back, imitating the position of her lips. They stared at each other, engrossed in their mirrored expressions. For just a moment, Janek thought, Beverly looked nonplussed.

As she ushered him into her office, she commented on his healthy appearance. "The last time I saw you, you were bleeding heavily on my bedroom floor. You look a lot better now." The same small, thin-lipped smile.

"You look better, too." He sent her a mental message: *I know you did it!* The idea that she might actually pick up on it filled him with a savage joy. "Last time I saw you," he said, "you were carrying on about what a failure you'd been as Diana Proctor's therapist."

At first she seemed confused. She recovered quickly. "Oh, of course," she said. "On the videotape. I've tried to regain my perspective since then."

"Have you?"

"What?"

"Regained it?"

"Oh, I've tried, Lieutenant. It's a terrible blow when a patient goes off . . . turns out . . . whatever. But there's only so much a person in my position can do. Psychotherapy's not a science; it's not exact. We know so little, you see. And we're all such frail creatures underneath, which, I think, may be the real lesson in all of this. The only thing to do after a failure like Diana is try to pick yourself up and go on as best you can."

"Still," Janek said, "I congratulate you on a remarkable recovery."

She looked at him curiously. "And *I* congratulate you."

"It was a pretty bleak night for both of us."

"I put a cushion under your head. Do you remember?"

"I must have been unconscious. Did you put it there before or after you discovered Diana was dead?"

This time her glance was sharp. "I don't recall. After, I suppose."

"I imagine you were pretty busy before Aaron Greenberg got to the scene?"

"I don't know what you mean."

"With three of us lying there. Two dead, of course. And you still had things to move around."

She stared at him. "I don't know what you're talking about, Lieutenant."

"Okay, Beverly, have it your way, let it go for now." He watched carefully for her reaction to his familiar use of her first name. She looked as if she were trying not to react. "Please forgive my informality, but since I nearly died in your bedroom and you were kind enough to cushion my head—well, I hope it's all right to call you Beverly. I'd like for you to call me Frank."

She smiled. "Thank you. That's fine. I'll feel very comfortable calling you that." She paused. "Now, what can I do for you . . . Frank?"

"I want to ask about the picture of your mother, the one upstairs."

"What about it?"

"I'd like to see it again if you don't mind."

"I don't understand." She was struggling, he could see, to regain her slightly rumpled composure. If there was one thing, it seemed, that Beverly Archer did not like, it was to be caught off guard by a man.

"It made a striking impression on me. I'd like to see it again."

She smiled sweetly, her composure restored. "I'm sorry, Frank, but no house tours today."

He stared at her. She stared back. *Now she knows I know,* he thought. Finally, when she spoke, her smile was guarded. "When you called, I assumed you wanted to talk about Diana. I already told everything to your Sergeant Greenberg and to that very kind Inspector Sullivan of the FBI. But I'll be happy to tell it all again to you—if that's why you're here."

"I didn't come to talk about Diana."

She blinked. "Why did you come?"

"To see you."

"Well, here I am!" She beamed.

"I wanted to look into your eyes."

She squinted. "I get the feeling you're trying to intimidate me, Frank." She paused. "I was told I was cleared."

"Not by me." He grinned.

He could see she didn't know how to react to that, didn't know whether she should grin back or scowl. In the end she tried to preserve her dignity. "Perhaps we should cut this short," she said.

"As you like," Janek said. "But I think you'll be interested to hear what I have to say."

She gazed at him. "I'm waiting."

"You're a very composed woman."

"I suppose I try to be."

"Your poise impresses me. Even the first time I came here, I was impressed. Even when you tried to make me think I had sexual fantasies about my goddaughter." He erased the half-smile from his lips; he wanted her to understand he was serious. "Jess was afraid of you. She left a message on my answering machine. She said she was deathly afraid." He paused. "If I hadn't been abroad at the time, I might have saved her life. But I was away, so she was killed. I hold you responsible for that."

Beverly Archer sat straight up in her chair, her features contorted by fury. "Oh, you're really impossible! That's just absurd!"

"I don't think so."

"Now you listen to me, detective. Before you emote any more garbage, you should know how impossibly stupid you sound. Jessica was *not* frightened of me. She had no reason to be. We were getting along very well. I was helping her. She told me I was. My only regret, and I can understand if you hold me responsible for this, is that I had no knowledge of what was going on between her and Diana. If I'd had any inkling, I assure you I would have taken steps."

She sat back, her lips still trembling. She didn't bother to disguise her anger. Even though he'd broken through her veneer, Janek was impressed. She came across as utterly authentic. *Perhaps she really didn't know,* he thought.

When she spoke again, her tone was more constrained. "For me the tragedy is having to live with my blindness to what was happening between two beloved patients. Neither girl said a word to me, not a solitary word about the other, except for occasional casual remarks. I had no idea they were involved on such an intense level. I wish I'd known. I think I could have done something if I had."

She was, he realized, apologizing to him the only way she knew. Not outright, without equivocation, as would have been appropriate, but tentatively, defensively. She wasn't capable of more.

"Perhaps you didn't know," he said. "Perhaps now you really are suffering over that. But it's hard for me to feel compassion when you speak about a 'tragedy,' and then it turns out what you mean is having to live with your personal failure as a therapist. Both girls are dead. As are seventeen other people. And you're responsible for all of them. I told you Jess was afraid of you. She had good reason to be. Diana told her a tale of being sent to various parts of the country to kill people who had offended you in the past. It was all for Mother, Diana told Jess—Mother, being, of course, your mother, the lady in the picture upstairs. An insane fantasy? Jess wasn't sure. She was just terribly, terribly scared. Well, I've had a lot of time to think about it, Beverly. Brushing close to death tends to focus your thinking. And I've decided that what Diana told

Jess wasn't an insane fantasy at all. I think it was true. I think you were behind every murder Diana Proctor committed, except maybe Jess. And because you weren't behind that one killing, you're able to work up sufficient emotion about it to convince people you had nothing to do with the rest."

He paused for effect. Her eyes were riveted to his. She hated him, of course; her eyes told him that. But no matter her hatred, she could not look away. He held her spellbound with his words.

"I came today to tell you to your face I'm not convinced at all. I see straight through your phony story and your transparent pack of lies. Now I promise you this: When I'm done with you, the whole world will see through them, too." He leaned forward. "You're a mind fucker, Beverly. You mind-fucked Diana. You designated the people she killed. You sent her out to do your dirty work because you didn't have the guts to do your killing for yourself. 'Mind murders' my chief calls them. 'How're you going to prove your case?' I'm not sure. I've got some ideas. We'll see how they turn out. You're sick. You're perverted. I think you're evil." He rose. "That's it. That's why I came, to tell you that, and to let you know I'll be working now full-time to put you away. The game's over, Beverly. No Diana around to protect you anymore. The real fight's about to start. It's just you and me, babe. And I don't intend to lose."

With that he turned on his heel and headed for the door. He opened it, didn't bother to shut it, just kept walking straight through her waiting room, past an attractive college-age girl who gazed after him with fascinated eyes, straight out the front door of her house and onto the street.

He maintained his pace as he walked down to Second Avenue, never once turning around. When at last he was certain he was completely out of view, he stumbled against the brick wall of an apartment building and then, arms extended, leaned against it and gasped.

His head reeled; his forehead was dripping.

God help me, he thought. *I just threw the gauntlet down.*

10

Broken Dreams

When he phoned Monika and told her what he'd done, she was startled and also a little angry.

"Why did you do that, Frank?"

"To unnerve her."

"I understand. But look what happened. You also unnerved yourself."

"Yeah, well, I think it was worth it."

"Listen to me." Her voice was urgent. "She's a dangerous woman. What if she comes after you?"

"With an ice pick and a pot of glue? Don't worry about that. She's the most contemptible type of criminal, a coward. There's nothing she can do to me now. Without her hatchet woman, she's impotent."

There was a pause at the other end. "I wonder if you aren't too close to this."

"Spare me, please, Monika. You sound like Kit."

"Maybe Kit's right. You despise Beverly Archer, don't you?"

"Let's say I don't like her very much." He paused. "Okay, I despise her," he admitted.

"Is that a healthy way to relate to someone you're trying to prove committed a crime?"

"I don't know whether it's healthy, Monika. But I assure you I'm under control. Anyway, there's no law that says I can't have feelings about my work."

"No one objects to your feelings, Frank," she said quietly. "I just don't want to see you . . . hurt yourself over this."

On New Year's Day Aaron called from Cleveland: "Time for you to come out here, Frank."

The next morning, the first workday of the new year, Janek flew to the Midwest. Gray skies, a vast frozen lake, plumes of industrial smoke, a furious late-winter storm. His plane circled Hopkins Airport for three quarters of an hour. Concerned stewardesses with glossy brows and frozen smiles paced nervously. After numerous unctuous announcements from the captain, the plane started down through impenetrable sleet, an endless descent, it seemed to Janek, until finally, unexpectedly, it landed hard. When it jerked to a stop, the relieved passengers applauded and shook their heads. The captain, face red, collar tight, stood nodding at the door. The collected crew wished everyone a happy New Year, a safe continuing journey, and, in the event Cleveland was the final destination, a most pleasant stay.

Aaron was waiting for him by the gate. He hustled Janek into his rental car, then drove into the city on an elevated highway.

"What kind of town is this?" Janek asked, looking down at gas stations, commercial strips, snow-crusted parking lots, endless blocks of drab gray buildings.

Aaron pondered the question. Then he looked up. "Mind if I wax poetic, Frank?"

Janek laughed. "Be my guest."

"Cleveland," Aaron intoned sonorously, "is a Rust Belt town of broken dreams."

Janek nodded; he liked that. And staring out the window, he also decided he liked the town. Perhaps because of the deliberate lack of any appliqué of glamour, he found it oddly glamorous.

Aaron laid out their schedule. He'd arranged three interviews for the afternoon. In his preliminary meetings with the people he hadn't told them much, just that a lieutenant of detectives was coming from New York to ask them questions about Beverly Archer. The case, he'd told them, was important and at this stage, highly confidential. As there were as yet no indictments, informants had been assured their cooperation would be held in confidence.

Something about the way Aaron was talking signaled Janek that he was holding back. "You found something?"

"Yep." Aaron grinned.

"Going to keep it a secret?"

"I think you're going to be surprised," was all Aaron would say.

Their motel, a standard low, sprawling complex, was situated beside a remote shopping mall. Janek checked in, unpacked his stuff, washed his face, then examined himself in the standard motel-room mirror. His tan, acquired in Mexico, had all but disappeared. What he saw was a middle-aged man in an inexpensive business suit with lines in his forehead and bags beneath his eyes. But he noticed something special about this man. *He looks like a guy who doesn't give up.* The idea of that made him feel good. He descended briskly to the lobby, then out to the portico.

"Okay, Aaron," he said, getting into the car, "I'm ready. Let's roll."

$\mathbf{T}$heir first stop was the Ashley-Burnett School for Girls. They drove awhile, entered a posh suburb of impressive homes, then came to an open gate which Janek at first took to be the entrance to a park. A discreet sign pointed the way down a winding, treelined drive. The campus extended on either side, athletic fields and lavish lawns covered with snow, crisscrossed by well-shoveled paths. Finally the school proper came into view, an impressive vine-covered red-brick building with two extended wings.

"This is one ritzy setup," Aaron said as he drove into the visitors' lot. "I didn't know real people sent their kids to joints like this."

As they walked to the administration building, Janek could hear the shrill cries of girls and the scampering of little female feet through the windows of what he took to be the school gym.

"How long did Beverly go here?"

"All twelve grades," Aaron said. "Old Bertha Parce was her high school English teacher." He glanced at Janek. "But later Beverly came back. It was just after she got her Ph.D. She spent a year in Cleveland trying to build up a practice. She was just starting out. Referrals were few and far between. To keep herself busy and make ends meet, she wangled herself a part-time job at her old alma mater as student counselor and school shrink."

The headmaster's secretary, a pretty young woman in a navy skirt, asked them if they wouldn't mind waiting a few minutes in the reception area. Aaron sat on a soft leather couch, while Janek inspected the display of school memorabilia on the walls.

There was a glass case full of trophies, most of them for arcane sports such as field hockey and equestrian dressage. There was an ornately framed wooden plaque emblazoned with the words "Head Girl" and the names of young women, student leaders in their respective years. There were also numerous class photographs. Janek asked Aaron what year Beverly was graduated.

Aaron checked his notebook. "Class of '68," he said.

Janek found the picture, inspected it closely. Two dozen girls, all wearing the same school uniform of white blouse and blue and red tartan skirt, were posed in two rows before the main building of Ashley-Burnett. He discovered Beverly in the second row on the end. She was standing slightly apart from her classmates. There was something separate, distant about her, something slightly alienated in her posture. But her face bore the same half-smile he had come to know so well, the thin-lipped half-smile that said "I have superior knowledge" and "Don't get too close."

"Mr. Bramhall will see you now."

Janek turned. The pretty secretary motioned them toward an inner door. Janek and Aaron followed her across polished parquet floors into a spacious cream-colored office. A handsome man in a beautifully tailored tweed jacket rose from behind an antique partner's desk.

"You must be Lieutenant Janek. I'm Jud Bramhall," he said, extending his hand.

Janek studied him while they made small talk about the brutal Cleveland weather. He and Bramhall, he decided, were about the same age, but there the resemblance stopped. Bramhall had the patrician good looks and arched eyebrows of an affable old-fashioned WASP politician, the kind that can't get elected in an American city anymore. He had the same kind of old money voice as Stanton Dorance, a voice that spoke of a fine eastern education and all the privileges attendant thereto.

"Sergeant Greenberg tells me you want a briefing on Bev Archer's sojourn here as school psychologist."

Janek was pleased by Bramhall's crisp announcement that it was time to discuss the matter at hand.

"A certain confidentiality implicit in our relationships with former staff precludes my getting too specific. But after consulting with our attorney, and based on the gravity of the matter, as explained by the sergeant here, I'm prepared to fill you in on a background-only basis. For anything more than that I'll require a subpoena."

Janek nodded. "That's fine. We're just trying to get a sense of what she was like."

Bramhall pulled a pipe from a rack on his desk, stuffed it with tobacco. Then he leaned back, a signal he was going to be expansive. Watching him, Janek had the feeling Bramhall would tell his tale well.

"It was a strange thing that happened with Bev. . . ."

The events he described occurred in 1977. The school, Bramhall didn't mind admitting now, was then a fairly troubled institution. There were drug problems, student pregnancies, a general breakdown in discipline. Nothing that wasn't going on at other independent schools at the time, but he, Bramhall, had been appointed headmaster only two years before, he was the first male head in the history of Ashley-Burnett, and he was anxious to make innovations and turn the school around. So the idea came to him that a trained psychologist ought to be available to any student needing help. He took it to the board of trustees, the concept was approved, and then someone brought up Beverly Archer's name. She was qualified, she had just gotten her degree, and, best of all, as a fairly young alumna she would be in a position to identify with the particular problems of Ashley-Burnett girls, pertaining to the school and also to their social lives outside.

"We are, after all, a fairly special group." Bramhall finally lit his pipe. "We have minority students, and we hope to recruit more as times goes on. But basically our function is to educate the daughters of Cleveland's older families. I make no apologies for that. Ashley-Burnett is an elite school. We consider ourselves the equal of any young women's academy in the East."

He made this last statement with uncondescending pride, a pride Janek could not help admiring. The man carried the torch for a world he must know was increasingly irrelevant, yet he did so without apology.

"That first autumn, when Bev came on board, I thought I'd made a pretty smart move. Here was an intelligent, well-motivated young woman eager to help her old school get back on track. And I have to admit that in the beginning at least things did seem to improve. As troubled kids turned to her for guidance, student and faculty morale tilted up. I got some calls from parents, too, always complimentary. A staff psychologist was a great idea. Why hadn't we thought of it before?"

But then, Bramhall admitted sadly, the euphoria of autumn began to turn. The winter term was always the hardest, he said, always the low point of the year. Cleveland's harsh climate was partially responsible. The gray skies and miserable cold forced everyone indoors. Kids caught the flu. Corridors resounded with sniffles and coughs. All educators are familiar with the phenomenon, a species of cabin fever that leads inevitably to a lowering of morale. But that particular winter, the winter of '78, seemed worse than usual. There was something indefinably miserable in the air. Bramhall, naturally concerned, called a number of staff meetings. Beverly, he remembered, kept fairly quiet. At the time he attributed that to shyness; she was new to the school and possibly intimidated by older staff. Then one weekend in late February disaster struck. A senior girl, a very popular one, too, hanged herself at home.

The suicide turned what had been a very dark winter term into a totally black one. In such a situation extensive counseling was called for, and Beverly seem to rise to the occasion. But then, ten days later, a second girl hanged herself, this time in the school gym. Her dangling body was discovered by a group of eighth graders, all of them deeply traumatized by the sight. And then the truth came out. Two other girls came forward and admitted to the existence of a "suicide club." Bramhall moved quickly to break it up.

"I still don't know exactly what it was about," he said, relighting his pipe. "Were the two hangings actually suicides or the result of a strange sex practice called autoerotic asphyxia that was then finding its way into various Ohio schools? But what did come out—and to me this was the most shocking aspect of the whole affair—was that not only had the two dead girls been seeing Bev Archer for counseling, but other members of the 'club,' in fact, a majority of them, had been seeing her as well. I want to make something clear. There was an understanding that if a girl wanted to see the quote school shrink unquote, she was under no obligation to tell anyone, nor would Bev report the consultation to either the school or the girl's parents. Total confidentiality was to apply; that was the whole idea. But I never expected Bev would take the rule so literally, especially after a girl who was in her charge took her own life. When I found out that *both* dead girls had been her patients, I couldn't believe my ears. The way it looked, Bev was the common thread in the affair." Bramhall angrily tapped his pipe against the top of his desk. "She might as well have been that damn suicide club's faculty adviser."

Janek could see that the shock of that revelation had still not abated, even after so many years.

"Bev was quite broken up by the suicides, of course. 'My fault,' she told me. 'Those girls were in my care, and I let them down.' She wept a lot and beat her breast. I felt she was sincere. But still, with her arrival, it seemed something almost . . . evil entered Ashley-Burnett. Well, whether she was responsible or not, I couldn't countenance her not keeping me informed. She clearly wasn't up to the job. I told her to take leave and that at the end of the term I'd have to let her go, as, of course, I did. . . ."

Bramhall fell silent for a time. Then he opened a file folder on his desk and removed a sheet of paper. "That spring Bev left Cleveland and moved to New York to start her career again. A couple of years later I received a letter from a Dr. Carl Drucker at a psychiatric hospital in Derby, Connecticut. He wrote that Bev had given my name as a reference and asked if I could recommend her for a part-time staff position."

Bramhall handed Janek the sheet he'd been holding. "Here's a copy of my response. I'm ashamed to admit it, Lieutenant, but as you can see, I recommended her."

As they followed a freshly shoveled path back to the visitors' parking lot, they ran into a group of Ashley-Burnett students walking the other way. The girls, red-cheeked, bundled in goose down coats, their tartan hats powdered lightly with snow, smiled demurely as they passed.

"Aren't they gorgeous!" Aaron exclaimed. "Aren't they the healthiest-looking kids!"

Janek nodded. The girls did indeed look healthy. The thought that Beverly Archer had brought her sickness into this academic Eden filled him with a sad and poignant fury.

Back in the car they didn't talk much. Bramhall's tale spoke for itself. Now they knew about two more young lives Beverly had screwed up. How many others, Janek wondered, could there be?

Aaron's next stop was a handsome slate-roofed, stucco-with-inset-timbers house on the edge of Shaker Heights.

"Beverly's kid sister's place," Aaron explained, as he parked in front. "Mildred Archer, now Mildred Archer Cannaday. Nice gal. Very informal. Two teenage kids. Local tennis champ. Call her Millie, Frank; she likes that. Her husband's a big shot cardiologist."

Millie Cannaday looked so different from her sister that at first Janek couldn't believe that they were siblings. He was persuaded only when he heard Millie speak; then he recognized Beverly's accent.

Millie was a tall, robust, handsome woman in her mid-thirties who moved with the light, liquid grace of an athlete. In certain ways she reminded Janek of Fran Dunning: her relaxed, friendly manner, so unlike the tense guardedness he'd observed in Beverly, and the straightforward way she made eye contact. But above all, there was a pervading aura of good health and of being comfortable within. After only two minutes in her presence, Janek knew that Mildred Archer Cannaday was not and never had been a wallflower.

The interview took place in a gracious, well-proportioned sunken living room with tall leaded windows at either end. French doors led out to a terrace with a view over a park behind the house. The furnishings consisted of twin chintz-upholstered couches, dark wood side tables, old-fashioned lamps, framed family photos displayed on the top of a baby grand piano, and fine Oriental rugs spread on a polished chestnut floor. Janek felt he was in the home of successful well-adjusted people, so unlike the effect of Beverly's minimalist office and her medieval bedchamber, dominated by the shrine to her mother.

When finally they settled down and Aaron brought up Beverly's name, Millie Cannaday sadly shook her head.

"Poor Bev. Such a miserable, unhappy woman. When I think of what she could have been . . . It's been a pretty long time since the two of us have really talked. It's not that we've become estranged. It's just that in the last few years she's become so *weird.* Oh, we exchange Christmas cards and call each other on our respective birthdays, and she usually remembers my kids' birthdays, too, and sends them a little check, four dollars or something ridiculous like that. I think last year she actually sent each of them five." Millie's eyes twinkled. "It isn't that she's stingy, you understand. Bev can't help herself. She was always tight, ungiving, retentive—isn't that the word? Well, I'm no psychologist, Lieutenant. I don't know the terminology. But I do know what happened to my sister and whose fault it was. Our mother's. Mama was the one who ruined Bev's life."

As Millie Cannaday launched into an extended monologue, Janek could feel the interview slipping into the kind of deeply felt reminiscence by which a speaker dredges up old memories and purges conflicts from his past.

"It's sad to say. But I'm afraid it's just that simple. Our mother was a totally self-centered person. Oh, she was beautiful. Everyone thought so. 'Victoria Archer's the most beautiful woman in Cleveland,' people used to say. And talented. Mama was very talented. At her height she was probably the best nightclub singer in town. With the right kind of luck she might have gone on to become a national star. God knows, she had the ambition for it, but I think underneath she was afraid of going up against the best. So she stayed out here, a nice enough place, as I'm sure you've noticed, Lieutenant. We actually have it pretty good in Cleveland. Great orchestra. World-class art museum. Fine university. But still, it's Cleveland, isn't it?" Millie's eyes twinkled again. "We can get pretty defensive about that. We don't like it when our town gets a cheap laugh on a talk show or when someone calls it the mistake on the lake with a knowing little sneer. Mama always said she hated it here. Funny, isn't it, that she stayed here her entire life? She was born here. And this is where she died."

She herself, Millie said, proceeding with her saga, had happily managed to escape her mother's domination.

"I was lucky. I broke away. I didn't need Mama so much, so I was able to stand up to her and make my break. But Bev couldn't do that. She needed Mama desperately. And so she got her, perhaps more of her in the end than she ever bargained for. I think Bev paid an awful price for her need. Mama used her terribly. She twisted and distorted whatever possible chance at happiness Bev might have had. I'll say it again because I believe it's true. Victoria, our mother, truly ruined Bev's life."

There was, Millie said, a kind of bizarre "contract" between her older sister and her mother, a contract which, although unspoken, was as binding and as forceful as if it had been cut in stone. Its basic terms were starkly simple: Victoria would live her life to the hilt, laugh, be beautiful, glamorous, thin, successful, and, most important, a sexually active and satisfied woman. Beverly, on the other hand, would be depressed, unhappy, plain, mousy, fat, mediocre, and asexual so as never to compete. And as in any personal services contract, there was a schedule of compensation: In return for not competing with her mother, Beverly would be "loved."

"It was a real lousy deal," Millie said. "The love Bev got was second-rate. Because the only person Mama was capable of loving was—yeah, you guessed it, Mama."

Millie excused herself. When she returned a few minutes later, it was with a tray, several glasses, bottles of beer, and a bowl of nuts.

"Have you met Bev, Lieutenant?"

Janek nodded. "I interviewed her a couple of times."

"How did she strike you?"

"Unhappy, plain, asexual—pretty much the way you just described."

"Well, you may find this hard to believe," Millie said, "but she was quite handsome as a girl. Still, I bet it's been twenty years since she's had a date. See, the more time she spent with Mama, the fatter and plainer she got. Then, when she dyed her hair red, it came out blah rather than glossy like Mama's. When they'd stand together near the end of Mama's life, they looked more like sisters than even Bev and me. Mama had had her face lifted several times, and Bev had really let herself go. Beautiful Vicky and drab Bev—the Archer girls. God!"

Millie believed that even though Bev worshiped their mother, she at times also hated her for imposing the awful contract. But every time Bev tried to break away, Victoria would pull her back.

"Can you imagine?" Millie asked. "Can you imagine how wasteful and stupid it is to allow your mother to rule your life?"

It was a rhetorical question, Janek realized; he made no effort to respond to it.

"I think that was Bev's tragedy," Millie said, "that she had a chance to live for herself, and in the end she wasted it."

Their father, Jack Archer, had been a distant figure. He and Victoria had married young and split up early, just after Millie was born. Jack, an engineer, had moved to Chicago, remarried, and started a second family. The girls had had very little contact with him, though Victoria had received substantial child support. Both girls were bright and had no trouble getting into Ashley-Burnett. Meantime, Victoria launched her career as a singer. Her success was instantaneous.

"Mama had an excellent voice. She was an accomplished singer. But there're plenty of good singers around. What Mama had that was extra was her incredible style. She could take a standard, a song everyone knew, and dramatize it, make it passionate. She knew how to reach people, put a song across. The glamorous nightclub singer—that was her public face. But there was so much more to her than what she showed her fans. Behind all the beauty and glamour there was one very hard-boiled lady. She was a great injustice collector, you know. Cross her and she'd never forgive. She had a kind of personal code, the gist of which went something like: If someone wrongs you, don't ever forget it. Nurse your anger and your hurt until it turns to bitterness and hate. But (and this was probably her most important tenet) never, never let your hatred show."

Millie sat back on the couch, her arms hanging limply. She had expended great energy describing her sister and mother; now she seemed exhausted.

Janek decided it was time to focus the interview. "Could Bev have inherited your mother's code?"

"Possibly." Millie smiled. "Oh, hell! I've told you this much. Why not the rest? Sure, she inherited it. Mama taught it to her. It became her code, too, for God's sakes."

In the last few years of her life Victoria started going mad. At least Millie thought she did. Beverly did not agree. For all her sister's background in psychology, her training and experience as a therapist, she refused to see what was obvious to all Victoria's friends—namely, that the singer was being eaten up by her hate.

"Eight years ago, when Mama died suddenly of a stroke, she was only fifty-five years old. But in the last five years of her life she carried on sometimes like a lunatic. At the lounge she'd be fine, her glamorous self. But in the afternoons before work she'd lie out on the chaise in her living room at the Alhambra Hotel, ranting and raving at the world. Out of nowhere she'd bring up someone's name, an old lover maybe or someone else she thought had done her wrong. Then she'd start in. Curses, pronouncements, spiteful value judgments. 'He's a prick.' 'She's a shit.' That kind of vulgar talk. And when she said something like that, it was usually about someone who really hadn't done anything particularly wrong. A man might have forgotten to send flowers, or one of her girlfriends might have forgotten to return a call. Trivial offenses to which she had these ludicrous reactions. It was truly awful to listen to. Meantime, there was Bev flying in from New York practically every weekend, rushing over to Mama's, listening to all her garbage, taking it all in, nodding her agreement. Sometimes Bev would stop by to see me afterwards. 'Isn't Mama wonderful!' she'd say. 'Aren't we lucky to have such a talented and brilliant ma!' God! The sick way she worshiped that woman, the weird way they fed off each other's madness." Millie peered straight into Janek's eyes. "I guess by now you know that's what I think: that Bev got as crazy as Mama in the end. . . ."

The time had come, Janek thought, to put some tough questions to Millie. "Did your sister ever have a run-in with a teacher at Ashley-Burnett?"

Millie smiled. "Sure. An old spinster English teacher. She was my teacher, too."

"Bertha Parce?" Aaron asked.

Millie nodded. "I'm amazed you know her name."

"What about two men named MacDonald—did she ever have any trouble with them?"

"Jimmy and Stu MacDonald? You call them men! They were just boys when I knew them. I think they moved east. That's what I heard anyway."

"What happened?"

"God only knows. Whatever it was, Bev was sensitive about it. Whenever their names came up, she'd start to act real antsy, then try and change the subject."

"Cynthia Morse?"

"Her roommate at Bennington. Yeah, they had a big falling-out. But I don't understand, Lieutenant." Millie smiled curiously. "How do you *know* about all of these people?"

"Let's hold off on that for now. I want to ask you about some others." Millie nodded. "Do the names Laura and Anthony Scotto ring a bell?"

"I don't think so. No."

Janek glanced at Aaron. "What about Wexler—Carla and Robert Wexler?"

Millie shook her head. Then she stopped shaking it. "Wait a minute! There was a *Bobby* Wexler."

Aaron smiled slightly. "Who was he?"

"A musician. Mama's accompanist one summer. There were so many of those guys. She went through them pretty fast. But I remember Bobby. It was the summer Mama sang at Cavendish. He was practically a kid. Actually I think he and Mama were involved. She usually screwed her piano players. That's probably why she tired of them so fast."

"Do you think you'd recognize this Bobby Wexler if you saw him again?"

"I might," Millie said.

Aaron showed her a photograph of the Wexler family taken several months before they were slaughtered. Millie studied it. "Yeah, that's him," she said. "It's been years, but the smile's the same, the old lecherous smile." She looked up at Janek. "Yeah, it's him, I'm sure. Now are you going to tell me what this is all about?"

"While you're at it, show her the picture of the Scottos," Janek gently instructed Aaron.

Aaron showed Millie the picture. They both watched as she studied it. "I may have seen the woman," Millie said. "What's her first name again?"

"Laura."

"And she was married to this guy?" Aaron nodded. "Do you know her maiden name?"

Aaron checked his notebook. "Laura Gabelli."

Millie nodded. "I may have seen her. Around Tufts College, I think. Bev transferred there from Bennington. Did you know about that?"

They didn't know. Millie filled them in. It was after the big falling-out with Cynthia Morse. Bev took a year off, came back to Cleveland, took a job as an aide at a psychiatric hospital, then for the next two years attended Tufts, where she majored in psychology. After that she moved back to Cleveland to get her doctorate at Western Reserve.

"Do you know of any falling-out she might have had with this Laura Gabelli?" Aaron asked.

"No. But it wouldn't surprise me. Just like Mama, Bev had fallings-out with damn near everyone." Millie paused. "Look, guys—all these questions about the two of them, then all these old names of people Bev didn't like. You're scaring me a little bit. I think the time's come for you to explain."

She looked to Janek, then to Aaron, and then back to Janek again. There was something so open and vulnerable about her that Janek was hesitant to fill her in. But he knew he had to. He owed her that, and he could see that she was the kind of person who'd rather know the truth, no matter how harsh, than be lied to or kept in the dark.

"Bertha Parce, the MacDonalds, Cynthia Morse and her two daughters, the Wexler family, and the Scotto family all had one thing in common," he said. "They all were murdered within the past fourteen months by a woman named Diana Proctor, who also happened to be your sister's patient."

Millie, mouth partly open, gazed at Janek. For a moment she appeared to be relieved. Then, abruptly, she sat up, as if the implications of what he'd said had hit her like a blow.

"But you don't really think—! I mean, you couldn't possibly believe—!" Her forehead creased; her pupils dilated. "You think Bev had something to do with . . . that Bev may have directed—?" And then: "You *do* think that, don't you? Yes, I see you do." She squeezed her eyes shut. "Oh, my God!"

Millie Cannaday began to scream. Her shrieks of anguish echoed through the house.

They stayed with her until she calmed down. Then Janek explained to her that yes, Beverly was a suspect, although so far no more than that. He and Aaron had come to Cleveland, he explained, on account of the portrait of her mother, which they'd seen in Beverly's bedroom. Certain objects, taken from the homicide victims, had been arranged in what seemed to be a votive offering style before the painting. Thus the question arose as to whether Victoria Archer had in some way been the inspiration for the Wallflower murders. Janek readily admitted that such a theory must seem farfetched; he was certainly not prepared to tell Millie her sister was a murderess. Still, the case remained open. By the way, did Millie know anything about the portrait?

"The full-length one of Mama in her red dress? Sure, I know about it. A man named Peter Aretzsky painted it about twelve years ago. It took up a whole wall of Mama's bedroom."

"Your sister inherited it?"

Millie smiled. "Bev wanted that picture something awful. That, Mama's red dresses, her miniature piano, and her big old four-poster bed." Millie rolled her eyes. "Bev always had her eye on the picture. She loved it, said it showed Mama the way she really was. Which is pretty funny . . . considering. You see, there's a story behind that painting." Millie turned to Aaron. "Are you taking him to see Melissa Walters?" Aaron nodded. "Ask her about the painting, Lieutenant. She can fill you in about that and a lot of other stuff. She was Mama's best friend . . . if in fact, Mama ever had one."

"Shit! She knew Bobby Wexler and Laura Scotto. That's proof she lied to us, Frank. So we got her, don't we?" Aaron hit the steering wheel with delight. "I'm starting to feel good about this case."

They were back in their rental car, driving to their final appointment of the day. The snow had stopped falling. Although it was only four-thirty, the sky was already turning dark.

Janek wasn't sure that proof of Beverly's lies quite meant that they'd "got her." But he did think it might be enough to persuade Kit to grant them more time. So far the trip to Cleveland was working out. *Now how the hell am I going to get a confession?* he wondered.

The lobby of the Alhambra Residential Hotel was a Moorish fantasy, a pastiche of thick walls, Arab columns, Córdoba arches, a central courtyard embracing a fountain, and a rectangular tiled pool stocked with carp.

Built in the late 1920s as a luxury establishment, the hotel was so well constructed that even now, after years of wear, it still emitted an aura of luxury and class. Palms planted in large terracotta pots occupied the corners. Ceiling fans, still now that it was winter, stood poised to whirl and cool perspiring guests.

A creaking elevator, paneled in mahogany and trimmed with brass, took them to the fifth floor. Here they followed a corridor, one side open to the courtyard, until they reached the door to Melissa Walters's suite.

A short old lady opened up, a lady who clearly did not wish her visitors to find her old. Her hair was blued, her forehead was powdered, her cheeks were rouged, her eyebrows were drawn, and her lips were waxed bright scarlet. Melissa Walters showed the soft smile and refined social mannerisms of another era.

It was so exciting to meet real live detectives! Would the gentlemen like something to drink? Port? Sherry? She had some fine old Madeira—could she tempt them with that? And she had taken the liberty of ordering in some prepared canapés, as well as a good selection of cookies from Damons, Cleveland's finest bakery.

Melissa Walters settled into her favorite chair.

Oh, yes, she remembered Vicky Archer. My goodness, they'd been the best of friends! Impossible to forget *her*. A great entertainer, a great personality. She'd been the life of this city for a time. Had the gentlemen been to the Fairmount Club Lounge? Perhaps they should go down there and take a look. Not that the place was anything now but a shadow of its former self. Still, at one time, not too long ago either, the lounge had been Cleveland's premier night spot and Vicky Archer had been its most glittering star. But please forgive her. She was rambling; she knew she was. She apologized for that. She had so few visitors these days, most of her friends having passed away. Vicky had been one of the first. It was tragic the way she died so suddenly and so young. They'd been confidantes even though she, Melissa, was fifteen years Vicky's senior. Oh, they'd had some great times together, wonderful times. . . . What? What was that they were asking? The painting, Aretzsky's painting? Of course, she remembered it! She'd seen it practically every day. Whenever she visited Vicky's suite, just two doors down the hall. A story? Oh, yes, there was a story about that picture, a scandal if they wanted to know the truth. Oh, they did, did they? What sly devils they were! Well, certainly, she'd tell them about it. In fact, it would be a pleasure. But would the gentlemen take a glass of Madeira first . . . ?

Janek and Aaron accepted her glasses of Madeira. They even licked their lips over her delicate canapés and grinned foolishly as they nibbled on her tasty little cookies. Anything to keep the old lady talking. Janek, who'd conducted thousands of interviews over the course of his career, recognized that Melissa Walters was a potential gold mine of information. If there was a secret about Beverly and Victoria, a secret even deeper than what he and Aaron had managed to dig up so far, this lady might reveal it if she were handled carefully enough. The way she sang Victoria Archer's praises suggested a profound ambivalence. He had picked up on undertones of anger, envy, even dislike.

"Aretzsky! Ha!" Melissa's scarlet painted lips parted in a smile. "He was smitten by her, of course. Utterly smitten! He would come around the lounge every night just to see her, watch her move, listen to her sing, perhaps be so fortunate as to be the recipient of one of her ravishing smiles. He was an excellent painter as it happened, probably Cleveland's best. But so temperamental! He'd refuse to paint a person he didn't like. He lost out on a lot of lucrative corporate work on account of that little peccadillo. Still, Aretzsky was your first choice if you wanted your portrait done. That's how he got Vicky's attention . . . although he didn't hold it very long."

Melissa asked if she could refresh their drinks. When they shook their heads, she shrugged and poured herself a double.

"I remember the night Aretzsky presented her with some drawings, quick little sketches he'd made of her right there in the lounge. She liked them, of course. She was no fool. And when he told her he wanted to paint her in oil, big, life size, maybe even bigger than life size, she certainly did not refuse him although she may have pretended to waver a little bit. Well, then he had her; at least he thought he did, the idiot! She began going to his studio to sit every afternoon. That dreary dump he lived in, near the lounge down at Carnegie and One Hundred Fourth, up four flights to a big, undusted room with his easel and messy paints at one end and his awful, smelly unmade bed at the other. They made love on that bed, of course. Vicky always knew how to inspire a man! I know he made nude sketches of her. She showed them to me once. But the big painting was the thing. Vicky in her red dress surrounded by a halo of reddish light. That's how they always lit her down at the lounge, you see. Oh, he made her look terrific—vibrant, bursting with energy and life. She was always glamorous, but he doubled her glamour. He idealized her. It was a picture painted by a lover. You couldn't look at it and fail to see that."

Melissa spread her arms. "Poor Aretzsky! That ugly, little, shrunken waif of a man with his bad skin and little wisp of a mustache—did he really think he was good enough to hold the interest of the Great Victoria Archer? Poor idiot! She ditched him, of course, soon as she got her mitts on his painting. Then he was heartbroken, or perhaps worse—a man destroyed. He started to become a nuisance, too. Long, reproachful, beseeching stares at the lounge. Silent phone calls to her suite in the middle of the night. He must have sent her fifty letters drenched in tears. She didn't bother to open them; just a glance at the envelopes and she'd toss them in the trash. I remember seeing him hanging around the stage door at the lounge or here, in front of the Alhambra, hoping to beg a precious moment of her time. And of course, the deeper he humiliated himself, the more disgusted she became, and the greater her disgust, the more cruelly she behaved. For make no mistake about it, gentlemen—Vicky Archer could be a real bitch!"

But, Melissa explained, there was a second act to the story, the scandal that arose later on. Aretzsky, heartbroken, disdained and scorned, turned bitter and took to drink. And, as is so often the case, the excesses of his infatuation were equaled by the intensity of his disillusionment. After several months, unable to rid himself of his obsession, he began work on a second portrait of Victoria far different from the first. It was the same size: enormous. She was in the same pose: singing. She wore the same clothes and jewelry: her diamond necklace and scarlet dress. But there the resemblance stopped. Instead of the heroic, idealized features he had painted the first time around, the features in the second picture were deeply characterized. That second portrait, painted out of heartbreak and bitterness, purported to show her as she really was: spiteful; self-ish; mean.

"I have to hand it to Aretzsky," Melissa said. "He caught something, no question about that. It wasn't the face Vicky showed the world, but it was a face I'd seen a couple of times when she was off her guard. Maybe it wasn't the real Vicky, but it did show a hidden side of her, particularly around the eyes and mouth. Aretzsky put everything he felt into it. It was truly a picture informed by hate. That's what people who saw it said. And people *did* see it! Aretzsky saw to that! He had a show at the Howard French Gallery at Shaker Square, and his big new picture of Vicky was the first thing you saw when you walked in.

"Well, she was furious! Who can blame her? Still, I think if Aretzsky's second portrait hadn't contained a certain amount of recognizable truth, she might have been able to laugh it off. But the way she went around expressing her outrage only made people eager to see it for themselves. And when they did, they began to talk. People were fascinated. The subject came up at dinner parties: Which picture showed the true Vicky, the first or the second? There were people who even reread that old Oscar Wilde story *The Picture of Dorian Gray* and then expounded on the parallels. And there was talk, too, that ugly though the second picture was, it was also, because of its passion, Aretzsky's greatest work. I remember Vicky coming in here at the time, sitting in the very chair you're sitting in now, Lieutenant, looking at me, shaking her head. 'Oh, Lisa'—she always called me that—'why did I ever let him paint me in the first place?' *Why?* "

Melissa turned to Janek, widened her eyes. Clearly she reveled in the effect of her tale.

"The answer, of course, was her insatiable vanity, which Aretzsky was more than happy to requite. But she didn't really want to know the answer to her question, so I kept my thoughts to myself. She did, however, try to do something about that second picture. She approached certain of her wealthy admirers and begged them to buy the portrait so she could have the pleasure of seeing it destroyed. From what I understand some fairly substantial offers were actually made. But no matter how much he was offered, Aretzsky refused. The man simply wouldn't sell. And why should he? Think about it. That picture was his revenge. You don't sell out your revenge, do you, Lieutenant? At least not if you feel wronged the way Aretzsky did . . ."

Peter Aretzsky, as it turned out, died just a year after Victoria

Archer. In Melissa's judgment, he never recovered from his obsession with the singer. The second portrait? Melissa had no idea where it was. The scandal subsided long before Vicky died. Wasn't it always like that? Melissa asked. People couldn't get enough of something, gossiped about it endlessly, then, a year later, wondered why they ever cared.

"Bev? Of course, I remember Bev. She's a psychoanalyst in New York, isn't she? Oh, just a therapist. Well, it's all the same to me. I don't know much about that kind of thing, but I know Vicky did a real job on the girl. The way she scampered around after her beloved 'Mama' like there was an invisible leash and collar around her neck! You had to wonder what she got out of it. The honor of being Vicky Archer's daughter, I suppose. Still, everyone thought it was pretty peculiar, but no one dared say a word. 'Oh, Bev's just going through an awkward stage right now'—that's what Vicky would say if you gingerly brought the matter up. A 'stage'! 'Right now'! You had to laugh! Vicky kept Bev awkward from the day she was born. I sometimes wondered if she kept her that way to make herself look better by contrast. Because, you know, the other daughter, Millie, wasn't drab at all. That's the way it is sometimes: One daughter serves the mother while the other strikes out on her own. I've seen it happen again and again. I just hope Bev has straightened herself out. Sometimes you can't do that, you know. You get twisted, and then, after the person who twisted you passes away, it's too late to change and have a normal life. . . ."

Janek decided to let her ramble on. Better that she reminisce at random, he thought, and add her little homilies about life than for him to question her too closely about Beverly and then be forced to explain why he was interested.

"How good a singer was Vicky Archer? You're really putting me on the spot, Lieutenant. Let's just say she was very good. Did you know she was on network TV once? The Carson show, I think. After that she played a club date in New York. But she wasn't quite good enough to make it there, so she came back here, where she could be sure she'd always be a star. And for a few years, at least, she had this city at her feet. Well, maybe I exaggerate. But you have to understand, the Fairmount Club Lounge, where she hung out and sang, was a kind of mecca for a number of us. Vicky was a goddess there."

Melissa shook her head. "If I close my eyes—"she closed them—"I can still see her standing in that cone of red light they always put on her, sultry, sexy, her hair red like a flame, crooning those great old songs, 'Black Coffee,' 'My One and Only Love,' 'Don't Smoke in Bed.' " Melissa opened her eyes again. "So, how good was she? Still want to know? Let's say she was Cleveland's answer to Peggy Lee. But let's face it, even at its height the Fairmount Club Lounge was no Persian Room. Cleveland just isn't New York, is it? I'm afraid not," Melissa added crisply, a ripe smile signifying a slightly mean satisfaction at finally being able to pin her old friend a little lower on the board of talent than perhaps old Vicky would have liked.

It was past seven when they got back to their motel. Aaron, who'd bought a Cleveland restaurant guide and had been eating his way through it since the day he'd arrived in town, wanted to try a highly recommended Chinese restaurant in a shopping center not far away. They drove there, ordered dinner, but didn't like it much. Every single dish was sweet.

Back at the motel Janek watched TV for a while, then went to bed. At 1:00 A.M. he was awakened by his phone. It was Melissa Walters. She sounded slightly frantic and very drunk.

"Sorry to wake you, Lieutenant, but I had to call. Something's been preying on me ever since you left. Then, when I phoned Millie Cannaday and found out why you're here, I just couldn't rest easy until we spoke."

Was she a crazy old lady, or did she really have something for him? "About what?" Janek asked.

"About Bev. I don't think anyone else knows it except for me. Anyone else living, that is."

"Knows what?"

"It has to do with her being a wallflower. It's a terrible thing,

Lieutenant. I'd rather not discuss it on the phone if you don't mind."

She suggested he join her for breakfast the following morning at a coffee shop around the corner from the Alhambra. She would explain everything then, she promised. Again she apologized for waking him up.

$\mathbf{H}$e had Aaron drop him off, feeling this was one interview he might handle better on his own. Melissa Walters was waiting for him, already sipping coffee. No powder, eye shadow, lipstick, or rouge was on her face that day. It was a ravaged old lady who sat across from him. Two plastic place mats, doubling as breakfast menus, decorated the table, along with a single rose lying on a dainty plate.

Janek ordered toast and coffee. Then he turned to Melissa.

"Well?" he asked.

"There was something Vicky told me once, back years ago. She was drunk when she said it. I'm sure she didn't remember afterwards." Melissa paused. "It was a terrible thing, Lieutenant. A truly terrible thing . . ."

It concerned the two MacDonald boys, Stuart and James. The brothers, it seemed, had had some kind of crush on Victoria. They came around to the lounge all the time, gazed at her intently, mesmerized by the way she sang. Vicky always liked young men, liked their fresh young bodies, but the MacDonalds, still in their teens, were too young even for her.

Still, Vicky was not a woman to waste a pair of infatuated boys. She'd been worried about Beverly at the time, feeling the girl was socially retarded, too shy with males, frightened even by the notion of sex. Her prescription for that was simple. "All Bev needs is a really good lay," Vicky said.

In the end that was how she decided to employ the MacDonalds: as studs to initiate Beverly into the rites and rituals of physical love.

"To use a couple of kids enamored of you to get your own

daughter hot and bothered—it was a rotten idea, and I think deep down Vicky knew it was." Melissa shook her head. She seemed highly disturbed by her story, a sign to Janek that it was probably true. "But once she got the notion into her head, she couldn't let it go. I don't know what happened exactly, except that there was a formal dance and she chose that occasion to sic the boys on to Bev. The whole thing went sour, as it was bound to do. First, there were two of them, which was crazy on its face. And second, the MacDonalds were just a pair of horny kids, not romantic at all. They made some kind of crude, clumsy pass, Bev got hysterical (at least that's what the boys reported to Vicky; Bev apparently never said a word), and the end result was just the opposite of what Vicky intended. Instead of learning what sex was about and how great it could be, Bev discovered it was horrible and never wanted to engage in it again.

"When Vicky told me what she'd done, she was practically in tears. She'd botched it, she admitted, and now she didn't know how to make things right. Even now I can remember her words: 'I didn't want her to be a goddamn wallflower, Lisa. Now I'm afraid that's what she's going to be.' "

That was what Melissa wanted Janek to know. She probably wouldn't have thought of it if Millie Cannaday hadn't mentioned that the MacDonalds had been murdered and their sex organs glued up by Beverly's patient. Then, when Millie mentioned the wallflower signature, the pieces just fell together in Melissa's mind.

As he listened, Janek couldn't help feeling sickened by the tale even as he was exhilarated by the knowledge that he had finally found a motive for at least one set of Wallflower killings. He thanked Melissa, paid the breakfast check, and went out to walk the cold, windy streets of Cleveland Heights.

He wandered aimlessly. The story haunted him. Everything about it rang true—except for Victoria Archer's tears. He could give no credence to her regrets. On the basis of everything he'd learned about the woman, he believed she probably *did* want Beverly to be a wallflower, and that was the real reason she'd set her daughter up. Monika would understand, Janek thought. She would analyze it clearly. She'd say that although Victoria may have *thought* she was sorry about the outcome, deep down in her subconscious she was pleased by it. *Very pleased.*

So Beverly had sent Diana Proctor out to kill and glue the MacDonalds in revenge for what they'd done to her after a dance years before. And the two toothbrushes Diana had brought back as trophies to be offered up to the image of Victoria on the wall— were they the symbols of the brothers' sex organs, sources of their mutual offense?

It was vile and sick, Janek thought, and also totally wrong. For, even if one believed in revenge, it was not the MacDonalds who deserved to be glued. It was Mama. That, Janek thought, was the ultimate irony in the whole grotesque and monstrous affair: that Beverly, the avenging wallflower, should have offered up trophies to the very woman who caused her to become a wallflower in the first place.

Janek made his way down to the University Circle area, then phoned Aaron at the motel. While he waited to be picked up, he was struck by a powerful idea. He pulled back from it; it seemed too perfect. Then he slowly brought it out again, rotated it, examined it, looked at it from every side. Perhaps, he thought, there *was* a way to break Beverly, induce her to confess. . . .

There they were, two Manhattan cops in a strange midwestern city, looking for a picture painted by an artist who had died seven years before.

"How do we find it? We go classic, Frank," Aaron said. And that's just what he did.

Although it was a textbook example of investigative work, later Janek would marvel at the elegance and speed with which Aaron brought it off.

He went straight to the Cuyahoga County Courthouse, where, after some mild flirting with one of the clerks, he obtained the estate file for Peter Aretzsky. Aretzsky's sole heir and executrix turned out to be one and the same person, his sister, a Mrs. Nadia Malkiewicz, who, as it happened, was conveniently listed in the

Cleveland telephone directory. Aaron called her. Yes, she was Peter Aretzsky's sister. Yes, she had inherited all his unsold work. Yes, she had the big picture of Victoria Archer. Yes, she would be willing to show it to the detectives. When would they like to see it? Now? Fine, they could come right over.

The entire process took Aaron just one and three-quarters hours.

Mrs. Malkiewicz, a widow, lived in Ohio City, a historical section on the west side of Cleveland which, after years of neglect, was in the midst of heavy gentrification. As Janek and Aaron drove in, they could hear the sound of sawing and hammering around the neighborhood. They saw Dumpsters on the street filled with the entrails of houses being gutted for renovation.

The Malkiewicz residence was the worst-looking house on its block, a narrow wood frame structure with peeling siding and an unshoveled path leading to a badly disintegrating front porch.

Nadia Malkiewicz looked as miserable as her house. A pale, drawn white-haired woman in a cheap, shapeless housedress, she had a bitter, puckered mouth and the beginnings of a mustache on her upper lip. Her greeting, too, was a good deal less effusive than Aaron expected after talking with her on the phone. Janek understood her transformation. A shrewd look in the old lady's eyes told him she saw them as vultures looking to pounce upon her late brother's work.

He also quickly understood something else: Mrs. Malkiewicz had contempt for said work. There were no original Aretzsky paintings displayed on her parlor walls, although there were pictures of another sort, including a large black velvet banner bearing a cloying reproduction of Da Vinci's *The Last Supper*.

"Yuk! That woman!" was Mrs. Malkiewicz's reaction when Aaron asked her about Victoria Archer.

"She ruined my brother's life, not that he had much of one. A failure and a drunkard was what he was! What's worse, tell me, than a failed drunken painter? Slapping paint on burlap all day long—is that any kind of life? My late husband, bless him, was a hardworking man. Forty-five years sweating it out on the flats. And what did he have to show for it when they laid him off? Nothing! Not even his promised pension. 'Sorry, we're bankrupt,' the company said. So that's what you get in this great United States of America. . . ."

They listened to her bitter gripes for half an hour before they could get her to escort them to the basement, where the treasure trove of art was stored.

The paintings, Janek could see at once, were being kept under appalling conditions. Forty or fifty canvases were piled unevenly against a rough stone cellar wall. Moisture oozed along the floor, and an old oil-burning forced-air furnace roared on the other side of the room.

When they began to pull the pictures out—the one of Victoria, being the largest, was at the bottom of the stack—he saw that many of the frames were warped and that there were mouse droppings in between.

Still, Janek found the work impressive. No matter that Peter Aretzsky had lived a miserable life, his drawing was authoritative and his palette was vibrant. When, finally, they pulled out the big portrait and set it up, Janek could tell at once that it was the artist's masterpiece.

Melissa Walters had been right: Aretzsky had put great feeling into it. His sense of his subject leaped off the canvas and struck the viewer hard. But it was not the painter's hatred that Janek felt so much, nor his bitterness and disillusionment. Although Victoria was harshly characterized, Aretzsky showed a good deal more of her than mere cruelty. It was, Janek thought, a portrait of an extremely unhappy woman, a woman ravaged by a vast and insupportable inner pain. Yes, she was mean, yes, she was selfish—the glare in her eyes and the set of her mouth made that clear enough. But what Aretzsky showed was a victim, a real human being in distress. And although Janek understood why Victoria had hated this picture and had wished to see it destroyed, he also understood how very wrong she'd been. Compared with the painting he had seen in Beverly's bedroom, the painting that had haunted his dreams, this was a mature work of art. That first portrait was a poster. This second one was a truly tragic image.

As Janek continued to gaze at the picture, many things became clear. He understood why Beverly had coveted the first picture and built her bedroom altar around it. It was a portrait of her mother as Beverly needed to remember her, while the second picture was too complex to inspire adoration. The Victoria Archer in the second picture was a woman who could make a wallflower of her own daughter. It was that true a likeness, Janek thought.

$\mathbf{L}$ater, upstairs, he and Aaron tried to strike a deal with Mrs. Malkiewicz, but the old lady wouldn't bargain. She acknowledged she'd been unable to sell a single one of her brother's canvases and admitted freely that he and Aaron were the first people to come around and express an interest in his work. Still, she held firm. Her price was nonnegotiable. Ten-thousand-dollars-take-it-or-leave-it. Not a penny less.

Why? they asked her. She couldn't explain it. She just knew the picture was valuable and she wasn't going to sell it cheap. But we're cops, they reminded her, civil servants; we don't have that kind of dough. Well, maybe not, she said. But ten thousand was still the price.

Janek understood even before Aaron that there was no point in further discussion. We'll think about it, he told Mrs. Malkiewicz politely. We'll let you know tomorrow.

$\mathbf{B}$ack in the car Aaron was explosive.

"You crazy, Frank? You'd even consider paying that? Screw her! And to hell with the picture!"

"Trouble is I want it," Janek said.

He explained to Aaron his conviction that the reason Mrs.

Malkiewicz set the price so high was that she didn't really want to sell.

"Sure she needs the money. And sure she acts like Aretzsky's pictures are shit. But the truth is she loved her brother, and his pictures are the only things of his she's got. To sell one off is to lose a part of him. Even if we agree to pay her price, I'm not sure she won't back out."

Aaron shrugged. "So what's the point?"

"The point is I need that goddamn picture. So I'll just have to get hold of the money, then handle her very carefully."

"Where're you going to get that kind of bread?"

"I think I know where I can raise it."

Aaron looked at him skeptically. "You're not thinking of Kit?"

"No, not Kit," Janek said. "I've got someone else in mind."

Back in the motel he dialed Stanton's office in New York. Mr. Dorance was in a meeting, his secretary said. Could he get back to Janek later on?

"No. Tell him it's an emergency."

A minute later a breathless Stanton came on the line.

"What's the matter, Frank? What's going on?"

"I need ten thousand dollars."

"Is this a joke? I'm kind of busy."

"No joke, Stanton. I'm out in Cleveland. I'm on the trail of the person who put that girl up to all those killings, including Jess's. I can't go into the details. It's a complicated case. The bottom line is that there's a painting out here I think I can use to put this person away. It'll cost me ten thousand dollars."

" 'Think' you can use?"

"Yeah, well, it's a long shot. But it's the only thing I got going. You said I should call you if I needed anything. I'm calling. This is what I need to catch Jess's killer."

A long pause. He knew what Stanton was thinking: Yes, he'd made that commitment, but ten thousand was a lot of money. Was there any way he could wriggle out of this? Was Janek off his rocker?

"You're sure the painting's worth it?"

"No. But that's what it's going to cost."

"Maybe you should have it professionally appraised?"

"Screw that. I need it now."

Another pause. "You're really calling in my marker?"

"I guess you could say that, Stanton, yeah."

"I didn't expect this. Not so soon."

"Neither did I. Believe me, if I had the money, I'd buy the damn thing myself."

"Well, all right. How soon do you need it?"

"Yesterday."

"I'll FedEx you a check. You'll get it tomorrow morning."

"No check," Janek said. "The seller's nervous. The only way I can close the deal is put cash down on the table."

"I can wire you the money, I suppose. To a local bank out there." He could hear the exasperation in Stanton's voice. "Jesus, Frank! I just hope you know what you're doing!"

"Yeah. Well, I'm just doing the best I can," Janek replied.

The following morning at eleven they were back at the Malkiewicz residence with ten banded packs of fresh hundred-dollar bills and a rented van big enough to transport the painting.

Mrs. Malkiewicz met them at the door. She looked at Janek nervously. "I didn't expect you back so soon."

"I've got the money. We're here to take the picture."

He knew the way to do it was to move as quickly as possible, ignore any hesitancy on her part, count out the cash bill by bill while Aaron wrestled the portrait out the door. That way, if she happened to have second thoughts, it would be too late; the transaction would be complete.

It worked out. Mrs. Malkiewicz didn't say a word, although

Janek couldn't help noticing her despair. He knew she'd get over it. Ten grand was enough to fix up her house. And she still had a thick stack of Aretzsky paintings rotting in her cellar.

That afternoon they found a carpenter who agreed to crate up the picture in time for the first flight the following morning to New York. Janek and Aaron would escort it back, the fruit of their investigation.

After the plane took off, Janek stared out his window at the sprawling city below. The sky was gray, broken by a few plumes of industrial smoke. Cleveland looked huge and flat, blocks of bleak gray buildings, a grid of iron-colored streets. The Cuyahoga River, famous for once having caught on fire, was crusted with snow, and Lake Erie seemed a vast white frozen waste. It was a strange and fascinating place, he thought, this city Aaron had described as a Rust Belt town of broken dreams. Here for many years iron and coal had been forged into steel, and here, too, the pathology of Wallflower had been forged.

11

The Portrait

The crucial move, Janek knew, would be the delivery of the portrait. Bungle that and he could botch his entire case.

He and Aaron war-gamed the problem. Since they couldn't break into her house and switch the new painting with the old (their preferred solution), they'd have to take their chances on a straight delivery. The trick, they agreed, would be to get Beverly to accept it.

"How about two guys in deliveryman uniforms. 'Parcel, Ms. Archer. Just sign here, please, ma'am.' "

"Yeah," said Aaron, "then they bring in this enormous box. 'Hey,' she yells, 'I never ordered this. Get this stinking thing out of here.' See, Frank, it's not like you want to send her a valentine that all we got to do is slip it under her door. That picture's fucking humongous."

"So there's only one solution," Janek said. "Deliver it ourselves."

"What if she won't take it?"

"We'll leave it on the stoop."

"So she ignores it. Or has it hauled away. There's no guarantee she'll look at it, even if she does take it inside."

"You're right," Janek said. "There're no guarantees about any of it. But if we deliver it to her in the proper context, our odds will improve. By a lot."

He called Monika, filled her in on his trip to Cleveland, outlined his plan, then asked her what she thought.

"Strange, a bit morbid, certainly daring," she said. She sounded less excited than he'd expected. "You say you want to shock this woman into a confession. But there's also a chance you'll shock her into a psychotic state. Have you considered that?"

"It's occurred to me," he said. "Frankly, the idea doesn't break me up. She goes to prison or she goes to the funny farm. I win either way. A third possibility is that she laughs the whole thing off. That's the one I'd just as soon not think about."

"Sounds to me like you're out for blood, Frank."

Why was she reproaching him? "Wasn't blood what *she* was out for?"

He imagined Monika shaking her head. "This is difficult for me. My profession is to heal, not to wound."

Suddenly he was irritated. "You say I sound like I'm out for blood—I'm not sure what that means. I'm certainly not about to pick up an ice pick and stick it in her ear. But if you mean tearing the mask off her face, then I guess you're right."

"Oh, Frank . . . I'm just not sure I can help you with this anymore."

But it wasn't her help he wanted now; it was her approval. And that, it seemed, she was not about to give. He didn't understand. She had told him to look to the past, that he would find the secret there. What secret, he wondered, did she expect he would find— the cure to Beverly Archer's disease?

"Look," he said, "she's a vicious, manipulative, dangerous murderess. My job is to put her away."

"Of course," she said sadly. "Of course. . . ."

He felt awful when he put down the phone. Would Monika now hold this against him? She said she understood, but did she? He was a detective, not a therapist. Now he had to do his job.

After much discussion and many rehearsals, he and Aaron agreed that since there was no way of knowing how Beverly would react, their best approach would be the simplest and most direct. No big dramatic production at the door. Just walk up the front steps picture in hand, ring the bell, offer to place it in the hall for her, then let the chips fall where they may.

Figuring she'd be tired and thus more vulnerable at the end of the day, they parked their van across from her house a little after 6:00 P.M. There they waited until 6:45, when her last patient left.

They had uncrated the picture earlier; it was now covered only with a sheet. They pulled it out of the van, picked it up, and together carried it across the street.

Aaron pushed the buzzer. It was a while before Beverly answered on the intercom.

"Who's there?"

"Janek."

A short pause. "Go away. I'm not in the mood today."

"I brought you something." He spoke cheerfully. "Something from Cleveland." He tried to entice her with his tone.

"Oh, really . . ." Her voice was lethargic. She certainly didn't sound upset.

"Open the door and I'll show you," he said. He paused again; he was getting into the rhythm of the thing. "You won't be sorry, Bev."

Aaron gave him a thumbs-up as they heard the lock mechanism being turned. Then the door opened and Beverly stood in the archway, hands planted on her hips. She looked a perfect little butterball as she stared at them and then at the sheet-covered picture in between.

"Is that great big thing for tiny little me?" She spoke with a sarcastic lilt.

Janek nodded. "Want us to bring it inside?"

"I don't know that I'm going to accept it. Remember the old saying: 'Beware Greeks bearing gifts.' "

"What're you afraid of? Think it's a Trojan Horse?"

She stared at the picture curiously. "What is it anyway?"

"A painting."

"What kind of painting?"

"Aretzsky's second portrait of your mother," Janek said.

She tut-tutted him. "Oh, Janek, you're so tiresome. I know all about that second portrait."

"Sure, you know about it. But did you ever look at it?"

"No. And I don't intend to."

As she started to close the door, he felt his case begin to slip away. *Do something! Razz her! Don't let her close you out!*

"Scared to look, Bev?" he taunted.

She hesitated. "No, I'm not scared to look."

"There are things in this picture you won't see in the one upstairs."

She nodded. "I know the story. A drunk old painter's revenge."

"Maybe something deeper than revenge, Bev. Maybe something true."

"All the truth went into the first portrait. The second was painted on the rebound. That's the way I heard it."

He shook his head. "You heard wrong. The first time Aretzsky was blinded by love. The second time his eyes were wide open."

She glared at him. "You're an ass, Janek." Again she tried to shut him out.

This is it, he thought. *Go for broke!*

He blocked the door with his shoe. When he spoke again he used no taunts nor was there any trace of sarcasm in his voice.

"The MacDonalds were a mistake, Bev. You sent Diana out to kill the wrong boys. Sure, they gave you a hard time. But it was your mother who put them up to it." He snatched the sheet off the picture, tilted it so she could see Victoria's face. "Look into her eyes. Check out her mouth. See the cruelty, the depravity, the selfishness? This is the lady who set you up. She told Melissa Walters she didn't want you to be a wallflower. But when you look hard at this picture you have to wonder if she meant it. Because that's what you are, Bev. A wallflower. Now and for the rest of your life." He thrust his finger at the painting. "And this is the lady who made you one. Not the MacDonalds. *Her!*"

He nodded to Aaron. They turned and walked away. The plan was not to look back, not to give her a chance to answer, or gesture at them, or show her contempt by slamming the door in their faces. By the time they heard it slam they were already at the curb. And still they walked. It was only when they reached the other side of the street and got into their van, that Janek turned and looked and saw with satisfaction that the door to the house was closed and the picture they'd left was no longer on the stoop.

Give her the night with her new mama, Janek thought. Let them cook together, heat each other up. Then, maybe, butterball will be ready to talk.

It was out of his hands now. It was between the Archers. Nothing for him to do but wait. He went home, ordered in some Chinese, watched a hockey game on TV, then retired early to bed. He did not sleep well. He tossed and turned, worried that Beverly would not take his bait, worried that if she did Monika would forever think less of him, because, as she'd put it, he'd gone for blood.

In the morning he spoke briefly with Aaron, who'd spent the night watching Beverly's house. Nothing yet, so Janek set to work methodically cleaning his apartment. He mopped his kitchen, vacuumed his rugs, waxed his furniture, and scrubbed his bathroom floor on his knees. He didn't clean up the place very often, but this day he did so with a vengeance. Perhaps, he thought, it was a way for him not to think about Monika, not to deal with the feelings she'd conveyed, the way she'd distanced herself after he'd revealed his plan.

A little after ten he received a call from a young lawyer, an associate at Stanton's firm, who was representing him on the Rusty Glickman assault suit.

"Glickman's got no case and Streep & Holster know it," the attorney said. "I told them: All you've got is a bunch of phony charges brought by a man Janek put away years ago. Unfortunately there wasn't any give, so my strategy now is to go into court and move for summary judgment. It may take a while but I'm pretty sure we'll get it. Then the whole miserable business will be done with."

Janek thanked him. The moment he set down his phone it rang again. He snatched it up.

It was Aaron. "Something's going on here, Frank. Beverly's not seeing her patients."

"What do you mean?"

"They show up on time, go to the door, ring, and stand there a while. When nobody answers the intercom, they sort of droop and slouch away."

"You're sure she's there?"

"Positive. I would have seen her come out. I tried to call her a minute ago. All I got was her answering machine."

He thought of what Monika had said, about the possibility Beverly could be shocked into psychosis. Maybe, just maybe, the portrait was having its effect.

"I'll be right over," he told Aaron. "Better get a police locksmith there too."

$\mathbf{H}$e would never forget the scene that confronted them when they finally got inside the house. The painting he and Aaron had delivered, at least what was left of it, stood in tatters in the front hall just inside the door. The image had been desecrated. The eyes, the cruel scheming eyes, had been stabbed straight through the pupils. The selfish mouth had been slashed across so that the lips hung in loose folds. The breasts, too, had been assaulted with a scissors or perhaps a knife. But by far the worst and most fiendish violations had been committed against the area between Victoria Archer's legs. That portion of the picture bore numerous stab wounds, a "pattern of fury," as medical examiners refer to a configuration of knife thrusts so rapid and vigorous that all vestiges of the reproductive organs are obliterated.

Janek and Aaron rushed up the stairs. At the bedroom door they stopped. The spectacle before them was so stunning and bizarre they could only stand before it and gape.

The room was bathed in reddish light. The original portrait, removed from its niche, lay flat across the great four-poster. Beverly, in the same scarlet dress her mother had worn in both paintings, lay upon the picture very still. There was blood on the canvas and the bed.

"I think she's dead, Frank," Aaron said. "It looks like she slit her wrists."

Janek walked forward and touched Beverly's forehead. The skin was cold as ice. He tried to lift her arm to check for wounds, but found he could not move her. Then he understood. She was stuck to the painting. She had glued herself to it.

"Jesus!" Aaron said. "Maybe she was trying to screw the picture. Do you think?"

Janek shook his head. He was sure that that was not what Beverly had been trying to do when she opened her veins, then glued herself to her mother—pelvis to pelvis, hands to hands, breasts to breasts. What she had attempted, he felt certain, was a terminal act of bonding. But then, perhaps in her last moments, she had writhed against the image, engaging in a final failed life-and-death struggle for release.

He circled the bed, and, when Bev's face came into view, Janek felt his rage subside. Her frozen expression, a mixture of panic and yearning, filled him with pity and terror.

He turned to Aaron. "Call the morgue," he said.

After Aaron went downstairs, Janek spotted an ivory-handled knife, blade open, on the floor. He picked it up, clasped the blade shut, then pushed a chrome button on the side. The blade sprang forward in his hand. It was the knife Bev had used to kill herself— Jess's knife, the knife that had haunted his dreams.

He looked back at Beverly, met her dead eyes head-on.

"What can I do for you?" he whispered.

The moment he heard his own voice, he knew the answer. He would use Jess's knife to cut the dead woman loose.

He imagined her screaming: "Cut, Mama! No!" But to cut them apart, he knew, was the only way. He straddled Bev, then sliced into the picture. How appropriate, he thought, that he was now separating her from the phony image she had worshiped. The painting was thick but the knife was sharp. The canvas parted before the blade like silk.

Beverly had been mad, of course, functional but mad, perhaps as far back as her girlhood. Confronted finally by the true nature of her mother, her madness had engulfed and destroyed her.

He waited until the medical examiner arrived, waited until the assistants carried Bev's body out. He sat alone for a while in the strange dark bedroom. And then it was time to leave.

Downstairs Aaron was standing before the damaged second portrait in the hall.

"Funny, isn't it, Frank, how now the two pictures look almost the same?"

Janek understood. The cuts he'd made in the idealized version upstairs matched almost perfectly the cuts Beverly had made in the cruel version before him.

"Too bad she killed herself," Aaron said. "It would have been a hell of a trial." He paused. "I wonder if she would have confessed in the end."

"She did confess," Janek replied. "She just didn't do it with words."

Aaron grinned at him. "Well, you got her, Frank. You nailed her."

"Yeah. . . ."

"Do you think Kit would say you did it straight?"

Janek shrugged. "Sometimes, when they're as crooked as this one," he said, "you have to use a slightly crooked nail."

There was, at first, a feeling of fulfillment. Having broken and destroyed the monster, he was no longer possessed by anger. There was the satisfaction, too, that came with understanding another person, adding another quantum to his store of knowledge of human beings and their mysterious capacity for evil.

But these good feelings fled quickly. The letdown descended within a day. It was like the Switch case: as soon as it was over, the passions that had fueled the quest began to die. And then he was left with himself, to ponder the meaning of his life—to wonder what Wallflower had meant to him, and whether it had cost him Monika's love.

He knew the case had changed him. He would never forget his horror as he felt the steel plunge into his throat, would never forget his conviction that he was going to die. But as he reexamined that moment, he recalled that it was not fear of death that had seized him, but a terrible frustration that he did not know who was attacking him or why.

Now that he had solved all that, he was left with his grief for Jess, a grief he knew he would always carry with him, though hopefully without the intensity of the past few months.

Redemption? He wasn't sure he'd achieved it. The seeds of his melancholy had been planted years before. There would be times throughout his life, he knew, when he must harvest their bitter fruit. And if, as he believed, he had driven Beverly Archer to suicide . . . well, he would have to live with that.

His cases always haunted him. Sometimes he felt as though his mind was filled with overlapping images from old homicides and the echoes of confessions of killers he had tracked and caught through the years. Now Wallflower, too, would become part of that montage. To be haunted, he understood, was the price he must pay for daring to explore the back alleys of tormented souls.

For two days after Wallflower was closed he walked the streets of New York. It was the second week of January, the coldest time of year. He felt himself buffeted by piercing winter winds.

On the afternoon of the second day he noticed something in the steamy window of a little antique store on Charles Street. He stopped before it, shivering, hesitated, then walked inside.

A small bell attached to the door tinkled as he entered. A bespectacled old man in a tattered gray sweater glanced at him from behind a battered desk. It was a warm, cluttered little shop, filled with sparkling objects. Janek nodded to the proprietor, then went straight to the object that had caught his eye. He picked it up, held it in his hand, stared at it, amazed. It was an almost perfect duplicate of the glass Monika had found for him in Venice.

He bought it at the old man's asking price. Surely finding such a glass was a wonderful omen that he must not spoil by haggling over cost. He hurried home, set the glass beside the one Monika had given him, and then peered into the pair as they broke the afternoon light into colors and stars, crystal fire.

The magic of Venice flooded back. In that enchanted city he had found himself a lover; in her arms he had found ecstasy and joy. After Jess was killed, Monika became more than his lover—she became his therapist and adviser too. But when he'd come back from Cleveland and told her of his intention to break Beverly with her mother's picture, Monika had responded coolly. She was a healer, not a wounder, she'd said. She'd told him she didn't think she could help him anymore.

He had gone ahead anyway, done what he had to do, and now that it was finished, he wanted desperately to be with her again. For a week he'd wanted to call her, but he'd hesitated. Would she still be reserved with him? Would she deny him her love?

Now, as he stared at the two glasses and the afternoon waned, he knew the time had come to call.

She sounded cheerful, said she was happy to hear his voice. They exchanged notes on the weather: Hamburg was chilly; that very evening a light snow had begun to fall. She was thinking about taking a week off, she said, perhaps driving down to Austria with some friends to ski. And how was he doing? When she hadn't heard from him, she wasn't sure what she should think.

As her voice trailed off, he began to speak. The Wallflower case was over, he told her. Beverly Archer was dead by her own hand. He wanted Monika to know that he owned up to his responsibility in the matter. He knew what he had done and why. He would not flinch from it; he felt no shame on account of it. Could she, Monika, accept him as he now accepted himself, for the person he was, without reservation or regret?

"Oh, Frank," she said, "how can you even ask?"

Suddenly his tension was eased. He felt he could step out from behind his detective's mask and speak to her as a man. He told her he wanted to tell her a story. He had been out walking that afternoon . . . had passed this little shop . . . had seen this glass . . . had bought it . . . it was nearly identical. . . .

"You know what this means?" he asked.

"Tell me, Frank."

"It means I want to be with you," he said, his longing for her pouring out through his voice. "Will you meet me in Venice? In three days? In two?"

There was a brief silence before she answered.

"Oh, yes," she said, and, as her words reached him, he imagined the sparkling affirmation in her eyes. "Oh, yes! Yes!" she said, and he could feel the glow of her warming him from across the icy sea.

ABOUT THE AUTHOR

WILLIAM BAYER'S last novel was the *noir* thriller *Blind Side*. He is also the author of the best-sellers *Switch* and *Pattern Crimes,* and the Edgar Award winner *Peregrine*. He and his wife, food writer Paula Wolfert, divide their time between homes in western Connecticut and Martha's Vineyard.